Praise for Kathryn Springer
and her novels

"It's a terrifically warm and joyous story."
—*RT Book Reviews* on *A Place to Call Home*

"A wonderful story [about] the joy of finding love again."
—*RT Book Reviews* on *Love Finds a Home*

"*Family Treasures* is extremely touching, effective and satisfying."
—*RT Book Reviews*

"The romance...will leave readers smiling."
—*RT Book Reviews* on *Longing for Home*

KATHRYN SPRINGER

A Place to Call Home

&

Love Finds a Home

HARLEQUIN® LOVE INSPIRED®CLASSICS

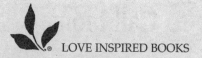 LOVE INSPIRED BOOKS

Recycling programs for this product may not exist in your area.

ISBN-13: 978-0-373-20843-2

A Place to Call Home & Love Finds a Home

Copyright © 2017 by Harlequin Books S.A.

The publisher acknowledges the copyright holder of the individual works as follows:

A Place to Call Home
Copyright © 2010 by Kathryn Springer

Love Finds a Home
Copyright © 2010 by Kathryn Springer

www.Harlequin.com

Printed in U.S.A.

CONTENTS

Kathryn Springer is a lifelong Wisconsin resident. Growing up in a "newspaper" family, she spent long hours as a child plunking out stories on her mother's typewriter and hasn't stopped writing since. She loves to write inspirational romance because it allows her to combine her faith in God with her love of a happy ending.

A PLACE TO CALL HOME

I sought the Lord, and he answered me;
he delivered me from all my fears.
Those who look to him are radiant;
their faces are never covered with shame.
—*Psalms* 34:4, 5

To Anna
Because I have no doubt there will come a day
when you dedicate a book to me! Remember,
"He who began a good work in you will
carry it on to completion." That's a promise!

Prologue

"Quinn? There's a headache waiting for you on line two."

Ignoring the phone, Quinn O'Halloran shot a wry look at his secretary and reached for the cup of coffee he'd poured over an hour ago instead.

"Mel Burdock," he guessed.

Faye McAllister shook her head. The movement sent the slender gold chains on her bifocals dancing. "No, Burdock's more like the tension headache that climbs up the back of your neck and camps out in your temples. This guy—instant migraine."

"Feel free to correct me on this, but I thought I hired *you* to intercept the migraines."

"You did. But this is the third time today I've intercepted this particular one." Faye aimed a scowl at the phone. "When I told Mr. High and Mighty that your policy is to return phone calls between four and five o'clock, he didn't seem to think it applied to him. He insists on talking directly to you but won't say what he wants. And—" another scowl "—he refused to tell me his name. Must be from out of town."

Quinn suppressed a smile. Faye took pride in her ability to deal with anyone who walked through the door of O'Halloran Security. It was one of the reasons he'd hired her. Quinn preferred to work behind the scenes and let Faye handle the customers. Those she didn't manage to scare away usually ended up signing a contract.

Glancing at the clock, he mentally scrolled through the rest of his afternoon schedule. If he ate lunch in his truck on the way to Mel's, it would give him an extra five minutes to deal with the anonymous headache on the line.

"I'll take it in my office."

"I'm sorry." Faye huffed the words. "If I let a salesman get through, I'll bring in doughnuts tomorrow morning."

Quinn grinned. "Are you kidding? If you let a salesman through, you'll bring in doughnuts for the next month."

After topping off his cup, Quinn followed the worn path down the center of the carpet to the oversize closet in the back of the building that doubled as his office. The red light on his desk phone continued to blink out a warning. A testimony to the caller's patience. Or stubbornness.

With a shake of his head, he picked it up. "O'Halloran."

"It's about time," a voice snapped.

Faye was right. Instant migraine.

"Good morning, Mr.—"

"Alex Porter." There was a significant pause, as if he expected Quinn to recognize the name. "Porter Hotels."

Now Quinn recognized the name.

The deluxe hotels had their roots in Chicago, where Quinn had lived for eight years before returning to Mirror Lake, Wisconsin. Under Alex Porter's management, offshoots now sprouted in other major Midwestern cities. Not only did they successfully compete against the larger, well-known chains, but the fact that Porter Hotels remained a family-run enterprise made it even more unique.

"What can I do for—"

"I want to hire you."

Quinn let out a slow breath. No wonder the guy had raised Faye's hackles. Everything Alex Porter said came out sounding like a command instead of a request. As if he expected his name would open doors that were closed to mere mortals.

The trouble was, Quinn thought with a trace of bitterness, it probably did. He'd dealt with people like Alex Porter before and had no desire to repeat the experience. Unfortunately, he wasn't in a position to turn down business. Any business.

Pride or a paycheck?

Over the past year, while trying to resurrect the business his father had spent the last years of his life determined to bury, Quinn had discovered the cause and effect relationship between the two. Sometimes the first one depended upon the second.

"Are you buying a condo? Building a hotel in the area?" Quinn searched his desk drawer—the Bermuda Triangle of office supplies—for a pen that actually worked. "O'Halloran Security custom designs security systems to fit the needs of each client. We can set up an appointment to discuss the details—"

"I don't need a new security system."

Quinn frowned. "I thought you said you wanted to hire me."

"I do. You recognized my name, and I recognized yours when I was researching businesses in the Mirror Lake area. I don't need an alarm system. This is… personal."

Personal.

Quinn's fingers tightened around the phone. "Sorry. You've got the wrong person."

"I don't think so."

"O'Halloran Security is strictly buildings. I don't provide personal security." Not anymore. "I'm sorry you wasted your time. But I have an appointment now, so you'll have to excuse me. There are other reputable agencies in the Chicago area. I'm sure you'll find someone."

To walk you to your limo, Quinn added silently.

"It isn't for me. It's for my younger sister."

Something in Porter's voice stopped Quinn from hanging up the phone. A hint of emotion that cracked the surface of the cool, CEO voice. "Just hear me out."

Don't ask.

"Please."

Coming from Porter, the word sounded as if he'd started speaking a foreign language. So, against his better judgment, Quinn asked.

"What's going on?"

"Abby turned in her letter of resignation at the hotel a month ago and bought a run-down lodge a few miles outside of Mirror Lake. She plans to turn it into a bed-and-breakfast." The disapproval leaking into Alex's voice told Quinn how he felt about his sister's decision. "You must have heard about it."

"Maybe." Quinn deliberately kept his voice non-committal as a conversation he'd overheard stirred in his memory.

Although he tried to keep to himself, he had heard a rumor about the sale of the former Bible camp while waiting for his breakfast one morning at the Grapevine Café, where local gossip brewed as fast as Kate Nichols's industrial-strength coffee.

"So far, Abby refuses to listen to reason and come back to Chicago where she belongs. It looks like I'm going to have to play this her way for a while."

"So why did you call me?" Quinn's lips twisted. "You need a bodyguard to keep the local riffraff away from her?"

That was ironic. At one time, his family portrait would have appeared beside the word *riffraff* in *Webster's Dictionary.*

Alex chose to ignore the sarcasm. "A few weeks ago, someone started harassing me. Vandalized my car. Painted some, shall we say, rather unflattering graffiti on the window of my office. There haven't been any overt threats made, but I want someone to keep an eye on Abby until my private investigator finds out who I angered."

"That could take a while," Quinn said under his breath.

To his amazement, Alex laughed. "It might," he admitted. "I'm not concerned about myself as much as I am about Abby. She is…fragile. I can't believe she's serious about opening a bed-and-breakfast, but it doesn't change the fact that right now she's miles away from civilization, living in a house with hook-and-eye locks on the doors and windows that won't close all the way. I want to be sure she's safe."

Some memories were so bitter he could taste them. "Then you should have done your homework. Because if that's the case, I guarantee you called the wrong person."

A tense silence stretched between them, and Quinn guessed it was because not many people had the guts to point out that Alex Porter made mistakes. Maybe he'd save Quinn the trouble and hang up first.

He didn't.

"You spent four years in the Marine Corps. Seven years with Hamlin Security," Alex recited evenly. "You moved back to your hometown a year ago to take over your father's locksmith business after he died. Since then, you expanded to specialized security systems designed for summer homes and luxury condos."

Apparently Porter *had* done his homework.

All those things were true. But Porter had left out a six-month gap in Quinn's employment history. "You forgot something."

"That you got a raw deal while you worked for Hamlin? Doesn't matter."

Didn't matter?

Under different circumstances, Quinn might have been flattered. Except that he couldn't believe someone could neatly condense the last thirteen years of his life and then dismiss the single event that had ripped it apart. Especially when it had cost him his career—and his reputation.

"I have a business. And it isn't babysitting the rich

and famous." *Been there, done that. Still pulling out shrapnel.*

"I need the best. That's you."

"What you need to do is buy your sister a rottweiler and remind her to lock the doors at night," Quinn shot back. "It sounds to me like you're overreacting to a threat that doesn't exist. And even if one does, it's in Illinois, not Wisconsin. She's probably safer here than anywhere."

"I'm not taking any chances when it comes to Abby's safety." A hint of steel sharpened the words. "I want someone with her who's experienced in sensing potential threats."

That was funny. Because Quinn was sensing one right now. A threat to the life he'd started to rebuild.

It was proving to be challenging enough to erase the stain of having the last name O'Halloran without people getting wind of the reason he'd returned to Mirror Lake. Quinn figured if they knew the truth, he'd have to start at square one again. If he was allowed to start at all.

From the sound of it, the only thing Abby Porter was in danger of was being smothered by an overprotective brother. Getting involved with the Porters would be a bad idea, for more reasons than Quinn could count.

"I can't help you."

"You mean you won't help me."

It boiled down to the same thing. "I can give you some names," Quinn offered reluctantly. "Talk to some people I used to know."

Not that he could guarantee those people would talk to him.

"You've heard of the White Wolf Run condominiums, right?" Alex asked. "Jeff Gaines happens to be a close friend of mine."

"Really?" Quinn's voice was stripped of emotion.

Apparently, Porter had not only done his homework, he'd done the extra credit. O'Halloran Security had put in a bid on that job.

A wave of frustration battered Quinn's resolve. This was the difference between the haves and the have-nots. When you belonged to the first group, all you had to do was open your wallet to get your way.

"I can put in a good word for you," Alex said.

The underlying message was clear. If Quinn agreed to work for him.

The confidence in Porter's voice rankled. And brought back that pride versus the paycheck issue again. Designing a security system for the White Wolf Run condos would boost Quinn's income enough to wipe out some of his start-up debt, install an air conditioner in the sweltering office and allow him to replace outdated equipment. It would also go a long way in securing his business's reputation in the area.

And your own.

Quinn ignored the mocking voice that infiltrated his thoughts.

"How does your sister feel about someone invading her personal space?" He wasn't agreeing to anything yet. Just…inquiring.

"It doesn't matter because Abby isn't going to know why you're there. Or that I hired you."

Quinn's internal alarm system went off. "What do you mean she isn't going to know why I'm there?"

"She can't find out that I'm involved in this. We

had a bit of a disagreement when she turned in her resignation. Abby refuses to accept any help from me. She can be a little…stubborn."

Apparently a Porter family trait.

"What a shock," Quinn muttered, silently adding that bit of information to what he'd learned about Alex Porter's younger sister so far.

Impulsive. Temperamental. Stubborn—Quinn translated that as *spoiled.* Oh, and what was the other word Alex had used to describe her?

Fragile.

All of them added up to one thing.

Trouble.

"Abby is focused on getting the place ready for her grand opening in August," Alex continued. "Her carpenter, Daniel Redstone, just won an all-expense-paid, two-week vacation with a professional fishing guide. You're going to take his place."

"How lucky for Daniel," Quinn said dryly.

"A person makes their own luck." Alex dismissed his comment. "You've helped Redstone out in the past when you were short on cash. That makes you an obvious replacement for him. No one will think twice about it. Neither will Abby. You'll be able to keep an eye on her and in between pounding nails and painting the outhouse, you can install a security system."

"You are…" Quinn paused. With so many issues to choose from, it was difficult to pick a winner.

"Thorough." Alex filled in the blank.

Quinn had been leaning more toward arrogant. Or smug. But he guessed that description fit as good as any.

"Two weeks. Until Daniel comes back." It was all

Quinn was willing to spare. Other than Faye, he only employed two part-time employees. Both men were responsible and would appreciate the extra work, but Quinn didn't want to look as if he were shirking his responsibility. People already told him that he resembled his father. The last thing Quinn wanted to do was act like him.

"Two weeks," Alex agreed. "24/7."

"You have got to be kidding." There was overprotective and then there was downright paranoid.

"That's my offer."

"The person harassing you hasn't bothered your sister." Quinn raked a hand through his hair. "Don't you think that's a little extreme?"

"I told you." Alex's voice was as cold as spring water now. "I'm not taking any chances when it comes to Abby's safety."

"You want me on-site. Round the clock. For two weeks."

"That's right." And before Quinn had a chance to turn him down flat, Alex proceeded to tell him what he would pay for the inconvenience. "Do we have a deal?"

Everything inside Quinn warned him to walk away. But he couldn't. Not if it helped O'Halloran Security succeed.

"We have a deal."

Quinn reminded himself that he'd walked through the fire before. Only this time he had an advantage. He knew how to avoid getting burned.

Chapter One

Abby Porter didn't realize she had company until Mulligan's tail began to thump a welcoming beat against the ground.

Swinging her feet over the side of the chaise longue, she began a hasty search for the sandals she'd kicked off. She'd located one and was in the process of looking for its mate when Mulligan lumbered to his feet.

As the dog trained his gaze on the corner of the house, Abby ignored the shiver that sowed goose bumps up her arms.

Thank you, Alex.

Her older brother's scare tactics were finally getting to her. All part of his plot to get her to come back to Chicago where he could keep a protective eye on her.

"Not a chance," she muttered, tamping down her unease. If she was going to be an innkeeper, she had to get used to people coming and going.

"Who is it, Big Guy? Who's here?"

In response, Mulligan let out a friendly woof.

Which told Abby absolutely nothing. The dog's instincts weren't exactly an accurate barometer when it came to assessing a potential threat. A week ago, she'd had to intervene before he got up close and personal with a porcupine during their morning walk around Mirror Lake. Mulligan loved everything, from the squirrels that scolded him from the branches of the oak trees to her reliable, good-natured carpenter Daniel.

Relief swept through her, causing the goose bumps tracking her arms to subside a little, when Abby remembered that Daniel Redstone was supposed to stop by to pick up his paycheck before he left on vacation.

For some reason, he'd expected Abby to be as excited as he was when he'd won an all-expense-paid trip with one of the best professional fishing guides in the state of Wisconsin.

Abby hadn't been excited.

The elderly handyman might have worked at a speed that hovered between slow and a dead standstill, but the final result of his effort was no less than breathtaking. If it hadn't been for Daniel's promise to send over a suitable replacement to fill in for him, Abby would have been tempted to offer a sizeable—but anonymous—donation to the fishing guide's favorite charity if he agreed to cancel the trip.

That the thought had even crossed her mind told Abby that she was already showing some early symptoms of "Alex Porter Syndrome." A disease characterized by an intense desire to control the universe.

In the end, she hadn't had much of a choice but to agree to send Daniel off with her blessing. And consider it another surprise to add to the growing list of surprises she'd encountered since her move to Mirror Lake.

Mulligan's low woof thinned to a whine, and Abby quickly figured out why.

The man rounding the corner of the house wasn't Daniel Redstone.

This man was younger. Much younger. He wasn't stoop-shouldered and thin as a fly rod, either.

Lost tourist?

Abby rejected the thought immediately.

There was nothing *lost* about the man. He moved with the kind of fluid, confident stride she'd always envied. The kind that said he didn't simply *know* his place in the world, he'd carved it out himself. Khaki cargo pants paired with a plain cotton T-shirt accentuated the man's lean, muscular frame but made it difficult to pinpoint what he did for a living.

Abby's eyes narrowed. It would be just like Alex to send one of his minions to keep an eye on her even after she'd told him not to. She loved her brother to pieces but he did have a tendency to bully people to get his way.

She hadn't expected Alex to take the news of her departure well, but she hadn't realized how strongly he would respond to what he labeled her "defection."

A few short months ago, his reaction would have caused her to give in, but this time it had only made her that much more determined to break out on her own. It was time. And the way things had fallen in place, it seemed that God Himself had gone before her to clear the path.

She could only pray that Alex would eventually come around and accept her decision. If Abby were

honest with herself—another thing she'd been practicing lately—she had to admit that it was partly her
fault that Alex didn't have a lot of confidence in her.
For a long time, she hadn't had much confidence in
herself.

The stranger spotted her and veered down the uneven brick path leading to the gazebo. As he drew
closer, the ruggedly handsome features became more
defined. Strands of silky, ink-black hair lay even with
the five o'clock shadow darkening his angular jaw.
Mirrored sunglasses—Abby had never been a fan—
concealed his eyes.

"Hello." Ignoring the second crop of goose bumps
that sprouted up her arms, Abby forced a smile. She
spotted her flattened sandal in the spot where Mulligan had been dozing and discreetly toed it back on.
"Can I help you?"

He stopped several feet away, close enough for her
to see her distorted reflection in his sunglasses. "Are
you Abby Porter?"

"Yes."

"Then I'm here to help you."

Abby blinked. "Excuse me?"

"I'm Quinn O'Halloran."

The name meant nothing to her. "I'm sorry. I—"

"Daniel Redstone sent me." He yanked off the
glasses and Abby found herself staring into a pair of
slate gray eyes. "I'm your new carpenter."

"My new…" Abby couldn't push the rest of the
sentence past the knot in her throat. She tried again.
"He didn't mention you'd be coming over today." Better. The squeak that had made her voice sound like a
rusty screen door was barely noticeable now.

He shrugged. "According to Daniel, you're under a tight deadline and need to keep the project moving along. I thought I'd stop by and take a look around to get a feel for things before I start."

"I am under a deadline but— Mulligan, no!" Abby lunged for the dog, who'd finally summoned the courage to inch close enough to swipe his tongue against Quinn's hand. She gave him an apologetic smile. "I'm sorry. We're still working on basic etiquette."

"You're a golfer."

"Golf?" At first the meaning behind his statement didn't sink in. When it did, Abby smiled. "No, I borrowed the term because I adopted Mulligan from the animal shelter an hour before he was to be euthanized."

"Another chance." The pale gray eyes lit with sudden understanding.

"It seemed to fit." Abby ruffled one of Mulligan's floppy ears. "And I happen to think everyone deserves a second one, don't you?"

Quinn didn't answer. Because Abby Porter's megawatt smile had momentarily short-circuited the hardware in his brain.

He knew her.

No, Quinn silently corrected the thought. He'd seen her before. On billboards strategically placed around the city of Chicago. Wearing black velvet and pearls. The reigning princess of Porter Hotels.

Only this princess looked different. And not only because of her smile. Honey-blond hair, caught in a casual knot at the base of her neck, accentuated delicate features dominated by a pair of eyes that were silver-green like an aspen leaf.

Instead of black velvet, she wore figure-hugging jeans, a paint-splattered T-shirt and a pair of sandals decorated with the gaudiest plastic daisies he'd ever seen.

But looks could be deceiving. He'd learned that the hard way. As far as Quinn was concerned, a diva in blue jeans was still a diva. Before she'd been aware of his arrival, he'd caught a glimpse of her reclining on the chaise longue with a book propped in her lap. Obviously she was so motivated to get the inn ready for her grand opening that she was taking a break before the day had barely started.

Quinn steeled himself against her smile, unnerved that it had had such an effect on him.

"Do you think you can spare a few minutes to give me a tour of the place?" He leveled a pointed gaze at the chaise longue.

"Of course." Abby's smile faded.

Quinn wasn't quite prepared for the direct hit to his conscience. If he'd forgotten the reason he'd changed his professional focus from providing security to buildings instead of people, a few seconds in Abby Porter's company had brought it crashing back. Buildings were easy to figure out. People, not so much.

They fell into step together, and Abby switched into tour guide mode.

"The main lodge started out as a private vacation retreat for a wealthy family, but eventually they donated it to a local church." She gestured toward the sprawling two-story split-log home that Quinn had passed on his way to the gazebo. "The congregation built five additional cabins on the water and turned it into a retreat center and Bible camp. Eventually, though, they couldn't keep up with the larger, more modern camps and had to turn it over to the bank."

Quinn could empathize. He knew all too well what it felt like to struggle to keep a business afloat.

"After that," Abby went on, "it ended up in the hands of a developer. He planned to replace the lodge with condos but later realized it wouldn't appeal to tourists who wanted a full recreation lake…and easier access to civilization. Most of the people who come back to Mirror Lake think of it as a second home rather than a vacation spot. They appreciate the slower pace."

"That's why you chose to turn the place into a bed-and-breakfast rather than a resort," Quinn guessed. "It will attract the type of clientele looking for peace and quiet."

Abby gave him an approving look. "It sat empty for almost five years until my Realtor happened to mention it a few months after I started looking. Believe it or not, I had to beg her to show it to me." Her voice dropped to a whisper. "But the first time I saw it, I knew it was perfect."

Quinn looked over at the lake, as clear and smooth as window glass, beyond a stand of towering white pines. He'd moved to Chicago after his tour of duty because he'd been ready to take on the world. Ready for a fresh start where no one knew the name O'Halloran. The energy and pace of the city had matched his lifestyle. Or so he'd thought. Until he moved back to Mirror Lake.

That first night Quinn spent in his childhood home, temperatures had dipped into the forties, but he'd crawled out the window of his old bedroom and sat on the roof.

He'd forgotten what it felt like to see the stars at night. To drive for miles without seeing a single house or apartment complex. Quinn may not have wanted to return to the town where he'd grown up but he hadn't expected to feel a tug on his soul, as if he were still connected to it. Especially when his memories of the place weren't exactly the Hallmark kind.

Sensing that Abby was waiting for a response, Quinn's gaze moved from the lodge to the weathered cabins strung like wooden beads along the shoreline. Work, work and more work. But he was reluctant to strip the sparkle from Abby's eyes. Again.

"It's got potential," he heard himself say.

Abby turned and smiled up at him. "I think so, too."

Once again, Quinn wasn't prepared for the force of Abby's smile.

Focus, O'Halloran.

"What time does the rest of the crew usually get here?"

Abby shot him a puzzled look. "The rest of the crew?"

"The *work* crew," Quinn clarified.

Abby's low laugh went straight through him. "Now that Daniel is gone, you're looking at it."

She couldn't be serious. "You and Daniel have been doing everything yourselves?"

"That's right." Abby reached down to fondle Mulligan's ears. "I hired some teenagers to do some painting, but they have other jobs so they're only available on the weekend." She skipped up the wide plank steps and opened the front door. "I moved in at the beginning of June and started working on the main house right away. It was in fair condition but I'm still in the process of…"

The rest of the words dissolved in Quinn's ears as he stepped through the doorway into the great room.

The place was a wreck.

Fair condition, Abby had said. The grand opening was a month away but Quinn saw three months of hard labor. At least.

No wonder her Realtor had tried to discourage her from purchasing the property and her brother had had a fit.

Quinn didn't have to be a professional carpenter to see that the hardwood floors needed to be varnished, the walls painted and another coat of stain applied to the tongue-and-groove pine ceiling.

Abby tilted her head and a strand of sun-streaked blond hair molded itself to the curve of her cheek. "So, what do you think?"

"Wow." That about covered it.

Abby grinned. "I'll show you the kitchen."

Can't wait, Quinn thought.

He followed her, silently adding projects to the list with every step. New baseboards. New trim. New light fixtures.

It didn't make sense. Abby Porter was an heiress. She had the resources to level the entire place and have it rebuilt in a week. So why was she doing the bulk of the work herself?

"The kitchen is original to the lodge when it was built in the 1940s, so it has a lot of vintage charm." Abby paused in the doorway.

Vintage charm. A Realtor's term for gold linoleum and chrome-trimmed Formica countertops.

He stepped past her, bracing himself for what was behind door number one.

"Your eyes are closed," Abby said.

So they were. Quinn opened them. "They're adjusting to the change in light."

He had to look. No getting around it.

Relief crashed over him when he stepped into a room that could have been featured in a home decorating magazine. Given the fact the place was going to be a bed-and-breakfast, it shouldn't have come as a surprise that Abby had devoted most of her time and effort to the kitchen.

She'd stayed true to the time period by keeping the original glass-front cupboards and painting the bead board walls a sunny shade of yellow. Old-fashioned dish towels had been recycled into valances.

The marble-topped island in the center of the kitchen blended seamlessly with the vintage decor but the granite sink and gleaming stainless steel appliances were definitely modern, state-of-the-art tools for the serious cook.

Quinn's gaze continued around the room and snagged on an ancient green oven, straight off the set of a seventies sitcom.

"I couldn't part with her." Abby followed the direction of his eyes and accurately read his expression. "She's an icon."

"She?"

"Mrs. Avocado."

She'd *named* the oven. "Does she…*it*…still work?"

"Sometimes."

"Correct me if I'm wrong, but if you're running a bed-and-breakfast, don't you need an oven that works *all* the time?"

"She's a little temperamental but we're getting to

know each other." Abby gave the appliance an affectionate pat.

Quinn steeled himself against the woman's infectious charm. Abby Porter was a *job*. He didn't want to think of her as a person. And he certainly didn't want to *like* her.

Maybe Faye didn't need a new air conditioner in the office that badly....

Unaware of his thoughts, Abby tapped the toe of one sandal on the ceramic tile beneath their feet, setting the plastic petals into motion. "The floor was a bit of a challenge because it wasn't even when I started."

"You did all this yourself?"

Abby's shoulders lifted in a modest shrug. "It wasn't that hard. I bought a book."

She'd bought a book.

"Are you ready to see the rest?" Abby was already on her way out the door. "I hate to rush the tour but I still have a hundred things to do today."

"More like a million," Quinn muttered.

"Excuse me?" Abby paused on her way out the door.

"Nothing. Lead on."

While Abby took him through the rest of the house, Quinn followed along, taking mental notes along the way. Alex, he discovered, hadn't been exaggerating. The windows on the first floor were the old-fashioned casement kind that had gone the way of the eight-track tape player. And a chimpanzee with a nail file could have picked the locks on the doors.

Abby wanted him working on the cabins but Quinn knew he'd have to come up with a plan that would put him alongside Abby at the lodge in order to make the house secure.

"This bedroom is called Serenity." Abby paused to open one of the doors. "I finished painting the trim this morning."

"This morning?" Quinn raised an eyebrow. He'd pulled in to the driveway at nine. "What time this morning?"

Abby tucked her full lower lip between her teeth before answering the question. "Mmm. I think it was around four."

"Four o'clock in the *morning?*"

One slim shoulder lifted. "And some people think insomnia is a bad thing."

Quinn didn't comment because he was trying to wrap his mind around the fact that Abby had been up before dawn. Working. He could relate. He'd done the same thing after he'd moved back to Mirror Lake. Slept a little, worked a lot. Especially because his father, in his final months, hadn't bothered to put money into anything other than the cash register at the local liquor store.

"So what do you think? Does it live up to its name?"

Abby's question yanked him back from the edge of those memories and he looked past her into the bedroom.

Quinn had expected Abby to copy the more popular rustic decor—characterized by an overabundance of largemouth bass and whitetail deer—used in other places that catered to tourists.

Instead, by combining cool blues and soft greens, Abby had brought the outdoors inside. And in the process, provided a comfortable oasis guaranteed to instantly lower a person's blood pressure.

"Very serene." Quinn's own blood pressure didn't agree with the assessment. Not with Abby standing close enough that he caught the faintest whiff of… *cinnamon?*…in the air. Not exactly a designer fragrance but oddly appealing. "Where is your room?" he asked abruptly.

Abby blinked. "On the third floor. I didn't want to take up space the guests could use. Plus, there's an enclosed, private staircase leading up to it, so I have my own entrance."

"There's a third floor?" Considering the two levels of windows on the house, Quinn wouldn't have guessed the house had an additional story.

"It's more like an attic, really, but if you don't count the cabins, I have the best view of the lake."

Quinn debated whether he should ask her to prove it but decided to wait for another time. When Abby was occupied with something else he'd take a look at it.

"Speaking of the cabins, maybe you should show me the one I'll be staying in so I can start unloading some of my things."

"The cabin you'll be staying in?" Abby echoed. "What do you mean?"

"I'll be living on-site until Daniel gets back. Didn't he mention that?"

"No." Abby's eyes darkened with an emotion Quinn couldn't quite identify. "As a matter of fact, he didn't."

Chapter Two

"Is there a problem?"

Definitely more than one, Abby thought as she tried to tamp down her rising panic.

She might have been rambling on like a cruise director who'd downed a shot of espresso, but she thought she'd done a pretty good job hiding her emotions after Quinn O'Halloran introduced himself as the new carpenter. But once again the man had thrown her completely off balance.

"You can't stay...*here.* I don't know what Daniel was thinking if he told you differently."

"Why not?" Quinn leaned against the door frame and tucked his hands into the front pockets of his jeans.

Why not?

Abby wasn't sure how to respond to the question. Was she being silly? Or worse yet, paranoid? Daniel had assured her that the carpenter he was sending over had worked with him before and came with excellent references. But having Quinn O'Halloran working on the property and having him *living* on the property were two different things entirely.

Over the past month, she and Daniel had settled into a pleasant routine. Abby concentrated on renovations in the main lodge while he tackled the cabins. During their lunch break, Abby coaxed Daniel to sample the results of a new recipe while the elderly carpenter entertained her with stories about small-town life. His off-key whistle provided comforting background music in the late afternoon when Abby moved outside to weed the flower beds.

She couldn't shake the feeling that Quinn's presence wouldn't be quite so comforting.

"You must have a place of your own," she stammered.

"I live a few miles north of town, so I would have a half hour's commute every day," Quinn said. "Look at it this way—I can put in longer days if I'm staying on-site. Shave some time off the project. Nothing against Daniel, but I work a little faster than he does."

"I don't—"

"And I could use the hours."

Abby's protest died in her throat. Quinn's voice had remained neutral but the subtle tightening of his jaw told her the admission had cost him. She felt a stab of guilt, knowing her hesitance had forced him to confess that he needed the extra income.

She could pay his mileage…

Just as she opened her mouth to make the offer, another thought pushed its way in.

Was it possible that Quinn was, in a roundabout way, an answer to her prayers? The grand opening was scheduled for the beginning of August but even

Daniel had been skeptical they'd make the deadline. Abby planned to focus her attention for the next few weeks on the great room but several of the cabins still needed work. If Quinn finished remodeling them, she could be at capacity opening weekend.

Just because God hadn't answered her prayer in the way she expected didn't mean that He hadn't answered it.

Okay, God, I'm going to assume Your hand is in this.

Abby forced a smile. "You might be ready to escape at the end of the day once you see what kind of shape the cabins are in."

"I'll stay until the job is finished." Quinn's eyes met hers. "You can count on it."

Abby's heart did a curious little flip and she backed away from that quicksilver gaze. Realizing her hands were clenched into fists at her side, she forced herself to relax.

Daniel, she reminded herself, was the closest thing she had to a friend in Mirror Lake. He wouldn't have asked Quinn to take his place if he didn't trust him. And with the grand opening looming, Daniel probably thought he'd done her a favor by suggesting that Quinn live on the grounds.

She released the breath she hadn't realized she'd been holding. "Two of the cabins are finished so you can take your pick. Both have kitchenettes and full baths…"

The cell phone in her pocket interrupted, playing the dramatic opening notes of Beethoven's *Symphony No. 5.* A special ring tone for a bossy big brother.

Abby took it out of her pocket but instead of answering it, she shut off the sound.

"I don't mind if you take a call," Quinn said.

"That's all right. I don't mind ignoring this one." Abby released a sigh. "My brother calls at least once a day to ask if I've come to my senses yet."

"Come to your senses?"

"He's a little overprotective." An understatement, but at the moment Abby couldn't come up with a better description. "He's part of the reason I bought this place. I love my brother but he doesn't understand that God might have a different plan for my life than the one *he* thinks I should follow."

God.

The comfortable way she said the word made Quinn…uncomfortable. Sure, he believed that God existed, but if the people living in Mirror Lake were reluctant to give an O'Halloran a second chance, Quinn didn't expect that God would, either. Especially when they'd parted company long ago.

"What does your brother think you should do?" he asked.

"Give in," Abby muttered under her breath.

Quinn raised a questioning brow.

"We have a…family business and he wanted me to stay there." A fascinating blush of pink tinted her ivory cheeks.

Interesting. Abby seemed reluctant to let him know just what that family business revolved around.

It seemed they both had their secrets.

"You didn't like it," Quinn prompted.

"I didn't say that."

He frowned. "Then why—"

Abby's phone rang again. Quinn gave her points for her sense of humor. It couldn't be a coincidence that the ominous opening notes from one of

Beethoven's most famous symphonies warned of an incoming call from Alex.

"Did I say overprotective?" Abby rolled her eyes. "I meant overbearing. And persistent. Which means I should probably get this over with or he'll keep calling."

And calling and calling, Quinn wanted to add. The normally unflappable Faye McAllister was still suffering from post-traumatic Porter syndrome. "Not a problem. I'll meet you down by the cabins."

"Thank you." Abby's bright smile surfaced. And lingered in his memory as Quinn left the room.

"Hi, Big Brother," he heard her say. "And yes, you can take that in the George Orwell *1984* way that I intended it."

As the screen door snapped shut behind him, a smile pulled at the corner of Quinn's lips.

Alex had mentioned that he and Abby had had a falling-out when she'd left Chicago, but Quinn didn't miss the exasperated affection in Abby's tone when she'd described her brother. And Alex's frustration over her decision to move to Mirror Lake hadn't overridden his desire to look out for her, no matter how stubborn he thought she was being.

They cared about each other.

Quinn ignored a pinch of envy. That kind of family loyalty was foreign to him.

Stepping onto the deck, he almost tripped over Mulligan, asleep in a pool of sunshine. He shook his head. Abby could have chosen a more protective breed, especially given the isolated location of the inn.

Abby thought everyone deserved a second chance.

If Abby Porter lived in the real world instead of an ivory tower, she'd realize that most people didn't share her view.

Mulligan rolled to his feet and trotted after Quinn as he crossed the lawn toward the cabins.

Home, sweet home. For the next two weeks.

Even though he'd agreed to Alex's terms, Quinn planned to play by his own set of rules. That meant he would satisfy the job requirements by being close enough to see the main house and yet be able to keep an eye on whoever was coming and going.

And on Abby.

The ease with which he shifted back into his former role surprised him a little. A little over a year ago, he'd emptied his locker at Hamlin Security, nodded to the former colleague who'd walked him out of the building and drove away without a backward glance.

Until Alex Porter had temporarily forced him back into the business.

Two weeks, he reminded himself. For O'Halloran Security, he could put up with anything.

Even Abby Porter's smile.

Quinn paused, silently judging the distance between the buildings before cataloging everything else around him. The lodge. The cabins. The boathouse. Even the trees. It gave him an immediate sense of what fit so he would instantly know if something didn't.

So far, the only thing that didn't quite fit was Abby's reaction to *him*.

She got as tense as a new bowstring if he got too close.

Her bright smile and unexpected sense of humor

rose easily to the surface but several times during the tour Quinn had sensed her retreating within herself. And the flash of panic in her eyes when he'd told her that he planned to stay on-site had bothered him, too. For a split second, she'd seemed...afraid.

Or he was imagining things?

At one point, Quinn had trusted his instincts about people. Not anymore. A six-month assignment working for the Raynes family had cured him of that.

Forcing thoughts of Abby aside for the moment, Quinn walked toward the cedar-sided cabin positioned closest to the house. The one with an unobstructed view of the driveway.

His foot touched the first step. And went right through it.

Perfect.

Quinn tugged his shoe free and continued the inspection. The wooden screen door sagged on its hinges and it looked as if a family of chipmunks had taken up residence in the fireplace.

He was prowling around the tiny kitchen when he heard Abby's breathless voice. "Are you in here?"

"Yup."

When Abby appeared in the doorway, her cheeks were flushed. Quinn wasn't sure if it was from a run-in with Alex or because she'd run all the way from the house. No matter what the reason, she looked way too fetching for his peace of mind.

Quinn turned his attention to the fieldstone fireplace instead.

That's right. Because you'll really be effective looking out for Abby when you can't even look at her.

"You'll probably want to move into North Star Cabin," Abby said. "Daniel finished it last week."

Quinn had seen the sign over the door of that particular cabin and it sat on a curve of shoreline, surrounded on three sides by a fortress of mature trees. "This one will be fine."

Abby's eyes widened. "The windows are broken and the screens need to be replaced."

"So?"

She laughed. *Laughed.* "Are you kidding? The mosquitoes will treat you like an all-you-can-eat buffet if you sleep in here."

"I'll install the windows this afternoon, then. I figure if I stayed in one of the cabins that needed remodeling, I'll be motivated to get it done faster."

Indecision skimmed through Abby's eyes. He'd used the magic word again. *Faster.* The pressure to be ready in time for the grand opening would convince her to let him have his way.

Her lips compressed. "I can't let you stay here, Mr. O'Halloran."

Or not.

"It's Quinn."

"Quinn." The color in her cheeks deepened. "What if it rains? The roof leaks."

He could tell she was wavering.

"Clear skies predicted through the weekend. And I'll replace the shingles on the roof after the new windows are in."

"The new furniture is on back order. You'd have to sleep on the couch and it's not very comfortable."

Tell that to the chipmunks, Quinn thought. They

seemed to be pretty comfortable there. "I've slept in worse conditions, believe me."

The indecision on Abby's face changed to curiosity, and Quinn mentally kicked himself. The less she knew about him the better. Granted, if she wanted to get an earful about the O'Halloran family history, all she had to do was ask some of the old-timers in town. But as far as Quinn knew, no one, not even Faye, knew what had happened while he'd been employed at Hamlin.

He planned to keep it that way. It was difficult enough to erase the stain from the name O'Halloran without bringing up the reason he'd returned to Mirror Lake after a fifteen-year absence.

"Fine." Abby finally gave in. "I'll make sure you have fresh linens. When will you be…moving in?"

"Today."

"Today?" Abby's arms locked around her stomach in a protective gesture that set off warning bells in Quinn's head.

"If that's all right with you," he added, watching her body language.

Abby's arms dropped to her sides but her fists remained clenched. "I suppose so."

On a hunch, Quinn took a few steps back and propped a hip against the antique trestle table in the center of the room. Abby's shoulders relaxed but the wary look in her eyes lingered.

Was she *afraid* of him? Or had she gotten skittish because her brother provided daily updates on the person harassing him, in an attempt to convince her to come home? Both possibilities left a bad taste in Quinn's mouth.

"Where did Daniel leave the tools?" Quinn hoped the subtle reminder that he was going to get to work right away would put the light back in her face.

It did. But not as quickly as he'd hoped.

"He didn't leave anything here. He probably assumed you'd use your own."

"Right." Because any self-respecting carpenter would use his own tools.

He'd have to stop in at the hardware store and pick up some new ones. And send Alex Porter the bill.

Chapter Three

Abby spent the rest of the afternoon in the kitchen, perfecting a recipe for the baking powder biscuits she planned to use to make strawberry shortcake that evening.

Some people escaped to the gym or a spa when their stress levels went off the charts. Abby escaped to the kitchen. Until she'd become friends with Jessica Benson, who'd joined the staff as a pastry chef at Porter Lakeside the previous winter, she hadn't looked at herself as anything more than a dabbler in the culinary arts.

Jessica was the one who'd dared her one evening to serve her chocolate mousse crepes with raspberry vanilla sauce to the hotel guests rather than the appreciative waitstaff that usually reaped the rewards of Abby's stressful day.

They'd been such a hit that Jessica had included them on the dessert menu. The next day, she'd asked Abby why she was wasting her talents, doing what was expected of her, rather than being in the kitchen doing what she loved.

Once Abby had gotten over her initial defensiveness, they had become the best of friends. Not only had Jessica encouraged her not to settle on the path of least resistance, she'd been instrumental in bringing Abby to a crossroads where she'd made the most important decision of her life. To surrender her heart to God and follow Him. No matter where He led her.

And Abby was convinced, in spite of her fears and the occasional setback, that He'd led her to Mirror Lake.

She tipped her face toward the ceiling.

Thank You, Lord.

She felt as if she'd been repeating those three simple words over and over, but nothing else seemed to fit. She *was* thankful.

Don't hold on to your fears, Jessica had told her the day she'd left. *Hold on to God instead.*

Sometimes that was easier said than done, but Abby was trying. While Jessica had sent her off with a hug and words of encouragement, Alex had lectured her. Warned her that sharing her home with the guests was a far cry from simply handing them a keycard and leaving them to their own devices. *No privacy,* he'd told her. *Your life won't be your own.*

If Abby hadn't understood the underlying reason for the warning, she might have been tempted to tell him that her life had never felt like her own anyway. But after she'd turned it over to the Lord, the excitement over what He planned to do with it overrode her fears. Most of the time.

Lost in thought, Abby stared down at the bowl of ingredients, wondering if she'd added the right amount of flour. With a sigh, she dumped it back into the canister and began to measure it out again.

This time, she couldn't hold Alex responsible for the dozens of biscuits cooling on wire racks around the kitchen. Or the reason she was so distracted today. This time, her new carpenter was to blame.

Quinn O'Halloran.

She'd seen him mask his dismay when he'd walked into the lodge that morning. Not that she could blame him. There was a lot of work left to accomplish.

The to-do list taped to the refrigerator filled one side of a piece of paper and half the other. Daniel's absence had already put her behind schedule. Which was the reason she'd agreed, against her better judgment, to let Quinn stay in one of the cabins.

As long as the cabins were ready for the grand opening, everything else would work out. Abby had discovered she wasn't ready to put guests in the main house right away. Years of having her privacy fiercely guarded had seeped into her personality in ways she hadn't acknowledged until she'd moved out from under the protection of her family's last name.

The rhythmic tap of a hammer paused for a moment and Abby couldn't resist peeking out the window. Quinn had left after she'd shown him the rest of the cabins but returned a few hours later and went straight to work. True to his word, he'd started with the cabin windows. Most of the building materials had been delivered before Abby arrived in Mirror Lake and she'd shown Quinn the musty garage where everything was stored.

His progress—and that, she told herself sternly, was what she was checking on—gave her a renewed hope that she would be open for business right on schedule.

Something moved near Quinn's feet and even from the distance separating them, Abby knew what it was. Mulligan. He'd whined at the door when Quinn's truck had returned, preferring to nap in the great outdoors at the new carpenter's feet than with her in the sunlit kitchen.

The traitor.

After removing the last batch of biscuits from the oven, Abby cleaned up the kitchen and then slipped out the back door, where she'd hung a load of sheets and towels on the line.

On warm afternoons, she preferred to put the sun to work instead of the industrial-sized dryer in the utility room. The Porter Hotels' housekeeping staff would have shaken their heads at the extra work but Abby found pleasure in doing things the old-fashioned way.

As she approached the cabin where Quinn was working, two dogs streaked toward her. Mulligan barked several times, as if introducing her to the lively, buff-colored cocker spaniel that bounced at his side as if it had springs in its paws.

Abby braced herself for impact but the dog pulled up short at the last second and sat down, lifting one dainty paw for her to shake.

Charmed, Abby set the laundry basket down and dropped to her knees. "Aren't you a little sweetheart? What's your name?"

"Abby, Lady. Lady, Abby." Quinn sauntered over, pushing the hammer into the leather tool belt that rode low on his narrow hips. He'd swapped the khaki pants he'd been wearing that morning for a pair of well-worn jeans. "We're roommates, so I had to bring her along."

Which meant that other than Lady, Quinn lived alone. For some reason Abby's heart—totally on its own accord—lifted and performed a brief pirouette at the thought.

"I know what you're thinking."

Abby sincerely hoped that wasn't true. "I wasn't thinking anything. But now that you mention it, Lady is…"

"She's what?" Quinn's eyes narrowed, as if he'd heard it before.

Not the type of dog Abby would have pictured riding shotgun in Quinn's pickup.

"Beautiful." Abby smiled as the spaniel tried to squirm into her lap. "Mulligan will love having company. If you ask him, I think he'd tell you that I'm pretty boring."

Not with that smile.

Quinn slapped the thought away as soon as it surfaced.

Apparently his former life wasn't as ingrained as he'd thought. Because he'd broken one of the cardinal rules of the trade. Don't get personally involved with a client.

You tried that once, remember? Look where it got you.

Frustration surged through him. Because nothing, beginning with his first glimpse of Abby Porter, had gone the way he'd expected.

First, he got another earful from Faye when he'd stopped by the office on his way through town. Even though the appointment book had a lot of white space, she'd been suspicious from the moment Quinn had informed her that he would be temporarily filling in for Daniel Redstone. He shouldn't have been surprised. Faye scolded him often enough about his tendency to micromanage the business, so his sudden decision to turn O'Halloran Security over to his part-time employees for two weeks had been out of character. The promise of a new air conditioner had finally appeased her, and he'd managed to escape.

Conscious of the time, Quinn had driven home, tossed some of his possessions into the back of the truck and boosted an ecstatic Lady into the passenger seat.

On the way back to the lodge, Alex had called him. Twice, because Quinn had ignored the phone the first time. He wanted to know why Quinn wasn't with Abby. He wanted to know how work on the inn was progressing. And he wanted Quinn to give him updates—*daily updates*—on how his sister seemed to be handling the stress.

The last request had given Quinn the opportunity to educate Alex on the difference between providing personal security and spying. Porter hadn't been happy with the lesson but Quinn knew he had to draw the line somewhere. Plus, Alex's attitude toward Abby had rubbed Quinn the wrong way. It was true she didn't seem like the type to take on a project as large as renovating an old former Bible camp but something in the determined set of Abby's chin made Quinn wonder if she wasn't up to the challenge.

Quinn had been tempted to tell Porter that, too, except he didn't know how to say it without sounding as if he were getting emotionally involved. And because he didn't *do* emotionally involved anymore, he'd simply cut the conversation short and decided he'd be screening his calls from now on.

There'd been no sign of Abby when he parked the truck in the driveway, but he'd heard her singing along with the music filtering through the open windows. Relief had poured through him. If Abby was inside, it meant that he could be outside. And Quinn welcomed the chance to clear his head.

It had worked. Up until the moment he spotted Abby walking across the yard, a laundry basket anchored against one hip. The sight of her felt like another kick to his solar plexus.

If possible, she looked even prettier than she had that morning.

Quinn tried not to notice the way the sunlight picked out the gold and platinum highlights in her hair. Or how the bright pink apron, fashioned to look like a slice of watermelon, accentuated her slender waist and the gentle curve of her hips.

"Have you had Lady since she was a puppy?" Abby asked, unaware that her smile scraped like sandpaper against Quinn's already frayed nerves.

"I inherited her."

"Inherited her?"

"My dad passed away last year. Lady belonged to him."

Quinn didn't bother to add that the dog had been another innocent victim of his father's neglect. The day before the funeral, Quinn had followed a rusty chain anchored around the post of the deck to a box made of scrap wood underneath an oak tree in the backyard. He knelt down to look inside and was stunned to see a pair of bright but wary eyes staring back at him.

Quinn hadn't known his father even owned a dog but it didn't surprise him a bit that he hadn't taken care of her. Mike O'Halloran's legacy was one of abuse and neglect. He'd let his family splinter apart, his house practically fall down around his ears and his locksmith business slide to the verge of bankruptcy.

While Quinn debated whether he should try and lure the dog out or simply call animal control, Lady had taken charge of the situation. She'd sidled up to him, her coat matted and dirty, and politely lifted a paw for him to shake.

Quinn had picked her up, taken her into the house and fed her. Then he gave her a bath. That night, Lady staked a claim near his feet when he went to bed.

She'd been there ever since.

"I'm sorry about your father." Abby rose to her feet and laid her hand on Quinn's arm. It took all his self-control not to jerk away from her touch. "My parents died when I was fourteen. They were flying home from a convention in a friend's twin-engine plane. There was some sort of mechanical failure…" Her voice trailed off, the memory—and the pain—as fresh in her eyes as if it had happened only the week before.

"You mentioned a brother. Alex. Do you have other siblings?" Quinn thrust his hands in his pockets, jostling her hand from his arm.

A heartbeat of silence preceded her answer. "No. Just Alex. He's eight years older than I am. He was finishing his last semester of college but he came home and took over the... I mean—" Abby caught herself. "He kept things going."

Took over, Quinn thought wryly, was probably a more accurate description. Still, he couldn't imagine the kind of pressure Alex Porter had faced after the death of their parents. Not only had he stepped into his father's shoes as CEO of Porter Hotels, he'd become an instant guardian to a much younger sibling. It went a long way in explaining why he was so protective of Abby.

Their eyes met and she backpedaled, almost tripping over the laundry basket in the process. "I'll put these sheets and towels inside the cabin for you."

Quinn released a sigh as the two dogs bounded after her. When he followed a few minutes later, he found Abby in the kitchen, eyeing the meager bag of groceries he'd dumped in the middle of the kitchen table.

"You brought...food."

"I don't expect you to provide my meals."

Abby's teeth tucked into her lower lip, a habit that Quinn had noticed seemed to coincide with her desire to say something she wasn't sure she should. The trait must have slipped through the cracks of the Porter DNA. Alex had no trouble saying what was on his mind.

"I know, but..." She picked up a can of ravioli and it looked to Quinn as if she shuddered. "It's silly to cook for myself when I can easily make enough for two."

Sharing meals with Abby. Quinn stifled a groan. Granted, it meant more time in her company but it also meant...more time in her company.

He scooped up a few cans of tuna and shoved them in the cupboard. "That isn't necessary. I'll make do."

"I've been trying out different recipes to serve to the guests." Abby paused to study the label on a loaf of white bread. "Daniel was my official food critic. And since you're taking his place as my carpenter, you might as well take his place as the taste tester, too."

The offer was reasonable. And generous. At the moment, Quinn wasn't sure he was in the mood to be either. He didn't *want* to get to know Abby better. "Thanks, but I'll get more done if I work at my own pace and don't have to stop for meals at certain times."

I'll get more done. He'd said the words deliberately but Abby didn't react the way he'd expected. Instead, she stared at him thoughtfully, as if he were a chessboard and she was studying her next move.

"Mmm." That was all she said. But instead of leaving, Abby began to sort through the groceries and put them away. Quinn joined in, only to speed up the process so he could get back to work. And put some distance between them again.

She clucked her tongue with something that sounded like disapproval.

Quinn slanted a look at Abby and caught her frowning at the can of soup in her hand. "What's wrong? Is it expired?"

"It's chicken noodle."

"So?"

"If you put chicken and water and some noodles into a pot, it turns into chicken noodle soup. Home-made. Which means it tastes better."

"That takes time."

"So?"

Quinn resisted the urge to smile when Abby tossed the word back at him. "So I work a lot. It's easier to open a can."

Both were the truth. He didn't work full-time as a carpenter, which was what Abby assumed he did for a living, but the long hours spent rebuilding O'Halloran Security called for sacrifices in other areas. Like his entire life. But that didn't appear to matter. Abby rolled her eyes and put it in the cupboard next to a box of generic macaroni and cheese.

"Macaroni. Cheese. This isn't hard to make, either," she muttered.

"Really?" Quinn raised an eyebrow. "Because I would think it's extremely challenging to locate fluorescent orange cheese, grind it into a powder and seal it in a tiny foil package."

Abby laughed. The lilting sound poured through the tiny kitchen. And swept right through his defenses. Fortunately, Abby's cell phone chirped, granting him a few moments to shore them up again.

"I'm sorry." She glanced at the number and a shadow skimmed through her eyes. "I should take this."

"No problem." Quinn retreated to the cabin deck and picked up one of the windows. Through the screen, he could hear one side of the conversation.

"I don't care and I don't think my attorney will, either." A long silence followed before Abby spoke again, her tone glacial. "Did he mention that Abby Porter is the one who called? No? Well, you might want to mention my name...yes. Thank you."

Quinn's lips twisted.

He'd never have put that autocratic, hand-me-my-crown-and-scepter voice with the woman in the paint-splattered T-shirt who'd offered to make him dinner.

What's the matter? You expected to see this side of her.

That was true. But he hadn't expected to be so disappointed.

Chapter Four

"In other words, the Lord is giving you another opportunity to trust Him. And to grow."

Abby sighed, knowing her friend was right. Jessica always had a wonderful way of cutting to the heart of an issue and letting God's light shine through the cracks.

"With all the opportunities He's been giving me lately, I should be growing as fast as Jack's beanstalk," Abby grumbled good-naturedly.

Jessica chuckled. "No one said opening a bed-and-breakfast would be easy. But do you still think it's worth it?"

"Yes." Abby didn't hesitate.

"There you go, then." Jessica's smile was evident in her voice. "So, what happened today that made you doubt it? Another pleasant phone call from Alexander the Great?"

Abby choked. *"Jessica."*

"Sorry. Did I say that with a lack of proper reverence? I didn't mean to."

She had and they both knew it. Abby grinned.

"I'm surprised Alex didn't fire you after I left. He suspects you were the one who put the idea of a bed-and-breakfast into my head, you know."

"But if he fires me he'll also lose one of his best managers. Who, by the way, happens to be my loving—and very loyal—husband."

"You're right about that."

Alex, for all his controlling ways, depended on Tony Benson to keep the cogs in all four hotels running smoothly. If he ever decided to leave, Abby knew that her brother would feel as if he were missing his right arm.

"Of course I am," Jessica said smugly. "So if I can't blame Alex, what was the challenge of the day?"

An image of Quinn's face flashed in Abby's mind before she could prevent it.

"I told you that Daniel Redstone won a vacation and took two weeks off, right?" Abby plucked a wooden spoon out of a ceramic crock on the counter. "His replacement showed up this morning."

"And you don't think he's going to work out?"

Abby hesitated. So far, she couldn't complain about Quinn's work ethic. The last time she looked outside, he'd already moved to the windows on the other side of the cabin.

Out of sight but definitely not out of mind.

"I'm sure he'll work out…fine." Abby dumped out the contents of the bowl and a cloud of flour rose into the air. She wrinkled her nose to subdue a sneeze.

"Uh-oh."

"What?"

"You're making bread, aren't you?"

Abby put her hands protectively over the mound

of yeast dough, as if Jessica was looking over her shoulder. "Maybe."

"Maybe," Jessica repeated. "So that's a big yes. You know you only make bread when something is bothering you."

"That's not true." At least, not always. But Jessica was right. There was something very therapeutic about pummeling—*kneading*—bread dough.

"So, what's this new carpenter like? What's his name?"

"Are we playing Twenty Questions?" Abby asked. "Because I prefer I Spy. Or Scrabble."

"Hold on a sec, Abbs." Jessica didn't bother to muffle her voice. "I'll be right there, honey. I'm on the phone with Abby. She's making bread."

"Uh-oh." Tony's baritone boomed in the background.

"Okay, I'm back. Continue. New carpenter…"

"Quinn O'Halloran." Abby punched down the dough with a little more force than necessary.

"What's he like?"

Reserved came immediately to mind. Confident. *Incredibly good looking…*

Abby put the brakes on her thoughts, refusing to let them continue down that path. Too dangerous. "He works faster than Daniel, so the cabins might be ready for the grand opening."

"Then what's the problem…" Jessica's voice trailed off, replaced by an audible smack as her palm connected with her forehead. "I'm sorry. Stupid question. Sometimes I forget."

"Don't apologize," Abby said quietly. "I want you to forget."

She wanted to forget.

"Does he make you uncomfortable?"

"Daniel recommended him."

"That doesn't answer my question."

Abby hesitated. She knew what Jessica was really asking but wasn't sure how to answer. Did Quinn make her uncomfortable? Yes. But not in the way her friend assumed.

"I'll talk to Tony." Jessica drew her own conclusion from the silence. "We can take a few days off. Drive up for the weekend."

Abby was touched by the offer. "And if you looked in the rearview mirror, you'd see Alex's Viper right behind you. We can't let him think that I'm afraid and calling for reinforcements."

"You're right," Jessica muttered. "He'd dispatch the deprogrammers and you'd be back in Illinois before sunset."

Somehow, her friend always managed to make Abby smile. "You should get back to Tony. He must be feeling neglected."

"It makes him appreciate me more."

The distinctly masculine snort that followed the comment made them both giggle.

"I'm praying for you," Jessica whispered.

"I know. I wouldn't be here if you weren't."

"You give me way too much credit. You're there because you listened to God and faced your fears."

Listened to God, Abby hoped so. Faced her fears? That was more difficult. Especially when they kept popping up like targets in a shooting gallery.

"One step at a time, remember?" Jessica said, as if she'd read Abby's mind. "And if this O'Halloran guy makes you nervous, you can find someone to take his place. It's okay."

"He doesn't make me nervous. Not like that." Abby had worked hard to overcome her wariness of strangers but there were times it crept back in, especially if she was in a confined space with someone she didn't know. Or if someone turned up when she wasn't expecting them.

With Quinn, it had been both.

The strange thing was, Abby had felt as if he'd somehow sensed her unease. There were times she could have sworn that he'd stepped away from her on purpose. Given her some space. And the few times they had been in close proximity, instead of feeling vulnerable, Abby had felt...safe.

She hadn't experienced that before.

That was what made her nervous.

Quinn flipped over on his back and swam leisurely to shore, letting the cool water flow over the kinks in his muscles. He'd replaced the last window in the cabin as the sun began to sink into the horizon, making the trees look as if they'd been planted in liquid gold. Venus, the first planet to appear in the evening sky, winked at him through a tear in the bank of apricot clouds above his head.

After working in the hot sun all afternoon, Quinn had looked forward to cooling off in the lake with a relaxing swim. The cooling off part was successful. The relaxing part, not so much. His thoughts weren't cooperating.

Not with Abby Porter all tangled up in them.

Two weeks. That's all I can spare.

The words he'd said to Alex came back to mock him. Because less than eight hours later, he was ready to bolt. Faye would understand about the air conditioner....

Who was he kidding? If that was the only thing at stake, he would be on his way back to town by now.

Reaching the dock, Quinn grabbed on to the ladder and pulled himself up. By the time he toweled off and started back to the cabin, the low drone in the bushes made him glad he'd repaired the hole in the screened porch.

There was no sign of Lady. She'd wanted to swim out to the raft with him but Quinn had made her stay behind. Because what the little dog lacked in size, she more than made up for in volume. If a car pulled into the driveway, Lady let him know about it. No one could get past her without sounding the alarm. Because she rivaled the best system O'Halloran Security had to offer, Quinn was willing to turn over guard duty to her for a while.

He'd never worked as a bodyguard with the intent of staying as far away as possible from the client before, but Quinn was up to the challenge this time.

Whenever his traitorous thoughts had started to conjure up Abby Porter's smile or her laugh, all Quinn had to do was squelch them by recalling the phone conversation he'd overheard through the cabin window. A glimpse into the woman's true nature. She was like so many of the people who'd hired him when he was with Hamlin. Sweet and personable as long as everything went their way. Ready to use the weight of their name and bank account number when it didn't. Like Serena Raynes.

Quinn's stomach rumbled suddenly, chiding him for turning down Abby's offer to cook for him. He ignored it. There was nothing wrong with a good old-fashioned can of sodium-saturated broth with pieces of mystery meat floating in it.

He stopped short as he entered the kitchen. And then looked around to make sure he hadn't walked into the wrong cabin by mistake. Nope. The canvas duffel bag containing his clothes was on the floor where he'd left it; flannel shirt tossed over the back of the sofa.

Quinn turned back to the old trestle table. It was covered with a crisp, white tablecloth that hadn't been there when he'd left the cabin to go for a swim. Some-one—and he had a pretty good idea who that someone was—had also taken the time to artfully arrange a place setting that rivaled the ones he'd seen in four-star restaurants. China plate. More silverware than Quinn knew what to do with. A crystal decanter filled with ice water.

The centerpiece was a covered casserole dish. Which Quinn eyed as if it were a ticking package that had been delivered in the mail.

Cautiously, he lifted the lid. And choked on a laugh.

Macaroni and cheese. At least Quinn figured that's what it was. It didn't look quite the same as what he was used to.

"Lady!" Quinn bellowed.

She appeared in the doorway, stubby tail wagging. A dog biscuit roughly the size of Quinn's tennis shoe clamped between her teeth. Still, Lady managed to make a noise that sounded more like a quack than a bark.

"Your timing is a little off." Quinn rolled his eyes. "You're supposed to make a ruckus before someone breaks in, not after."

Not in the least concerned by the reprimand, Lady turned and trotted off to finish her supper.

Quinn decided it would be foolish of him not to do the same.

It didn't mean he'd changed his opinion of Abby Porter.

Abby's alarm clock—the dozen crows that perched in the pine tree outside her bedroom window every morning—went off at quarter to five.

Right on schedule.

Ordinarily, she loved to wake up to the sound. As soon as the sky began to lighten, they met in the branches and held what would probably be considered a lively coffee klatch in the aviary world. Minus the coffee. The noise level reminded her a little of the people who crowded into the booths at the Grapevine Café to exchange news. Abby relied on the birds to wake her up every morning but in this instance, morning had come way too soon.

Rolling over, Abby fought the temptation to pull the quilt over her head and close her eyes for a few more minutes. She could blame the total absence of sleep on the gigantic bowl of Moose Tracks ice cream she'd eaten at midnight…or on Quinn O'Halloran.

The ice cream was the obvious choice. Quinn the more honest one.

Abby shifted restlessly as she recalled the abrupt

change in his attitude after she'd excused herself to speak to Derek Carlson's landlord.

A month before she'd left Chicago, Tony and Jessica had introduced her to Derek, a young man who had recently joined their congregation and was trying to turn his life around after serving time in jail for theft.

Abby had not only arranged for the hotel to hire Derek as a line cook but she'd found an apartment for him in a building near the hotel so he could ride his bicycle to work. Unfortunately, when Derek's record came to light, the landlord had changed his mind about renting to him.

Derek had left a message on her phone, telling her the landlord had added an amendment to the contract. He wanted a year's lease, backed up by a two-month security deposit, or he wouldn't let Derek take the apartment.

The landlord's latest obstacle forced Abby to perform her best imitation of Alex at his most autocratic, hoping she could pull it off. But when she ended the conversation and had gone outside to find Quinn, he barely spared a glance in her direction.

On her way back to the lodge, it occurred to Abby that he might have taken offense at her less than enthusiastic response to what he considered edible food.

Abby groaned and buried her face in the pillow, once again scolding herself for her lack of sensitivity.

Quinn had come right out and said he wanted to work as many hours as possible because he needed the additional income. If a man was forced to be frugal with his finances, then canned soup was not only easy but it didn't strain the budget, either.

Abby believed that actions spoke louder than words but she had her own little twist on the saying.

The best kind of apology was served warm from the oven.

Hence the double batch of gooey, homemade macaroni and cheese.

There'd been no sign of Quinn when she'd knocked on the door of the cabin, so she'd bribed her way past Lady with a jumbo, whole-wheat dog biscuit.

A single bare lightbulb flickering in the kitchen ceiling was the only thing holding the evening shadows at bay. The room looked so stark and unappealing that Abby hadn't been able to resist the urge to spruce things up a bit. She'd set the table, left the casserole dish where Quinn couldn't miss it and then spent a restless night wondering how he felt about the peace offering she'd left.

"You're *still* thinking about it," Abby muttered.

Mulligan's impatient woof at the bottom of the stairs reminded her that the grace period for delivering his breakfast kibbles had officially expired.

"Five more minutes," Abby called, reaching for the Bible on her nightstand.

After moving into her new home, Abby had taken Jessica's advice and started reading through the Psalms. Her friend must have known she'd find encouragement in the verses that reminded her not to be afraid. To trust God.

And there were a lot of them. She would pick one out and think about it while taking Mulligan for his morning walk around the lake.

The peaceful lap of the water against the shoreline and the whisper of wind in the trees provided the perfect start to the day. Time to memorize one of her "walking verses." As much as there was to accomplish, Abby didn't want to get so focused on fixing up the lodge that she neglected to seek out the One who'd led her there in the first place.

As she got dressed, she heard the staccato tap of a hammer outside the window. For some reason, it didn't surprise her that Quinn was an early riser, too. She resisted the urge to look out the window and went downstairs to the kitchen.

She filled a thermos with coffee and grabbed one of the biscuits she'd made. When she opened the door, two dogs stood there, looking up at her with hopeful expressions.

Abby smiled.

"The more the merrier, I suppose. Let's go."

Chapter Five

"**W**here is my sister?"

"Porter." Quinn removed the nail pinched in the corner of his lips. He wouldn't have answered his cell except for the fact he'd decided to allow Abby's brother one phone call a day. He'd also decided to get it over with as soon as possible. "What's wrong? Your satellite imagery isn't working this morning?"

"Funny," Alex growled. "Now answer the question."

"Is this a test?"

"Yes."

Quinn eyed the board, held the nail in place and gave it a solid whack with the hammer. "I haven't seen her yet, so my guess is that she's still sleeping."

"Your guess." Alex repeated the words. "It's your job to *know.* It's seven-thirty and Abby's routine is to be awake and going by five."

"I've been here twenty-four hours," Quinn pointed out mildly. "Not quite enough time to get to know her routine." Other than forcing her way into his kitchen and offering her opinion about grocery lists. Breaking and entering, armed with macaroni and cheese…

Quinn stuck another nail between his lips to circumvent a smile.

"She goes for a walk around the lake every morning."

"If you're six hours away and you know that, what do you need me for?"

"The only reason I know is because Abby *told* me she does. A prayer walk, whatever that is." Alex's tone made it clear he didn't much care. "And you should be with her."

"Abby is fine." Quinn might not be sure where Abby was at the moment, but he was convinced of that much. "And you're spending an awful lot of money for no reason."

"I have a reason." Alex's voice tightened. "It's called peace of mind."

Quinn's gaze drifted to the curve of the shoreline, where the trees formed a living wall that blocked out the sunlight. "If it makes you feel better, I'll check on her."

"I'd appreciate it." Sarcasm leaked into Alex's voice. "Why do I get the feeling that you aren't taking this seriously, O'Halloran."

"You're taking it seriously enough for both of us. If you aren't happy, maybe you should find someone else." *Sorry, Faye,* Quinn thought. *I'll get you a bigger fan.*

"You agreed to keep an eye on Abby. You can't do that unless you're *with* her."

Quinn didn't appreciate the reminder. Because it was true.

"Is your private investigator having any luck?"

"He's narrowed it down to three possibilities."

"No kidding? Only three?"

Alex laughed. "O'Halloran…"

"I'm fired?" Quinn interrupted hopefully.

"You're quite the comedian."

"But still employed?"

"Yes."

Quinn was afraid Porter was going to say that. What he didn't understand was why. So he asked.

"I told you. I wanted the best."

"You didn't ask Ken Raynes for a reference, did you?" Quinn dropped the question like a gauntlet.

Alex didn't pick it up. "I hired the right person."

Quinn wished he felt the same way.

"'The name of the Lord is a strong tower. The righteous runs into it and is safe.'"

Abby said the words out loud, letting them soak into her soul.

For too long, she'd taken refuge in the Porter name. Hidden behind the wealth and privilege—and protection—it afforded. Although both she and Alex worked hard to ensure the success of the business their parents had started, Abby knew their inheritance gave them access to resources most people didn't have.

It was the reason she'd been determined to do things on her own when she purchased the property on Mirror Lake. And why she hadn't told anyone in town about her connection to Porter Hotels.

Alex thought she'd lost her mind, but Abby knew that something different had happened. She'd found *peace* of mind.

She wasn't going to trust the Porter name to keep her safe anymore. Or to define who she was. There were other names she put her hope in now.

Savior. Deliverer. Prince of Peace. Shield. Fortress.

Reading through the Psalms and discovering the names of God was like panning for gold. The verses helped her sift out her old way of thinking— the doubts and fears and insecurities—until the truth remained.

It felt like an adventure. One she wouldn't have had the courage to embark on without finding strength in God's promises.

Her thoughts drifted back to Quinn. Something that had been happening on a frequent—and rather disturbing—basis over the past twenty-four hours.

Was he a believer?

Quinn seemed so…guarded. And a flicker of doubt had appeared in his eyes when she'd told him that Alex thought he had a better plan for her life than God did.

Jessica's husband had mentioned that some men had a difficult time surrendering their lives to God because it was hard to relinquish control. Abby had discovered the irony in that when she'd examined her own heart. She *didn't* have control. Accepting that hadn't been scary, it had set her free.

She'd been praying for months that Alex would discover that same truth.…

And Quinn, Lord. If he doesn't know You.

Rounding a corner, Abby stepped off the worn path that meandered along the shoreline to follow the one she'd discovered a few weeks ago. Mulligan, who knew their destination, played tag with Lady through the underbrush.

As the trees opened into a clearing, Abby's heart lifted at the sight of the chapel. It hadn't been listed in the property description, so when Abby had stumbled upon it one day while chasing after Mulligan, who'd been chasing after a rabbit, it felt as if she'd been given a gift. The tiny, fieldstone building was empty except for six wooden pews arranged in front of a cross fashioned from rough-hewn timbers.

Along with the kitchen, it had become one of her favorite retreats.

"Sorry, you two. No dogs allowed."

Mulligan and Lady, who'd been waiting for her to catch up, seemed to understand because they flopped down in the grass a few feet away from the weathered door.

Abby left the door open a few inches to let some fresh air circulate inside the building as she slipped past them.

The scent of lemon oil lingered in the air. She'd polished the pews until she could see her reflection, but other than that she'd left the chapel the way she'd found it. Even though it would benefit from some simple repairs, Abby was reluctant to change a thing. At first she wasn't sure she wanted to let the guests know about it, but decided it would be selfish to keep it a secret.

She slid into the first pew and closed her eyes, trying to remember her walking verse.

The name of the Lord is a strong tower...

A hand clamped down on her shoulder and Abby surged to her feet, her instincts fueled by the adrenaline coursing through her veins.

In the time it took Abby to draw her next breath, she had flipped the person onto his back, neutralizing the threat.

Quinn.

* * *

Quinn lay flat on his back, staring up at the beamed ceiling.

A blurry image of Abby's face appeared above him, the silver-green eyes wide. He blinked. Because incredibly enough, it looked as if she were...

"Smiling," Quinn groaned. "Why are you smiling?"

"Because it worked." Abby dropped to her knees beside him.

He tried to lift his head but little white spots danced in front of his eyes. Suddenly there were two Abbys. And *both* of them were smiling. "What worked?"

"The takedown. It's a self-defense move—"

"I know what it is." Quinn pushed his fingertips against the floor to get some leverage so he could sit up. And chase the spots away. "But why did you practice it on me?"

Abby looked a little uncertain now. "You...surprised me."

"I surprised *you?*"

When he looked through the opening in the door and saw Abby sitting in the pew, he'd thought she was crying. Her head was bent, chin against her chest. Shoulders slumped. It had propelled him to her side in an instant.

The next thing he knew, he was flat on his back, staring up at the ceiling.

"Are you all right?"

"Too late," Quinn muttered. "I think those are the first words I should have heard. Not 'it worked.'"

"I'm sorry." Abby tried unsuccessfully to subdue her excitement. "It's just that I studied that move in a book and I wasn't sure it would really work."

"Glad I could help... *Ouch.*" Quinn pushed himself into a sitting position and lifted a hand to explore the lump he was sure had to be sprouting from the back of his head. But Abby's hands got there first, tunneling through his hair. Exploring his scalp.

Making him see spots all over again.

Quinn swallowed hard. "Next time just knock me unconscious."

"What?"

"Never mind." Time for a countermove. He inched away.

Abby scooted closer. "No blood. I don't think there's any swelling, either."

Quinn gaped at her. She actually sounded a little disappointed. "Just a mild concussion, huh? I guess I'm lucky this concrete floor has some give to it."

"It's pine, not concrete." Abby leaned in until they were almost nose to nose. Close enough for Quinn to see an intriguing emerald fleck in one of her silver-green eyes. Breathe in the fresh scent of her shampoo—along with that intriguing hint of cinnamon. "Your pupils aren't dilated."

The side effects from being so close to Abby were proving to be greater than any caused by a bump on the head.

Ignoring the pain that streaked up the back of his neck, Quinn lurched to his feet. "Thank you, Dr. Porter. Did you read a book on how to diagnose the damage you caused after you read a book on how to cause the damage?"

"Okay, maybe you do have a concussion." Abby reached for him and Quinn drew back. "I won't flip you again. Promise." The engaging smile she flashed in his direction was more dangerous than her amateur ninja skills.

Now that the spots had begun to fade—and Abby no longer had her hands in his hair—his thoughts began to clear. "I'm not sure why you *flipped me* in the first place."

"I told you. You surprised me." Abby bit her lip and turned away. "How did you find me up here? Did you need something?"

An explanation, that's what he needed.

Quinn stared at her; the instincts he no longer trusted kicked into red alert. Most people, even if startled, would have reacted differently. An involuntary jerk. A gasp. Abby, on the other hand, had felt his hand on her shoulder and treated him as a…threat.

Why?

"A how-to book on self-defense," he ventured casually. "Is that what you consider light reading?"

"Oh, you know…" Abby's gaze slid away from him. "Because you never know."

As far as explanations went, it meant nothing. And everything.

Quinn rubbed the back of his head, wondering if he should push the issue.

Abby noticed the gesture and had the good sense to at least *pretend* she felt guilty about tossing him onto a hardwood floor. "Does it still hurt?"

"Only my pride."

Abby smiled again. "If that's all, then *Dr. Porter* guarantees you'll make a full recovery."

Quinn wasn't so sure. The damage to his head was minimal. At the moment he was more concerned about the potential damage to his heart.

Chapter Six

Abby spent the remainder of the morning staining trim in the library and berating herself for her response when Quinn had shown up at the chapel and touched her shoulder.

She wouldn't have blamed him if *his* response had been to quit on the spot.

If Quinn questioned her sanity for converting a dilapidated former Bible camp into a bed-and-breakfast—and there was evidence to support that theory—then what did he think of her now?

All he'd done was put his hand on her shoulder to get her attention and she had sent him sprawling.

And then, to make matters worse, she'd smiled.

Smiled.

And touched him, an inner voice reminded her, adding another item to her list of crimes.

Checked for bruises, Abby corrected, even as a memory pushed its way in. The silky slide of Quinn's hair between her fingers. The warmth of his skin. The way his eyes had darkened to charcoal—okay, possibly due to pain—when she'd knelt down next to him to see if he was showing signs of a concussion.

Stain dripped off the end of the foam brush and landed on her shoe instead of the drop cloth.

That did it.

A change of scenery was in order. Something to keep her mind off Quinn O'Halloran. Maybe it was time to devote some attention to the list of errands she'd been putting off for the last few days.

Abby poked her head out the door and called for Mulligan, jingling her car keys as an added incentive. He loved to sit in the passenger seat and stick his head out the window, lips turned inside out in a grin, while his ears flapped in the breeze like miniature wind socks.

After waiting another sixty seconds, it was clear that her faithful companion had abandoned her for the adorable cocker spaniel that had moved in next door.

Abby paused on her way to the garage, wondering whether she should walk down to the cabin and let Quinn know she would be gone for a few hours.

Since she'd barely seen him after they'd parted company that morning, she decided against it. He wouldn't even notice she was gone.

Coward.

True. But in this situation, Abby decided she could live with that. Her formal apology was cooling on the kitchen counter, so although she knew she had to face Quinn sooner or later, Abby picked later. She couldn't face him at the moment.

"Going somewhere?"

Abby froze. And turned toward the familiar voice. Quinn stood several yards away. Looking better than anyone had a right to in a plain white T-shirt and faded jeans. His hands were raised above his head as if he were surrendering.

A bubble of laughter escaped before she could prevent it. "Not funny."

"Who said I was joking? Never let it be said that Quinn O'Halloran doesn't learn from his mistakes." Something moved through Quinn's eyes like sunlight skimming the surface of the water. On anyone else, Abby would have recognized it as amusement. On Quinn…

No, it couldn't be. He couldn't actually be *teasing* her.

While she was trying to wrap her mind around that, his lips hitched up at the corners.

Abby's heart did a free fall to her toes.

It wasn't the polished, make-sure-you-get-my-best-side kind that she was used to having bestowed upon her. Not even close. And as far as smiles went, it probably wouldn't even register on a smile scale. If there was a smile scale. But none of that mattered because even the *hint* of a smile on Quinn O'Halloran's face packed enough punch to steal the breath from a woman's lungs.

While Abby struggled to draw a breath, the pointed look Quinn aimed at the keys dangling from her fingers reminded her that he'd asked a question.

"I have some errands to run in town."

"Mind if I tag along?"

It was the last thing she expected Quinn to say. And the last thing she wanted him to do. After all, the whole point of putting some distance between them was so she wouldn't think about Quinn for a few hours. It defeated the whole purpose if she actually brought him with her.

"I need a few things from the hardware store if I want to start the roof this afternoon," he added. "I was going to drive in later, but when I saw you walking to your car..."

He knew it would be silly to take separate vehicles to the same place. Abby knew it, too. That's why she gave in.

"I suppose."

Some of her reluctance must have crept into her voice because Quinn's eyebrow lifted. "Can you give me five minutes to wash up and put Lady in the cabin?"

"I don't mind if you bring her along."

The elusive smile came and went again. "You'd have her on your lap. Lady doesn't like the backseat."

"Neither does Mulligan. If we take your truck, we can all fit in front."

"My truck?" Quinn's expression was as astonished as if she'd suggested they fly to Mirror Lake.

"What's wrong with your truck?"

"Nothing. Except it's probably not as comfortable as your vehicle." The pointed look Quinn aimed at her lipstick-red convertible severed the connection his unexpected smile had created between them.

Before Abby could explain that the car hadn't been her choice, but a gift from Alex on her twenty-first birthday, Quinn was already striding back to the cabin.

Five minutes later, the four of them were wedged together into the cab of Quinn's pickup. Lady curled sedately up in her lap while Mulligan sat in the middle, content to give up his usual window seat for the entertainment of watching the tree-shaped air freshener dance from Quinn's rearview mirror.

Abby pulled a piece of paper out of her bag and skimmed the contents. "Have you lived in Mirror Lake very long?"

Quinn didn't answer so Abby wasn't sure he'd heard her. She tried again. "Have you—"

"A while."

A while.

What did that mean? A month? A year? Ten years? The shuttered expression on Quinn's face made her curious.

"How much time will you need in town?" He neatly tried to change the subject. Which made Abby even more curious.

"Not more than two hours. A friend of mine recommended that I buy from local artists when it's time to put the finishing touches on the inn. Do you know anyone in the area I could talk to?"

"Artists? Not that I can think of." Quinn slanted a look at her over Mulligan's bushy head. "Stop in and ask at the Grapevine Café. I'm sure someone there would know."

"I love that place."

"Why?"

"It reminds me of the diners on those old TV shows. Vinyl booths. Plastic ferns in the window. An old-fashioned soda fountain. A jukebox. Everyone talks to everyone else. It's like stepping back in time."

Exactly why Quinn avoided it.

What he had a difficult time believing was that Kate Nichols's café appealed to Abby, whose last name opened doors to the best of the best. The Porter Hotels' in-house restaurants boasted four-star ratings and required a tie to get past the mâitre d'.

Abby might view the "everyone talks to everyone else" as a quaint, small-town feature but from Quinn's perspective, it was gossip, plain and simple.

The locals loved the café because a cup of coffee was cheaper than subscribing to the *Mirror Lake Register* and the news more timely. They also had the place to themselves, as the tourists who migrated north in the summer usually bypassed the Grapevine on their quest to find something a little more upscale.

It had also become a popular teenage hangout over the years, even before Kate's parents had turned the place over to her. Quinn had avoided it back then.

The same way he did now.

He shouldn't have suggested to Abby that she go there for the information she was seeking. Not that Quinn expected his name to come up, but it had before. Thanks to his father, the O'Halloran name had been the topic of conversation more times than Quinn wanted to remember.

"I have to talk to Mayor Dodd." Abby nibbled thoughtfully on the end of a pen. "Something about a community celebration that's coming up."

"Labor Day weekend. Reflection Days," Quinn muttered, barely avoiding another pothole as he tore his gaze away from the velvet-soft curve of her lower lip.

Laughter flowed through the cab of his truck. "Clever."

Quinn wasn't surprised Abby had made the connection so quickly, but a lot of people didn't get it. "I suppose that's one word for it."

"What would you call it?" She tilted her head and a wisp of hair drifted across her cheek. Quinn tightened his grip on the steering wheel so he wouldn't do something stupid. Like brush it away.

A two-day forced march down memory lane, that's what he would call it. But he couldn't tell Abby that. Not without opening a Pandora's box full of questions he didn't want to answer.

"An excuse for the Chamber of Commerce to increase their annual budget." There. That was safe. It also happened to be the truth.

Abby clucked her tongue. "Were you born this cynical?"

"You could say that." Quinn had been born an O'Halloran, so the two kind of went hand in hand.

"Well, I think you're blessed to live in a town like Mirror Lake. Even if it's only been for *a while*."

Quinn didn't miss the emphasis Abby put on the last words and a reluctant smile tugged at his lips. Her sense of humor and buoyant personality continued to surprise—and, if he were honest—charm him.

Except that Quinn didn't want to be charmed.

He kept his eyes focused on the road, hoping Abby would take his silence as an indication that he didn't want to talk.

She didn't.

"So what does Reflection Days involve? Other than padding the town budget?"

"Mirror Lake started out as a logging town in the 1800s. A lot of the families can trace their ancestry back to the original founders." Quinn found it more than a little ironic that he should be the one to explain the history of Reflection Days. "There's not much holding it together anymore. When businesses started to close and kids grew up and didn't come back, the city council got nervous. They decided to hold an annual community pride celebration to remind people of the values Mirror Lake was originally founded on."

"I think it's a wonderful idea."

"You might change your mind when Mayor Dodd tries to guilt you on to one of his committees. That's the thing about Reflection Days. All the local businesses are expected to participate."

Except for O'Halloran Security, of course.

When Quinn had moved back to Mirror Lake the summer before, no one had approached him about contributing in some way to the weekend-long celebration. If he'd had any doubt the community wasn't eager to throw out the welcome mat for another O'Halloran, there was his proof.

"Do you think so?" Instead of looking concerned, something Quinn would expect from a person who had enough work to keep her busy round the clock for the next year, Abby's eyes sparkled with anticipation.

Quinn had never been so relieved to see the Welcome to Mirror Lake sign up ahead. "I'll find a place to park the truck and meet you back there in a few hours. Don't worry about the dogs. Slim Peterson keeps his Irish setter at the hardware store so they'll have a chance to stretch their legs running up and down the paint aisle."

"Thanks. I'll try not to take too long." Abby slipped the list back into her purse. "I still have to finish staining trim when we get back… Quinn, look. There's a parking space."

Right in front of the Grapevine Café.

He cruised past it. "Sorry." Not a bit. "Missed it."

"Because you stepped on the gas instead of the brake," Abby said under her breath.

Quinn found another spot farther down the street. In front of Happy's Engine Repair and as far from the café's enormous plate-glass windows as possible.

If word hadn't already gotten out that he and Abby were working together, Quinn wasn't going to deliberately provide grist for the local rumor mill.

Abby pulled down the visor and frowned. "Where's the mirror?"

"Mirror?" Quinn echoed.

"The mirror that comes as a standard feature on every visor," Abby said. Slowly. Enunciating her words as if explaining something to a very small child.

"There is no mirror."

She sighed and shifted in her seat so she was facing him. "Well?"

"Well, what?"

"You're going to have to be my mirror. How is my face?" She stared straight ahead, schooling her features until she resembled one of the marble statues he'd seen in the Chicago Institute of Art.

Quinn eyed her suspiciously. "Is this a trick question?"

"Of course not." Abby's sigh stirred the wisps of sun-streaked hair on her forehead. She rephrased the question. "How do I *look?*"

Stunning was the first word that came to Quinn's mind before he could put it on lockdown. "Fine."

"You're sure?" Abby looked more anxious than a trip to the Grapevine Café warranted. "My hair isn't a mess? My lipstick hasn't worn off? No one knows me very well so I want to make a good impression."

"Your hair is…fine. Lipstick…" Quinn's breath hitched in his throat. To answer the lipstick question meant he had to look at her lips. Something he'd deliberately avoided for the entire ten-minute car ride into town. And had planned to deliberately avoid for the next two weeks. "Also fine."

"That wasn't so bad, now was it?" Abby grinned, tucked her purse under one arm and hugged her smelly old dog with the other.

She had no idea.

Quinn needed to do something to restore his equilibrium and since cynicism had always worked well for him in the past…

"But if you wanted to make a good impression, you should have driven your convertible into town."

Alone.

Abby wrinkled her nose. "Shame on you," she scolded lightly. "That sounds like something someone who judges a person by the kind of car they drive—or don't drive—would say."

She marched away, the heels of her cute little sandals clicking against the sidewalk.

Quinn stared after her in disbelief.

If he wasn't mistaken, Abby Porter had just accused him—Quinn O'Halloran—of being a snob.

Chapter Seven

"What can I get for you, Abby?" Kate Nichols slid into the seat across from her with a welcoming smile.

Abby, who couldn't imagine her brother ever joining his guests at their table with such unaffected ease, smiled back. The owner of the Grapevine Café couldn't have been more than a few years older than she was, but the lively snap in Kate's shamrock-green eyes hinted she was up to any challenge that came her way.

Abby felt a pinch of envy.

We're working on it, aren't we, Lord?

"Just coffee." Abby's gaze drifted to the slices of pie rotating in a dessert carousel a few yards away from the booth.

Kate arched a copper brow. "Strawberry, peach or apple?"

"Strawberry."

"Strawberry it is." Kate leaned forward. "So what brings you into town? I haven't seen you since the service last Sunday morning."

Abby winced at the memory.

Exhausted from working well past midnight, Abby had started to nod off during the video clip Pastor Wilde had played during the adult Sunday school hour. A discreet nudge from Kate's elbow had saved her from acute embarrassment.

Abby would have scooted away right after the class ended but Kate had caught up to her at the door, blocking her escape with an enormous leather study Bible. Something in the young woman's warm personality and mischievous smile had reminded her of Jessica, so she'd accepted Kate's invitation to sit with her during the worship service.

"I still can't believe I did that."

"Don't worry about it. I know what exhaustion feels like. I'm up by 4:00 a.m. making pies three times a week. Believe me, you'll have a chance to return the favor someday." The soft laugh that followed the promise put Abby instantly at ease.

"I will."

Kate turned toward a pack of adolescent boys jostling their way between the tables, their destination the jukebox in the corner. The movement set her cap of fiery red corkscrew curls bouncing.

"No music for five minutes. We're trying to have a conversation here," she barked out.

The boys froze in their tracks and did an immediate about-face, slinking back to the booth they'd occupied moments before.

"If I have to listen to 'Born to Be Wild' one more time, I'm pulling the plug on that relic," Kate muttered. "Missy! Read that book during your break. We need two cups of coffee and a piece of strawberry pie over here."

The willowy teenage girl behind the counter snapped to attention, blushing, and hurried to obey.

"My brother would love you," Abby said without thinking.

"What?" Kate's eyes widened.

"As an employee," Abby amended quickly. "Alex owns a...restaurant." Or four. Restaurants which happened to be located in the hotels he also owned, but she saw no point in mentioning that. "He appreciates 'highly motivated people.'"

Unless it was his sister, of course. When it came to her, Alex appreciated it when Abby was highly motivated in a place where he could keep an eye on her.

Kate shrugged. "If you aren't highly motivated around here, you don't survive. Which is why you'll do just fine. It was sheer genius to buy that old camp and turn it into a bed-and-breakfast."

Abby hadn't expected the compliment but it bloomed inside her. "There's still a lot of work to do."

"When isn't there?" Kate aimed a wink at Missy, who'd sidled up with the pie and two cups of coffee. "Refill the boys' glasses and take ten, sweetheart. You're not going to be any good to me if you spend the whole afternoon wondering what's going to happen at the end of chapter three."

Missy's wide smile exposed twin rows of metal braces. "Thanks, Kate!" She darted away.

"Chapter three?"

"I facilitate a book club for high school girls. It meets here once a month during the summer," Kate explained. "They get homemade pizza and chocolate cake and I get a chance to reread the books I loved at that age. It's a win-win situation."

"It sounds like a lot of fun." Abby emptied the contents of a sugar packet into her coffee. "And I think it's great you take the time to organize something for them."

Kate waved her spoon in the air, as if brushing aside the compliment. "The kids' main complaint is that there isn't a lot to do around here. This is my way of encouraging them to 'bloom where they're planted,' so to speak. You don't know how many times I hear the girls say they can't wait to graduate and move away, never to return."

"Did you ever feel that way?"

"Call me crazy, but no. I never did. I happen to think Mirror Lake has a lot to offer—but I guess it depends on what you're looking for." Kate smiled. "You must know what I'm talking about. I mean, you moved here on purpose, you brave girl."

Brave? It was a word Abby never would have chosen to describe herself. Her faith had given her the courage to start a new life in Mirror Lake but there were times she still battled doubt.

"The book club is always open to new members," Kate continued. "If you're interested."

"It's tempting…" Abby hesitated, not wanting to be rude.

"But totally unrealistic," Kate finished. "I understand. You've got your hands full with that place. I suppose it's slow going without Daniel Redstone there."

Abby wasn't surprised Kate had heard about Daniel's windfall. As much the carpenter talked about fishing, he'd probably turned cartwheels down the middle of Main Street after he'd won the vacation.

"He sent over his partner yesterday, so I'm still on schedule for the grand opening."

"Partner?"

"Quinn O'Halloran."

"Quinn—" Kate, who'd taken a sip from her cup, suddenly began to cough.

"Are you all right?" Abby plucked a napkin out of the metal holder and pressed it into Kate's hand.

"I think so," she wheezed, dabbing the cloth against her streaming eyes.

"Do you know Quinn?" Abby asked, hoping the question didn't sound like shameless curiosity. It was merely…curiosity. Without the shameless.

"A little. He grew up here but we were a few years apart in high school." Kate's voice crackled and she tried to smooth it out with another sip of coffee. "He left town right after graduation. No one saw him for years and then he showed up after his dad died. I didn't realize he was working for you."

"Only until Daniel comes back," Abby said, still processing what Kate had just told her. If Quinn had grown up in Mirror Lake, why hadn't he mentioned that when she'd asked him how long he'd lived in the area?

"He's helped Daniel out in the past, I suppose," Kate murmured. "But Quinn isn't—"

"Kate," a plaintive voice interrupted. "Can we play a song now?" One of the boys she'd shooed away appeared beside the booth. "It's been more than five minutes."

"Sure. Streisand or the Beach Boys. Your pick."

Glowering, the teenager stomped back to the booth.

"It's important to give kids choices." The twinkle in Kate's green eyes belied her serious tone. "Now, what were we talking about?"

"Quinn." Abby leaned forward, more than ready to return to the previous topic of their discussion.

She wanted to know the reason behind Kate's strange reaction when Abby had mentioned that Quinn was filling in for Daniel. And what Kate had been about to say right before they'd been interrupted.

"Miss Porter!" The bells on the door accompanied Mayor Dodd's boisterous greeting. "I knew I'd find you here!"

"Not that a person has a whole lot of options in a town this size," Kate whispered as she picked up her cup and slid out of the booth. "I think this is the perfect time to check over the dinner menu."

A half hour later, Abby knew why her new friend had made a quick getaway. While Quinn had managed to condense the purpose behind Reflection Days in a few short sentences, Mayor Dodd expounded on it as if he were standing behind a pulpit on a Sunday morning.

Abby had been introduced to him briefly after she'd moved to Mirror Lake. As round as he was tall, the mayor bore a striking resemblance to a garden gnome. Blue eyes blazed beneath snow-white eyebrows that merged together like an unclipped hedge over the bridge of his nose. Sideburns connected a flowing salt-and-pepper beard to the thick mustache that obscured his upper and lower lip. What it didn't obscure was the toothpick that jutted out of the corner of his mouth and kept time with every word he spoke.

"...the Chamber of Commerce welcomes new businesses to the area. You give to the community, you get back." Mayor Dodd's coffee cup came down between them like a gavel to emphasize the point.

"I'd be happy to—"

"Good. Good." The toothpick bobbed in approval. "We're one judge short for the Reflection Day parade."

Behind the counter, Abby saw Kate make a slashing gesture against her throat. "Um—"

"Good. Good. I'll have my wife call you with the details. She's in charge of the parade committee."

Abby decided that Kate must have been directing the gesture toward the boys crowded around the jukebox. Judging a parade didn't sound like a huge responsibility. And she was looking forward to getting involved in the community.

Abby happened to glance at the clock and gasped. "I'm sorry, Mayor Dodd. I have to go."

The toothpick drooped like a cat's tail on a rainy day. "But we haven't talked about your nomination for the Main Street beautification project yet—"

"Mayor?" Kate breezed up to the booth. "I've got one slice of apple pie left. On the house, if you're interested."

The blue eyes brightened. "On the house? Good. Good."

Abby sent the café owner a grateful look as she snatched up her purse. "How much do I owe you for the coffee?"

"Forget about it." Kate lowered her voice. "You earned it. FYI, the mayor's won the pie eating contest five years in a row. Six slices in three minutes and twelve seconds. Now go."

As Abby made a break for it, the opening beat of "Born to Be Wild" followed her out the door. Stepping into the warm afternoon sunshine, she scanned both sides of the street but there was no sign of Quinn. Or the truck.

Great. He'd kidnapped her dog and left her stranded in Mirror Lake.

"It's about time."

Quinn caught the wadded-up piece of paper that came sailing toward him as he walked into the office.

"That bad, huh?"

"Let me count the ways." Faye crossed her arms. "Your part-time guys are struggling for dominance. If this was *Survivor,* I'd vote them both off the island. Mel Burdock calls every few hours, complaining his house isn't getting the *undivided attention* you promised when he hired you…and it's five hundred degrees in here today because my stubborn boss won't swallow his pride and let me buy an air conditioner for the office."

"Don't exaggerate. It can't be more than a hundred and fifty." Quinn raked a hand through his hair. "But go on."

"Thank you. I will." Faye picked up an envelope and waved it at him. "This letter from Jeff Gaines came in the mail and every time I get tempted to steam it open, I eat a piece of candy instead. I've gained three pounds in the last two hours."

Quinn held out his hand.

"Candy or the letter?"

"Both."

Faye complied. "Now be a good boy and stand still while I read it over your shoulder."

"What would I do without you and your total disregard for the fact that I'm the one who signs your paycheck?"

"Is that what you call it?" she asked tartly. "To my way of thinking, a paycheck should cover more than a cup of coffee at the Grapevine."

"Kate's coffee *is* expensive." Quinn grinned, used to Faye's acerbic sense of humor. "I'll be back in a few minutes."

She reached up and patted his cheek. "I hope it's good news, honey."

He did, too. But it took two laps around the office before Quinn opened the envelope. If his bid was accepted, he could tell Alex Porter he wouldn't have time to work at the lodge, looking for threats that didn't exist…and be forced to deal with the unexpected feelings Abby stirred inside of him.

She continued to astonish him. Her response to his comment about the car had left him reeling. To Quinn's knowledge, no one had ever accused *him,* even teasingly, of being a snob before.

No one had ever dropped him on the back of his head with a basic move from chapter one of an amateur's guide to self-defense book, either.

Or cut through his defenses with a single smile.

The sooner he was done with this assignment— and, he reminded himself, Abby Porter *was* an assignment—the better. Alex had hinted that she had moved to Mirror Lake on a whim; once she realized that the grim reality outweighed her dreams, she would return to Chicago.

Quinn didn't doubt it for a second. And he had no intention of letting Abby take a piece of his heart when she jumped into that little red convertible and drove away.

He took a deep breath and opened the envelope. Inside was an official letter from Gaines Developers. With Jeff Gaines's official signature at the bottom. Officially telling him that the deadline for the bid on the White Wolf Run condos had been adjusted due to extenuating circumstances.

Extenuating circumstances otherwise known as Alex Porter.

Quinn closed his eyes briefly.

Should he admire the guy's tenacity or withdraw the bid and walk away with his pride still intact? Quinn hadn't been guaranteed that O'Halloran Security would win the contract, but if Porter put in a good word for him with Jeff Gaines, it would level the playing field a little. Give the business a fighting chance.

Quinn wished he didn't need one.

But Mike O'Halloran had dragged the family name through the mud and every time Quinn took a step forward, it felt as if everyone's eyes were on him— watching to see if he left footprints.

The bells over the front door jingled, announcing the arrival of someone Quinn hoped was a potential customer. If it wasn't, he had no doubt that Faye would convince the person that O'Halloran Security had something they needed.

He wasn't sure what he'd do without her.

Quinn hadn't forgotten the day she'd shown up because it was the day he'd almost given up.

He'd only been in Mirror Lake a week but was already overwhelmed by the monumental task of repairing all the things that had suffered due to his father's neglect. The house. The business. A needy cocker spaniel. A stunted, dried-up rhododendron bush planted next to the front door of the office that looked to be in the same shape as everything else he'd inherited.

While Quinn had been kneeling in front of the rhododendron, examining it for signs of life, someone's finger had tapped his shoulder with the force of a woodpecker searching for its next meal.

It had been years since he'd seen her, but Quinn recognized Faye McAllister immediately. She was one of the people he'd told Abby about, a member of a family who could trace their origins to the founders of Mirror Lake. She'd driven a Cadillac almost as long as Main Street and made a full-time career out of being a doctor's wife.

Everyone in Mirror Lake respected Faye— although Quinn suspected there was a thin line between respect and terror. If she was a little brash and outspoken, people were willing to overlook it because Doc McAllister was just the opposite. A quiet, even-tempered man who made house calls.

Shortly after his return to Mirror Lake, Quinn had heard that Doc had passed away the previous fall, but he hadn't seen Faye around.

Until she'd found him.

"You don't answer the phone or the door," she snapped. "Shouldn't you be helping your paying customers?"

Quinn wanted to say that he would, if he had paying customers to help. Instead he'd asked, "Can I do something for you, Mrs. McAllister?"

"I don't know." Faye had glowered at him. "I locked my keys in my car. Is this place open for business or not?"

He'd almost said no.

"Yes."

"Then why is there a closed sign in the window? Why isn't someone in the office answering the phone?"

"Because I haven't hired someone to answer the phone yet." Quinn's frustration had reached its limit and spilled over into the next question. "When can you start?"

He'd waited, expecting Faye to club him over the head with her purse. To his astonishment, a smile had spread across her face.

"Tomorrow morning."

She'd arrived at eight o'clock the next day, a brown bag lunch in one hand and an African violet in the other, and took over the front office with the efficiency of a four-star general.

Faye had no computer skills and knew nothing about office management. Quinn kept her on anyway. Because his first two honest-to-goodness paying clients played bridge with her on Tuesday nights.

A coincidence? He didn't think so.

Staring down at the letter in his hand, Quinn tried to figure out the best way to explain the delay to Faye. One that would convince her not to call Jeff Gaines and demand an explanation of the "extenuating circumstances" herself.

On cue, the desk phone chirped at him.

"Yeah?"

"What's taking you so long?" Faye demanded. "Is the letter written in Chinese?"

He laughed. "No, it's in English."

"Then get out here and tell...wait a second. Someone is walking up the sidewalk."

She sounded disappointed. Quinn, on the other hand, was relieved. He'd slip out while Faye was occupied with the customer. Abby had asked for two hours and it was close to that now....

As he took a step toward the door, a familiar voice made Quinn's heart slam-dunk against his rib cage.

Abby.

She'd found him.

Chapter Eight

She'd gone to the wrong address.

Which meant Abby had five minutes to find the right one before it was time to meet up with Quinn again.

Plunging one hand into her purse, she tried to locate her list as an elderly woman, whose hair matched the sleeveless red blouse she wore, zipped toward her with an energy that was impressive, given the fact the building felt like a sauna.

"Can I help you?"

I doubt it.

Abby bit back the words before she said them out loud.

The address scrawled on the piece of paper had led her to a cement block eyesore two blocks off Main Street.

The sparsely furnished reception area, with its water-stained ceiling and dark paneled walls, gave Abby no clue as to what kind of business went on there but it couldn't have been the one she was looking for.

She mustered a friendly smile, an attempt to offset the grim work environment the poor woman had to deal with. "I hope so. I must have written down the wrong address."

"Maybe, maybe not. What are you looking for?"

"Fourteen Maplewood. There's supposed to be a locksmith there."

"Then you're in the right place."

"Really?" Abby caught herself. "That's…great." The floor sank beneath her foot as she took a step forward.

"Faye McAllister. Office manager." The woman extended a hand. "And you're in luck because the boss is in this afternoon. I'll let him know you're here."

"Oh." Now Abby was down to three minutes and counting. "I thought I'd make an appointment. I don't have a lot of time."

"That's all right. Neither does he." Faye McAllister tossed the cryptic words over her shoulder as she marched toward a crescent-shaped desk wedged between the counter and the wall.

Abby gnawed on her lower lip. Maybe she should call Quinn and let him know she'd be a few minutes late. As she searched in vain for her cell phone, which proved to be as elusive as her list, she heard the soft tread of footsteps coming toward her.

Abby looked up, the smile dying on her lips when she saw Quinn standing there.

Guilt zapped her conscience. She'd taken so long he'd been forced to track her down.

"I'm sorry, Quinn. I was just about to call you." Too bad she couldn't offer her phone as proof. "I need to hire a locksmith to key the rooms in the lodge but it shouldn't take long. I can meet you outside in a few minutes."

"Abby—"

"Abby?" Faye McAllister jumped into the silence and her eyes narrowed. "Abby *Porter?*"

"Y-yes." Abby's heart pitched. Was it possible the woman had recognized her name? She hadn't deliberately tried to keep it a secret, but she hadn't gone out of her way to tell people about her connection to Porter Hotels. She liked having people treat her the same way they would anyone else.

"And you need a locksmith."

"Y-yes."

"This is *O'Halloran* Security," Faye said.

"O'Halloran…" Heat that Abby couldn't blame on the sweltering air branded her cheeks.

There wasn't a sign in the yard. No logo on the door. Not even a number on the mailbox. As a newcomer to the area, how was she supposed to know who owned what?

Her gaze slid to Quinn. "One of your relatives is a locksmith?"

Absolute silence followed the question.

"She doesn't know?" Faye aimed an accusing look at Quinn.

Abby looked from one to the other. "Know what?"

"You didn't *tell* her?"

"Tell me what?"

Quinn finally looked at her, the expression on his face similar to the one she'd seen earlier that morning. When he'd been lying on his back in the chapel.

"I'm the O'Halloran in O'Halloran Security."

Quinn saw the confusion darken Abby's eyes. "I don't understand."

"Get in line," Faye grumbled.

"Come back to my office so we can talk." Hopefully he'd come up with an explanation on the way there. But the first order of business was to separate Abby from the thoughtful gleam in his secretary's eyes.

"Office?" Abby repeated the word. "You have an *office?*"

"This way." With a stern look at Faye—who looked ready to follow—Quinn ushered Abby down the dim hallway.

He'd considered his office fairly passable but as they stepped inside, Quinn tried to see it through Abby's eyes.

Plaster and a fresh coat of paint didn't completely conceal the outline of fist-sized holes in the walls, evidence of Mike O'Halloran's frustration when things didn't go his way.

The oak desk was scarred but solid—and no one but Quinn would ever know that his initial sweep had revealed a cache of empty vodka bottles in the drawers.

The curtains Faye had strung up—without his permission, of course—not only provided color but concealed the hairline cracks in the glass that fanned out like a spiderweb along the top of the window casing.

Quinn had done what he could to make the office more customer-friendly, but replacing the business's outdated technology had been more of a priority than replacing the carpeting. Or the furniture....

"Abby, wait. Don't sit—" Down.

Before Quinn could finish the sentence, Abby had dropped into the captain's chair opposite his desk. When it immediately began to tilt like a faulty amusement park ride, she anchored one sandaled foot against the floor and looked up at him, waiting for an explanation.

Because Quinn was still working on that, he tried to stall.

"You didn't mention that you needed a locksmith."

"Maybe if you would have mentioned you *were* a locksmith, I would have mentioned that I needed one."

He couldn't argue with that logic.

"I can't believe—" Abby shook her head and Quinn sucked in a breath, waiting for the barrage of questions he knew would follow "—how amazing God is."

He blinked. "How what?"

"Amazing God is." Abby grinned. "I shouldn't be, should I? Amazing is just part of who He is… It shouldn't surprise me when things like this happen. I mean, think about this."

Quinn had been. And all those thoughts centered on how to convince Abby that there was a valid reason why he was moonlighting as a carpenter.

She opened her arms and kicked off with her foot, sending the chair spinning in a wobbly circle.

Quinn would have leaped forward to stop her if he hadn't been so mesmerized by the sight. And the sound of her laughter.

"Every time I start to have doubts that I'm doing the right thing, He shows me that I'm on the right path." Abby planted both feet and stopped the chair midspin. "You don't know what I'm talking about, do you?"

"Not a clue."

"You. A locksmith. I can't believe it. You're already working on-site and you're familiar with the lodge and the cabins." Abby shook her head in wonder. "I don't have to meet with someone new and go over what needs to be done. You're there all day anyway. You can take some time to put new locks in, can't you?"

The chair had stopped spinning but Quinn still felt dizzy. Lack of oxygen prevented a person from thinking clearly, didn't it?

"Sure." The word almost got stuck in his throat. He'd expected Abby to be suspicious as to why he'd left his business to help get hers off the ground. But she was looking at him as if…

"You, Quinn O'Halloran, are an answer to prayer."

Quinn stared at her in disbelief. He wasn't an answer to prayer. In fact, he wasn't sure a man whose future at the moment was one big question mark could be an answer to anything.

He rejected the claim with a shake of his head. "I'm just the hired help."

Alex Porter's hired help.

"That's not true." Abby said it with so much sincerity that for a moment, Quinn was actually tempted to believe her. But what shook him even more was the realization that he *wanted* to believe her. "And I don't believe in coincidences."

"What do you believe?" The words were out before Quinn could prevent them.

Abby's gaze locked with his, as if she were trying to decide whether he really wanted to know. And then she nodded once—and smiled—as if she'd gotten the answer. "That God has a plan—a purpose—for our lives."

The simple response tugged at Quinn's soul in a way he hadn't expected it to.

He did believe that God had a plan—for other people. People who amounted to something. That was the reason, when Quinn turned eighteen, that he'd felt responsible for coming up with one of his own.

In Chicago, no one had known anything about his background. They hadn't known that Mike O'Halloran was drunk more than he was sober. They didn't know Jean O'Halloran had walked out on her husband. Not that Quinn blamed his mother for leaving—it just would have been nice if she'd taken him along.

No one in Chicago was watching, waiting for him to make a mistake that would prove he was destined to "turn out just like his old man."

When Hamlin Security hired him, Quinn felt as if he'd been given the second chance that Abby claimed everyone deserved. His colleagues respected him, his employers trusted him…until circumstances had forced him to return to Mirror Lake.

Ken Raynes, the CEO of a software company, had contracted him to provide personal security for his youngest daughter, Serena, who was being harassed by a former boyfriend. The seventeen-year-old was spoiled and rebellious, a potentially combustible combination. Although it was company policy to keep a professional distance from his clients, Quinn had felt sorry for the girl. Serena's parents didn't have time for her and her friends seemed to come around only when they wanted something.

He'd befriended her. Listened to her problems. And when he discovered Serena was hooked on prescription drugs, Quinn went directly to Ken, hoping her father would get Serena the help she needed. When Serena's family confronted her, not only had she denied ever using drugs, she'd informed her parents that

Quinn was the one who'd offered to score some for her if she was interested.

In a perfect world, Quinn's word would have carried more weight than that of a troubled teenager. But he didn't live in a perfect world. Ken Raynes traced Quinn's roots back to Mirror Lake and found Mike O'Halloran. An alcoholic. The town troublemaker. It didn't matter that Quinn had a spotless record.

Quinn wanted Serena to get help, but Ken Raynes, who had political aspirations, didn't want a scandal. The only way to make his family look good was to make Quinn look bad.

Quinn had tried to do the right thing and it cost him his career. Not only that, it had forced him to return to the place where he'd always felt he *didn't* belong.

Was he supposed to believe God had a purpose in that?

"So…" The lilt in Abby's voice nudged Quinn out of the shadows. "What do we do now?"

I have no idea, Quinn wanted to say. Until he realized she was asking about locks for the inn, not his past. Or the condition of his soul. "Tell me what you want and I'll write up an estimate."

"Don't bother with an estimate. I trust you."

Why?

The question ricocheted around Quinn's head. Because she believed he was an answer to prayer?

In the past, he would have deliberately tried to gain Abby's trust. It came with the job. Quinn had found when his clients trusted him, they were more willing to listen to his instructions. Follow his recommendations.

If anything, Quinn knew he should feel relieved—

not guilty—that Abby's initial reticence toward him seemed to be fading.

Unless she discovers the reason you've been helping her.

For the first time since Quinn had agreed to Alex Porter's terms, fear skated down his spine as he considered how Abby would react if she discovered the truth.

No more trusting looks. No more heart-stopping smiles....

She won't find out, Quinn told himself.

Alex's PI would figure out who was harassing him and realize there was no threat to Abby. Daniel would come back to finish the cabins and Quinn would return to his real job. Abby would be none the wiser. No harm done.

Now all Quinn had to do was believe it.

"How long have you been in business?" Abby asked.

"About a year. Why?"

Color tinted her cheeks. "I can tell you're in the process of...fixing things up. And you work with Daniel, too. I thought..."

He was an answer to prayer who was having trouble making ends meet.

Quinn tried not to wince. Now it made sense. Why she hadn't peppered him with questions about the reason he was dividing his time between O'Halloran Security and the inn.

Abby's next question confirmed his suspicions.

"Do you require a deposit?" Her slender fingers traced a crescent-shaped gash on the corner of his desk. "For materials?"

Quinn frowned. "That's not necessary."

"But—"

"We can hash out the details later."

"Translation—we can argue about it on the way home." Abby flashed an impish smile.

It wasn't the smile that got to him this time. It was the word *home* that opened the door to a host of images Quinn hadn't known lay buried in his subconscious.

What was more unsettling was that he'd never experienced the kind of pictures his imagination was painting. They weren't memories of the ramshackle house he'd grown up in a few miles outside of Mirror Lake. These were different—and yet all too familiar.

In his mind's eye, Quinn saw a fire crackling in the great room. A sunlit kitchen with yellow walls. A nest of cushions in the hammock near the deck… and Abby. In every single one.

Quinn pushed the thoughts from his head before they could take root in his heart.

The future was too uncertain. If O'Halloran Security didn't start turning a profit, he would have to sell it and move on. Quinn was already halfway into his two-year plan.

God has a purpose. A plan.

The conversation he'd had with Abby cycled through his mind again.

She believed that God's plan included converting a rustic camp into a bed-and-breakfast.

Quinn didn't know if that were true or not, but he did know one thing.

God's plan for Abby didn't include him.

Chapter Nine

Abby pushed the heels of her hands into the bread dough and heard an air bubble pop.

Quinn had lied to her.

He didn't "hash" out the details on the drive back to the lodge. He didn't argue about them, either. Because in order to do those things, a person had to be willing to *talk* first. And Quinn hadn't.

Abby didn't count two growls and a harrumph as meaningful conversation.

When they'd arrived back at the inn, Quinn dropped her off at the house and drove down to the cabins. With *her* dog.

She knew he was sensitive about having to work two jobs, although Abby didn't think that was anything to be ashamed of. It proved he wasn't afraid of hard work. That he was committed to making his business succeed.

Come to think of it, they had a lot in common. Quinn would recognize that if he'd put his male pride aside and...

And what?

Smile at you again. Admit it, you want him to like you....

She wasn't going to admit anything. Abby pushed that thought away, only to have another one take its place.

Because you like him.

Over the next hour, three dozen cloverleaf rolls, a chef's salad and a lemon torte formed a line on the counter. Sorting through her recipe card file proved to be much easier than sorting through her feelings for Quinn.

That she even *had* feelings for Quinn was disturbing.

Abby had never been in a serious relationship. In her social circles, she'd never been sure if men were as attracted to her as they were to her last name. And the fortune that went with it.

If, in some rare instance, she did show a spark of interest in someone, Alex swooped in and circled the poor guy like a hawk until he ran for cover.

If a girl mixed those things with a troublesome tendency to be leery of strangers, it added up to a lot of evenings alone.

Not exactly the kind of lifestyle the average person who saw Abby's face on a Porter Hotel brochure would assume she was living.

Although there was a certificate on the wall of her "office" proving she had a business degree, Alex brushed aside her suggestion that he let her take a more active role in the hotels' day-to-day operations.

Six months ago, a feeling of discontent had seeped in. She was tired of being the poster girl for Porter Hotels.

As the corporation's official spokesperson, her face was featured in all the marketing campaigns. A symbol of the type of person who chose to stay at one of their hotels.

Sophisticated. Discriminating. Refined.

Frequent appeals to Alex, asking for more responsibility, fell on deaf ears. He didn't understand her frustration. Tried to assure her that her role as the company spokesperson was important. Abby knew it also served another purpose, although Alex wouldn't have admitted it. It cut down her interaction with people. A billboard was as close as anyone could get to her.

Abby had wanted more. And then she felt guilty for wanting more because she already *had* so much.

Restlessness with life in general drove Abby to her favorite place to reduce stress—the kitchen.

Jessica Benson was the first person who had recognized Abby's restlessness for what it really was. Not a search to "find herself," but to find God. The One who'd created her.

The day Abby surrendered her heart to the Lord and took that first tiny step forward in faith, she hadn't expected to begin a journey that would change the entire landscape of her life.

Skyscrapers for towering white pine. A penthouse apartment for a room tucked under the sloping eaves of a former attic. A small town where people recognized her face—but not because they'd seen it on a billboard. Where they called her by her first name— and weren't intimidated by her last.

Abby had lived in Chicago all her life, but the

first time she'd visited Mirror Lake, there had been a heart-to-heart connection.

A place she'd lived for a little over a month now felt like home.

It was no coincidence that she'd found the perfect piece of property to convert into a bed-and-breakfast inn. Or fallen in love with the sleepy little town that curved around the shoreline on the opposite side of the lake.

When doubts crept in, all Abby had to do was look back and count what Jessica called "spiritual signposts." Evidence that she was following the right path. God's path.

The road had its share of potholes, bumps and curves, but whenever she was discouraged, it seemed as if God was ready with a new signpost.

Like the amazing discovery that Quinn was a locksmith.

Once again, Abby's thoughts moved back to him like a needle seeking North on a compass.

He'd seemed uncomfortable when she'd shown up unexpectedly at his office that afternoon, but Abby understood why.

Kate told her that Quinn had moved back to Mirror Lake a year ago. That would have made it near the time his father had died. Abby didn't have to be a detective to make the connection.

Not only had he inherited Lady, his father's dog, he'd inherited his business.

Abby's respect for him had risen another notch.

What had Quinn given up in order to revive a business that was obviously struggling? What had he left behind?

The questions plagued her as she added a dozen cookies to the already crowded wicker hamper on the table—bait to lure him down from the roof of the cabin.

The sun was setting, and in an hour Quinn would have to hold a flashlight in one hand and a hammer in the other.

Time to send him home.

Shrugging into a lightweight sweater, she grabbed the basket and started across the lawn.

The dogs dozed in the grass. Mulligan's nose twitched as she walked past him, but he made no move to get up.

Abby's initial confidence faded a little as Quinn pushed back the brim of his ball cap and peered down at her.

She could use one of his heart-stopping little half smiles right about now to bolster her courage.

"I brought you a little something."

Quinn's gaze shifted to the picnic basket she'd lugged across the yard. "A little something, huh?"

Abby relaxed when she saw a hint of amusement in his eyes. She'd been afraid he would view it as charity. "All right, there's a lot of little somethings."

Quinn swung down from the ladder and landed right in the middle of her personal space.

Abby's breath stalled when his fingers grazed her palm as he took the basket out of her hand. "Thanks."

"You're welcome."

"Even though I told you that you didn't have to go to any trouble for me."

Come to think of it, he *had* told her that.

"You brought a lot of your food here so I wanted

to make sure you had some—" *decent* "—food to tide you over until I see you on Monday."

Quinn stiffened. "Are you going somewhere this weekend?"

"No. You are."

His expression didn't change.

"It's Friday." She tried again. "The day before the weekend. Weekends generally mean time off."

"You're taking the weekend off?"

"Of course not. But I don't expect you to be here 24/7." Abby saw some unidentifiable emotion flare in the depths of his pewter-gray eyes. "*You* have the weekend off."

"I don't need the weekend off."

"I'm giving it to you anyway." She smiled. "You've accomplished more in the past two days than I thought was humanly possible. You earned a break. Besides that, I'm sure you have things of your own to catch up on."

Abby had seen his office. She knew he did.

Quinn wasn't sure how to get past this new complication. "It's covered."

"Well, then—"

"Abby, I don't *want* the weekend off." Quinn waited until he saw understanding dawn in her eyes.

But she only *thought* she understood. And what she thought she understood was that he wanted to work as many hours as possible before Daniel came back.

"You can take Sunday off, then."

Quinn buried a sigh. Abby was determined to give him a day off. Along with a picnic basket loaded with food to pass the time.

"Trying to get rid of me?"

To his amazement, Abby blushed. "N-no."

Once again, Quinn tried to reconcile the woman standing in front of him with the sophisticated woman featured on the billboard advertising Porter Hotels.

It was almost as if there were two Abby Porters. He didn't know which woman was the real Abby Porter, but decided he liked the one with the windswept golden hair and winsome smile better.

"I'd feel guilty if you worked on Sunday," Abby continued. "Because I don't. It's my…rest and refresh day."

Great. Another complication. But thanks to his agreement with Alex Porter, where Abby went, Quinn followed.

"So, what do you do on your rest and refresh day?" He hoped it didn't include shopping. Or socializing.

"In the afternoon, Mulligan and I take a walk around the lake or I try to catch up on some reading…"

Hiking. No problem. He'd tag along. Reading would keep her close to home. It could be worse, Quinn decided. Neither of the things she'd just mentioned involved leaving the property.

"And I go to the early service at Church of the Pines."

"Church of the Pines."

"Have you been there?"

Abby's innocent question opened a floodgate of memories.

As a kid, Quinn had attended Sunday school there one summer. Not long after his mother left, his fourth grade homeroom teacher, Miss Anderson, had pulled him aside and invited him to go to church with her. She drove past their house on Sunday mornings and must have seen him playing outside.

Quinn, willing to grab any opportunity that would take him away from home, had said yes.

There'd been whispers and sidelong glances from the rest of the children when Miss Anderson gently pushed Quinn into the room that first day. They'd subsided when he was put in charge of smoothing tiny felt figures on a flannel board while she told a story about a little man named Zacchaeus, who climbed a tree to see Jesus.

The story stuck in Quinn's mind because no one else liked the man and they wondered why Jesus wanted to go to his house for supper.

Quinn knew exactly how Zacchaeus felt.

After that, he'd looked forward to Sunday mornings. He listened to stories and sang songs he'd never heard before. At snack time, Miss Anderson would put extra crackers on his napkin and refill his glass of juice.

Quinn didn't even mind sitting for another hour in the sanctuary—where the stories were longer and there was nothing to eat. Other kids grumbled and fidgeted if the sermon went longer than it was supposed to, but not Quinn. Sometimes he listened to what the pastor was saying, but most of the time he was content to soak in his surroundings.

The whole room always seemed to be filled with light. Stained glass windows painted rainbows on the gleaming hardwood floors. Tall white candles glowed on a table by the piano.

Quinn had felt safe within the walls.

The stories the pastor told made him feel strong on the inside, too. Quinn had prayed with Miss Anderson one morning and asked Jesus to come into his heart, so he figured that was the reason he felt different. For a little while, he'd imagined it meant that things would *be* different.

They weren't.

Because he always had to go home.

And his father, who was used to Quinn giving him a wide berth, didn't appreciate the change in him.

"Quit pestering me about your ma. I told you, she isn't coming back."

"Yes, she will."

A split second later, Quinn was yanked off his feet.

"Did she tell you that? Did she call you?"

"No." Quinn had gasped the word, wishing he hadn't said anything. In the past, he would have made up a lie. He couldn't this time. Now he knew lying was wrong. *"I've been praying she comes home."*

"Praying?" His father's scornful laugh was somehow more frightening than his rage. *"You think God listens to you?"*

"Miss Anderson said He does."

As soon as he saw his dad's expression, Quinn knew he shouldn't have talked back. Shouldn't have said anything about his teacher. It had only made things worse.

"You've been sneaking out."

"Miss Anderson takes me to church with her."

The laughter faded to a sneer. *"Those people feel sorry for you. You're like a stray mongrel dog they feed once a week so they can feel better about themselves."*

"That's not true." But doubt slithered through Quinn's mind when he remembered the extra crackers Miss Anderson gave him every week.

He tried to remember some of the verses that he'd memorized, the ones Miss Anderson said would give him strength, but Mike O'Halloran had pushed his face close to Quinn's. *"You stick close to home from now on or I'm going to have to pay that pretty schoolteacher of yours a visit. Tell her to mind her own business."*

Quinn had recognized the look in his dad's bloodshot eyes.

The next day at school, he told Miss Anderson he didn't want to go to church anymore. She'd asked him why, but Quinn hadn't told the truth that time. He told her it was boring. To prove his point, he kicked the wastebasket over on his way out the door.

The remainder of the day was spent in the principal's office, waiting for his dad to pick him up. He'd spent the night on the roof, staring up at the heavens. The things his father had said made Quinn wonder if Miss Anderson hadn't gotten it wrong about the kind of people God listened to.

When the snowflakes started to fall, Quinn stopped praying that his mom would come back. By the following summer, he'd stopped praying about anything at all.

"Quinn?"

The light touch of Abby's hand on his arm made him snap to attention. "What?"

She chuckled. "Where did you go?"

"Nowhere." Nowhere he wanted to revisit. And definitely nowhere he would ever take Abby.

But, he thought with an inward sigh, there was somewhere he *would* have to take her.

"I asked if you'd ever gone to church there," Abby reminded him.

"A few times. When I was a kid."

She didn't look surprised. Nor did she ask why he didn't attend anymore. "Do you want to go with me?"

"Sure. Why not?" He didn't have much of a choice so he might as well let her think it was her idea.

A smile backlit Abby's eyes. As if she were genuinely happy he'd agreed to go.

What are You doing, Lord?

The prayer formed in Quinn's soul and took flight before he had a chance to catch it.

It wasn't until later that night, while staring up at the ceiling, Quinn realized he'd actually talked to God again. Asked Him a question.

And now here he was. Lying awake, waiting for an answer.

Chapter Ten

Abby slipped out of the house, a coffee cup in one hand and her walking verse in the other.

Dew glistened in the grass and it was early enough that wisps of fog, soft as cotton candy, hung over the lake.

Mulligan and Lady ran circles around her, ready to go.

"Shh." Abby put a finger to her lips. The shades in the windows of Quinn's cabin were still drawn. "Not everyone likes to get up this early on a Saturday morning, you know."

She hadn't been able to talk Quinn into taking the weekend off but it didn't mean he had to be up and working at the crack of dawn, either.

The dogs streaked ahead and disappeared into the woods. Abby followed at a more leisurely pace, keeping an eye on the grid of roots poking from the ground beneath her feet as she recited the verse out loud.

"'I sought the Lord, and he answered me. He delivered me from all my fears. Those who look to him are radiant.'" Abby peeked at the slip of paper in her hand. "'Their faces are never covered with shame...'"

A branch snapped behind her.

She glanced over her shoulder and saw Quinn closing the distance between them at an easy lope.

There was no escaping the man.

Not that you want to, an inner voice teased.

Before she had time to form a snappy inner comeback, Quinn reached her side.

"What are you doing out here so early?"

Funny, Abby had been about to ask him the same thing.

"I take Mulligan for a walk around the lake every morning," she explained. "Lady followed us again. I hope you don't mind."

"Not a bit." He shrugged. "She's probably happier with the pace you set. I tried to take her with me once, but I ended up carrying her back. We were four miles from home."

Abby pictured Quinn toting the pudgy dog for that distance and laughed. "I won't be offended if you leave us behind in the dust. I've got cinnamon rolls in the oven, so I can only go halfway around this time." She stepped to the side to give him some room, but instead of going on ahead, Quinn fell in step beside her.

"I think you dropped something." He pointed to a piece of paper tumbling down the path in front of them, propelled by a mischievous breeze coming off the lake.

By the time Abby chased it down, she was out of breath. And laughing so hard her ribs ached.

"I admire your dedication to keeping the environment clean," Quinn said when she limped up to him.

"I didn't want to lose it," Abby gasped. "It's my walking verse."

"I'll take your word for it. Because it looked to me like you were running." Quinn's lips curved, a repeat of the rare but potent smile she'd caught a glimpse of the day before.

Abby pressed a hand against the stitch in her side. "Don't make me laugh," she pleaded. "It hurts."

Quinn held out his hand. "Okay. Let's hear it."

"Hear it?"

"Your *walking* verse."

Abby's fingers curled protectively around the piece of paper. "I didn't get much of a chance to look at it." *Before you distracted me.*

"You're stalling." Quinn plucked it from her hand and started down the trail again.

Leaving her with no choice but to follow. "Fine. But you have to start me out."

Quinn looked down at the paper. "'I.'"

Abby made a face at him. "A bigger start."

"'I sought.'"

Abby bumped him with her hip. "Be serious."

He laughed instead.

The sound washed over her—and through her—as warm and unexpected as a summer rain. Bringing the feelings that Abby had been trying to deny into full bloom.

"Sorry." Quinn's laughter faded but a smile continued to dance in his eyes as he looked down at her.

Abby made the mistake of making eye contact with him. The toe of her shoe caught in a root and she pitched forward. Quinn's hand shot out to steady her.

His touch was as warm as his laughter and she was

struck by an overwhelming urge to turn into the circle of his arms. Rest her head against his chest.

Whoa. Where did that come from?

She pulled away instead and stumbled up the path, trying to concentrate once more on the verse she'd written down.

"'I sought the Lord, and he answered me. He delivered me from all my fears. Those who...'" Abby paused, waiting for Quinn to prompt her.

When he didn't, she glanced up at him.

The smile on his face had disappeared, replaced by...disbelief?

Abby's heart sank.

Quinn stared down at the piece of paper, aware that Abby was waiting for him to give her another clue.

He couldn't say a word.

Her "walking verse" was the answer to the question that had cycled through his mind over the course of a sleepless night.

He'd asked God if He was still there. If He was still listening.

I sought the Lord, and He answered me.

Now he understood Abby's reaction the day before when he'd told her that he owned O'Halloran Security. She'd been amazed by what she'd viewed as God's intervention on her behalf.

Quinn was a little amazed himself. So amazed that he couldn't push out another word.

"I'm going to turn around now." Abby's voice intruded softly on his thoughts. "But you can keep going. I don't want to hold you back."

Hold him back? Quinn was beginning to wonder

if Abby Porter wasn't responsible for moving him *forward.*

"Did you say something about cinnamon rolls?"

"Yes, I did. But what about your run?"

Quinn shrugged. "I can fit it in later."

"Or…" Abby's eyes held a sparkle of mischief. "I'll race you back." She whirled around and sprinted down the uneven trail.

Once Quinn's initial shock melted away, he started after her. The dogs took up pursuit and all four of them burst into the clearing a few minutes later.

The rusty car parked in the driveway immediately set off Quinn's internal radar. The three teenage boys lounging against the hood looked as questionable as the vehicle.

Abby started in their direction.

"Abby, wait."

She quickened her pace instead. "That's my Saturday painting crew. They're early today. They don't usually show until noon."

The boys intercepted them halfway across the yard but by the time they met, Quinn made sure he got there before Abby.

Abby went down the row, introducing him to Tim and Zach Davis, but hesitated when she got to the third one, a lanky boy who looked to be several years younger than the brothers. He squirmed under her welcoming smile and Quinn had the feeling the kid would have bolted for the car if he hadn't been wedged between the other boys.

"I don't think we've met before," she said.

The boy's dark-eyed gaze couldn't seem to find a

place to light. It bounced from Abby to Quinn and back again until it finally settled on the ground.

"This is Cody." Tim finally spoke up. "He wants to paint, too."

"Wonderful." Abby sounded as if she meant it. "This place needs all the help it can get. I know Daniel usually gets you started, but I'll show you the painting supplies—"

"I don't mind playing foreman today," Quinn interrupted. "I know you're anxious to get started on the library."

"I think I'd rather be outside today." Abby tilted her face toward the sun and closed her eyes. "It's going to be a perfect summer day. Beautiful."

When she opened them again, all three teenagers were staring at her.

"What?"

No one said a word. They shuffled and muttered and looked everywhere but at her. Until Quinn intervened. He pointed at the garage. "Thataway. *Boys.*"

With sheepish grins and furtive glances in Abby's direction, they stumbled away.

"Strange." Abby's brow furrowed. "Daniel never mentioned they don't like to talk."

Was Abby really that naive? One smile from her had left them totally tongue-tied.

"That's probably because they talk to him," he said dryly.

"I scared them away, didn't I?" She sighed. "Chalk it up to a lack of experience with kids."

Call him a glutton for punishment, but he wanted to see her smile again. "You could always buy a book."

It worked.

"Maybe I will." Abby grinned. "Right after I finish the one I'm reading on effective communication."

Quinn sucked in a breath.

Maybe it wouldn't be a bad idea to read that one himself.

He knew exactly how the boys had felt. Abby had a way of leaving him tongue-tied, too.

It took all of Abby's willpower to stay inside the lodge and not find a chore to do outside. Other than delivering cold drinks to her work crew, who'd set to work painting the boathouse shortly after their arrival, she'd spent the afternoon in the library.

She planned to turn it into a gathering room, where guests could play board games in the evening or settle into the comfortable chairs with a good book.

Like the other rooms, it boasted a fieldstone fireplace with a raised hearth. A perfect place either to invite conversation or encourage solitude....

Beethoven's *Symphony No. 5* suddenly broke through her musings.

Abby would never feel the same way about classical music again.

"Hi, Alex."

"Change your mind yet?"

"No. Have you?"

It had become their standard greeting over the past few days.

The amusement in Alex's voice, rather than disapproval, gave Abby hope that he was starting to accept her decision.

Abby wasn't sure why, but she'd sensed a change

in her brother over the past week. He hadn't been quite as dogged in his attempt to convince her to return to Chicago.

Not that she was complaining. A change like that she could live with. Alex was the only family she had and they'd always been close. The tension between them hadn't been easy to deal with.

"How are things going up there?"

"Great. This has been a productive week." Thanks to Quinn.

"That's good."

"Okay, who are you and what have you done with my brother?"

Alex didn't see the humor in the question. "I only have your best interests at heart."

It was a familiar refrain. One Abby had never been able to argue with. Until now. "Maybe that's part of the problem, Alex. Maybe it's time you followed some of your own interests for a change. You put your life on hold in order to raise your kid sister. But your sister isn't a kid anymore."

She waited for a snappy comeback. There was a reason Alex had been appointed captain of the debate team in college.

"I'm doing what Mom and Dad would want me to do," he finally said.

The hint of uncertainty in Alex's voice tugged at her conscience.

"I know." Abby couldn't argue with that. From the time she was six years old, protecting Abigail Marie had become the Porter family's personal cause. After their parents' death, Alex had continued to carry the torch.

He had to be as tired of bearing that burden as she'd finally become of being the one responsible for it.

"Why don't you come home for the weekend and we'll talk about it."

"I am home."

"I miss you, Abby."

"Now you're inviting me to go on a guilt trip?"

"Is it working?"

She laughed. "You don't give up, do you?"

"You know I don't."

The doorbell came to life, sending out a series of tinny, off-key notes that reminded Abby of a jack-in-the-box.

"I'll call you back later, Alex. There's someone at the door."

"You're going to answer the door?"

"Yes, Alex. I live here," Abby explained patiently. "I'm the logical person to answer the door…." As she pulled it open, the rest of the words died on her lips.

"Who is it?" Alex demanded. "Who's there?"

Abby finally found her voice.

"A police officer."

Chapter Eleven

"I'll call you later, Alex." Abby ignored her brother's squawk of protest as she closed the phone.

The officer swept off his hat, exposing the shiny dome beneath it. "Good afternoon, Miss Porter."

"Good afternoon." Abby opened the door and stepped onto the porch. There was no logical reason for her to be nervous, but the butterflies that took wing inside of her didn't seem to care. "Is there something I can do for you, Officer?"

"Sergeant," he corrected. "Sergeant West. I'm with the county sheriff's department."

"It's nice to meet you, Sergeant. Would you like to sit for a few minutes?" Abby gestured toward the pair of wicker rocking chairs. "I made a pitcher of lemonade this morning, if you'd like a glass."

The deputy cleared his throat. "No, thank you, Miss Porter. I'm here on official business."

Abby's heart dropped to her feet. "What is this about?"

"It's been brought to my attention that Cody Lang is working for you."

Something about the man's tone immediately put Abby on the defensive. "Tim and Zach Davis brought Cody with them today to do some painting. This is the first time I've met him."

"Lang's name came up this past week. We've had a rash of burglaries in some of the cabins on the other side of the lake. The sheriff's department has good reason to think he was involved."

"But you aren't sure."

The deputy's eyes narrowed. Maybe he heard something he didn't like in *her* tone. "My source is usually reliable. When there's trouble, it's a safe bet one of the Lang boys is in the middle of it. It looks like this one is following his brother's footsteps."

"I'm sure Cody will be all right. He's just looking for a chance to earn some extra money like other boys his age."

"Or he wanted to check things out." Sergeant West shrugged. "If I were you, I'd send him on his way, not give him the run of the place."

Goose bumps rose on Abby's arms. "I appreciate your concern but Zach and Tim vouched for Cody and he seems like a polite boy—" in spite of his inability to look her in the eyes "—and since you don't have proof that he was involved in the burglaries, I think I'll keep him on, at least for today. I have more than enough to keep him busy."

Stereo speakers suddenly launched an attack of pounding bass, drowning out the birdsong in the trees.

Perfect timing, boys, Abby thought.

Sergeant West's gaze swung toward the lake, locking on the four figures near the dock. "I understand O'Halloran is staying with you."

Abby stiffened. Apparently the officer had more than one reliable source. "I'm on a tight deadline. Mr. O'Halloran is able to put in longer days if he stays in one of the *cabins*." She put some weight on the last word, just in case there was any confusion as to where Quinn was staying.

"How is that going?"

"He's making a lot of progress—"

"That's not what I meant," the sergeant interrupted, not taking his eyes off Quinn. "Does he… keep to himself?"

Abby frowned. She didn't understand the question but she didn't appreciate his tone. "I thought you drove out here to check on Cody Lang."

"Like I said, you haven't lived in Mirror Lake long enough to be privy to certain…information."

"Or swayed by prejudice."

Sergeant West's gaze swung back to her. "Mike O'Halloran, Quinn's father, was bad news. Everybody around here knows it."

Abby had noticed the way Quinn's expression hardened whenever he spoke of his father. For the first time, she had some insight into the reason why.

"I thought we were talking about Quinn."

The officer shrugged, as if that detail didn't matter. "Same family."

"Different men." Abby dug her nails into her palms to stop her hands from shaking.

"The apple doesn't fall far from the tree, so the saying goes."

Abby had only known Quinn for a few days, but

she knew it didn't apply to him, no matter what his father had been guilty of.

"I'll keep that in mind," she said politely. "Thank you for stopping by, Sergeant."

The officer gave her a sharp look, as if judging her sincerity. "You keep an eye on Lang. If he causes any trouble, let me know." Sergeant West's gaze strayed to Quinn again. "Something else you might keep in mind, Miss Porter. A man who doesn't talk about his past…well, he usually has a reason."

Quinn watched the squad car pull away.

The tension in Abby's shoulders told him the deputy hadn't stopped by for a social call.

"What do you think he wanted?"

Quinn glanced at Cody Lang, wondering if the boy had read his mind. The kid looked a little tense himself; the hunted look in his dark eyes all too familiar.

The boy's last name wasn't familiar but then again, Quinn had been gone a long time. It was possible the Lang family had migrated to the area after he'd left town.

"I don't know." But he planned to find out.

"She looks upset," Cody whispered.

Quinn thought so, too, but he was surprised by the intuitive comment. He glanced at Cody and saw the raw fear banked in his eyes before he averted his gaze.

The kid must have come to his own conclusion as to why the deputy had stopped by to talk to Abby.

"You tell Tim and Zach that break time is over, okay?" Quinn planned to give Cody a light, reassuring cuff on the shoulder but when his hand came up, the boy flinched.

Quinn silently berated himself. He should have known better.

"I'll be back in a few minutes."

Lost in thought, Abby didn't seem to be aware of his approach.

Quinn's vow to keep a professional distance disintegrated when he saw Abby's hands clenched at her sides.

Had the deputy delivered bad news?

"Problem?" He tossed out the question to let Abby know he was there.

She thought he'd been teasing the day before, when he called out a greeting to warn her of his presence. He hadn't been. Abby's vague response that day in the chapel when he'd asked why she had read a book on self-defense techniques still chewed at the edge of his thoughts.

"Not anymore."

"Sergeant West."

"You know him?"

"I remember him." An answer that wasn't quite an answer, but it was the best Quinn could do. The deputy had been fresh out of the academy when he was a kid. "I'm not surprised he stopped by to say hello. He likes to keep tabs on things." Which probably explained why the deputy hadn't retired yet.

"He didn't stop by to say hello," Abby said. "He heard Cody Lang was here. It sounds like Cody was implicated in some burglaries that happened a few days ago. Cabins on the other side of the lake. Sergeant West wanted to make sure I was aware of it."

It had been fear he'd seen on Cody's face, not guilt, but he didn't think that would matter to Abby. If West pegged the boy as a suspect, Abby would believe him.

His jaw tightened. "Do you want me to tell Cody?"

"Tell him what?" Abby looked up at him, a question in her eyes.

"That you want him to leave?"

"Why would you do that? I need him," Abby shocked him by saying. "And there's no proof Cody was one of the boys who broke into the cabins."

Laughter rolled across the lawn as the Davis brothers began to wrestle in the grass like a pair of frisky puppies. Quinn noticed that Cody was still staring in their direction, as if he knew they were talking about him.

"There's no proof he wasn't involved, either," Quinn pointed out.

Doubt surfaced in Abby's expressive eyes. He could almost read her thoughts.

Maybe the sergeant was right. He could be checking out the place to see if there's anything worth coming back for. When you're alone…

"Cody will understand," Quinn said. "In fact, he's probably expecting it."

Abby's chin lifted, as if in answer to an unspoken question. "Don't say anything to him."

"Are you sure?"

"I'm sure."

"What about Sergeant West?"

"What about him? He was just doing his job. Warning me about Cody." Abby started across the yard.

Quinn caught up to her in less than a stride.

"What else did he warn you about?"

* * *

Quinn's tone was even; it was the bleak look in his eyes that stopped Abby in her tracks.

He knew.

Maybe, like Cody, he'd also expected it.

If Sergeant West hadn't made that disparaging comment about Quinn's father, Abby might have missed the shadow that skimmed across his face.

Had Quinn experienced the same kind of mistrust? Judgment?

Part of the reason Abby loved the idea of living in a small town was because of the "everyone knows your name" charm it represented. She hadn't thought of that in terms of the negative.

She sensed that Quinn was waiting for her answer.

"He thought he should fill me in on a little area history." Abby's indignation, on simmer, began to bubble up again as she recalled the conversation with Sergeant West.

"And how it repeats itself." It wasn't a question.

Abby took another step forward but Quinn's hand caught her wrist.

She didn't pull away, although she could have. Quinn wasn't holding her captive. His grip was too loose, too gentle, for that.

How could she explain that she knew what it felt like to have people make assumptions based on her family? On her last name?

It had happened all the time. As the "face" of Porter Hotels, some people had treated her as if she didn't have a brain. Assumed she had a personality as shallow as the piece of paper the brochure was printed on.

"I prefer to make up my own mind," she finally said. "Based on what I see, not what people say."

Quinn stared down at her, searching for the truth. "And what do you see?"

They weren't talking about Cody anymore.

Quinn hadn't let go of her wrist. Without thinking, Abby squeezed his hand. His eyes darkened and his fingers closed around hers...

"Miss Porter?"

They jerked apart as Cody sidled up. His gaze riveted on his feet. "I wanted to say thanks. For letting me paint today."

Abby felt a rush of compassion. It was obvious from the set of the boy's narrow shoulders that he expected to be sent on his way. So he'd decided to leave on his own to save himself more embarrassment.

She pretended not to understand. "Do you have to go now?"

Cody looked taken aback by the question. "I—I thought you'd want me to," he mumbled.

"Actually, I've got another job for you. If you're interested."

Cody's shoulder lifted and fell. "I don't have anything else to do."

Abby wasn't fooled by the casual tone or the matching shrug. He knew the reason Sergeant West stopped by and was doing his best to hold his tattered pride together.

"I want to try out a new recipe but in order to do that, I need some fish," she said briskly. "I was having pretty good luck last weekend casting for sunfish in those lily pads at the end of the dock. Are you willing to give it a try? I'll pay you for your time."

"You're going to pay me? To fish?" Cody's voice thinned out and cracked on the last word, reminding her, for all his forced bravado, how young he was.

"It's something that needs to be done and I don't have time to do it." Abby mustered a stern look at having her motives questioned. "So, what do you say?"

Cody darted an "is this for real" look at Quinn. What he saw must have reassured him because a wide grin split his face.

"I say yes."

"Ask Zach and Tim if they want to help. There are enough fishing poles in the storage shed for all three of you."

"Okay. I'll tell them." Cody backed up three steps, turned around and sprinted across the yard as if he were afraid Abby might change her mind.

"They'll be here all evening now," Quinn predicted.

"I know." Abby couldn't help sounding a bit smug. But Cody's expression was worth an adjustment in her plans.

"They're not going to get another thing accomplished the rest of the afternoon."

"I know."

"And they're going to tell all their friends that Abby Porter pays her employees to fish." Quinn sighed. "But I guess it doesn't matter what I think. You're the boss."

"You're right. And because I'm the boss, I can order you to supervise them."

Quinn tunneled his hand through his hair and gave her an impatient look. "I've got work to do."

"Yes, you do." Abby pressed her lips together to flatten a smile.

He spotted it anyway. "Abby—"

"Boss." She tapped an index finger against her chest.

"Bossy, you mean," Quinn muttered. "You're determined to give me some time off this weekend, one way or another, aren't you?"

Apparently nothing got past the man!

"I have no idea what you mean," Abby denied primly.

"Uh-huh." He didn't look convinced.

She sensed Quinn was going to continue the argument, but the series of whoops erupting from the Davis brothers told her that Cody had relayed the news about the change in their job description.

"I better show them where everything is." Abby chuckled. "And they *do* need supervision. I have no idea how to harness that kind of energy."

Quinn fell into step with her. He didn't even have to touch her and every nerve ending in Abby's body began to hum in response to his closeness.

"What made you decide that Cody wasn't involved in the break-ins?" he said after a moment.

Abby slanted a look at him. Nothing in Quinn's expression gave away his thoughts, but she sensed that her answer was important.

She told the truth.

"I didn't."

Chapter Twelve

"Look at this one, Abby!" Cody called, holding up a bluegill the size of Quinn's hand.

"It's definitely a keeper."

Quinn heard Abby's lilting voice and glanced over his shoulder. She was making her way down to the dock, balancing a tray loaded with snacks.

He was beginning to think she had a kitchen full of elves that did all her baking.

"Is anyone hungry?"

The three boys immediately abandoned their fishing poles, with Cody Lang leading the stampede toward the picnic table.

Quinn had a feeling the younger boy craved attention more than food.

The change he'd seen in Cody over the past two hours was startling. With every fish he caught—and brought to Quinn for approval—a glimmer of pride had begun to burn away his initial wariness like sunlight pushing its way through a storm cloud.

Quinn had no doubt the credit for the boy's transformation belonged to Abby. In spite of her claim not to understand kids, she'd somehow managed to come up with the perfect plan to convince Cody to stay. With his pride still intact.

He'd been wrestling with the fact that, in spite of her misgivings, she hadn't sent the kid on his way with Sergeant West's blessing.

And asked you to go along.

Quinn released a quiet breath.

What had the deputy said about him?

The rose tint blooming in Abby's cheeks affirmed that West hadn't missed an opportunity to fill her in on what she'd tactfully referred to as "local history."

I believe what I see. Not what people say.

Abby's response should have put Quinn's mind at ease, not given birth to a dozen more questions.

"There's plenty." Abby waved at him. "At least there is now. I can't guarantee if that will be true in five minutes."

Quinn, who'd found a loose plank on the dock to fix while the boys fished, raised the hammer in response to her invitation. "I'll be right there."

"You snooze, you lose!" Zach Davis shouted.

Abby's laughter followed the teenager's challenge and it was all Quinn could do not to roll his eyes when he saw the shy but adoring looks the boys cast her way. It was clear she'd won them over—and not just with her cooking skills.

Quinn watched her fill glasses of lemonade, chatting easily as if they'd known each other for years.

It was possible that her self-proclaimed ignorance of knowing how to relate to kids was actually working to her advantage. She didn't try to win them over.

Abby was just being... Abby.

Friendly. Generous. Hospitable.

It occurred to Quinn that she possessed all the qualities of a great innkeeper. She had a way of making people feel...welcome. Accepted.

The first conversation he'd had with Alex Porter pushed its way, unbidden, into Quinn's mind. Abby's brother didn't think she was capable of running a bed-and-breakfast. In fact, Quinn had gotten the distinct impression Alex didn't think Abby was capable of much of anything.

He'd described her as fragile.

Quinn hadn't thought much about it at the time, other than to add that particular trait to the list of reasons why he shouldn't have accepted Alex's proposition. He assumed that no one would know better than one of Abby's own family members what she was, or wasn't, capable of doing.

But over the past few days, without Quinn even being fully aware of it, the sophisticated figurehead of Porter Hotels had gradually started to be replaced by... Abby. A woman who tackled difficult projects with a gleam of determination in her eyes and a how-to book in her hand. A woman with a smile that shimmered like sunlight on water. A woman whose faith wasn't the cardboard kind—it was the wide-eyed, childlike kind that expected God to do amazing things.

Didn't Alex see any of those qualities?

One of them was dead wrong about her and Quinn was beginning to have an unsettling feeling that it wasn't him....

"Last piece of chocolate cake!" Abby ignored the

chorus of protests as she held the plate above her head—and out of the boys' reach.

Quinn rose to his feet, reluctant to join them. His crowded thoughts didn't leave much room for making polite conversation. He didn't have Abby's talent for putting people at ease.

Cody scooted over on the bench to make room for him. A smear of chocolate frosting bracketed his mouth and Quinn plucked a cloth napkin out of the basket and handed it to him.

"Thanks," Cody mumbled around a mouthful of cake.

From there, the conversation dwindled as the teenagers got serious in their attempt to sample everything on the tray.

Abby filled a glass and handed it to him, the smile on her face reflected in her eyes. Eyes that didn't hold a smidgen of doubt or suspicion. Wisps of sun-streaked hair had escaped the apple-green bandana on her head. The color matched the patchwork apron tied around her waist.

She looked totally...*kissable.*

The piece of cake Quinn had just swallowed lodged in his throat.

"I see you found the loose board on the dock."

Abby's words buzzed in his ears like a tree full of cicadas. Great. He was acting like the rest of the adolescent boys at the table!

"Actually, it found me." The board had cracked beneath his weight when he'd stepped on it.

"I caught some nice perch." Zach gulped the remainder of his lemonade and reached for the pitcher.

Abby beat him to it and refilled his glass.

"So did Cody," Tim chimed in.

Cody's ears turned red. "They were okay."

"I can't wait to try them." Abby put one hand on Cody's shoulder.

Quinn saw him shrink from her touch and wondered if Abby had noticed.

Tim snagged the last slice of watermelon from the bowl. "We have to go pretty soon. We're taking our grandma out for dinner tonight.

"Yeah." Tim sighed. "If she doesn't eat right at six-thirty, she says it messes up her constitution. Whatever that is."

"But we can come back tomorrow," Zach added, his expression hopeful.

Over the boy's head, Quinn aimed a what-did-I-tell-you look at Abby.

She crossed her eyes.

Quinn choked.

Tim leaned over and obligingly thumped him on the back.

"I don't think tomorrow will work out," Abby said. "There's church in the morning and I'm afraid I have plans for the rest of the afternoon."

Silence fell, along with the boys' faces.

Abby tilted her head thoughtfully. "But why don't you call me on Monday? I'm sure Quinn and I can come up with a few other things for you to do this week."

That, and the fact that Abby passed around the plate of cookies again, cheered them up.

"Come on, Code." Tim rose to his feet and snaked an arm around Cody's neck, seizing him in an affectionate headlock as he pulled him off the bench.

Abby discreetly doled out white envelopes to each boy as they got up to leave. "Thank you for all your hard work today."

All three nodded and shuffled their feet. And blushed. Then they trooped away, pushing and jostling each other with every step.

"Are boys always like that?" Abby whispered.

"Like what?"

"In perpetual motion."

"You have a brother."

"Alex was never like that." Abby sounded certain as she began to gather up the dishes. "He was seriously…serious."

"I should clean the fish they caught." Quinn wouldn't have minded, except that Sergeant West's visit had made him start thinking about getting those locks changed. "You might not have noticed they didn't get around to that part of the job."

"They didn't have time." Abby winked. "Because of Grandma's, um, constitution."

The impact of that mischievous wink shot through Quinn like a lightning bolt and left him reeling. While he tried to recover from the impact, a car horn blasted.

Abby twisted around, lifting her hand to wave goodbye. Her face clouded. "I think something's wrong."

Quinn turned in the direction of the driveway and saw Cody loping back.

"Zach's car won't start," he gasped once he was within earshot.

"I'll take a look at it." Quinn should have known Abby would follow. Mulligan and Lady, curious over what the fuss was about, trailed along, too.

Twenty minutes later, after Quinn had pronounced the engine dead, the boys circled the ancient Impala like mourners at a graveside service.

"I can't get ahold of Dad. He's not answering the phone," Tim complained. "They must be waiting for us at the restaurant."

"Grandma has a rule against using our cell phones in the restaurants," Zach explained. "She makes Dad turn his off, too."

"That's okay…" Abby looked at Quinn.

He couldn't read minds but somehow he knew what she was going to say next.

"I'm sure Quinn can drop you off."

Yup. That was exactly what he knew she would say.

And he had no way to get out of it. He couldn't suggest she ride along because there wasn't room in his truck—or her convertible—for the five of them.

Silently, he figured out how much time it would take to run the Davis brothers back to Mirror Lake and drop off Cody at home. A half hour. Tops. Quinn weighed that against the possibility of Alex calling for an update on Abby's location.

"Sure. No problem."

The boys piled into Quinn's pickup and he gave them a moment to adjust before he squeezed into the front cab next to Cody. At least the dogs hadn't tried to hitch a ride.

The last thing Quinn saw when he looked in the rearview mirror was Abby. Laughing.

"You're meeting your family at the Grapevine Café, right?" Quinn asked once they were on the road.

"Nope." Zach shook his head. "The Cedars."

Quinn's back teeth ground together.

The Cedars was located ten miles west of Mirror Lake. It would add another half hour onto the trip.

Abby will be fine, Quinn reminded himself. There was still a good hour of daylight left.

He tried not to think about the break-ins across the lake but put a little more pressure on the gas pedal, hoping Sergeant West wasn't running radar on one of the side roads.

Zach and Tim's parents appeared the moment Quinn's truck pulled up by the front door of the restaurant, resulting in another delay. Quinn spent five minutes explaining who he was and why he'd given the boys a ride and another five minutes offering their father a possible diagnosis as to what was wrong with the car.

Forty-five minutes later, he turned down the private road that wound through an archway of maple and oak to the lodge.

The first thing Quinn noticed was that the house was dark. That in itself struck him as odd. The moment the sun began to set, Abby turned on every light until the place glowed like a Chinese lantern.

Quinn parked the truck by the cabin and got out. The peach and pink sunset spilled from the horizon onto the lake as if someone had tipped over a paint can. Everything was calm. Quiet.

Too quiet.

There was no sign of Abby. Or Lady and Mulligan.

Quinn's next breath stayed in his lungs.

Because what he did see was a ribbon of black smoke curling over the roof of the lodge.

* * *

It wasn't working.

Abby cupped one hand over her mouth and, with the other, tossed another handful of sticks into the ring of stones.

According to the book there were supposed to be flames, not smoke.

"What am I doing wrong?" she murmured.

Lady and Mulligan, who'd camped a safe distance away from the fire pit and were sharing one of Abby's homemade biscuits, both stopped chewing and raised their heads.

But they weren't looking at her.

Abby turned her head just in time to see Quinn round the corner of the house. At a full run.

She vaulted to her feet, startled by the wild look in his eyes and half expecting to see a black bear at his heels.

Dread bloomed in Abby's chest. She couldn't imagine what would rattle a man like Quinn.

Had he seen something?

Someone?

As much as she'd tried to put it out of her mind, Deputy West's warning about the break-ins had whittled away at her confidence. After Quinn had left with the boys, she'd needed something to prevent fear from highjacking her inner peace.

The thought of taking a walk to the chapel wasn't as appealing as it usually was, which discouraged Abby even more. She wanted to enjoy God's creation, not worry about vandals using the woods as a hiding place.

She'd decided to tackle one of the projects on her to-do list until Quinn came back.

The expression on his face, however, drained away her initial relief at his return.

"What's wrong?" She was almost afraid to ask.

He skidded to a stop a few feet away from her. "Saw. Smoke."

She frowned, because it looked as if he were having trouble breathing. Which didn't make sense given the fact that *she* was the one whose lungs had been seared by the smoke!

"I know." Abby coughed. "But it's supposed to be a fire."

Quinn looked at her. And the fire pit. And then he dropped to the ground and covered his face with his hands.

Strange.

"Are you all right?"

"Yes." His teeth snapped together on the word.

"You don't look fine. You look…upset. Did something happen?"

He lifted his head, peering at her through narrowed eyes. "Apparently not."

Not sure how to interpret that, Abby picked up a sturdy branch and poked at one of the logs. Another cloud of smoke billowed into the air.

"What are you doing?"

Abby would have thought it was obvious.

"Making a campfire. And believe me. It's not as easy as it looks in the picture."

"Picture."

Maybe, Abby thought, she shouldn't have mentioned the picture. But it was too late. Quinn was already reaching for the manual, facedown on the grass and open to page thirty-four.

He squinted at the camouflage cover and read the title out loud. *"How to Survive and Thrive in the Woods."*

Something in his tone put her on the defensive. "There's a really interesting chapter on edible plants, too."

Quinn set the book down. Carefully. "Why are you making a campfire?"

"Because…" Abby wasn't sure she wanted to confess it was because she'd read that an evening campfire was considered standard entertainment for any respectable country bed-and-breakfast. "The guests are going to expect a campfire. For sing-alongs. Roasting marshmallows. I figured I better practice so I don't embarrass myself."

Well, in front of anyone else, Abby silently amended. It was too late for that with Quinn.

She was thankful the shadows hid her face. She couldn't blame the heat in her cheeks on her pitiful attempt to start a fire. Once again, discouragement punched holes in her confidence and drained away some of the initial enthusiasm she'd felt while following the step-by-step directions in the manual.

"I know. I'm a city mouse in the country." Abby's attempt at humor fell flat. She fiddled with the knot at her waist where she'd tied the tails of her shirt together.

"You don't look like a city mouse." Quinn's gaze swept over her and Abby cringed.

She could only imagine what she looked like. Her faded cutoff jeans and denim shirt were more white than blue. She'd stuffed her bandana in her back pocket when it got snagged in a branch—the same branch that didn't want to let go of her hair when she'd searched for sticks to burn.

"You look more like… Huckleberry Finn."

"Thank you." Abby smiled.

"Most women wouldn't take that as a compliment." He rose fluidly to his feet and studied the smoldering logs.

"That's good. I don't think I want to be *most women*."

"You're not." A reluctant smile tugged at Quinn's lips.

She took that as a compliment, too.

"The book doesn't say you have to use dry wood, not green," he said after a moment. "You wouldn't know that by looking at a picture."

There was not an ounce of condescension in his voice.

"Oh." Abby didn't know why, but that made her feel a little better. A smile tipped her lips. "So maybe I *can* survive and thrive in the woods?"

Quinn's gaze shifted back to her.

"I think…" He paused and Abby braced herself to accept his criticism. "That Abby Porter can survive and thrive anywhere."

Chapter Thirteen

Quinn couldn't believe he'd said the words out loud. But he must have, because Abby lit up like a Fourth of July sparkler.

His pulse, which had finally started to even out after discovering the source of the smoke, picked up speed again.

That was his cue to leave. Retreat. *Escape.*

Maybe a few hours of sleep would restore the ten years that had been stripped from his life when he'd seen the smoke and thought Abby's house was on fire.

Somehow, he doubted it.

Four years in the U.S. Marines and seven as a bodyguard with one of the most prestigious personal security firms in the Midwest and he'd practically collapsed in the dirt at the bright yellow daisies on Abby's sandals.

Practically? An inner voice gibed.

Okay, he *had* collapsed in the dirt at the bright yellow daisies on Abby's sandals.

That was another thing Quinn couldn't explain. He'd been in dangerous situations before, but his knees had never turned to liquid the way they had when he'd spotted Abby, safe and sound by the fire pit.

Quinn wasn't sure if he could thank Sergeant West or Alex Porter for his overreaction to a nonexistent threat. What he *was* sure of was that he wouldn't get any sleep until Abby was in the house for the night.

"The fire will go out on its own," he said. "There isn't much of a breeze tonight, so the sparks shouldn't be a problem."

Abby kicked at one of the logs with the toe of her shoe, a thoughtful look on her face.

"Good night." Quinn waited for her to take the hint.

"'Night." Abby dusted her palms against her jeans. And glanced toward the woods.

He should have known. "Let's go."

"Go where?"

Quinn knew he was going to regret this.

"To find some dry wood."

"No wonder people like campfires. I didn't understand it until now."

Not content simply to prove that she could start a campfire, Abby had settled down to enjoy it, too. She leaned forward, holding her palms out to capture the heat. The firelight played over her features, turning her porcelain complexion to gold.

Quinn cast a longing look in the direction of his cabin and lowered himself onto one of the wool trapper blankets Abby had spread out next to the fire instead.

For a few minutes, the only sound was an occasional snap as the flames spread through the kindling.

Abby put a hand over her mouth to stifle a yawn. And failed.

"You're tired." Quinn wasn't surprised. She rose at dawn and lights glowed in the windows of the lodge well past midnight.

"Yes." Another yawn slipped out. "But I don't want to move." She drew the corners of the blanket over her legs and scooted closer to the edge of the stones. A blissful smile stretched across her face. "This feels too good."

Quinn silently agreed. Which was another reason to call it a night.

"I should clean the fish the boys caught." He'd had to put that task aside in order to play chauffeur. "We have to get up early for church, right?" he added, hoping Abby would take his second not-so-subtle hint.

Across the fire, he saw her catch her lower lip between her teeth.

"What?"

"I, um, let the fish go."

"You…" Quinn couldn't have heard her right.

"Let them go. They were still alive when I pulled the stringer out of the water so I thought—"

"You'd give them another chance," Quinn finished.

"So they could get a little bigger."

Unbelievable. But so… Abby.

"I am not going to tell the boys what you did." Quinn smiled and heard Abby catch her breath. He frowned. "Cold?"

Mutely, she shook her head. Drawing her legs up

against her chest, she rested her chin on her knees and met his gaze across the fire.

Uh-oh.

Quinn had been afraid of this. The intimate warmth of a campfire didn't only lend itself to sing-alongs and s'mores. Like a quiet nook in shadowy, candlelit corner of a restaurant, a campfire also created an optimal environment for conversation.

For *sharing.*

Exactly the kind of thing he'd promised himself that he would avoid when it came to this assignment.

"Do you think Cody will be all right?"

The question took him by surprise. Although it shouldn't have. Abby, who didn't know if the boy she'd fussed over that afternoon was guilty of breaking and entering, had fussed over him anyway.

Unfortunately, Quinn couldn't give her any guarantees. "He has Zach and Tim looking out for him."

"Do you know anything about his family? Sergeant West said something about him following in his brother's footsteps."

Apparently, Sergeant West had had a lot to say during his ten-minute conversation with Abby.

"I don't know anything about the Langs," Quinn said truthfully. He could make a few guesses—none that would guarantee Abby a good night's sleep, however.

"Do you think Cody was involved? In the break-ins?"

"No." Although Quinn wouldn't have been surprised to find out the boy knew the names of the people who were.

He decided not to mention that, either, but Abby

must have drawn her own conclusions because her eyes darkened with concern.

Not wanting her to worry that her cabins might be a future target, Quinn tried to think of something to put her mind at ease.

"I'm planning to put the new locks in on Monday. If my boss gives me a thumbs-up, that is."

As he'd hoped, a smile worked the corner of Abby's lips. "I suppose so. As long as you don't shirk your other duties."

His other duties.

Quinn closed his eyes briefly at the innocent reminder.

It was becoming too easy to forget what those "other duties" were when they were together.

"Quinn?"

His eyes snapped open. Abby was leaning forward. This time, the concern in her eyes was for him.

"You can't even keep your eyes open." She clucked her tongue. "I'll see you in the morning."

Quinn should have been relieved she'd finally decided to turn in for the night...except for one nagging detail. While she was eager to send him on his way, she'd scooped up the manual and begun to page through it.

There was no telling what she was planning this time.

"I'm not that tired." He crossed his arms behind his head and got comfortable. "In fact, I think I'm getting my second wind."

Abby's heart did a somersault when Quinn unfolded his lean frame next to the fire.

In spite of what she'd said earlier, her reluctance to retire for the night wasn't only because she didn't want to leave the warmth of the fire. She didn't want to leave Quinn, either.

As guarded as he could be, once again she'd witnessed his softer side when he'd interacted with Cody and the Davis brothers that afternoon.

She hadn't been spying on them, but the library windows did overlook the lake, after all.

Abby had seen Quinn patiently untangling Cody's fishing line. Pausing in his work to admire the latest catch. Laughing at the boys' antics.

No matter what Quinn's father had been like, she knew without a doubt that Sergeant West was wrong about Quinn. Quinn's actions affirmed the kind of man he was.

When he'd returned and witnessed the disaster of a fire she'd made, he hadn't made her feel like an idiot. Or taken control of the situation, the way Alex would have.

I think Abby Porter can survive and thrive anywhere.

While she'd struggled to absorb that astonishing— and unexpected—compliment, Quinn had led her into the woods, showed her which kind of wood burned the best and then left her alone to find it. When she met him back at the fire pit with an armload of birch, Abby felt like a prospector who'd struck gold. Not only because she'd managed to start a respectable campfire, but because of Quinn.

There was no denying it. She was drawn to him. And not just physically, although his rugged good looks were incredibly easy on the eyes. She was drawn to his strength, which made her feel safe rather than vulnerable. To the sense of humor that surfaced at unexpected times and made her laugh.

She didn't feel pressure to have to conform to certain expectations when she was with him. Abby had found few people she could be herself with and it was a little unnerving to discover that Quinn, in the space of a few short days, had become one of them.

Abby glanced up and found him watching her. The intensity of his gaze made her wonder what he was thinking.

Quinn seemed to have an uncanny way of knowing her thoughts so she quickly averted her gaze and tossed a handful of pine needles into the blaze.

"Now that I know how to make a fire, I think I'm going to start one every night. This is a very nice way to end a day." *You're rambling again, Abby,* she chided herself. Knowing that, however, didn't make it any easier to stop! "It's like a little piece of paradise here. I'm not surprised you came back to Mirror Lake."

"I didn't plan to."

Abby couldn't believe she'd heard him right. "I thought you came back to take over your father's business."

"I came back to sell it."

The words hung in the air between them. As tempting as it was to push, to ask Quinn why he'd changed his mind and stayed, Abby waited.

Would he trust her?

"The veteran's hospital called to tell me that Dad's liver and kidneys were failing," he said at length. "I didn't know he was that sick. Whenever I called, he wouldn't talk to me more than a few minutes. By the time I got there, he'd slipped into a coma. Two hours later, he was gone."

Abby felt her heart wrench as Quinn paused, knowing he was reliving that moment.

Her mind flashed back to a hospital waiting room. Alex had walked in, his face a pale canvas, shaded with gray. He'd reached for her and she'd instinctively backed away, as if she could escape the truth of what he was about to say.

Both of them. Gone.

"I know what that's like," she murmured. "Not to have a chance to say goodbye. There are things you wish you could have said. Things you wish you would have done. I'm sure your father felt the same way."

"You didn't know my father."

There it was again. The tension in Quinn's jaw. The bleak look in his eyes.

Mike O'Halloran was bad news. Everyone around here knew it.

"What was he like?"

"Sergeant West didn't tell you?"

Abby caught her breath at the challenging look in his eyes. It was almost as if he'd read her thoughts.

"I'd rather hear it from you," she said simply.

"The story isn't all that unique." Quinn shrugged. "Dad spent more time at the tavern than he did at home. He liked whiskey because it made him feel powerful. But all that meant was that he had the strength to break things. Furniture. Dishes. His business." A pause. "People."

The shuttered look on his face warned Abby not to feel sorry for him.

His story might not be unique, she thought, but that didn't mean it hadn't been an incredibly difficult one for a child to live out.

Alex had taken care of her after their parents died. Who had been there for Quinn? He hadn't mentioned his mother, leaving Abby to assume that she hadn't been a significant part of his life.

"I'd left Mirror Lake after graduation and hadn't planned to come back. When I found out how sick Dad was, I had to. He didn't have anyone else."

He made it sound so simple but Abby knew it must have been difficult to come back. Even more difficult to stay, if people shared Sergeant West's opinion about his family.

From what Quinn had told her, his father hadn't been there for him. And yet he hadn't let that determine his actions. Abby wondered if Quinn realized what that said about his character.

A log collapsed, sending a shower of sparks into the air.

Quinn didn't seem to notice.

"Like I said, I got there too late. After he died, I inquired about arrangements and found out it had already been done. He didn't even need me for that." Quinn shook his head. "I also found out that, for some reason that only made sense to him, Dad had left everything to me. A house on the verge of foreclosure. A business about to go bankrupt."

The undercurrent of bitterness in his voice told Abby that he hadn't welcomed the news.

"But you accepted the challenge. You stayed in Mirror Lake."

"I didn't have much of a choice. A week before

Dad died, I…lost my job." Quinn shifted, as if to dislodge the memories pressing in on him. "When I found out he'd left everything to me, it was as if he had the last laugh. Like having someone toss you an anchor when you're out in the middle of the lake, treading water."

Abby moistened her lips. Quinn's body language warned her that he wouldn't welcome someone else's perspective on the matter but she had to obey a soft, inner prompting.

"Your dad might not have had your best interests at heart, but you have a heavenly Father who loves you and He does," Abby said softly, feeling her way. Praying for wisdom. "Maybe inheriting the business wasn't an anchor meant to drag you down. Maybe it was God's way of giving you a lifeline."

Chapter Fourteen

The aroma of freshly brewed coffee swept over Quinn the moment he reached the deck.

He'd already gone through half a pot but wouldn't turn down another cup. The caffeine surfing through his veins was the only thing lifting the fog from his brain.

The conversation he'd had with Abby had gone through his mind so many times during the night that it had worn a permanent rut there.

He hadn't meant to talk about his father. Especially with Abby. Opening up the door to his past was dangerous on more than one level, for both of them. Before he realized what was happening, he'd let it slip that he had lost his former job. If Abby hadn't been focused on Quinn's relationship with his father, she could have questioned him about where he'd lived. What he'd done for a living.

Not only had Abby managed to sneak through his defenses, once she'd gotten through, she'd dropped that bombshell on him guaranteed to alter the terrain of his beliefs. And then left him alone to assess the damage.

There'd been plenty.

Quinn had stayed by the fire until the embers faded from red to gray. When he finally walked back to his cabin, he saw the sliver of light shining under the eaves where Abby's bedroom was located. Did Abby have a difficult time falling asleep, too? If the coffee tasted as strong as it smelled, it was a good indication that she had.

He tapped on the screen door.

"Come in." Abby's voice floated down the stairs. The official lilting cadence of a morning person. "I'll be right down. Pour yourself a cup of coffee."

Quinn made his way to the kitchen and stared in disbelief at the array of baked goods on the table. The inn hadn't opened and it looked as if Abby were already cooking for a dozen people.

"Have a…" Abby came around the corner as he was reaching for a sample. She smiled. "Cinnamon roll."

Quinn's mouth went dry.

He'd teased Abby the day before about her resemblance to Huckleberry Finn. This morning, she was the woman on the billboard for Porter Hotels.

The white sundress Abby wore made her sun-kissed skin appear even more golden. Pencil-thin heels replaced the plastic daisy sandals. Her hair was subdued in a neat coil at the nape of her neck, showcasing a diamond cross necklace and matching earrings. The stones weren't large or gaudy but they glowed with a soft fire that told Quinn they were genuine.

If it hadn't been for the familiar, luminous smile, Quinn might not have recognized her.

"Are you bringing a mid-sermon snack?" He dragged his gaze away.

She smiled. Call him an idiot, but he couldn't get enough of Abby's smile. "This is my contribution for the potluck after the service."

"There's a potluck?"

"Mmm." Abby tilted her head. "I thought I mentioned that."

"No. You didn't." Quinn's plan to arrive late and leave early began to unravel.

"Don't worry about bringing something. I have enough for both of us."

That wasn't what Quinn was worried about. He was worried about spending more time than absolutely necessary under the scrutiny of the people who attended Church of the Pines. He was used to people talking about him; he didn't want to cast a shadow on Abby's reputation.

She poured two cups of coffee and handed him one. "Have two cinnamon rolls if you'd like. We're celebrating."

"Celebrating?"

"Last night when I came in, there was a message on the answering machine from a woman named Lydia Thomas. She and her husband are missionaries in the Philippines, but they're here on furlough for the summer. Apparently, her cousin lives in Mirror Lake and mentioned that I was opening a B&B here." Abby paused to take a breath. "She and her husband, Simon, met and fell in love when they were camp counselors one summer. They'll be celebrating their fiftieth wedding anniversary and they want to renew their vows. *Here.*"

"Your first guests." Quinn thought of all the work that still needed to be accomplished but didn't want to dampen her excitement.

"That's not all." Abby's eyes shone as bright as the diamonds around her neck. "They want to rent out all five cabins so they can invite their friends and family to witness the vow renewal—in the chapel." Abby performed a graceful ballerina twirl, the filmy skirt of her dress swirling around her knees. And, Quinn couldn't help but notice, she did it without spilling a drop of coffee. "Can you believe it? The chapel, Quinn! That's where her husband proposed."

The dreamy look on her face told Quinn that she was caught up in the romance of it all. His thoughts took a more practical turn.

All five cabins. He did some quick calculating in his head. Three of them were finished. Installing new locks and a security system would take up the bulk of his time the first part of the week but it was possible he could have another cabin done by the time Daniel returned.

"Which weekend are they going to reserve?"

Abby bit her lip. "That's the tricky part."

"The *tricky* part?" Quinn's stomach contracted. "Don't tell me they want to rent out the place the weekend of your grand opening?"

He remembered her mentioning that she hadn't taken any reservations yet because she initially planned to rely on word of mouth rather than formal advertising. The grand opening was supposed to provide people with an opportunity to tour the grounds, view the rooms and sample some of the food Abby planned to prepare. If she took in guests that weekend, visitors wouldn't have the freedom to explore.

"No. They're scheduled to go back to the Philippines. Lydia wanted to know if there was any way I can accommodate them the weekend before."

It took a moment for her words to sink in. "They want you to open the inn a week *early?*"

"Yes."

Amazingly, a sparkle danced in Abby's eyes instead of the panic Quinn should have seen there.

"What did you tell her?"

"Nothing yet. It was too late to return her call last night but I plan to call her back right after church."

"To tell her no, right?"

"You should have heard Lydia's voice, Quinn. She sounded thrilled at the idea of renewing their vows in the chapel where Simon proposed to her."

Lydia and Simon.

Abby had never met the couple but the warmth in her tone made it sound as if she'd known them forever.

"That's two weekends from now." Someone had to be the voice of reason and Quinn figured since he was the only other person in the room, the task fell to him. "You aren't even sure you'll have things ready in time for the grand opening."

The voice of reason, however, didn't put a dent in Abby's enthusiasm.

"I prayed about this a lot during the night and I really think it's what I'm supposed to do," Abby said. "Lydia and Simon have spent fifty years together on the mission field. If I can do something special for them, I'm trusting that God will give me the means to accomplish it."

The closer they got to church, the quieter Quinn became.

Not, Abby thought, that he'd been Mr. Talkative

since she'd told him about the Thomases' vow renewal. He hadn't argued with her decision but she could tell he wasn't happy with it, either.

But, she reminded herself, he hadn't heard Lydia's voice on the answering machine. The woman had sounded as breathless and giddy as the seventeen-year-old girl who'd fallen in love that summer over fifty years ago.

How could she say no?

There was no denying, however, that it would take a tremendous amount of time and energy to have the inn ready for guests a full seven days earlier than Abby had originally planned. Not to mention the food preparation. Lydia had asked if she would consider catering a small reception after the vow renewal.

She hadn't told Quinn that. He already thought she was crazy for even *thinking* about opening the inn early. Fortunately, he'd let the subject drop after she'd reminded him that she believed in God's plans and purposes, not coincidences.

You'll have to help me, Lord. There is no way I can do this without You.

"Are you coming?"

With a start, Abby realized they were in the parking lot.

"Sorry." She slipped out of the car and smoothed the wrinkles from her skirt. "I was thinking about Lydia and Simon Thomas."

"How you hate to disappoint them this time around but you would love to see them the next time they're in the States?"

"No." Abby swatted Quinn's arm with her purse.

And heard a polite cough.

She glanced up and saw Pastor Wilde standing several feet away, watching them with interest.

The first time she attended Church of the Pines, she'd been a little shocked to see a handsome man in his early thirties take the pulpit at the beginning of the service. It suddenly made sense to Abby why every single woman between the age of eighteen and eighty crowded the front pews, which were typically the last to fill up on a Sunday morning.

According to Kate Nichols, Pastor Wilde came to Mirror Lake to serve as a temporary interim pastor the summer before but had stayed on when the elders, impressed by his easygoing personality and passion for the Lord, offered him the full-time position.

"Pastor Wilde." Abby felt Quinn freeze beside her. She linked her arm through his, took a step forward and felt instant resistance. "Good morning."

"Morning, Abby." The pastor smiled at her before his gaze slid to Quinn. He extended his hand. "I don't believe we've met. I'm Matthew Wilde."

Just when Abby began to wonder if she had to step on Quinn's toe to get him to make a noise, he shook the pastor's hand. "Quinn O'Halloran."

"I'm glad you're joining us today."

Quinn's chin jerked once in acknowledgment.

Abby couldn't understand his response. If he'd attended Church of the Pines in the past, why did he seem so uncomfortable?

"You asked for prayer last week." Pastor Wilde looked at her. "How are things going out at your place?"

Abby smiled up at Quinn. "Actually, my prayers were answered. Quinn came to my rescue. He took

Daniel's place and he's already finished one of the cabins."

"Only two more to go," Quinn muttered.

"God does care about the details." Pastor Wilde's gaze bounced between the two of them. "I hope you're both staying for the potluck after the service."

"Oh, that's right. I almost forgot the salad. It has to be refrigerated." Abby turned and dove into the backseat to retrieve it.

So much for Quinn's hope that he and Abby would arrive late and avoid the pre-service meet and greet. But then again, he'd also hoped to avoid the pastor and yet here he was, making nice with the guy in the parking lot.

Pastor Tracey must have retired. That shouldn't have surprised him. For all Quinn knew, the church could have seen several ministers come and go over the past fifteen years.

He hadn't missed the appreciative look in Matthew Wilde's eyes when he greeted Abby. Not that Quinn could blame him. Abby's smile gave the sun a run for its money. The pastor hadn't ogled her in an inappropriate way but it still bugged him. Quinn took a perverse satisfaction in knowing that Abby hadn't seemed to notice.

"Quinn used to attend here a long time ago." Abby returned, a large covered bowl in her hands. A strand of hair worked its way out of the pins and dropped to her shoulder like a silky yo-yo. "Now where did that come from?" she grumbled.

Without thinking, Quinn reached out and tucked it back into place.

The pastor's eyes narrowed. Like a shepherd who had just spotted a wolf stalking one of his lambs.

Stupid, stupid, stupid, Quinn silently berated himself. *Not exactly the way to fly under the guy's radar, O'Halloran.*

Abby unwittingly came to his rescue. "I suppose we should go inside. The service can't start if we keep the pastor standing out in the parking lot."

"I can take this." Quinn reached for the bowl and Abby handed it to him with one of her signature bright smiles.

"Thank you."

Matthew Wilde gave him a measured look as he picked up the thread of conversation again. "I've been trying to get to know everyone in the congregation, but I don't remember seeing your name on the membership roster."

"Like Abby said. It was a long time ago. I was in fourth grade."

"Then you're originally from the area?"

The pastor's casual tone didn't fool Quinn a bit. There might be not a bright light shining in his face, but he was definitely in the hot seat. "Born and raised. I left after graduation."

"Where did you go?"

Abby darted a look in his direction as they began to walk toward the doors. It was clear she was as interested in his answer as the pastor was. "The marines," he said reluctantly.

"Four years?"

Quinn nodded and quickened his pace. If he was lucky, he'd make it to the man handing out bulletins before the next question.

An elderly woman bustled up to them, running interference as she planted her tiny frame in front of the pastor. Quinn would have hugged her, except he was afraid the ushers would think he was going for her purse.

Quinn took a bulletin, ignored the usher's bulging eyes as he recognized him and started down the aisle.

Only to face another complication.

The only empty pews were close to the front of the church. Which meant he and Abby had to walk up the center aisle—in front of everyone—to find a place to sit.

Abby, who seemed oblivious to the curious looks they were receiving, waved to Kate Nichols, who promptly shifted everyone over to create enough space for them for join her.

The two women, who couldn't have known each other for more than a few weeks, hugged as if they were lifelong friends. Over Abby's shoulder, Kate winked at him. The brat.

She knew he avoided her café and she knew why. He refused to provide more grist for the rumor mill.

"Hi, Quinn."

"Kate."

A smile danced in her eyes at his less than enthusiastic reply. "It's good to see you."

Quinn was saved from having to respond when a woman joined the pianist and began to sing.

As the words of the praise song flowed through the sanctuary, Quinn felt as if he were transported back in time.

The church, like the town, hadn't changed in the past fifteen years.

Sunlight streamed through the stained glass windows, painting the floor with swashes of crimson, emerald and gold. While other churches sought to modernize with comfortable chairs and PowerPoint displays, Church of the Pines remained the same.

Quinn hadn't expected to find comfort in that.

"Quinn?" Abby touched his hand.

With a start, he realized the congregation was rising to their feet to join together in the last verse of the song.

He didn't know the words but was content to listen to Abby sing them in her clear contralto.

When the song ended and they'd taken their seats again, Matthew Wilde stepped up to the front.

"Good morning, everyone." His smile swept over the congregation. "Welcome to the Church of the Pines. For those of you who are guests, I'm Pastor Matthew Wilde. And today, we're going to a place called Gilgal."

Chapter Fifteen

Quinn studied the fresh flowers on the piano. The young mother discreetly doling out animal crackers to her children in the next row. Counted the number of candles on the altar.

He even tried to come up with a way to convince Abby to tell Lydia Thomas they couldn't hold their vow renewal at the inn. But in spite of his best efforts, like the bluegill Cody had hooked and played until it finally gave up, Matt Wilde's sermon slowly began to reel him in.

"Do you know what was between the wilderness and the Promised Land?" Matt paused. "Well, if a person checked out the Scriptures, they might say it was the Jordan River. And they'd be right." He smiled. "But I think I'm right, too, when I say it wasn't only the river, it was faith.

"The Israelites, children of the Promise, had been wandering in the desert for forty years. I don't know about you, but I've done my share of wandering—even after I trusted Christ as my Savior. Like they did, I had a habit of looking back instead of forward. Sound familiar?"

Quinn saw heads begin to nod. Abby's was one of them.

"Joshua wanted to lead the people to the Promised Land, but in order to do that, they had to take that first step of believing God and trusting Him. The water didn't part before they stepped in. It parted *after* their toes touched the water.

"Even though life in the wilderness is barren and difficult, there are times we are tempted to stay there. We start to set up camp like it's our home." Matt lifted his hands. "This is it. This is all I can expect from myself. All I can expect from God. But it isn't our true home. It's not the place we're *supposed* to dwell. God wants us to cross over into all that He has for us, not live in defeat, wandering in the wilderness.

"He had an amazing plan for His people. A plan they discovered when they stopped wandering and started trusting. The word *Gilgal* means circle. God gave the people a do-over, in a sense. Brought them full circle. The reason they'd spent forty years in the desert was because they'd disobeyed Him, but He gave them another opportunity to trust Him. He'll do the same for you. I know, because He did it for me.

"My question for you today is this, are you going to trust Him? Are you going to take that step of faith and believe His promises? You don't have to stay in the wilderness. God has something special waiting for you, too. Be brave. Take that first step of faith and find out what it is."

Instead of rising with fire-and-brimstone intensity,

Pastor Wilde's voice dropped. To Quinn, it had more of an impact than if he'd shouted the words.

"Will you pray with me?"

Quinn automatically bowed his head with everyone else, but his thoughts were scattered in a dozen different directions...and then he felt Abby take hold of his hand.

"You aren't getting a root canal, you know." Abby tugged on Quinn's arm but it was like trying to move a mountain.

Quinn didn't budge. He noticed the pastor had finished praying.

Abby sighed and closed her eyes.

"What are you doing?"

"Shh. I'm praying for you."

"For me?" He sounded as if he were choking.

Abby nodded but didn't open her eyes. "Jesus said if we have faith like a mustard seed, we can move a mountain. Compared to that, moving you to the fellowship hall should be a piece of cake."

She peeked up at Quinn through her lashes and saw his lips tilt.

"Come on," he growled. "I suppose if we don't get in line, the only thing left will be those salads made out of Jell-O and cottage cheese."

"I always go to the dessert table first," Abby whispered.

"Lead the way." Quinn's smile kicked up another notch and Abby caught her breath.

She saw a few curious looks as they made their way to the buffet table but most of the people smiled. At both her and Quinn. Still, she could feel the tension emanating from him. As if he were expecting a lightning bolt to find him at any moment. Or someone to shoulder their way through the crowd and tell him that he didn't belong here.

Quinn hadn't commented on Pastor Wilde's sermon but she knew it had to have moved him.

Listening to Matthew's message, Abby had prayed that God would speak to Quinn. Touch his heart. The words the pastor had spoken were like a benediction to the conversation she and Quinn had had the night before.

When Quinn talked about his father, underneath the bitterness was regret. And underneath the regret, grief. The emotions layered below the surface like striations in a rock.

It was important to her that Quinn take the step of faith that would set him free from the past…because Quinn was important to her.

Abby swallowed hard as the truth washed over her.

She'd known him less than a week and yet every conversation they'd had, every smile they shared, every moment they spent together acted like invisible threads knitting her heart to his.

She had no idea if he felt the same way. But it had to mean something that Quinn had confided in her about his childhood. Sat with her by the campfire. Brought her to church…

"Can't decide?" Quinn whispered. "Take one of each. That's what I'm going to do."

Abby blinked. If she could stand in front of a table laden with mouthwatering desserts and not see them, she was in worse shape than she thought!

"I'm glad you haven't left yet, Abby." Kate rushed

up to her. "There's someone I want you to meet and don't you dare slink away, Quinn O'Halloran," she added in the same breath. "Pastor Wilde is looking for you."

Before Abby knew it, Kate had whisked her away. She glanced over her shoulder and saw Quinn bookended by Pastor Wilde and a tall, dark-haired man she didn't recognize.

"You asked me about local artists when you were at the café a few days ago," Kate said. "I don't know why I didn't think about Emma Barlow. You're practically neighbors. She lives on Stony Ridge Road about a mile away from you."

"She's an artist?"

"Emma probably wouldn't call herself that," Kate said with a low laugh. "She considers what she does a hobby, although I disagree. She has a gift. I talked her into selling three of her mosaic garden stones to me last summer and each one is a work of art. They're absolutely beautiful."

Abby could already picture a path made up of one-of-a-kind stones winding through the kitchen garden she had designed. "I'd love to meet her."

"She's right over there." Kate pointed to a slender woman sitting at a table in the corner. Her sandy brown hair and delicate features matched those of the boy sitting next to her. Brother and sister? Abby wondered. Emma looked too young to have a child that age.

The woman rose to her feet as they approached.

"Emma, this is Abby Porter. Abby, Emma Barlow and her son, Jeremy."

"Please, sit down," Emma said. "Jeremy and I are almost finished."

"Oh, we don't want your table," Kate said cheerfully. "We want you. Abby is opening a bed-and-breakfast on Mirror Lake and she's interested in buying from local artists."

Emma gave Kate a look. "I hardly qualify as a local artist," she protested.

"Don't be so modest." Kate pulled out a chair for Abby and plunked down into the one beside it. "I was telling her about the mosaic work you do."

The color in Emma's cheeks matched the carnation-pink blouse she wore. "It's just something I do in my spare time," she murmured. "To relax."

"They are good, Mom," the boy piped up. "Maybe if you start selling some of them, I can get a new bike."

"Jeremy Barlow!" Emma looked as if she wished the floor would open up and swallow her.

"Sorry." Jeremy grinned. "But it's true."

Abby took pity on her. "I'm sorry about the ambush," she said. "But I really would like to see some of your work."

"It's not…" Emma paused and the indecision in her wide blue eyes collided with Kate's scowl across the table. "I suppose that would be all right. For you to look at it, I mean."

Something in Emma's expression told Abby that even though she was giving in, she didn't want her to purchase anything out of a sense of obligation.

"Great." Abby pushed away from the table. Not only because she didn't want to give Emma an opportunity to change her mind, but because she wanted to check on Quinn.

Maybe it had been her imagination, but she had felt some strange vibes between him and Pastor Wilde in the parking lot. Abby trusted that Matthew wouldn't say or do anything to make a visitor uncomfortable, but Quinn might not perceive it that way. Judging from what he'd told her the night before, he didn't think anyone would see him as anything other than the offspring of Mike O'Halloran.

Was it possible that Quinn believed God felt the same way?

"Earth to Abby." Kate snapped her fingers a few inches from Abby's nose.

"I'm sorry." Now it was Abby's turn to blush. "I was…somewhere else."

"I'm sure you were," Kate teased. "And I should probably take you back there, or he's going to think you've been kidnapped."

Abby managed a wan smile. Knowing it was just an expression didn't prevent the knot that formed in her stomach.

She reminded herself that she wasn't wandering aimlessly in the wilderness anymore, tangled in the thorns of painful memories. Like Pastor Wilde, she had taken that step of faith into a land of abundant living that God promised.

"Mom?" Jeremy's face lit up as he turned toward his mother. "It looks like some of the guys are going to play baseball. Can I go, too?"

Emma shook her head. "We're going to be leaving soon."

Instead of arguing, Jeremy slumped lower in the

chair and bulldozed a forkful of corn into what was left of his mashed potatoes.

Kate looked as if she were about to say something but changed her mind. An awkward silence descended.

"I'll call you, Emma," Abby said. "Is your number in the book?"

Emma averted her gaze. "It's listed under Brian Barlow."

Abby hadn't missed the shadow that skimmed the surface of the other woman's eyes. If she wasn't mistaken, Emma Barlow had spent some time in the wilderness, too.

To her credit, Kate didn't say a word about Emma as they left to find Quinn. Abby was relieved. Quinn thought the Grapevine Café lived up to its name, but Kate didn't seem like the type of person who considered gossip an acceptable form of conversation.

"I don't see Quinn."

Kate chuckled. "He's a big boy. I'm sure he's still with Pastor Wilde."

Or else, Abby thought, he'd left her stranded at the church potluck.

Her suspicion increased after they took another lap around the fellowship hall. There was no sign of Quinn anywhere. Or Pastor Wilde, for that matter.

"Let's check outside," Kate suggested. "We have picnic tables set up in the yard and a lot of people take their food out there when the weather is nice."

Abby had a hard time not charging ahead of her friend as they made their way back upstairs and out the double doors into the sunshine. Kate was right. At least half the congregation had gone outside. The older members of the congregation balanced paper plates in their hands while they chatted with friends and the younger ones sprawled on their stomachs in the grassy area off the parking lot.

"See, there he is… Oh, no."

"What?" Abby's gaze bounced from the group of boys playing touch football in the grassy field adjacent to the church to a circle of young mothers with babies in their arms and toddlers attached to their skirts like barnacles.

She couldn't see Quinn anywhere.

"I think you've been replaced."

"Replaced?" Abby frowned.

Kate pointed to a path of asphalt near the corner of the building, where a line of giggling little girls had formed, each waiting to take a turn.

Pastor Wilde held one end of the bright pink jump rope.

Quinn held the other.

Abby watched in fascination as an adorable little girl, with ink-black hair and skin a soft shade of caramel, tugged on the hem of Quinn's shirt. He continued to turn the rope with one hand and scooped her up with the other, settling her onto his hip.

Kate looped an arm around Abby's shoulders and gave them a squeeze.

"And you were worried Quinn wouldn't make friends."

Chapter Sixteen

He wasn't Superman.

Who was he kidding?

He couldn't even claim to be a real carpenter, although at least Quinn knew one end of the hammer from the other.

Not that his thumb would agree. It was still throbbing in response to being mashed a time or two. Okay, maybe more like a dozen.

It was Abby's fault he was so distracted. Thoughts of her created a hazardous work environment. Quinn was tempted to call OSHA and turn her in. Maybe that would stop her from carrying out her crazy plan to open the inn early.

On second thought, he doubted it.

Raking a hand through his hair, Quinn stepped back to survey the porch rail.

If he didn't finish soon, he'd be working in the rain. An ominous bank of clouds had unrolled on the horizon, blocking out the sun and kicking up a breeze that curled the tops of the waves that slapped the shoreline.

As soon as he and Abby had gotten back to the inn, he'd started working on the next cabin. If she was serious about opening up a week early for the Thomases, he couldn't afford the luxury of a "rest and refresh" day.

Abby must have come to the same conclusion. She'd disappeared inside the house right after church and he hadn't seen her the rest of the day.

Quinn was hoping that once she took off her rose-colored glasses and acknowledged the staggering amount of work left to be done, she would admit defeat.

Like you did?

The mocking question rerouted Quinn's thoughts to the conversation they'd had the night before, where it dovetailed with the sermon Pastor Wilde had delivered that morning.

Like a two-by-four to his thick skull.

No coincidences, Abby said.

Quinn was starting to think that God did have a plan. And a sense of humor.

When Matthew Wilde had suggested they "take a walk and get to know each other," Quinn braced himself for part two of the interrogation the pastor had started in the parking lot.

Quinn had been a little shocked when the pastor started to talk about himself instead. And he wasn't sure how, but not only had he gotten roped—literally—into playing with a group of giggling little girls, he had also agreed to meet Matthew for breakfast on Thursday morning. At the Grapevine Café, no less.

He was about to pick up the hammer again when

Lady planted herself at his feet and barked, a polite reminder it was time for her supper.

"Got it." Quinn bent down to ruffle his pet's silky ears. "Where's your sidekick?" He looked around for Mulligan. The two dogs had become inseparable during the week.

As if she understood the question, Lady looked toward the house and whined.

Quinn's eyes narrowed.

It wouldn't hurt to check on Abby and make sure she wasn't working too hard. And snag another one of her killer cinnamon rolls at the same time.

If Abby insisted on feeding him like this, he'd have to put in a few more hours of work every day to burn the extra calories off.

Not that there was a lack of work to find.

Lady followed him over to the cabin and Quinn filled her dish, shutting the door quietly behind him before making his way to Abby's.

Mulligan must have realized his buddy was missing, because when Quinn stepped onto Abby's porch, the dog's howl drifted through the open windows.

Usually Abby had praise music blasting while she worked, but other than Mulligan's mournful song, everything was quiet.

"Abby?" He opened the door and stuck his head inside.

No response.

Frowning, Quinn took a step into the foyer. The tangy odor of lemon cleaner stung his eyes.

Abby definitely hadn't been lounging around all day with her nose in a book. He could practically see his reflection in the floor.

"Abby? Are you in here?"

Mulligan heard his voice and dashed around the corner, all four paws scrambling for purchase on the glossy hardwood floor. The momentum sent him skidding toward Quinn like a baseball player sliding into home plate.

Quinn caught the dog before he took out a lamp.

The commotion didn't lure Abby to the great room. Quinn felt the blood thicken in his veins as he made a sweep of the first floor and then the second.

He took the narrow staircase leading up to the third floor and found his path blocked by a bright green door.

Had she decided to take a nap?

"Abby?" He tapped his knuckles against the wood and turned the knob at the same time. The door swung open.

Quinn had a split second to take in the neat but tiny living quarters—pale green walls, an antique wardrobe and the sleigh bed covered in a simple patchwork quilt—before something else registered.

The bed was empty.

Now what?

There was nowhere else to look. And there was no sign of Abby. Anywhere.

Abby untied the lightweight sweater she'd knotted around her shoulders and pushed her arms through the sleeves to cloak the goose bumps rising on her skin.

The morning had started out hot and muggy, but the temperature had dropped over the past hour as a front moved in, making Abby question her decision to take a walk so close to sunset.

But scrubbing and waxing the floors for the better part of the afternoon had given her plenty of time to formulate ideas on how to decorate the chapel for Lydia and Simon's vow renewal.

Talking with Lydia on the phone had affirmed she was doing the right thing. Abby had felt an instant rapport with the elderly woman as they discussed the arrangements.

Following the old adage about honesty being the best policy, Abby explained to Lydia that the inn wasn't officially open for business for several more weeks. When Lydia immediately began to apologize, Abby assured her that she felt blessed to be part of the anniversary celebration.

It took a few more minutes to convince Lydia that she and Simon and their guests wouldn't be an imposition—as long as the couple could overlook some minor imperfections.

Even as she'd said the word, Abby wondered if leaky roofs and rotting floors could be considered imperfections.

Not, she thought as she made her way down the trail, that Lydia would even notice. When she realized Abby was offering to open the inn early, the woman's voice had thickened as she assured her that being able to renew their vows at the chapel was all the "perfect" she needed.

Abby couldn't wait to meet the couple. And she couldn't wait to tell Quinn what Lydia had said.

Guilt shot through her as Quinn came to mind.

She hadn't seen him all day. Here she'd spouted

off about setting aside Sunday to "rest and refresh" and then she'd spent every minute of it up to her elbows in lemon polish.

He must have known she wouldn't change her mind because shortly after he'd dropped her off at the house, the tap of the hammer punctuated the air. As far as she knew, he hadn't even stopped for a break.

Not that Abby had, either.

As if on cue, her stomach rumbled. Ignoring it, Abby veered off the trail and followed the worn footpath that led to the chapel just as fat droplets of rain began to fall.

The eerie stillness that had settled in the air was disrupted by a pair of crows, who sounded the alarm as she approached the stone building. Their cry was taken up by a red squirrel who shimmied up the nearest oak, perching there to act as sentry.

Abby slipped inside and let her eyes adjust to the gloom. She was used to stopping at the chapel on her daily walk, when sunlight flooded the one-room sanctuary. Now, shadows stretched across the floor and up the walls.

A low rumble of thunder broke the silence and Abby's stomach pitched. She looked up at the ceiling.

"Lord, help me not to be afraid," she murmured. "I know You're here with me."

Instead of giving her courage, the hollow echo of her voice sent another shiver gliding through her.

Determinedly, Abby took a walk around the interior, fixing her gaze on the stained glass windows rather than the dark corners.

As she paused to run the tip of her index finger around the dusty sill, a jagged spear of lightning ripped through the clouds, opening a seam in the sky for the rain to pour through.

Abby backed away from the window. Stranded. At least until it let up a bit.

The chapel didn't have electricity and she wished she would have brought a flashlight along. Not that she'd planned on having the last hour of daylight snatched away by the bank of dark clouds that had unrolled across the sky.

The wind picked up in intensity and pushed against the door, like someone trying to shoulder their way inside. Abby's mouth went dry and she tore her gaze away from it.

"Twenty guests." She said the words out loud, trying to find some comfort in the sound of her own voice. The people would be almost shoulder to shoulder in the pews, a comfortable but cozy fit.

In her mind's eye, she could see the sides of the wooden pews decorated with fresh flowers, ivy and ribbons; candles on pedestal stands lining the front of the chapel.

Abby's gaze shifted from the pews to the narrow door behind the altar that opened into a small storage room. When she'd first discovered it, she'd found stacks of old programs and a box of props that must have been used for skits the campers put on during the summer.

She blinked in the gloom.

It looked as if the door were open a crack.

Don't be silly, Abby scolded herself, taking a tentative step back. *It's your imagination. The way the shadows are falling makes it look like it's open....*

The inside of her mouth turned to chalk.

It *was* open.

Abby backpedaled a few more steps, her eyes riveted on the door to the storage room.

She had two choices. Head back to the house in a thunderstorm or open the door and prove to herself there was nothing on the other side.

"Don't hold on to your fears. Hold on to God."

Jessica's words cut through the storm going on inside her.

Her feet felt like waterlogged sponges as she put one foot in front of the other. The shadows had swallowed most of the natural light and the door wavered as Abby reached out a hand.

It swung open at the barest touch of her fingers and she took a tentative step inside. Her gaze swept the interior of the room and she released a ragged breath.

Empty.

Relief poured through Abby and she sagged to her knees, laughing weakly. In the past, something like this would have either paralyzed her or sent her running. This time, she'd faced it.

And she knew why.

Thank You, God.

Quinn was halfway up the trail when the beam from the flashlight flickered and died.

Not that he needed it. The constant flashes of lightning were doing a pretty good job of illuminating the way.

He stopped and worked the button a few times, just to be sure. Nothing. The temptation to turn around was strong.

If Abby had gone to the chapel, a distinct possibility since he'd found her car parked in the garage, then she was waiting out the storm there. Nice and dry.

Unlike him.

If he showed up there, soaked to the skin, she was going to think he was crazy.

And she'd be right.

A shard of lightning, too close for comfort, nicked the top of one of the pines near the lake. The ground hummed under his feet.

That did it.

Even if Abby was warm and dry, there was no way he was leaving her alone up there.

He'd barely taken another step when something hurtled against him.

Quinn staggered under the impact and his feet shot out from under him as if someone had greased the trail. He fell, taking Abby with him.

As he looked up into her eyes, something about the scenario seemed strangely familiar.

"What did I do this time?" he groaned.

"What are you doing out here?" Abby scolded, raising her voice above the shriek of the wind. "It's dangerous to be under the trees in a storm."

As if to emphasize her words, another cymbal crash sounded in the treetops.

Quinn surged to his feet and brought her with him. "Let's get back to the house before we get turned into human shish kebabs."

He kept one arm around Abby while they slipped and slid their way down the trail, locked together like a pair of amateur figure skaters until they reached the safety of the lodge.

They stumbled into the kitchen and Abby sagged

against the counter, her shoulders shaking as a small lake formed at her feet.

Was she hurt? Scared?

She pushed the wet hair off her face and lifted her head.

"You're smiling again." Quinn stared at her in disbelief.

"Am I?" Abby swiped a soggy sleeve against her face and giggled. "That didn't help."

He'd just had another ten years stripped off his life and she was acting like a baby duck who'd found a warm puddle to splash around in!

"What on earth possessed you to go for a walk in a storm?" Quinn said, a little amazed he was able to talk with his back teeth clamped together.

"I had some things to do at the chapel." Abby's teeth began to chatter but she grabbed a teapot off the stove and began to fill it with water. "Do you want some t-tea?"

The perfect hostess.

Quinn felt the anger drain out of him. In two strides he was by her side. Plucked the teapot from her bluish hands.

"I want you to change into dry clothes and curl up with a fuzzy blanket and read the chapter in *Survive and Thrive in the Woods* about thunderstorms," he said softly.

Abby wasn't intimidated by his scowl. If anything, her smile brightened. "And then I'll pass it on to you. I wasn't the only one out in that storm, you know. What's your excuse?"

"I went to find you," he admitted with a growl. "Because I knew you'd skip that chapter."

A droplet of water burst and ran down her cheek. Quinn stopped it with the pad of his thumb. Of their own accord, the rest of his fingers splayed over the delicate curve of her jaw.

Leave. Now.

Quinn's brain sent out an urgent SOS to his heart. He would have enough memories to keep him awake at night without adding another one. What it would feel like to kiss Abby.

"What were you thinking anyway?" He scraped up some anger. At the moment, that emotion was safer than the other ones swirling around in his head. "You could have been hit by lightning. You could catch pneumonia—"

"Quinn?"

He barely heard her over the jackhammer of his heart.

Abby came up on her tiptoes and touched her lips to his. Smiled into his eyes.

"Thank you."

Chapter Seventeen

"Good news."

Quinn rolled over and scrubbed his eyes with the back of one hand. "Porter?" he said into the phone.

"Of course." Alex sounded irritatingly cheerful at—Quinn squinted at his watch—five o'clock in the morning.

He felt as if he'd just fallen asleep. Probably because his conscience had kept him awake most of the night.

"This better be good," Quinn muttered. "And it better not have anything to do with attaching tiny surveillance cameras to squirrels."

"You're fired."

It took a moment for the words to register. "Fired?"

"Out of a job. Let go. Terminated," Alex clarified almost cheerfully. "The police took the guy who's been harassing me into custody last night. Caught in the act of sticking a wicked-looking knife into the back tires of my Viper, by the way."

Wide-awake now, Quinn propped himself up on one elbow. "Who was it?"

There was a pause, as if Alex was surprised by the question. "The younger brother of someone I fired about a month ago. Apparently he took issue with my decision and wanted to get revenge. He's fifteen, though. Old enough to be charged as an adult."

Alex sounded as if he wished he were able to sentence the teen himself. Quinn couldn't help but compare that to the compassion Abby had shown Cody Lang.

"You know what this means, don't you?" Alex continued. "You can pack up your tools and get back to the security business."

Pack up his tools.

A week ago, he would have already been on his way back to Mirror Lake. But a week ago, he hadn't known Abby.

"Great." Quinn winced at his own lack of enthusiasm as he turned away from the sunlight streaming through the window.

He thought of all the work that needed to be done in the next two weeks so that Abby would have the inn ready for the Thomases' anniversary celebration.

"What kind of strings are you going to have to pull to get Daniel to come back early?"

Silence. And then, "I'll think of something."

Something in Alex's tone made Quinn wonder if he had another plan in mind. A prickle of unease skated down his spine.

"Daniel is going to come back, isn't he?" he pressed. "Abby won't have the inn ready in time if he doesn't."

"Really?" Alex didn't sound surprised. "I warned her she was taking on too much."

Everything clicked into place and Quinn's frustration swelled. "You're a master at pulling strings but you aren't going to get Daniel to come back, are you? You *want* Abby to fail."

"I want her to come to her senses," Alex retorted. "I told you that she's fragile. It's my job to protect her."

"Fragile?" Quinn repeated. "Abby is one of the strongest people I know. She's been putting everything she has into this place. And it isn't your job to undermine her decisions. It's your job to support them."

"You don't understand what my job is. It's not that I don't support her decisions. It's this particular decision. Abby doesn't have what it takes to run a bed-and-breakfast. I want her to realize that before she gets in over her head."

Were they talking about the same person here?

Quinn's frustration propelled him out of bed and he stalked to the window. "I think you're underestimating her. Quit playing the protective big brother card. If you loved her, you'd be spending your time and energy helping her get this place into shape, not trying to think of ways to get her back to Chicago." Quinn didn't bother to sugarcoat it. It wasn't as if Porter could fire him twice.

"You don't know anything about my family. And you've only known Abby a week. You don't know anything about…"

"About what?"

"Her past."

"She told me about your parents. I realize that you feel responsible—"

"I'm not talking about that," Alex said tightly.

"Then what are you talking about? You got me into this. I think you owe me an explanation."

"Fine." Alex snapped the word. "Maybe if I do, you'll understand where I'm coming from. Abby was abducted by a hotel employee when she was six years old."

The air emptied out of Quinn's lungs.

Abducted.

A dozen possible scenarios played out in his mind and every one of them added to the weight on his chest. "What happened?"

"My parents fired Sid after they caught him stealing. He bet on the horses. Had gambling debts that needed to be paid. The thing was, if he would have asked instead of taking the money, my dad would have helped him out."

"He asked for a ransom."

"No. He lured her away out of revenge. To prove to my parents that they weren't untouchable. That bad things could happen to them, too. It took the police almost two days to find Abby. I was only thirteen at the time, but I remember the look on our parents' faces when they found out she was missing. I think it was the first time they realized success comes at a price."

Alex's soft laugh, stripped of humor, hinted that he was under no such illusion. "Things changed in our family after that. No more open-door policy at the hotels. No more treating the employees like family. They enrolled us in private schools. Mom and Dad couldn't undo the past, but they did everything to make sure something like that would never happen again."

They'd closed ranks, with Abby in the middle.

"Dad took me aside one day and told me that it was up to us to do everything we could to make sure nothing like that ever happened again."

Alex had taken it to heart. Abby had been a teenager when their parents died, leaving her brother to carry that burden alone. No wonder he'd lost it when someone had started to harass him.

Quinn wondered if the Porters' attempt to shield Abby from further harm had done just the opposite. They'd insulated her in an attempt to ease her fears—but Abby had been a child at the time. What if their actions had only served to affirm there was a reason to be afraid? A reason not to trust people.

He let out a slow breath. It hurt. "Does she remember?"

"Enough to cause a mild panic attack on occasion. She described it to me once. Sometimes they're triggered when there are a lot of people around or someone she doesn't know gets too close to her. She doesn't trust easily. I've seen her at a party, laughing and having fun, and the next minute she leaves. Just like that. Now do you understand? Can you imagine her running a bed-and-breakfast? Strangers showing up at her door night and day. Living in the same house with her. It isn't a good fit."

Quinn plowed a hand through his hair and inadvertently touched a sensitive spot on the back of his neck. The place where his head had connected with the floor of the chapel the week before.

The first time he'd met her, she did seem uncomfortable when he got too close to her. And hadn't he questioned Abby's strong reaction when he'd surprised her that day in the chapel?

Not that this was the answer he'd wanted to hear.

"You've seen it, haven't you?" Alex asked quietly. "You know what I'm talking about."

Quinn had seen it. But he'd also seen other things. He'd seen Abby put aside her own misgivings and give a troubled boy a chance to prove himself. He'd seen her giving one hundred and ten percent to a business that would showcase her gifts and talents…and challenge her deepest fears.

He'd seen her faith.

"Believe me," Alex continued. "This is what's best for Abby. If she puts all this time and effort into the bed-and-breakfast and then realizes she can't do it, she's going to feel worse than if she hadn't tried it at all."

A movement caught Quinn's eye. Abby and Mulligan were walking down to the lake. Given the fact that Abby had another long day ahead of her, there shouldn't have been a bounce in her step. But there was.

In spite of all the obstacles, she believed God had brought her to Mirror Lake. Abby was doing exactly what Pastor Wilde had encouraged the congregation to do. To step forward in faith.

"I think you're wrong," he heard himself say. "You should come up here and take a look at what she's done to the place. You'd be surprised."

"No offense, O'Halloran, but she isn't your problem anymore. It's over. Mission accomplished. You can get back to your own business now."

And stay out of his.

Quinn got the message, loud and clear.

So that was it. He was supposed to walk away. It's what he'd planned all along. So why did the thought twist his stomach into a knot?

Because you thought Abby would be an assignment. You never thought you'd start to care about her.

Unbidden, the memory of her impulsive, petal-soft kiss came to mind. It had taken all Quinn's self-control not to follow up with one of his own. Instead, he'd left a millisecond after he saw the dazed expression in Abby's eyes when she realized what she'd done.

"I don't have to remind you that our arrangement stays between the two of us," Alex said.

"You just did." Quinn's gaze remained riveted on Abby. She'd kicked off her sandals and waded in the shallows, arms outstretched, face tilted toward the sun.

Was her brother right? Maybe being the proprietress of a bed-and-breakfast wasn't the best career choice for someone who'd been through what Abby had. And if that were true, wouldn't it be better to accept that now? To cut her losses and close the place down before she invested even more of herself?

Alex's dry chuckle jerked him back to reality. "I have to admit, it's been interesting working with you."

Quinn didn't need one more reminder that the past few days had been a job. Keeping an eye on Abby simply a means to an end.

"By the way, don't be surprised if you get a phone call this morning."

"Jeff Gaines." The last thing Quinn wanted to think about was the condos. The bid he'd thought would solve all his problems.

Right.

"No. From your old boss at Hamlin Security."

Quinn's fingers tightened around the phone. "What did you do?"

"You give me way too much credit, O'Halloran," Alex said dryly. "If you kept up with the news down here, you'd know that Serena Raynes checked into a private rehab facility over the weekend. Her older brother was formally charged with providing her with prescription drugs. You were right. And I'm pretty sure your old boss is going to call you and tell you that. After he swallows that mouthful of humble pie."

Quinn braced one hand against the wall and closed his eyes.

Hamlin Security might want him back. He'd spent seven years of his life there—close to a promotion when Serena's accusation had cost him his job.

"You have a chance to get your life back," Alex said. "Everything you wanted."

A week ago, Quinn thought he knew what he wanted.

Now he wasn't so sure.

"I know you miss her." Abby paused to pat Mulligan's head, sympathetic to the mournful look in his eyes. "And no, I don't know when they'll be back."

While supervising the deliverymen who'd arrived to unload the new furniture for the cabins, she'd seen Quinn put Lady in his truck and drive away.

Five hours ago.

Abby couldn't shake the feeling that something was wrong.

He'd spent the entire morning and the better part

of the afternoon putting dead-bolt locks on the doors of the lodge. Abby had bribed him into stopping for a lunch break with her, but Quinn used the time together to explain a design for a security system that would warn her if a car passed a certain point in the driveway. He'd also suggested surveillance cameras so she could see who was outside the door after regular business hours.

She'd been impressed, but not surprised, at how knowledgeable he was. Quinn would make a success out of O'Halloran Security.

When she'd told him that, he hadn't looked as if she'd given him a compliment. Just the opposite.

The only reason she could find for the sudden change in his behavior was her decision to open the inn early for the Thomases' anniversary party.

Or because you kissed him.

She groaned at the reminder.

Maybe she could plead temporary insanity, because she still wasn't sure what had come over her. The gentle caress of his hand against her cheek? The velvet roughness of his voice while he lectured her about the danger of wandering around the woods in a thunderstorm?

The look of stunned surprise in his eyes after she'd kissed him remained etched in her memory. So was his response. By the time she drew another breath, the door had already closed behind him. Leaving her alone to deal with the fallout of her decision.

It was ironic, really, Abby decided now that she'd had a chance to think about it. The woman leery of men, the woman who looked for ulterior motives and tested their sincerity, had been the one who'd thrown caution to the wind and initiated their first kiss....

First, last and only kiss, she silently amended as she peeled back a corner of the dish towel to check the bread dough.

She must have done something wrong because it remained as flat as her mood.

Maybe she should call Quinn's cell phone and find out where he was and when he planned to return...

Ack.

Abby caught herself.

"Repeat after me. You are *not* Alex."

And Quinn wouldn't have left without a good reason. More than likely, he'd gone back to his own office to work on the security system he'd designed for the inn.

She gathered up some supplies and a cookbook. "Come on, Mulligan. We miss them but it doesn't mean we should sit around and sulk all evening."

The droop of the dog's ears said that sulking was fine with him, thank you very much, but he trailed behind her as she went out the back door and headed toward the fire pit.

Thanks to Quinn's helpful suggestions, Abby had a fire going in no time.

She fed tiny sticks into the flames and waited for that familiar feeling of contentment to sweep away the restlessness in her soul. The first stars winked above her. The mournful cry of a loon drifted across the lake. It was a perfect evening...except for one thing.

Quinn wasn't with her.

A few nights ago, they'd sat together in this very spot and Quinn had told her about his father.

Abby hadn't brought it up again but she'd been asking God to speak to Quinn's heart. His bitterness over his dad's shortcomings held him captive. Until six months ago, she'd been there. Dragging that kind of chain around was hard work. Freedom, Abby knew, felt a lot better.

If only Quinn would see it…

The marshmallow on the end of the stick she was holding over a cluster of embers suddenly burst into flame. Frantically, Abby started to wave it around in an attempt to put it out.

"The Fourth of July fireworks were a few weeks ago."

Abby dropped the willow branch into the fire, marshmallow and all, as Quinn emerged from the shadows. The sight of him set off a few fireworks inside of her.

She hadn't realized until now that a tiny part of her had been afraid he wouldn't come back.

"Hi, stranger." Abby tried to keep her smile under control but failed.

"Hi." Quinn stopped several feet away and pushed his hands into his pockets.

"I was wondering what happened to you."

Quinn didn't pick up the hint. "What are you doing?"

"Making s'mores. When I was talking to Lydia, she said it was one of the things she and Simon had done together when they were camp counselors. I'm practicing so I can make them one evening while they're here. As a surprise."

"You're practicing? Making s'mores?"

"I keep burning the marshmallows. Not that Mulligan minds," she added with a laugh. "There must be a trick to it. I'm open to suggestions…"

Quinn moved closer but with obvious reluctance. Unexpected tears scorched the back of Abby's eyes and she looked away. The awkwardness between them was her fault.

Her and her impulsive kiss.

"Where is the chocolate?" He surveyed the ingredients strewn on the blanket beside her.

Abby's fingers curled around the empty foil wrapper in the pocket of her sweatshirt. "I'm practicing without chocolate."

Because she'd eaten all of it while waiting for Quinn's return.

A ghost of a smile touched his lips. "Uh-huh."

The smile gave Abby courage. She patted the blanket next to her. "Well? Are you going to help me sharpen my s'more-making skills?"

"Abby—" The rest of the sentence broke off in a sigh. Quinn didn't move but she felt his retreat. Knew what he was going to say before he said it. "I'm pretty beat tonight."

It wasn't the whole truth and Quinn could tell by the look on Abby's face that she *knew* it wasn't the whole truth.

He'd spent the last few hours driving aimlessly down pitted county roads, wondering what to do.

Praying about what to do.

He wasn't sure how, but he'd ended up back on a very familiar road.

He'd seen the relief in Abby's eyes when he and Lady had returned. Heard the question in her voice when she asked what had happened to him.

Quinn could hardly wrap his mind around it. In the course of a single day, his life had been turned upside down.

Alex Porter had fired him. Bob Hamlin wanted to meet with him.

But here he was. Back at the lodge.

Because Abby needed him.

Chapter Eighteen

Finished.

Abby stepped back to admire the new valances. The crisp blue curtains, bordered by a jaunty stripe of white grosgrain ribbon that gave them a nautical look, were the finishing touch on the cabin Lydia and Simon would be occupying during their stay.

The last two cabins were still a long way from being ready but it felt good to check this one off the list.

Quinn's personal belongings were lined up neatly by the door, waiting to be relocated to the next cabin.

Tim and Zach Davis had shown up right after breakfast. Quinn assigned one of them the task of mowing the grass and the other trimming weeds around the buildings. It was obvious from their disappointed expressions that they'd hoped Abby needed more fish.

She'd tried to cheer them up the best way she knew how. With a piece of homemade cinnamon streusel coffee cake. It seemed to work...until she'd asked about Cody.

The brothers had exchanged a look and then explained they hadn't seen him since Quinn had dropped him off at home on Saturday evening.

Abby had tried not to let her concern for the boy show but decided to ask Quinn if there was something they could do.

If she had a chance to talk to him.

Abby had hoped if she knocked on the door of his cabin early enough, they would have a few minutes to talk. But Quinn had opened the door for her and kept right on going, muttering something about checking on Zach and Tim.

The past few days had been a whirlwind of activity but it was clear that Quinn was still avoiding her. Whenever he saw her approach, his expression turned wary. Guarded. And she lost her nerve.

Maybe he was afraid she was going to kiss him again.

The trouble was, she wanted to kiss him again. And talk to him. Laugh with him. Sit by the fire with him.

Every day that brought her closer to reaching her goal of finishing the cabins brought her one day closer to losing Quinn. Daniel was scheduled to return on Monday and Quinn would go back to O'Halloran Security.

The temptation to ask him to stay on and help her and Daniel finish the cabins for the Thomases' party was strong, but Abby knew she couldn't bring herself to put that kind of pressure on him. Quinn had more than enough work of his own to catch up on.

She had a plan, though. Quinn had given up so much of his time that Abby wanted a chance to repay him somehow. She had even gathered her courage and called Faye McAllister the day before. She suspected that having Quinn's office manager on her side would guarantee her success.

Faye was enthusiastic about the idea but warned her that Quinn had stubbornly refused any offers she'd made over the past year to spend her own money on anything related to his business. The only thing he'd allowed her to do was donate curtains for the office—and that was only because she'd put them up before she asked him for permission.

Abby wasn't worried. Under certain circumstances, she could be just as stubborn as he was. Like it or not, there were times when the Porter DNA prevailed.

She was about to leave when Quinn's cell phone began to hum on the coffee table next to her.

He'd been in such a hurry to avoid her that he must have forgotten it.

She grinned.

Here was her excuse to talk to him.

Abby swiped up the phone and automatically glanced at the tiny screen. Blinked when she saw the familiar name.

Alex Porter.

It couldn't be. Why would her brother be calling Quinn?

There was one way to find out. She flipped open the phone.

"Hi, Alex."

The silence on the other end was a dead giveaway.

"Abby?"

"Don't sound so surprised. How did you get this number?"

"I—" Alex hesitated.

Alex *never* hesitated.

Her hands suddenly felt cold. "Why are you calling me on my carpenter's phone."

"O'Halloran is still working for you?"

Wait a second…

"You know Quinn?"

"Not…personally."

"Alex."

"It's not what you think."

Abby hadn't been thinking anything. Until now.

"You weren't trying to get in touch with me, were you? You called this number on purpose. To talk to Quinn."

"Ab—"

"Don't lie to me, Alex." The shrillness of her own voice made Abby wince. "How did you know about him?" A thought occurred to her. "You had a background check done on him, didn't you?"

It was the only possible explanation. She couldn't remember if she'd mentioned to Alex that someone was filling in for her carpenter temporarily but if she had, her brother would have wanted to make sure Quinn's record was clean.

"I hired him."

Abby frowned. "How could you have? He took Daniel Redstone's place…"

When Daniel mysteriously won a contest he hadn't even remembered entering.

Abby sank into the closest chair and pressed a hand against her churning stomach.

"Listen to me, Abby. I was worried about you being alone up there. Someone started harassing me a few weeks ago and when the police couldn't catch the guy, I admit that I freaked out a little. I needed to know that you were safe. That's why I hired O'Halloran."

"To watch me."

"It's not as bad as you make it sound."

No, it was worse.

The pieces began to fall into place even as Abby's heart began to fall apart.

How Quinn seemed to put aside his initial reserve and spent more time with her. Inviting himself along on her trip to town. Meeting up with her at the chapel. His insistence on going to church with her Sunday morning.

The campfire…

Tears burned the backs of Abby's eyes.

She'd been foolish enough to think of him as a friend. That he'd sought out her company because he wanted to be with her. That he was beginning to care about her. Not because Alex had paid him to.

"Why Quinn? How do you know him?"

"That isn't important."

It was to her. "You owe me an explanation." She couldn't believe her voice sounded so firm. So even.

"I recognized his name when I was looking for someone in your area who could help me out," Alex finally admitted. "Someone I could trust to be discreet."

Discreet. In other words, he needed someone willing to deceive her by pretending to be a carpenter.

"What do you mean you recognized his name?"

"He was a bodyguard for Hamlin Security in Chicago before he moved back to Mirror Lake," Alex said reluctantly. "One of their best."

"A bodyguard." A bubble of laughter burst out even as tears leaked out the corner of Abby's eyes. "Of course he was."

"Let me explain—"

"I've heard all I want to." More than she'd wanted to. But she still had to ask. "Does he know? About me?"

Alex knew what she meant. "Yes."

So not only did Quinn assume she wasn't capable of looking after herself, he felt sorry for her, too.

Abby Porter. Poor little rich girl.

"He didn't want to take the job, Abby. I didn't give him much of a choice."

As if that somehow made it okay.

"Goodbye, Alex."

"Abby, wait—"

"I've been waiting, Alex. Waiting for you to stop treating me like I'm still that traumatized six-year-old. That was one of the reasons I left Chicago. I realized that I was never going to get past what happened because you wouldn't let me." She drew a ragged breath, not sure at the moment whose betrayal hurt the most. Alex's or Quinn's.

The screen door opened and Mulligan and Lady clattered in, Quinn a step behind them. In his hands was a bouquet of Queen Anne's lace and brown-eyed Susans.

The smile on his face faded when he saw the tears tracking her cheeks.

"Abby? What is it?" He was at her side in an instant.

"It's for you."

She handed him the phone and walked out the door.

* * *

"Hello?" Quinn barked the word into the phone as he started after Abby.

"Why are you still there?"

Porter.

Quinn's feet suddenly melted to the floor. "What happened? What did you say to her?"

"She saw my name come up on your phone," Alex said. "And wondered why I was calling *her* carpenter."

"What did you tell her?"

"The truth."

The truth.

Quinn's throat closed.

"You stayed, didn't you?" Alex made it sound more like an accusation than a question. "Why? I told you that I didn't need you anymore…" His voice ebbed away and then came back stronger. "You stayed because *Abby* needed you."

"I have to talk to her." Quinn saw Abby sprint across the yard and disappear into the house.

"You need to talk to me first," Alex shot back. "Is there something going on between you and my sister?"

"No." At least, not anymore.

The stricken look in Abby's eyes flashed in Quinn's mind.

The past few days he'd been trying to find a way out of the mess he'd gotten himself into. He hadn't expected it to blow up in his face.

"I'm trying her cell from my other line. She isn't picking up." Alex's own frustration spilled out. "This wouldn't have happened if she hadn't picked up your phone. The phone that wouldn't have been there if *you* hadn't been there."

Quinn didn't bother to come to his own defense. He didn't have one. "I'll talk to her."

"She won't talk to you," Alex predicted.

He had to try anyway.

Porter had been wrong about a lot of things. Quinn prayed he was wrong about that, too.

Abby took a deep breath when she heard the front door open.

Five minutes hadn't been enough time to prepare herself to face Quinn. Not that it mattered. Abby doubted if a month would have been enough.

She stood behind the small check-in area, an antique buffet she'd converted into a counter, so there would be something solid between her and Quinn. He wouldn't be able to see her knees shake, either.

The anger she'd felt while talking to Alex had drained away, leaving her feeling numb. And incredibly stupid.

The irony of the situation had begun to sink in. In the past when a man tried to get to know her, Abby would look for ulterior motives. Signs of a hidden agenda. Quinn had been the exception. She knew she was falling in love with him. But now? Now it just felt as if she were falling.

He appeared in the doorway. Abby waited for him to say something. An excuse. An apology. An explanation. Instead, he seemed to be waiting for her to speak.

So she did.

"I want you off my property. Now." Abby was

amazed her voice wasn't quivering like the rest of her. "My brother might have hired you, but I think I have the right to fire you."

"All right." Quinn nodded once. Pivoted toward the door.

He was leaving. Just like that.

"That's all you're going to say?" How could he look so calm when Abby felt as if she were bleeding to death on the inside?

Quinn paused. "Alex is worried about you. Talk to him."

From his remote expression, Quinn might as well have been a stranger standing in the doorway. Abby looked for the man whose smile had melted her heart like chocolate in the sun. The one who'd worked tirelessly from sunrise to sunset so she could open the inn on schedule…

Because Alex paid him to.

"I guess Alex was right about you." Abby tossed the words at Quinn's back as he turned to walk away. "You were the best one for the job."

Chapter Nineteen

"I haven't been stood up since fifth grade, when Tammy Higgins didn't meet me at the monkey bars during recess like she promised."

Quinn flicked an impatient glance at the man sauntering up to him. "I forgot."

Matt Wilde grinned. "I believe you. But only because you know that lying is bad."

"Tell me about it," Quinn muttered.

The pastor propped a hip against the woodpile, where Quinn had been taking out his frustration on a helpless cord of oak in the backyard.

"Maybe you should tell *me* about it."

"No, thanks."

"Why not?"

"I'm not, how do you say it? A member of your flock. Not anymore, anyway."

"If you know that expression, there's a good chance you are." Matt grinned. "So, spill your guts, O'Halloran."

Quinn speared him with a look. "Are you sure you're a minister?"

"Yes, but let's put that little detail aside for the moment and pretend I'm your friend."

Quinn winced. "You're doing this on purpose, aren't you?"

"Tell me what's going on and I'll tell you if I'm doing it on purpose."

"I don't know where to start."

"You can start by telling me why you didn't show up at the café this morning. Leaving me at Kate Nichols's mercy, by the way."

"Better you than me." Quinn picked up the ax and attacked another log. So what if it was only the end of July? Winter came early in northern Wisconsin.

Without asking, Matt picked up another ax and joined in. For a few minutes, the only sound was the dull thwack of the two axes turning logs into kindling.

"Abby Porter."

The second Matt Wilde said the name out loud, Quinn's ax missed its mark and sank into the ground.

"There." Matt's smile was smug. "I started. Now it's your turn."

"You don't give up, do you?"

"Do you?" Wilde neatly turned the tables on him.

Quinn's frustration fled, replaced by relief. "You talked to Abby."

It had been difficult enough to leave the day before. More difficult knowing that she had to sort through everything alone. The way things stood with Alex, Quinn didn't think she would talk about it with him. Her friendship with Kate Nichols probably hadn't reached the point where Abby would consider her a confidante, either. Which meant that Abby was alone.

"No." Matt denied it. "As a matter of fact, I haven't

seen Abby since Sunday, when the two of you came to church together."

"Then how…" Quinn stopped when he saw the wry look on the other man's face.

"I took a guess." The pastor propped the ax against the woodpile and clipped Quinn on the shoulder. "And I was right. That means you owe me a cup of coffee."

"Well?" Quinn stopped pacing long enough to aim the question at Matt. He wasn't a pacer by nature but he'd practically worn a rut through the floors of his house over the past twenty-four hours.

After Abby ordered him off her property, he'd loaded up his things, put Lady in the truck and went home. He hadn't even made an appearance at the office to let Faye know he was officially back to work.

"Well what?"

"I stopped talking. Isn't this when you tell me everything will be all right?"

Quinn had spent the last hour telling the pastor everything that had happened. Spilling his guts, just like Matt had encouraged him to do. He'd heard that confession was good for the soul but Quinn didn't buy that anymore. If anything, saying the words out loud—telling someone what he'd done—had only made him feel worse.

Matt blew out a sigh. "I don't know that it will be. She found out that two people she cared about—two people she trusted—weren't honest with her. That's a lot to process, especially considering what Abby has been through. She needs people to encourage her to move forward, not try and hold her back."

Quinn didn't need the reminder. When his imagination wasn't tormenting him with images of Abby's expression when she'd handed him the phone, it was conjuring up pictures of her as a child, taken away from her home and family.

"Why didn't you tell Abby that you came back after her brother told you he didn't need you anymore?"

"It wouldn't have mattered." Quinn knew it was true.

Weighed against the rest of the things he'd done, why would Abby believe him if he told her the reason he'd gone back to the lodge that day?

Matt considered that. "So, what happens now?"

"You're the pastor. I was hoping you could tell me."

"Are you going to give her some time to cool down and then talk to her?"

If Matt had heard Abby's parting comment, Quinn thought, he wouldn't even ask that question. It had found its mark. Knowing he'd deserved it kept the wound from healing.

"I can't." He didn't deserve her forgiveness. It was the reason he hadn't tried to make excuses or explain that he'd agreed to Alex's terms because he'd wanted O'Halloran Security to be a success.

It was more important to him now that Abby was successful.

"Do you think her brother's concerns are valid?" Matt asked carefully.

Quinn had asked himself that same question at least a dozen times. And every time, he came up with the same answer. "No. I think some of Abby's doubts about herself, some of her fears, were actually magnified because of the way her family treated her after the abduction. She told me that God changed her. I don't know why her brother can't see it."

"Unfortunately, we see what we want to." Matt's expression clouded slightly.

"Abby wants to have the inn ready for the Thomases' anniversary party. Alex won't try to get Daniel Redstone to come back because he wants her to fail. Unless she hires a crew, which is going to be difficult around here on such short notice, she'll have to tell them it won't be ready."

"Alex might not try to get Daniel to come back early but that doesn't mean *you* can't."

Quinn stared at him, turning the idea over in his mind before rejecting it. "Daniel does great finishing work but he isn't fast. If I could clone the guy, maybe." A thought suddenly occurred to him.

"What? I see the wheels turning in there."

"Nothing. I doubt it would work."

Matt leaned back and laced his fingers behind his head. "Humor me."

"Abby goes to your church. The congregation is supposed to help each other out, right? What if a group of volunteers showed up at the lodge this weekend for a workday?"

Matt smiled. "That's a great idea. You can bring it up tonight at the leadership meeting."

"Me?"

"It's your idea."

"But that kind of stuff is in *your* job description," Quinn pointed out. And he doubted people would listen to anything he had to say.

Matt was already shaking his head. "You've been out there. You know what needs to be done. If you make the appeal, I'll take it from there."

"Fine." At the moment, Quinn would have agreed to walk up and down the sidewalk in front of the

Grapevine Café holding a sign if it meant getting Abby the help she needed.

"If we get this organized, are you going to be there?" Matt asked.

"I don't have the right to set foot on her property," Quinn said. He wouldn't blame Abby if she called Sergeant West to haul him away, either.

Abby had trusted him and he'd taken advantage of it. Of her. She'd shocked him to the core with that kiss. That was the moment he'd realized exactly what was at stake if she found out who he was and why he was there.

Everything.

He'd tried to put some distance between them over the next few days but Abby had only seen him pulling away from her, not the reason he had to.

"She doesn't know how you feel about her, does she?"

He opened his mouth to deny it, but Matt cocked an eyebrow.

Lying. Bad. Remember?

Quinn gave in. "I wasn't honest with her about anything else. Why would she believe me if I told her that?"

"You know the saying. Actions speak louder than words."

"I know. That's why she won't believe me." Quinn paused in front of the kitchen window and drummed his fingers against the sink. "I'll call Daniel and ask him if he'll come back. I'll show up at your meeting this evening, too. But I can't do anything else."

"Fair enough."

"I appreciate you coming over." Quinn stretched out his hand.

Matt ignored it.

"Not so fast." The pastor pushed one of the chairs

away from the table. "We talked about Abby. Now it's time to talk about you. And then, I suggest we talk to God."

The sound of a vehicle coming up the driveway sent Mulligan on a mad dash to the front door.

Abby resisted the urge to follow him.

It wasn't Quinn. She would have recognized the ragged purr of his truck.

But you wish it was.

Abby pushed the thought away. Now that she knew the truth, she understood why he'd started to avoid her after she kissed him.

After Quinn walked out the day before, Abby had plenty of time to sort through the pieces and put them together. Alex had told her that he'd pushed Quinn into accepting the job. She knew why he'd agreed. O'Halloran Security. Her brother had obviously made Quinn an offer he couldn't refuse. One that made him turn back to his former career.

As a bodyguard.

Alex had hired him to watch her and she'd unknowingly crossed a line. A professional boundary. He'd operated within the parameters of the job. In her naiveté, she hadn't.

Mulligan began to whine, and Abby could almost feel the dog's disappointment. Instead of his friend, he must have realized the vehicle belonged to Zach and Tim Davis.

When she'd talked to the boys the day before, they'd agreed to put in extra hours at the lodge whenever they were free. As much as Abby appreciated their willingness to help out, she'd already decided to call Lydia Thomas and explain that although she was still willing to provide refreshments after the vow renewal at the chapel, she wouldn't be able to host the anniversary party for the entire weekend.

Mulligan clattered into the kitchen, tail wagging, as if to question why she wasn't at the door yet to greet their company.

"I know." Abby dried off her damp hands on a towel, turned the music down and stepped onto the porch.

Zach and Tim waved a greeting. So did the four other teenage boys that bailed out the side door of the green minivan parked in her driveway. Cody Lang was one of them.

"You brought reinforcements this morning," Abby said. "That's great."

Tim grinned. "This is nothing."

Cody offered a shy smile of his own. "Yeah. We just got here first."

"First?"

Zach pointed and Abby saw the wink of sunlight striking chrome. Another car cruised down the driveway. Followed by another.

"What's going on?"

"We'll let him tell you."

"H-him?"

"Pastor Wilde," Zach said. "He told everyone to be here at eight o'clock Saturday morning. So here we are."

Abby recognized the pastor in the driver's seat of the second car. He gave her a friendly salute as he hopped out and opened the passenger door for Kate Nichols.

"Morning!" Kate waved a lime-green feather duster in Abby's direction.

"What are you doing here?"

"Reporting for duty, of course," Kate sang out.

"You don't mind a few extra hands today, do you?" Matthew asked in a low voice as a caravan of vehicles began to line the driveway.

A few extra hands? The number of people gathering on the lawn reminded her of the volunteer crews that her favorite home makeover show drew. Abby recognized some of the people from church, but others were complete strangers.

"Mind?" Abby echoed. "I can't believe it. How did you know? Why would you—" Her voice broke off when she caught sight of a familiar figure making his way through the crowd.

"Daniel!" Abby rushed up to him. "What are you doing here? You're supposed to be on vacation!"

"Fish weren't biting that great." His eyes twinkled. "'Sides that, I missed your cooking."

"Is that so." His wife, Esther, swatted Daniel's arm but gave Abby a warm smile.

By the time everyone was assembled on the lawn, Abby estimated there were fifty people who had put aside their own Saturday to-do lists to check something off hers.

Humbled by the unexpected gift, Abby didn't know what to say as the chatter subsided and everyone looked to her for direction.

"Here. Maybe this will help." With a mischievous wink, Kate presented Abby with a bright yellow ball cap with the words *I'm the Boss* embroidered on it.

"That belongs to her, you know," someone said in a stage whisper.

Abby put it on and blushed when the noisy crew began to applaud.

Matt stepped up and put a hand on her shoulder. "Let's dedicate this project—and this day—to the Lord."

Abby would have thought her tear ducts would be completely dry by now. She was wrong. While Matt prayed, the grass blurred at her feet.

This morning, she'd felt completely alone.

God had just reminded her that she wasn't.

"Amen." Matt lifted his head and turned to Abby. "Okay. Put us to work!"

With Daniel's help, Abby divided everyone into smaller work groups and put one person in charge of each project. Matt had spent a summer on a roofing crew in college, so he pulled some of the older teens from the church youth group together to help him tear shingles off the cabins.

Esther Redstone and some of the older women in the congregation took over Abby's kitchen, filling pitchers with cold drinks and making sandwiches.

As the official foreman, Abby moved from crew to crew throughout the morning, taking time to answer questions, give instructions or hand out bottled water until it was time for lunch.

She and Kate were hauling coolers to the picnic tables when Kate suddenly paused and gave a low whistle. "Who is that?"

Abby followed the direction of her friend's finger as it traced the path of the silver Viper cruising up the driveway.

Abby folded her arms across her chest.

"That," she said, "is my brother."

Chapter Twenty

"Can we talk?"

Her brother sounded so uncertain that Abby hardly recognized his voice. Very un-Alex-like.

"I don't know," she murmured truthfully.

Without waiting for an invitation, Alex sat down on one of the low wooden benches by the campfire. She almost smiled. This was the brother she knew and loved.

And because Abby did love him, she handed him the stick she'd been holding, with its perfectly browned marshmallow on the end.

The last of the volunteers had left an hour ago. Abby went to the kitchen to clean up and found it in spotless condition, thanks to Esther and the rest of the seniors who belonged to the Knit Our Hearts Together ministry at Church of the Pines.

She'd needed a quiet place to regroup. To thank God for His provision.

To try not to think about Quinn.

"You wouldn't return my calls," Alex said. "I figured you couldn't ignore me if I showed up here." He examined the marshmallow suspiciously before easing it off the stick. "I guess I was wrong."

"I didn't ignore you. There was a lot going on today." Abby refused to feel guilty.

"That's one of the things I wanted to talk to you about. Where did all those people come from?" Alex sounded so mystified that Abby couldn't suppress a smile.

"They're members of the church I attend."

"I guess that explains the sermon I heard on the roof," her brother muttered.

"Pastor Wilde gave a sermon? On the roof?"

"No, this one was delivered by a little fireball who gave me a hammer and told me to, and I quote, 'make myself useful.'"

Abby choked back a laugh. "That would have been Kate Nichols."

Alex shook his head and Abby waited for him to make a disparaging comment of some kind.

She'd known it was only a matter of time until he voiced his opinion about the inn, which was one of the reasons she'd avoided him all day. Well, that coupled with the fact that she knew her brother hadn't made the six-hour drive to Mirror Lake simply because she'd refused to return his phone calls. Alex had another agenda.

He would have talked to Quinn and found out she'd asked him to leave the property. Alex knew she would be feeling discouraged. Hoped he could catch her in a moment of weakness.

And maybe he would have, if she hadn't experienced such an outpouring of generosity that morning.

"They seem like good people, Abby."

She blinked, not sure she'd heard him right.

Alex smiled. "Yes, you heard me. This place doesn't look anything like the pictures you showed me. I have to admit I'm impressed."

"They did get a lot accomplished, didn't they?" Abby couldn't help the hint of pride that crept into her voice. The volunteers had worked together so efficiently that she hadn't had to make that phone call to Lydia Thomas after all.

"They did. But it's *you* I'm impressed with."

Abby's gaze flew to her brother's face. "Me?"

"Quinn told me that I underestimated you."

Her breath stalled. "Quinn said that?"

"When I talked with him on Monday morning." Alex's eyes narrowed, as if he were remembering the conversation. "He also said that if I loved you, I would support your dreams, not try to sabotage them."

"I can't believe…" Abby paused. "Did you say Monday?"

"That was the day I fired him."

"But… I fired him on Wednesday." Abby stared at her brother, stunned.

Monday was the day Quinn had disappeared. He hadn't told her where he was going or why. She'd been sitting by the fire, making s'mores. And then…

"He came back." Alex made the connection before she did.

"Why?" Abby pressed her hand against her mouth.

"I think we can rule out that it was because of me," Alex said wryly. "Or because he needed the money or the extra work. I think he came back because of *you*, Abby."

Some of the old doubts surfaced.

"Because he felt sorry for me."

"Because he's in love with you," Alex corrected her.

"Then why did he leave?"

"From what I know about O'Halloran? It was probably for the same reason."

"Looks like you're going somewhere."

Quinn turned toward the gravelly voice. "Hi, Daniel. Come on in."

The pleats fanning out from the corners of Daniel Redstone's eyes deepened. "I knocked. Guess you couldn't hear me with your head stuck in a suitcase."

"How did things go out at the lodge today?" It had taken all Quinn's self-control not to call Matt Wilde and ask him about the workday at the lodge. "Did anyone show up?"

"Musta been fifty people out there. I think we got most everything done, except for some odds and ends."

"Abby will be able to host the Thomases' anniversary celebration?"

"I expect so." Daniel settled his wiry frame into a cane-back rocking chair. "You accomplished a lot in the amount of time you were there. But then, you always did work circles around me. Maybe you should have been a carpenter."

"Maybe." Quinn tossed a pair of socks into the suitcase.

"Taking a vacation?"

"I don't know yet."

"Abby's brother told me you might get your old job back."

Quinn's mouth dropped open. "You know Alex Porter?"

"Not until he showed up at the lodge today. We had a nice little chat about fishing trips and being honest with people." Daniel's gold tooth flashed with his smile. "He's not bad with a hammer, either. For a city boy."

"He *helped* you?"

"Kate didn't give him much of a choice, from what I saw."

Knowing that Quinn had left and Abby was without a carpenter, Alex had probably driven up to make a last-ditch effort to convince her to return to Chicago. If the volunteers hadn't showed up, would she have agreed?

No coincidences, Abby was fond of saying. God has a plan. A purpose.

Quinn was finally accepting that as truth. He was convinced Abby was right when she claimed that God had brought her to Mirror Lake. What he wasn't sure about was where *he* fit in God's plan.

"I appreciate you coming back, Daniel." Quinn tried to stow his emotions but it wasn't as easy as it used to be.

"We help out our own, you know."

"That's good. It's important to Abby that she's part of the community."

"I was talking about you."

"Me? No." Quinn instantly rejected the notion. "I've been back for over a year and everyone still treats me like an outsider."

"You get treated like an outsider because you act like one." Daniel harrumphed. "You know folks round here. You hold yourself back and people leave you alone. You reach out a hand, there'll be someone there to grab it. You just never reached out until now. They wanted to help Abby, sure. But they went because *you* asked them. Your roots are here."

Quinn fixed his gaze on the suitcase. "What if I told you that the only reason I came back to Mirror Lake was to see what I could get for this house and Dad's business?"

"Then you would have waited until after the funeral. Truth is, you came back to stand by a man who was dying. A man who never stood by you while he was alive." Daniel cleared his throat. "That shows what kind of man you are."

"I'm no hero, Daniel."

"You hired Faye, didn't you?" Amusement danced in the other man's eyes.

A reluctant smile curved Quinn's lips. "She made me."

"You saw what no one else did. That woman was like a boat without a rudder after Doc died." Daniel smiled. "You paid off your dad's debts. Cleaned things up around the place. People had you pegged right away. They've just been biding their time, waiting for you to figure out where you fit."

Quinn tried to process what Daniel was telling him.

All this time, he'd thought people avoided him because of his last name. Daniel was implying it was because they had taken their cue from him.

Either way, it didn't matter. Not anymore. He had a meeting with Bob Hamlin in Chicago the next day.

Quinn's hands balled into fists at his side. "I can't stay in Mirror Lake."

"Because you don't want to? Or does your decision have something to do with Abby?"

"You talked to Alex," Quinn said roughly. "You know he hired me to take your place. Not as a carpenter. As a watchdog. There was no noble purpose behind it. I did it because I needed the money—and a shot at the Gaines condominium bid." Quinn almost hated to admit it. Hated to see the look of disappointment on his friend's face. "I went there under false pretenses."

"Are you afraid she won't forgive you?" Daniel's eyes met his. "Or are you afraid she will?"

Quinn felt the impact of both questions. "What are you talking about?"

"For years, I watched Mike O'Halloran sabotage his life. It was like he couldn't accept any good thing that came his way. Your mother. You. A paycheck for a job well done." Daniel's voice softened. "You say you don't want to be like your dad? Then don't let the past keep you from the future God has for you."

It sounded a lot like the sermon Matt had preached the previous Sunday.

"Did you and Matt Wilde compare notes?"

"We read the same book." Daniel smiled. "And it's full of people who stumbled and fell but they got back up again with God's help. Had the courage to go forward."

People like Abby, Quinn thought. She'd demonstrated that kind of courage when she'd moved to Mirror Lake.

"God doesn't give us one chance and then turn His back on us if we mess it up," Daniel said.

"I know." Quinn pressed his fingers against his eyes. "But I really blew it with Abby. How do I know that *she* won't?"

"You don't. That's where the courage part comes in." Daniel chuckled. "She named her dog Mulligan after all, didn't she?"

Chapter Twenty-One

"**A** campfire! I can't believe you thought of it, Abby!" Lydia Thomas reached out and reeled Abby in for another hug. "Doesn't this bring back memories, Simon?"

"Yes, it does. This is a real treat, Abby." Simon, a handsome man whose blue eyes hadn't lost their sparkle since the couple had arrived the day before, smiled at her. "Almost makes me feel seventeen again. We can't thank you enough for opening the inn for us early."

"He's right," Lydia chimed in. "This is the perfect end to a perfect weekend."

"You're welcome." Abby returned the smile, pleased that her attempts to re-create some of the couple's favorite experiences while they'd been camp counselors all those years ago had been so warmly received.

Within an hour of their arrival, Abby felt as if she'd known the couple forever.

Lydia and Simon's three adult children and a small contingent of grandchildren arrived shortly after they did, along with several members of the original bridal party.

Abby had given everyone a tour of the lodge and showed them to their cabins. While they settled in, she prepared an old-fashioned cookout, serving up hamburgers and hot dogs along with potato salad and homemade vanilla ice cream for dessert.

Afterward, the older grandchildren had discovered the croquet set in the boathouse and coaxed their parents into teaching them how to play.

Any concerns Abby might have had about whether she was ready to open her home to strangers were put to rest. She loved catching a glimpse of them walking along the shoreline. Watching the kids play tag with Mulligan in the yard. And she knew it wasn't a coincidence that her first guests were a small group of people who loved her home as much as she did.

Lydia and Simon had renewed their vows earlier that afternoon and it had taken all of Abby's self-control not to break down and cry. Not only because Simon and Lydia couldn't take their eyes off each other, but because they exchanged more than vows during the ceremony. The look of love and understanding that passed between the two of them held fifty years of memories.

She'd planned the campfire as a final send-off for the family and their friends after hearing Simon mention the counselors had gathered together there every evening to recap the day's events. Lydia's blush told Abby that there was more to the story and she was hoping to find out what it was.

"This is a great fire, Abby," Simon complimented.

Thanks to Quinn, Abby thought before she caught herself.

She cringed inside.

Was everything going to remind her of him? He'd only been in her life a little over a week and yet memories of him were connected to the smallest things.

"Sit with us for a while." Lydia motioned her over. "You must be exhausted."

"Are you sure?" Abby hung back. "I don't want to intrude."

"Don't be silly." Lydia scolded her in the same affectionate tone she used with her children and grandchildren. "We want you to stay."

The murmurs of agreement from the rest of the group convinced her. And Abby couldn't think of a better way to spend the evening.

"This can't be the same fire pit that was here when you and Mom worked at the camp all those years ago." Lydia and Simon's daughter, Shelly, eyed the circle of bricks skeptically.

"It sure is. I remember your mother right where you are—" Simon pointed to one of his grandsons. "And sticking her tongue out at me while I played the guitar during evening devotions."

To Abby's astonishment, Lydia didn't deny it. Instead, the woman laughed. "That's true."

"Sticking your tongue out at Grandpa doesn't sound very romantic." Eleven-year-old Lexie Thomas aimed a disapproving look at her grandmother.

Simon chuckled. "I would say it's about as romantic as the skunk she and her friends tried to chase under my cabin one night."

"Simon!" Lydia clucked her tongue. "We came here to reminisce about the good times, remember?"

"And we are." Simon winked at Abby. "We might not be here today if it weren't for that skunk."

"A skunk?" Abby looked from Simon to Lydia, trying to decide if he was kidding.

"Lydia took an instant dislike to me the moment we met." He lowered his voice to a stage whisper. "She thought I was a bit, what's the term? Full of myself."

"He was." Lydia gave her husband a fond look. "My friends and I decided to take him down a peg. There was a skunk that liked to lurk around the garbage cans near the cabins. We snitched brooms from the supply closet one evening and tried to herd it toward Simon's cabin."

From the indulgent looks the adults exchanged, it was obvious the story was a familiar one. But their children leaned forward, eager to hear the rest. So did Abby.

Simon picked up the thread of the story. "I heard a commotion and flipped the porch light on. That startled the poor little critter, but instead of running under my cabin like it was supposed to, it ran into the bushes."

"The bushes where I was hiding," Lydia added.

"Her plan, needless to say…backfired." Simon grinned.

"Literally." Lydia sighed as their grandchildren snickered. "The head counselor banished me to solitary confinement in a separate cabin for the rest of the weekend. Simon was the only one brave enough to visit me. Every night, he would show up and hand me an ice cream bar through the window. Then he would sit on the step and talk to me through the screen. He turned out to be so sweet that I started to feel guilty and finally confessed what I'd done."

"I had a confession of my own," Simon said cheerfully. "From the moment I met her, I started asking God to give me a chance to win her over. I had no idea He would use a skunk."

Everyone laughed, including Abby.

They spent a few more hours around the campfire reminiscing until Simon caught Lydia yawning and announced it was time to call it a night. The parents collected their sleepy children and drifted back to the cabins, but Abby lingered by the fire.

The time spent listening to the couple share memories of their life together was bittersweet.

It made her miss Quinn even more.

After her conversation with Alex, Abby had dared to believe that her brother was right. That Quinn shared her feelings. And when she had called Kate to thank her again for being part of the work crew, her friend confided that the workday had been Quinn's idea.

Those things had given Abby hope.

Until she discovered that Quinn had gone back to Chicago.

Alex told her how he'd lost his job with Hamlin because of Serena Raynes's accusation and remembered him saying he took over his dad's business because he didn't have a choice.

Now Quinn had been given another opportunity to decide which life he wanted to live. And he'd chosen the one that didn't include her.

Mulligan, who'd been stretched out at her feet, suddenly stood up, his gaze fixed on something in the shadows. His tail began to wag.

"Oh, no, you don't—" With all the talk about

skunks, Abby wasn't going to take any chances. She made a grab for the dog's collar but he was too fast for her. "Mulligan!"

She scrambled after him, almost tripping over the rubber ball one of the Thomases' grandchildren had left in the yard.

Mulligan stopped at the edge of the shadows, looked over his shoulder at her and barked, as if waiting for her to be the brave one.

"Who is it?" She chuckled. "Friend or foe?"

"I guess you'll have to decide."

Abby's heart rolled over when Quinn stepped out of the shadows.

He'd stayed away as long as he could, but when Quinn saw the color drain from Abby's face, it made him wonder if he shouldn't have waited another day.

He'd wrapped up his business with Bob Hamlin in Chicago and made one last stop before returning to Mirror Lake. Ken Raynes had requested a meeting with him. As part of Serena's recovery, she wanted to apologize for lying to her parents about him and had asked her father to pass on a letter she'd written to Quinn.

When Ken had asked Quinn what he planned to do, Quinn hadn't hesitated.

"I'm going home."

On the long drive back, Quinn had gone over and over what he planned to say to Abby. Which, he realized now, had only worked when he wasn't *facing* Abby.

Silence weighted the air between them. Until Abby broke it.

"I thought you went back to Chicago."

Quinn hated to see the confusion in her eyes, knowing he was to blame for it.

"I came back."

"Why?" Abby's eyes darkened. "Alex said you'd been offered your old job back. You have a chance to start over."

"I do want to start over." Quinn drew a ragged breath, knowing that what he said next would determine whether that would happen. "With you. Here, in Mirror Lake. You said you believed in second chances. I'm asking for mine."

Abby didn't say a word.

Was he getting through to her?

"I should never have agreed to work for your brother, but I told myself I had to. For the business. About twenty-four hours after we met, my loyalties changed." His expression was rueful. "I started to work for *you*. I wasn't honest before but this is the truth. I've never felt this way about anyone. You were right about God having a plan and a purpose—I was too blind to see it before. But when I picture my future, you're there. In every part of it. What can I say to make you believe that—"

"Nothing."

"Nothing?" Quinn's heart bottomed out.

Had Daniel been wrong?

Abby was so shocked to hear the husky rumble of Quinn's voice—to see him standing several feet away—that his words had barely registered.

When regret darkened his eyes, she realized Quinn

had misinterpreted her silence and reached out a tentative hand to touch his face.

"I mean, you don't have to *say* anything," Abby said softly. "I believe you. Because you're here."

"Abby." Quinn drew her into the warm circle of his arms and rested his chin against her hair. "I had a nice speech all prepared but when I saw you, I couldn't remember any of it. Except—" he looked down at her, his smile suddenly turning roguish "—the way it ended."

Abby wondered if there would ever come a time when that smile wouldn't send her pulse into a delighted skip.

Having witnessed the looks that still passed between Simon and Lydia Thomas, she doubted it.

Abby peeked up at him from under her lashes, a little giddy now that the barriers between them had fallen. "And how did it end?"

An answering spark flared in Quinn's eyes.

"Like this." He lowered his head and kissed her.

When they finally broke apart, the look in his silver-gray eyes stole her breath away.

"Quinn O'Halloran," she teased, her voice sounding a little breathless even to her own ears. "That felt more like a beginning."

"A beginning it is, then." Quinn's arms tightened around her. "Any objections?"

He didn't give her a chance to answer, but Abby didn't mind.

She couldn't think of a single one.

* * * * *

Dear Reader,

I hope you enjoyed your first visit to Mirror Lake—
a small town with a big heart.

As Quinn discovered, experiences from the past
can color our perspective…and make it difficult to
trust God with the future. It took Abby, who had
taken that step of faith, to show him that sometimes
you can go home again!

I love to hear from my readers. Please visit my
website at kathrynspringer.com and sign up for my
quarterly newsletter.

Blessings,

Kathryn Springer

LOVE FINDS A HOME

And I pray that you, being rooted and established in love, may have power, together with all the saints, to grasp how wide and long and high and deep is the love of Christ.
—*Ephesians* 3:17–18

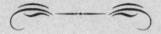

To Colleen, my "third" daughter, who has
a special place in my life and in my heart. Love ya!

Chapter One

"Flowers?" Police Chief Jake Sutton spotted the enormous bouquet of roses the moment he stepped into the break room, where the officers roosted near the coffeepot before heading out on patrol every morning. "I'm touched, guys, but you shouldn't have."

The three men staring morosely at the fragrant centerpiece snapped to attention at the sound of his voice.

"We didn't," Phil Koenigs muttered, the droop of his narrow shoulders more pronounced than usual.

"No offense, though, Chief," Tony Tripenski added quickly. "We would have brought you flowers if we knew you liked them." His eyes widened when he saw Jake's eyebrow lift. "I mean, not that you look like the type of guy who likes flowers…"

Phil rolled up the fingers on one hand and cuffed Tony on the shoulder. "Put the shovel away, Trip. All you're doing is digging yourself a deeper hole."

Glowering, the younger officer folded his arms across his chest and slumped lower in the chair.

Jake paused long enough to pour himself a cup of

coffee before making his way to the table. Something warned him that he was going to need the extra caffeine. The last time he'd seen the men in such a dismal mood was the day he'd officially been sworn in as Mirror Lake's new police chief.

He flipped an empty chair away from the table and straddled it. "If one of you has a secret admirer, you'd look a little happier. That means someone must be in the doghouse with the wife."

"The doghouse would be easier," Steve Patterson, one of the part-time officers, grumbled.

"Yeah." Trip nodded. "*Much* easier. I'd rather face Sherry when she's in a mood than..." His voice dropped to a whisper. "You know who."

No, Jake didn't know. He hadn't been born and raised in the area, something more than a few people had been quick to point out since his arrival.

His gaze cut back to Phil. If he wanted a straight answer, it would most likely come from the senior officer. As second in command, Phil had been the most likely candidate to step into the shoes of the former police chief, who'd opted for an early retirement. Instead, he'd astonished everyone by turning down the position.

Any concern that Phil's decision would make the transfer of power a rocky one had been put to rest when Jake found out Phil was the one who'd pulled his resume from the stack of applications and given it his personal stamp of approval.

He still wasn't quite sure why. But he did know that if it weren't for the dour officer's willingness to fill him in on the local—and sometimes colorful—history of the town and the people who lived there,

Jake might still be suffering from an acute case of culture shock. Within the first twenty-four hours, he'd discovered that what Mirror Lake lacked in population, it made up for in quirks.

He had a feeling he was about to add another one to the list.

He glanced at the officer, surprised when Phil averted his gaze. "Phil? Flowers?"

The officer scratched at a coffee stain on the table with his thumbnail. Sighed. "They're for Emma Barlow."

"Okay." Jake drew a blank on the name. "I'll bite. Who is Emma Barlow?"

The three men exchanged looks but none of them seemed in a hurry to enlighten him. Jake waited, drawing on the patience that had become second nature while working as an undercover narcotics officer.

"Brian Barlow's widow," Phil finally said. "Brian was a good man. A good...cop."

Was.

Jake didn't miss the significance of the word. Or the flash of grief in the older officer's eyes. It was the first time he'd heard about the department losing an officer. Apparently that was one bit of local history Phil hadn't been eager to share.

"What happened?"

"He was killed in the line of duty six years ago. High-speed chase." Steve picked up the story with a sideways glance at Phil, who'd lapsed into silence again. "On the anniversary of his death, one of us takes flowers to his wife..." He caught himself. "I mean his widow."

"That's thoughtful of you." Jake wasn't surprised.

From what he'd learned about the town over the past few weeks, an annual tribute to a fallen officer was the kind of thing he'd expect from the tightly knit group of people who lived in Mirror Lake.

No one agreed or disagreed with the statement. But if anything, they looked more miserable than they had when he'd walked in. For the first time, Jake noticed three plastic straws lined up next to the vase.

Absently, he picked one up and rolled it between his fingers.

The *short* one.

His eyes narrowed but no one noticed. Probably because they'd all found a different focal point in the room to latch on to.

The evidence in front of him and the officers' expressions could only lead Jake to one conclusion.

"Don't tell me that you're drawing straws to see who gets to deliver the flowers?"

"No." Trip almost choked on the word.

Jake might have believed the swift denial if the tips of Trip's ears hadn't turned the same shade of red as his hair.

He turned to Steve and raised an eyebrow.

Steve's Adam's apple convulsed in response. "We draw straws to decide who *has* to deliver them," he muttered.

"Let me get this straight. You buy Emma Barlow flowers every year but no one wants to *give* them to her?"

Absolute silence followed the question. Which, Jake decided, was an answer in itself. Under any circumstances, it was difficult to lose a fellow officer, but in a small community like Mirror Lake, he guessed it had shaken the town to its very foundation.

He buried a sigh. "I'll drop them off. Where does she live?"

The officers stared at Jake as if he'd just volunteered to walk into a drug deal wearing a wire on the *outside* of his clothes.

"You?" Steve's voice cracked on the word.

Not quite the reaction Jake had expected.

"Is there something I'm missing here?" he asked. "Don't I just knock on the door, express my condolences and give Emma Barlow the flowers?"

Phil opened his mouth to speak but Trip and Steve beat him to it.

"That's pretty much it, Chief." A hopeful look dawned in Trip's eyes.

"Yup." Steve's head bobbed in agreement. "That's all there is to it."

"Phil?"

The officer's fingers drummed an uneven beat against the table. "That's usually the way it goes," he said cautiously.

Usually?

"So you think she would be more comfortable if someone she knew brought them over—" Jake didn't have a chance to finish the sentence. Phil's radio crackled to life as a call came in from dispatch.

The three officers surged to their feet.

"Better go." Phil moved toward the door at an impressive speed, Steve and Trip practically stumbling over his heels in their haste to follow.

"Wait a second." Jake couldn't believe what he

was seeing. "It takes all three of you to respond to a *dog* complaint?"

Phil had already disappeared, leaving Steve and Trip glued to the floor as if Jake had aimed a spotlight on them.

"It might be a *big* dog," Trip mumbled.

"Huge." Steve nodded.

"And vicious," Trip added. "You never know."

"That's true." Jake suppressed a smile. "So, in the interest of maintaining public safety, I'll expect a full, *written* report on this large, vicious dog and details of the encounter before you leave today."

The officers' unhappy looks collided in midair.

"Sure, Chief." Trip plucked at his collar. "Not a problem."

He vanished through the doorway but Steve paused for a moment. "Emma Barlow lives in the last house on Stony Ridge Road. It's a dead end off the west side of the lake—"

A hand closed around Steve's arm and yanked him out of sight.

Jake shook his head.

Definitely one for the list.

Emma Barlow sat at the kitchen table, palms curled around a cup of tea that had cooled off more than an hour ago.

Ordinarily, she could set her clock by the arrival of an officer from the Mirror Lake Police Department. Nine o'clock sharp, as if the stop at her house was the first order of business for the day.

Or something to get over with as quickly as possible.

Sometimes Emma wondered if the officers dreaded August fifteenth as much as she did.

After six years, she knew exactly what to do. As if every moment, every movement, were choreographed.

Emma would open the door and find one of the officers, most likely Phil Koenigs, standing on the porch with a bouquet of red roses.

Always roses.

They didn't speak. Emma preferred it that way. She accepted the flowers more easily than she would have awkward condolences. Or even worse, a pious reminder that God loved her and she should accept Brian's death as His will.

Emma had often wondered why no one else saw the contradiction there. If God really loved her, would He have left her a widow at the age of twenty-four? Wouldn't He have somehow intervened to save Brian?

Those were the kinds of questions that ran through Emma's mind during the sleepless nights following the funeral, but she'd learned not to voice them out loud. It hadn't taken her long to discover that most people, no matter how sympathetic or well-meaning, seemed to give grief a wide berth. As if they were afraid if they got too close, it would touch—or stain—their own lives somehow.

No one liked to be reminded how fragile life could be. Especially another police officer, who looked at her and saw Brian instead. A life cut short.

Maybe that explained why the officers remained poised on the top step, waiting for her to take the flowers. She would then nod politely. Step back into the house. Close the door. Listen for the car to drive

away. The roses would be transported to the cemetery and carefully arranged, one by one, in the bronze
vase on Brian's grave.

What she really wanted to do was throw them
away.

If it weren't for Jeremy, she probably would. Although her ten-year-old son had very few memories
of his father, he took both pride and comfort in knowing that an entire community did.

Jeremy had lost enough; Emma wasn't about to
take that away from him.

Unlike her, Brian had been born and raised in Mirror
Lake. He'd left after graduation, only to return two
years later with a degree in Police Science and a gold
wedding band on his left hand, a perfect match with
the one now tucked away in her jewelry box.

The snap of a car door closing sucked the air from
Emma's lungs. Lost in thought, she hadn't heard a
car pull up the driveway. Through the panel of lace
curtains on the window, Emma caught a glimpse of
a light bar on top of the vehicle.

Rising to her feet, she tried to subdue the memories that pushed their way to the surface. Memories
of the night she'd fallen asleep on the sofa, waiting
for Brian to come home. But instead of her husband,
a visibly shaken Phil Koenigs had shown up at the
door...

You can do this, Em. Open the door. Take the
roses. Nod politely. Close the door.

Her fingers closed around the knob. And her heart
stumbled.

It wasn't Phil who stood there, a bouquet of long-
stemmed roses pinched in the bend of his arm.

It was a stranger, empty-handed.

"Emma Barlow?"

A stranger who knew her name.

Emma managed a jerky nod. "Y-yes." Her voice sounded as rusty as the screen door she hadn't found time to replace.

"I'm Jake Sutton." He extended his hand. "The new police chief."

Before she knew what was happening, Emma felt the warm press of his fingers as they folded around hers.

She'd heard a rumor about Chief Jansen's upcoming retirement but hadn't realized he'd been replaced yet. Replaced by a man in his midthirties, whose chiseled features and tousled dark hair gave him an edgy look. A faint web of scars etched the blade of his jaw, as pale and delicate as frost on a window. If it weren't for the white dress shirt and badge, he would have looked more like someone who walked the edge of the law, not a man who dedicated his life enforcing it.

Emma pulled her hand away, no longer sure what she should say. Or do.

Jake Sutton had just changed the rules.

Chapter Two

Jake felt Emma Barlow's hand flutter inside his like a butterfly trapped in a jar. Before she yanked it away.

His first thought when the door opened was that he'd gone to the wrong address. The woman standing on the other side was young. Younger than he expected.

Too young to be a widow.

Fast on the heels of that thought came a second. In an instant, Jake knew why the officers let the short straw decide who delivered the flowers. It wasn't the painful reminder of losing a friend and colleague they didn't want to face.

It was Emma Barlow.

He recognized the anger embedded in her grief; flash-frozen like shards of glass in the smoke-blue eyes staring up at him.

She didn't want flowers. Or sympathy.

She wanted him to leave.

It was a shame that Jake rarely did what people wanted—or expected—him to do.

"Do you mind if I come in?"

Instead of answering, Emma Barlow made a strangled sound.

Was that a yes or a no?

Jake took a step forward. She took a step back... and bumped into the person who'd materialized behind her. A boy about ten or eleven years old, with sandy blond hair a shade or two lighter than hers. Eyes an identical shade of blue.

Jake released a slow breath.

No one at the department had mentioned a child.

Steve had said that Brian Barlow had died six years ago. If this was his son, and the boy had to be, given the striking physical resemblance to Emma, he must have lost his father before he started school.

Something twisted in Jake's gut when Emma put a protective hand on the boy's shoulder. He'd gotten used to the suspicious looks cast his way while he worked undercover, hair scraped back in an unkempt ponytail and a gold stud in one earlobe. He'd gotten rid of both after leaving the force, but Emma Barlow's wary expression still unsettled him. Made him feel like the bad guy.

"Jeremy, this is... Chief Sutton." Emma's husky voice stumbled over the words. "Chief Sutton—my son. Jeremy."

Jake extended his hand. "It's nice to meet you."

The boy hung back, his gaze uncertain. "Where are the flowers?"

The question broadsided Jake. If Emma's son had expected him to show up with a dozen roses, he obviously hadn't followed standard protocol.

Okay, God, I thought I was following Your orders.

Jake's silent prayer went up with a huff of frustration. Not at God, but at himself. The trouble was, he'd been a cop longer than he'd been a follower of Jesus, so he wasn't always sure he was getting the faith stuff right.

Over the past six months, he'd tried to tune in to what some referred to as "a still, small voice" or a "gentle inner nudge."

His younger brother, Andy, without mentioning names, of course, claimed that if "someone" had a thick skull, God sometimes had to shout to get their attention. And if that "someone" also possessed a thick skin, the "gentle nudge" might feel more like an elbow to the ribs.

Jake had felt that elbow when he'd reached out to steady the vase on the seat beside him at a stop sign on his way to Emma's. He studied the flowers, as if he'd just been given a piece of evidence, but found nothing unusual about a dozen roses mixed with lacy ferns and a few tufts of those little white flowers he couldn't remember the name of. The standard arrangement a woman received for Valentine's Day or an anniversary. To remind her she was loved...

Another jab.

Jake had closed his eyes.

Did a bouquet of red roses honor her husband's memory? Or was the sight of them one more reminder of everything Emma Barlow had lost?

Jake had turned the squad car around and headed for the florist shop.

Once inside, he'd bypassed the cooler filled with pink and blue carnations, ready and waiting to celebrate the next newborn baby, and dodged a display of vases filled with single-stemmed roses, the grab-and-go kind, best offered with an apology.

His foot had snagged the corner of a wooden pallet, almost pitching him headfirst into the sturdy little tree in the corner.

The clerk explained it had been part of a late-summer shipment that hadn't sold because most people planted trees in the spring. A mistake.

Jake had seen it as divine intervention.

Now he wasn't so sure.

"I brought something else this time."

Jeremy ducked his head and Jake waited, hoping the boy's natural curiosity would trump his fear.

Jeremy scraped the toe of his tennis shoe against the porch, sloughing off a blister of loose paint. His voice barely broke above a whisper but Jake heard him.

"What is it?"

Emma resisted the urge to echo the question.

"Come on. I'll show you." Jake Sutton stepped off the porch and strode toward the squad car. Without asking for her permission, Jeremy bounded after him.

Leaving Emma no choice but to follow.

The police chief opened the back door of the vehicle and pulled out a bucket.

Emma blinked.

He *had* brought something else.

A spindly coatrack of a tree with leaves that looked more like pieces of damp crepe paper glued to the drooping branches.

"What's that?" Jeremy's nose wrinkled as he sidled closer.

"This…" Jake anchored the container against one

narrow hip and bumped the door shut. "Is an apple tree."

Jeremy gave it a doubtful look. "I think it's dead."

"It'll be good as new once it's planted. All it needs is some water and sunlight." Jake tilted his head. "I was going to offer to dig the hole, but you look strong enough to do it."

He sounded so certain that Jeremy's chin rose. "S-sure."

Before Emma could protest, Jake transferred the bucket to her son's arms. Jeremy's shoulders sagged under the weight, but to her astonishment his eyes glowed with pride when he turned to look at her.

"Should I find a place to plant it, Mom?"

Emma nodded, not trusting her voice. Although they lived in the country, her son shunned the rough-and-tumble antics that most boys his age enthusiastically embraced. Emma knew she was partially responsible for that. After Brian's death, she'd had no choice but to take Jeremy to work with her at the library, where he'd been forced to find quiet things to occupy his time.

By the time he was old enough to pursue some of his own interests, Jeremy had seemed more content to observe things rather than experience them. Emma had been secretly relieved when it looked as if he hadn't inherited his father's love of a challenge. Brian's desire to push the limits had burned like a flame inside him. One that marriage and becoming a father had only tempered, never fully quenched.

Jeremy flashed a shy smile in the man's direction before trudging away, arms wrapped as tight as insulation around the bucket.

Emma couldn't get her feet to move. Or her vocal cords.

She didn't know what to do with an apple tree. Jake Sutton should have brought roses. Never mind that she didn't *like* roses… It was what he was *supposed* to do. And he should be driving away now… not watching her with golden-brown eyes, as calm and measuring as a timber wolf's.

Those eyes locked with hers and Emma had the uneasy feeling he could read her thoughts. "Do you have a shovel handy?"

Afraid of where the question might lead—possibly to Jake Sutton staying longer?—Emma didn't respond.

Unfortunately, Jeremy did. "There's one in the shed," he called over his shoulder, his mood a whole lot more cheerful than hers.

"Good. You find a spot for the tree while your mother and I round one up."

Didn't she have a say in this?

Emma's hands clenched at her side. "That's not necessary, Chief… Sutton." Her mind was still having a difficult time adjusting to the change. Not only in the name but the man himself. "You must be busy. Jeremy and I don't want to keep you from your work."

"It's Jake. And don't worry about me getting into trouble." A glint of humor appeared in his eyes. "I'm the boss."

Said, Emma thought a bit resentfully, with the confidence that police officers seemed to wear as comfortably as their uniform. And if that weren't enough, the amusement bloomed into laughter, causing a chain reaction. It spilled into the creases fanning out from those amber eyes and tugged at the corners of his lips. The result was a charming, if slightly lopsided smile.

He wasn't supposed to smile, either.

Emma tried to ignore her uninvited guest as they made their way around the corner of the house, past the rusted swing set Jeremy had already outgrown. Weeds sprouted at the base of the poles, a reminder that she'd been neglecting the yard work.

She caught a sigh before it escaped.

Not for the first time, she wished there were more hours in the day.

Between working at the library and her responsibilities at home, Emma didn't have a lot of time to devote to general maintenance around the property. There had been times when she'd thought about selling the place and leaving Mirror Lake for good…if memories of Brian hadn't become fragile threads that held her there.

And if she'd had somewhere else to go.

She tried to see the property from Jake Sutton's eyes. Did he notice some of the shingles had begun to peel away from the roof like the soles of a worn-out shoe? That dandelions dotted a shaggy backyard in desperate need of a lawn mower?

In spite of his easy stride and that disarming smile, something warned her that the man didn't miss much.

"How about right here, Mom?" Jeremy waved to them from the spot he'd chosen. Smack-dab in the middle of the yard.

Emma looked around, not sure if she wanted it in such a conspicuous spot. Before she had time to respond, Jake nodded.

"Good choice. It'll get full sun there."

Jeremy seemed to grow several inches, basking in Jake Sutton's approval as if *he'd* been the one exposed to sunlight.

It didn't make sense. Her son, ordinarily shy around strangers, was responding to the police chief as if they'd known each other for years.

Emma changed direction, veering toward the shed in search of a shovel. The knot in her stomach loosened when Jake didn't follow her. Facing any critters that might have taken up residence inside was more appealing than facing *him* at the moment.

When she returned a few minutes later, brushing cobwebs from the rusty shovel she'd unearthed, Jake was kneeling beside Jeremy. Heads bowed together, shadow and sun, as they studied the planting directions printed on a ragged piece of paper attached to one of the branches with a piece of twine.

Her lips tightened.

The sooner she started digging, the sooner Jake Sutton would leave them alone.

Emma aimed the shovel at a random spot in the grass but Jake plucked it gently from her grasp. "Jeremy's got it." He aimed a wink in her son's direction, as if the two of them had already discussed how to deal with the possibility of any maternal resistance.

"We haven't had much rain. The ground is pretty hard." She reached for the tool again but Jake handed it to Jeremy, who reacted as if he'd been given the Olympic torch.

Emma worried her bottom lip between her teeth while she watched Jeremy's face scrunch in concentration as he threw his weight against the handle. The ground barely cracked beneath the blade.

"I can—" Emma started to say.

"It's okay, Mom," Jeremy gasped. "I got it."

"You're doing great." Jake smiled again. At *her*. As if he knew how difficult it was not to take over. To watch Jeremy struggle.

The next five minutes seemed like an hour. Finally Jake stepped forward. "Looks great, Jeremy. Why don't you take the tree out of the bucket while I clear some of this loose dirt out of the hole?"

"Okay," Jeremy panted the word, relinquishing the shovel with a grin.

Emma felt something shift inside her. She had a feeling that by the time Jake cleared some of the "loose dirt" out of the hole, it would be deep enough to plant the root ball.

Jeremy wrestled the apple tree out of the bucket, and together he and Jake dropped it carefully into the hole.

If possible, the sapling looked even more forlorn than it had in the bucket.

Jeremy must have thought so, too. "I'm going to get some water."

He scampered away, leaving Emma alone with Jake Sutton.

"I hope you don't mind." The rough velvet of his voice scraped across Emma's frayed emotions. "I thought you might like a change this year. Something that will last longer than a vase of flowers."

Change?

Emma almost laughed.

She'd been through enough changes to last a lifetime.

Chapter Three

"So, how are you adjusting to small-town life?" Matthew Wilde slid into the booth opposite Jake.

"Did we have an appointment?" Jake feigned confusion. "Because I'm pretty sure I wouldn't choose to answer that question during the morning rush at the Grapevine Café."

"I don't wait for my congregation to make appointments." The pastor shrugged. "I've discovered it's more effective to go where they are. Like Jesus did."

"Mmm. That explains why you spend so much time out on the lake."

"Jesus did say something about becoming fishers of men." Matt grinned. "What better place to find them?"

"What can I get you, Pastor?" Kate Nichols, the owner of the café, appeared beside their table, her smile as vibrant as the auburn curls that poked out like rusty bedsprings under the yellow bandana she wore.

"Just coffee."

Kate propped one hand on her hip. "You know as

well as I do that as soon as I leave you're going to change your mind and want the special with a side of hash browns and bacon. Why don't you save me the trouble and put the order in now?"

"I'm surprised you stay in business, Kate. The way you treat your customers. And your pastor," Matt added piously.

Kate arched a brow. "Eggs?"

"Over medium."

She turned to Jake. "Chief?"

"Just coffee, thanks."

Kate tucked the pen in her apron pocket and flitted away. She reminded Jake of a hummingbird. Always in motion. From what he'd heard, Kate Nichols was Mirror Lake's own five-foot-two generator, keeping the town running.

"Why did she believe you and not me?" Matt complained.

"I never change my mind."

The vinyl booth crackled as Matt leaned back and folded his arms behind his head. "Your name came up yesterday."

"Let me guess. Delia Peake." From the way the woman had glared at him from the back row of the choir on Sunday morning, Jake guessed she was still steamed that the animal who'd trampled her garden and sampled the produce as if it were a buffet had eluded capture. As far as Delia was concerned, if Jake was worth his salt as a police chief, he would have apprehended the furry little vandal himself. Never mind that he'd been out at the Barlow house at the time of the "attack."

Jake jerked his thoughts back into line as they

strayed to Emma Barlow. Again. Almost a week had gone by since he'd tossed protocol out of the window and presented her with an apple tree instead of a bouquet of roses. The memory of that morning should have started to fade. Instead, the opposite had occurred. Jake found himself thinking about it—about *her*—even more. Emma Barlow had a way of sneaking into his thoughts before he realized what was happening...

Like right now.

"No, it wasn't Delia. This time." From the amusement lurking in Matt's eyes, Jake knew the pastor had heard about the garden fiasco. "A few months ago, Harold Davis, one of the church elders, met with me about starting a mentoring program. Matching men from the congregation with boys from single-parent families in town. The initial feedback from everyone was positive, so we researched the success of similar programs in other churches and wrote up a mission statement. I've been compiling a list of men willing to serve as positive role models for boys who don't have one in their lives."

Jake could see where this was going. "And you want to add mine to the list."

"I already did."

"This is where I remind you that I'm new to the area. You don't know anything about me." Only what Jake had told the pastor the first time they'd met, and he'd deliberately left out a few details of his former life.

"I know the important things." Matt's gaze remained level. "You're a believer. You're growing in your relationship with Christ. And you mentioned that you wanted to get involved in one of the ministries at Church of the Pines."

Jake could have argued every point. He was a *new* believer. He had a long way to go when it came to relationships, not only with the Lord but with everyone in general. And he'd had no idea that a casual comment about serving in the church would bring about such quick results. Jake had meant it, but thought he would have more time to prepare for the task. Like a few months. Or years.

"Has anyone ever told you that you're awfully pushy for a preacher?"

"Can't honestly say I've heard that one," Matt denied cheerfully.

"Only because people won't say it to his face," Kate interrupted. She slid a steaming plate in front of the pastor and checked the level on Jake's coffee cup before moving to the next table.

"We have a picnic planned for this coming Saturday," Matt went on. "Not only to give potential parents information but as a meet and greet so the mentors can get to know the boys and vice versa. We'll match up the pairs after that."

"I don't know," Jake hedged. "I would have to know more about what's involved."

"It's easy. You just take a kid who needs a little time and attention under your wing."

Under his wing.

That, Jake thought, wasn't as easy as it sounded. Not for someone like him, anyway. Not too long ago, the only thing he could claim to have "under his wing" was his duty weapon.

Maybe he should have thought it through a little

more when he'd told God he would say "yes" to whatever He asked.

Especially considering that he *had* been about to die when he'd made the promise.

"Listen, Mom! Do you hear that?" Jeremy's head popped out from behind the colorful screen that separated the children's area from the rest of the library.

He had volunteered to reorganize the picture-book section, literally turned upside down by a rambunctious pair of four-year-old twin boys who had visited the library with their teenage babysitter earlier that morning.

Emma didn't bother to tap her finger against her lips, a gentle reminder for her son to keep his voice down. For the past two hours, they had been the only ones in the building.

"Hear what?" She tipped her head, pretending to be unaware of the faint but unmistakable sound of music drifting through the open windows.

"The ice-cream truck." Jeremy abandoned his post and rushed toward her. "Can I get something? Please?"

Emma was already reaching for her purse, stashed on the bottom shelf of the circulation desk. Apparently Charlie "The Ice-Cream Man" Pendleton had decided to take advantage of another hot August afternoon. His ancient truck, with its equally ancient sound system, drew children into the streets with an enthusiasm that transformed the local Christmas tree farmer into a Pied Piper in denim bib overalls.

The music grew louder, a sure sign that the ice-cream truck had just turned the corner as it cruised toward its destination—a shady spot in front of the Grapevine Café.

"Here you go." Emma handed him some change. "Be careful when you cross the street."

Jeremy stuffed the money into the front pocket of his khaki shorts. "I will."

"And remember not to go any farther than the café."

"I won't."

He'll be fine, Emma told herself as the heavy door swung shut behind him.

Charlie Pendleton didn't have a lot to say but below the dusty brim of the man's faded cap were eyes as sharp and watchful as a school crossing guard. Not to mention that his first stop was located kitty-corner to the police station…

Emma's heart dipped as an image of Jake Sutton flashed in her mind. And she didn't appreciate him intruding on her thoughts like this, any more than she had his unexpected appearance on her doorstep.

Although he had left a few minutes after Jeremy had returned with the bucket of water for the apple tree, his departure hadn't given Emma much relief. Because for some reason, Jake Sutton had become Jeremy's favorite topic of conversation over the past few days.

He hadn't even been disappointed that there were no flowers to take to the cemetery. Jake's unexpected but creative gesture had impacted Jeremy in a way that Emma hadn't anticipated.

It had impacted her, too, but not in the same way.

From what she had seen, Jake didn't seem to care about things like rules or expectations or even simple protocol, for that matter. He reminded her of the timber wolves that had been introduced into the heavily wooded northern counties, but gradually migrated into more populated areas, unmindful of any boundaries, natural or man-made. Not necessarily dangerous, but unpredictable.

Only Emma didn't *want* unpredictable. Not anymore.

On his way back to the department, Jake spotted Charlie Pendleton's truck parked in front of the Grapevine Café. Unlike his route, the man's appearance in town never followed a set pattern or schedule.

The ice-cream truck had rattled through town on several occasions, each time pulling Jake into a surreal Mayberry moment. A year ago, Jake wouldn't have believed that a town like Mirror Lake actually existed.

Or that he would be living there.

He slowed down as he got closer and noticed a group of larger, middle-school-age boys push their way through the children patiently waiting to place their order. Jake recognized them immediately. Too young to get jobs and yet too old for babysitters, the boys' favorite pastime seemed to be hanging out at the park or getting into mischief.

By the time Jake pulled over and hopped out of the squad car, they had formed a tight circle around someone at the back of the line.

One of them spotted Jake and sank his elbow into his friend's side.

"Hey…" The boy's voice snapped off when he saw Jake walking purposefully toward them.

The circle parted immediately, giving Jake a clear view of the unlucky kid who had been trapped inside.

Jeremy Barlow.

The boy looked more worried than hurt, but Jake's protective instincts—instincts he hadn't known that he possessed until now—kicked into high gear.

"What's going on?" He turned his attention to the largest boy in the group.

"Nothing. We're just goofing around." As if to prove his point, he gave Jeremy a friendly cuff on the shoulder.

Jeremy winced but remained silent. Jake stepped between them, forcing the others to fall back. "Doesn't Charlie have a rule that the youngest kids get to go to the front of the line?"

"Yeah, but it's stupid," one of the boys muttered. "It should be whoever gets here first."

"If that's the case, then from what I saw Jeremy would still be ahead of you." Jake folded his arms. "Right?"

The oldest boy looked as if he were going to argue the point when Charlie's voice, as crackly as the speakers, broke through the hum of chatter around them.

"Okay, that's it! There are kids waiting for me at the next stop." The elderly man closed up the back of the truck and jumped inside, deaf to the chorus of protests that rose from the boys who had been harassing Jeremy.

Jake's eyes narrowed. "You can go. But at the next stop, I'm going to assume you'll go to the end of the line and there won't be any more 'goofing around.'"

Mumbling their agreement, the boys made a beeline for the pile of bicycles on the sidewalk in front of the café.

The rest of the children began to disperse. Jeremy's pensive gaze followed the truck as it chugged away.

"Are you going to catch up with him at the park?" Jake asked, knowing it was the second stop on Charlie's route.

He shook his head. "Mom doesn't want me to go farther than the café."

Jake frowned. When he was Jeremy's age, he and his best friend had practically worn the rubber off their bicycle tires on summer afternoons like this. His mother had seemed to accept the nomadic lifestyle of adolescent boys. Her only rule was that Jake eat breakfast before he left the house in the morning and be back in time for supper. And what happened during the hours in between he didn't need to account for.

Given the way Emma had hovered close to Jeremy the first time they'd met, Jake had a hunch she wasn't as lenient.

"Mom is still at the library. I should go back." Jeremy squared his thin shoulders.

Jake couldn't help but be moved by the boy's valiant attempt to hide his disappointment. "Do you want a ride?" he heard himself say.

The blue eyes widened. "In the police car?"

"That's what I'm driving." Jake couldn't help but smile at his reaction. "Hop in."

Jeremy didn't have to be told twice. He was sitting in the passenger seat with his seat belt buckled before Jake opened the driver's side door.

"My dad drove a car like this, didn't he?"

The innocent question took Jake off guard. Did

Jeremy remember his father? "I'm sure it was similar," he said carefully. "But it probably didn't have a laptop like this one."

"It's important to keep up with changes in technology," Jeremy said seriously as he leaned forward to study the radar gun mounted to the dash.

"That's right." Jake's lips twitched as he turned the car around. "How is the apple tree doing?"

"I think it's going to live. And it's better than flowers, even if we didn't have anything to take to the cemetery."

Jake's hands tightened on the steering wheel. He hadn't considered that the bouquet the police department gave Emma would end up on Brian's grave.

Further proof that he'd made a mistake.

"There's Mom." Jeremy pointed out the window.

Emma stood on the sidewalk in front of the library, her willowy figure accentuated by the white blouse and knee-length denim skirt she wore. Her gaze was riveted on the squad car.

The expression on her face warned Jake that he'd just made another mistake.

The sight of a squad car cruising down the street caused Emma's hands to clench at her sides. It was silly, she knew, to have such a strong reaction to a vehicle.

She steeled herself, waiting for it to go past. Instead, the car glided to a stop in front of the library.

The sight of a familiar face in the window squeezed the air from her lungs.

What happened?

The words stuck in Emma's throat as she watched

Jake Sutton's lean frame unfold from the vehicle. He prowled around to the passenger side and opened the door.

"Chief Sutton gave me a ride in the squad car, Mom." Jeremy was smiling as he jumped out. "It's pretty sweet."

"But…" Emma struggled to find her voice. "What about the ice cream? Didn't you catch up to Charlie in time?"

The smile faded. "Yeah."

Emma sensed there was more to the story and her heart sank. "Was someone bothering you again?"

"You know Brad and his friends. They just like to show off," Jeremy mumbled.

She glanced at Jake and found him regarding her with that measuring look. The one that made her want to run for cover.

"Everything is fine," he said. "Jeremy mentioned you were at the library, so I offered to give him a ride back."

"And he let me turn on the lights." Jeremy's smile returned.

Emma caught her breath as a memory surfaced, momentarily breaking through the grief that had formed like a crust of ice over her heart.

On Brian's official first day with the Mirror Lake police department, he had stopped home and handed her a camera, shamelessly turning his lunch break into a twenty-minute photo session. His attempt to strike a serious pose had made Emma laugh—which had sparked Brian's laughter in return.

Every one of those moments had been captured in heartbreaking detail except for one difference.

That carefree young woman was someone Emma no longer recognized. Someone who no longer existed.

Watching Emma's eyes darken, Jake realized he'd done more than cross a line. He'd inadvertently stirred up something in her past. It was possible that in order to cope, Emma had found it easier to tend her grief instead of her memories.

"Mom?" Jeremy tugged on her arm. "It's got a really great computer, too. They can look up all kind of things. I'm not in it, though, so we looked up you instead."

Jake winced as Emma snapped back to the present and turned on him.

"Me?"

Jake smiled, hoping she would realize that running her name through the system had been a harmless illustration to satisfy Jeremy's curiosity, not an invasion of her privacy. "Date of birth March fifteenth. And you have a very clean driving record."

Emma took a step back. "Jeremy, it's time to go. I have to lock up now."

The message in her blue eyes was clear.

If Emma had her way, that was all he would know about her.

Chapter Four

Emma was up to her wrists in wet cement when her cell phone rang. She managed to dry off her hands and wrestle the phone from the pocket of her jeans on the fourth ring, seconds before the call went to voice mail.

"Hello?"

"Mrs. Barlow? This is Pastor Wilde from Church of the Pines."

Emma's fingers tightened on the phone.

She should have expected this. Jeremy had been drawn into the church's fold by a colorful flyer he'd seen stapled to the bulletin board at the library, advertising a special weeklong children's program. Emma had agreed to let him participate, assuming her son's interest would end once the seven days were over. She hadn't considered that Jeremy would want to start attending the worship services, but at his insistence they'd gone to Church of the Pines the past few Sundays.

For his sake, she'd endured the sermons that reminded her God loved her, and smiled politely at peo-

ple while keeping a careful distance. But while Emma
had ignored the little white cards the ushers handed
out, asking for the name, address and phone number
of visitors, she remembered that Jeremy had diligently
filled one out each time.

Emma looked at the pieces of colored glass scattered on her worktable, silently calculating how much
time she had before the mixture began to set up.

"I'm right in the middle of something…" She
paused, hoping the pastor would take the hint.

"When would be a good time to call back?"

The pleasant voice remained cheerful but firm,
letting Emma know that her hesitance was only pro-
longing the inevitable. "I suppose I have a few minutes right now. What is it you wanted to talk about?"

"I'm calling people to let them know about the
mentoring ministry picnic on Saturday afternoon. It
starts at noon—"

"Mentoring ministry?" Emma knew it wasn't polite to interrupt but she couldn't prevent the words
from spilling out. "I'm sorry, but I'm not sure what
you're talking about, Pastor Wilde." And the last thing
she wanted to do was get involved with Church of the
Pines. Sitting through the Sunday morning services
was proving difficult enough.

A moment of silence followed. "I'm sorry, Mrs.
Barlow." Pastor Wilde sounded a little confused.
"There was a short write-up in the bulletin this past
Sunday. Local boys from single-parent families are
matched with men from the congregation who com-
mit to spending several hours a week with them. It
can be helping with homework, grabbing a burger or
shooting hoops together. Whatever the pair decides

to do. My job as the coordinator is to pray for any specific needs they might have and oversee the group activities once a month."

Single-parent families.

There it was. No matter how hard she tried to be both mom and dad to Jeremy—to meet all his needs—their home fell into that category. It didn't matter that they hadn't had a choice. That Brian's death had pushed them there.

"I doubt that Jeremy would be interested. He's very shy and wouldn't be comfortable meeting with someone he doesn't know." *And neither would I,* Emma added silently.

Pastor Wilde cleared his throat. "Ah, Jeremy is interested, Mrs. Barlow. In fact, he turned in a registration form already."

The phone almost slipped through Emma's fingers. "Are you sure it was Jeremy? Maybe it was his Sunday school teacher. Or another adult."

Emma heard the sound of papers rustling.

"I'm, ah, looking at his signature right now."

She released a quiet breath, unwilling to believe that Jeremy had signed up on his own. One of the older boys must have decided to play a practical joke on her introverted son. It wouldn't be the first time. "I'll talk to Jeremy. Thank you for calling."

"Mrs. Barlow?" Pastor Wilde must have sensed she was about to hang up. "Attending the picnic on Saturday doesn't mean Jeremy is obligated to join the program. Abby Porter offered to host the picnic at Mirror Lake Lodge and there will be an informal question-and-answer time after lunch.

"I should add that I've personally met with all the

prospective mentors and they've had extensive background checks done. It's a blessing we've got men who are willing to donate their time and energy to be positive role models."

Positive role models to boys without fathers.

"It sounds like a good idea," Emma murmured.

For someone else's child.

She couldn't imagine letting Jeremy spend time with someone she didn't know, background check or not.

"Then we'll see you and Jeremy on Saturday?"

"I'll think about it."

Emma hung up the phone. At least she hadn't lied. She did think about it.

And the answer was no.

Why had she said yes?

Emma took one look at the people milling around the immaculate, beautifully landscaped lawn and almost turned the car around.

She glanced at Jeremy, who was already wrestling his seat belt off. Her son's eager expression answered the question.

After that disturbing phone call from Pastor Wilde, Emma had waited until dinnertime to bring up the subject of the mentoring ministry, still convinced there had been a mistake—that someone else had turned in the registration form with her son's name on it.

Jeremy's whoop of excitement, however, had immediately proved Emma's theory wrong. She hadn't been prepared for his enthusiasm when he learned about the pastor's invitation to the picnic...or his reaction when she told him they wouldn't be able to go.

Emma winced at the memory.

He'd been crushed.

So Emma had explained—quite patiently she'd thought—the reasons why she didn't think that being involved in the mentoring program was a good idea.

Jeremy had listened. And then her quiet, sensitive little boy had leaned forward, looked her straight in the eye and suggested a compromise.

A compromise!

"Mom, you're always telling me that it isn't a good idea to jump to conclusions, right? That a person should do some research before making a decision. I think we should go to the picnic and find out the facts. If you decide you don't want me to do it, then I'll be okay with that."

How could she argue? Especially since it was obvious which member of the Barlow family was guilty of "jumping to conclusions" this time!

The request was fair. Reasonable. But now, watching a group of preadolescent boys zigzag across the lawn in hot pursuit of the one carrying a football, Emma was convinced she'd made a mistake.

"Jeremy—" The car door snapped the sentence in half.

Tension curled in Emma's stomach.

There was no turning back now. Not only had Jeremy escaped, but Abby Porter had spotted their car and was making her way across the yard.

Somehow, the innkeeper managed to look stunning in faded jeans and a pale green T-shirt that matched her eyes. With her blond hair pulled back in a casual knot and a colorful apron tied around her waist, Abby looked far different from the sophisticated woman in velvet and pearls who had appeared in the ad campaigns for her family's elite hotel chain in years past.

Emma, who'd chosen to wear a navy twill skirt and white blouse, felt positively dowdy by comparison.

"Emma!" Abby appeared at the window. "I'm so glad you're here."

Emma wished she could say the same. She slid out of the driver's seat, resisting the urge to dive back inside the vehicle. Abby immediately linked arms with her, almost as if the other woman had read her mind.

"The turnout this afternoon is higher than we expected." Abby smiled. "I'm glad Pastor Wilde and Harold Davis realized there was a need for something like this in our community."

The need for boys to have male role models in their lives.

The reminder scraped against Emma's soul. She was doing her best to raise Jeremy. He was all she had left in the world. After Brian's death, her son's presence had warmed her heart like a tiny flame, keeping her emotions from growing cold. Over the years, Emma had tried to make sure Jeremy didn't feel as if he were missing out on something, and yet now he wanted to spend time with a mentor.

A *stranger.*

"I'm not sure it's the right thing for Jeremy," Emma said stiffly. She didn't want to offend Abby but she needed to make it clear that she hadn't made a decision whether or not he could join the program.

"Then I'm glad you came to check it out." Abby didn't look the least bit ruffled by her honesty. "And

I've been hoping for a chance to talk to you. One of my guests asked for your business card last weekend."

"I don't have a business card," Emma murmured, trying to keep track of Jeremy as he bounded ahead of them.

Abby gave her a playful nudge. "I know you don't, silly. That was a hint."

"The number for the library is in the phone book."

Abby's laughter caused several heads to swivel in their direction. "You're so funny, Emma. And humble, too. I'm not talking about the library. Gloria Rogers saw the mosaic table in my perennial garden and she couldn't stop raving about it. Of course—" Abby's smile turned impish "—I might have mentioned that even though Mirror Lake Lodge has an exclusive contract with the extremely gifted artist who crafted the piece, you might be persuaded to take on more commissions."

"Abby!" Emma didn't bother to hide her shock. "It's a *hobby,* something to pass the time. It's not a business. I already have a job."

Abby looked smug rather than repentant. "That's exactly what I thought when I was sneaking into the hotel kitchen at midnight to make raspberry lemon tarts." She made a sweeping gesture with one arm that encompassed the refurbished lodge and cabins. "Look where that 'little hobby' took me."

But, Emma wanted to argue, that was different. Raspberry lemon tarts were *meant* to be shared. The mosaics she created had sprung from a need to fill long hours and hold painful memories at bay. And like her grief, she'd tried to keep that part of her life private. But in a town as small as Mirror Lake, word had gotten out.

"You can't compare what we do," Emma murmured. "You have a business degree. Experience. I don't have any formal training."

"You have a gift." Abby's tone left no room for argument. "And when God gives you a gift, it's part of His plan."

Doubt flared from the embers of Emma's grief, snuffing out the unexpected flicker of longing that Abby's words stirred in her heart. There had been a time in her life when she had believed it—before she began to wonder why, when it came to her, did God seem to take away more than He gave?

When she'd met Brian, he had swept her off her feet. She had become a wife at nineteen. A mother at twenty. But Emma's dreams had encompassed a lifetime. They would make a home. Raise a family. Grow old together.

And then she'd lost him.

If all that had been part of God's plan, it seemed safer to keep her distance from Him, too.

"Why don't you and Jeremy find a table and I'll get you both a glass of fresh-squeezed lemonade?" Abby offered.

"All right." Emma looked around but there was no sign of Jeremy. Anywhere. "I don't see him."

"He must have found someone to play with," Abby said.

"Jeremy doesn't care for sports." And was often teased because of it. Tension cinched the muscles between Emma's shoulder blades as she scanned the faces around her.

"Maybe he went down by the lake. Some of the boys were fishing from the dock earlier."

Abby's words, meant to calm her fears, had just the opposite effect. "Jeremy doesn't know how to swim."

Emma felt a pang of guilt at the quickly veiled surprise she saw reflected in Abby's green eyes. She knew what the other woman was thinking. What parent, who lived in a town built on the shore of a lake, wouldn't insist that their child learn to swim?

Emma tried to swallow the knot of panic forming in her throat as Abby gave her arm a comforting squeeze. "I have an idea," she said. "There isn't a boy—or man, for that matter—who will ignore the sound of a dinner bell. I'll give it a ring and I guarantee that you won't have to find Jeremy—he'll find you."

"Thank you." Emma gave Abby a grateful look but didn't wait to see if her idea would work.

She headed down to the lake.

Jake heard the clang of a bell, rallying the troops for lunch, and knew he was running out of time.

The team of mentors would be introduced right after Abby served the meal. If he wanted to let Matt know that he would be more comfortable volunteering in another area of the ministry, he had to do it soon.

Jake had come to the conclusion that he wasn't mentor material only minutes after he'd shown up for the picnic. He had rusty social skills and rough edges his newfound faith hadn't had time to hone. And to top it off, he didn't know a thing about kids. Call him crazy, but wasn't being able to relate to kids an important qualification when it came to being a mentor?

He had taken a walk down the shoreline to think. And to pray.

You know I'm willing, Lord, but I don't think I'm cut out for this. Guys like Matt are better at it. Kids love him—I'd probably scare them away. You must have something else in mind for me, so let me know what it is and I'll do it.

Maybe the prayer team could use another volunteer. He had as much experience in that area as he did interacting with kids, but at least the chance of doing any significant damage remained smaller.

As Jake turned to go back to the lodge, a movement farther down the shoreline caught his attention. He paused, wondering if the flash of color had been a red-winged blackbird searching the cattails for something to eat.

Until he heard a splash.

Knowing how mischievous boys could be, Jake doubted that Matt had given them free rein of the premises for the picnic. The pastor and Quinn O'Halloran, a local businessman and member of the congregation, had planned a variety of games, part of an ingenious strategy for deterring them from creating their own entertainment.

If it *were* boys from the picnic who'd wandered out of sight.

Off duty or not, Jake had no choice but to check it out. He'd received several complaints earlier in the week from some of the local fishermen, who claimed their vehicles had been broken into while parked at the boat landing. Jake couldn't prove it—yet—but he had a sneaking suspicion that whoever was responsible for breaking into the summer cabins had decided to broaden the playing field.

Jake bypassed the trail and created his own route, one running parallel to the marked hiking path that curved around the lake. As he reached the shore, he saw a boy standing knee-deep in the water, tugging on a rope attached to a makeshift raft bobbing in the waves. He was in no immediate danger that Jake could see, but because the kid's frame looked as thin as one of the reeds growing along the shoreline, Jake decided to lend a hand.

"Hold on!"

At the sound of Jake's voice, the boy turned to look at him.

Jake, who'd always prided himself on keeping his emotions in check, felt his jaw drop in disbelief.

There was no mistaking that pair of serious blue eyes and unruly hank of sandy blond hair.

Jeremy Barlow looked just as astonished to see him. "Chief S-Sutton."

Chapter Five

Without a second thought, Jake kicked off his shoes and waded into the water. Together, they began to pull the raft into the shallows.

"Thanks," Jeremy gasped.

"Does this belong to you?"

Jeremy shook his head, spraying Jake with droplets of lake water. "I saw it floating out there. I was afraid a boat might hit it."

That answered one of his questions. But Jake had another, more important, one. "What are you doing down here by yourself?"

"I'm not by myself," Jeremy said quickly. "I'm with my mom."

"Really?" Jake refused to give in to the sudden urge to look around and see if there was another familiar face close by. A familiar face dominated by smoke-blue eyes and hair the pale golden-brown of winter wheat. "Where is she?"

"She's, um, talking to Miss Porter. At the lodge."

So Emma and Jeremy hadn't come to Mirror Lake Lodge for the picnic. That shouldn't have come as a surprise. Emma was as protective as a mama bear with a cub. Jake couldn't imagine she would trust her son's care to someone else, even for a few hours.

Especially someone like you, an inner voice mocked.

Jake couldn't argue with that. Emma had managed to express her opinion of him the day they'd met without saying a single word. And it wasn't, he reminded himself, as if being Jeremy's mentor was even an option.

Prayer team, remember?

But that didn't mean he was going to leave Jeremy alone by the water. "Does she know you're down here?"

The guilty look on Jeremy's face said it all. "I didn't mean to go this far."

"I'll tell you what—I'll walk back there with you."

His officers might question his sanity, but the thought of seeing Emma again actually lightened Jake's mood. Although given her response when he'd brought Jeremy back in the squad car, he doubted she would be anxious to see *him* again.

"Thanks." Jeremy bit his lip as he looked down at his shorts. "I don't think I was supposed to get wet, either."

"The sun is shining. You'll air-dry in no time," Jake said lightly. "And though I appreciate the fact that you fished this thing out of the lake, the next time—"

"Look!" Jeremy let go of the rope, his startled cry interrupting Jake's lecture on water and the "buddy system." He pointed to a black canvas bag riding along the bottom. As the raft had bumped along the rocks, the bag had ripped open, leaving a trail of tools in the water.

Jeremy began to collect them while Jake hauled the bag onto shore to examine it more closely. He frowned when he saw the name FIELDING stamped on the side of the fabric. Rich Fielding had been one of the people whose cabins had been broken into.

Jeremy knelt beside him, clutching a hammer and wrench against his damp T-shirt. His eyes widened when he read the name on the bag. "I know Mr. Fielding. He teaches science at my school."

"Well, I guarantee he's going to be happy to have his property returned."

"You mean this stuff was stolen?"

"That's right." Jake lifted one side of the raft and looked underneath it to see if they'd missed anything. "You have pretty good detective skills."

"Really?" Jeremy's eyes shone with the same pride Jake had seen when he'd let him dig the hole for the apple tree.

Jake didn't have an opportunity to answer because Emma burst into view.

"Jeremy Brian Barlow!"

Emma's gaze locked on the boy standing at the edge of the water. At the moment, she wasn't sure whether to scold him or hug him. Or both.

"What are you doing down here?" The panic that had fueled her frantic search drained away, leaving her weak with relief. As Emma took a step forward, the wet sand gave way beneath her feet. She would have stumbled if a hand hadn't shot out to steady her.

"Careful."

Emma's head jerked up. Her relief at finding Jeremy safe and sound was so great, she had barely spared a glance at the man standing a few feet away from him.

Not that Jake Sutton was easy to overlook. Both times Emma had seen the police chief, he'd been in uniform. Today he wore plainclothes suitable for a Saturday afternoon picnic, but the faded jeans and black T-shirt only accentuated the man's rugged, almost untamed, good looks.

For some inexplicable reason, the touch of his hand sowed goose bumps up her arm.

What was he doing here, of all places?

Emma pulled away and turned toward her son. "You know the rules, honey." She wasn't sure if the crackle in her voice was the aftershock of relief from finding Jeremy, or because the warm imprint of Jake's fingers lingered on her skin. "You're supposed to ask for permission if you want to go somewhere."

"I found Mr. Fielding's tools, Mom," Jeremy said. "Someone hid them under the raft. Chief Sutton said I have good detective skills."

"You went out on a *raft?*" Emma directed the question at Jeremy but cut an accusing look at Jake.

"Not in it, Mom," Jeremy said. "I pulled it out."

"It was in the shallow water. Jeremy wasn't in any danger," Jake interjected quietly.

Emma turned back to Jeremy, hoping Jake Sutton would take the hint that this matter was between her and her son. "You have to be careful by the water," she reminded him, all too aware that Jake could hear every word.

"I know." Jeremy released a gusty sigh as he pulled

on his socks and tennis shoes, a reminder that he'd heard this particular lecture before. "But if I knew how to swim, you wouldn't have to worry so much."

Emma felt the weight of Jake's gaze and her cheeks flamed. She wasn't about to explain that it was impossible to teach her son something that she didn't know how to do.

That responsibility should have fallen to Brian. After all, her husband had loved to brag about how much time he and his friends spent in the lake every summer.

One of the high-school athletic coaches offered lessons at the beach every summer, but Emma's job prevented her from leaving to transport Jeremy there and back—and she was hesitant to trust someone she didn't know with his safety.

Discouragement settled over her, the weight of it all too familiar. "We should get back to the lodge." And away from the censure Emma was afraid she would see in those amber eyes. "I'm sure everyone has started eating lunch already."

Emma hoped the thought of food would divert Jeremy's attention. Over the summer, his appetite had increased to the point where she'd started to wonder where he was putting it all. But instead of charging toward the lodge, Jeremy turned a hopeful look toward the very man Emma wanted to get away from.

"Aren't you coming, Chief Sutton?"

She stifled a groan. From what Jake had said, Emma assumed he and Jeremy had met by accident. She hadn't considered he might be a guest at the picnic.

Relief poured through her when Jake shook his head.

"I'm on my way back to the station." He must have seen the disappointment on Jeremy's face because he knelt down until they were eye to eye. "But I'll tell you what. How about we go with 'Chief Sutton' when we're out in public, but if it's just the three of us, you can call me Jake. Is that a deal?"

Jeremy grinned. "It's a deal."

"But only if that's okay with your mom." Jake looked at her. "Emma?"

Why, she wondered in frustration, did Jake Sutton have to have such an attractive voice? The rich timbre washed over her, stirring her senses like the jazz she played on the radio while working on a mosaic.

"I suppose." Emma saw no point making a fuss about it. She couldn't think of any occasion where it would be just the three of them.

The thought should have been accompanied by relief, but the emotion that skittered through Emma felt, strangely enough, like...disappointment.

Jake watched Emma stumble in the sand again, only this time in her haste to get away from him.

You charmer, you.

Not that he'd *tried* to charm her. Jake was as out of practice at that particular skill as he was at making polite conversation over a glass of lemonade. Fortunately, what he did know how to do was diffuse a tense situation. And Emma had been strung as tight as a new bow when she'd discovered Jeremy by the lake.

Her panic may have faded, but she obviously hadn't changed her opinion of him. She'd barely been able to make eye contact. And when Jake had taken hold of her arm, she had reacted as if he'd burned her.

What did Emma see when she looked at him? Did she see a man or a badge? Was he a person or the symbol of a career that had robbed her of a husband?

The thought chafed.

When he'd asked Phil about Emma after delivering the apple tree, the older officer had still been reluctant to talk about what happened. Jake had pressed a little, asking if Emma had changed after Brian died.

"Can't say for sure." Phil had looked troubled by the question. *"Brian grew up in Mirror Lake. He was an outgoing guy. Liked to be in the middle of things. Emma stayed close to home, especially after Jeremy came along. She wasn't from around here, so no one really got to know her."*

Or no one had tried. Which meant that Emma, a young mother, had been alone in her grief. From what he could see, it still held her locked in a cold grip.

Lord, you can get into the places people shut off from everyone else. You did it for me and I know you can do the same thing for Emma.

That Jake even thought to pray for Emma confirmed the change in *his* heart.

"There you are."

Jake looked up and saw Matt striding down the trail toward him.

"I've been looking for you." Relief surged through Jake and he silently thanked God for giving him the opportunity to let the pastor know that he'd decided against being a mentor.

"That's funny, because I was sent to find *you*." Matt grinned. "Rounding up strays comes with the job."

"Duty calls." Jake jerked his head at the tool bag. "These were stolen from one of the cabins last month."

"Hey, this is your day off," Matt reminded him, a teasing glint in his eyes. "You weren't supposed to be investigating anything more serious than the dessert table."

"Says the man who also chose a career that keeps him on call 24/7."

"Touché." Matt rolled his eyes. "So now what?"

"Steve Patterson is working the day shift. I'll give him a call and have him meet me at the department with the stolen property."

"You're going to miss the meeting." It wasn't a question.

"I'm afraid so." Jake hesitated, torn between not wanting to disappoint the pastor and knowing that the sooner he got this over with, the sooner Matt could look for someone to take his place.

Matt slanted a knowing look at him. "You're having second thoughts, aren't you?"

"You remind me of my brother." Jake raked a hand through his hair in frustration. "Andy can read minds, too. Do they teach you how to do that in the seminary?"

"I like your brother already."

"Everyone does." Jake could say it without a twinge of envy. "It's too bad you got stuck with me instead of him." He was only half joking.

Matt chuckled. "I'm pretty sure God didn't look down from Heaven and say, 'Pops, I sent the wrong brother to Mirror Lake.'"

Sometimes, Jake wasn't so sure.

* * *

"Before we get started, would everyone please join me in a word of prayer?"

Conversation around the table subsided as Pastor Wilde stepped to the front of the group. His easy smile swept over the people gathered together under the shade of the willow trees.

Emma bowed her head but didn't close her eyes, choosing to focus on a maple leaf near her foot. Scarlet trimmed the delicate edges, a sure sign that autumn was on its way.

She blocked out the pastor's words until she heard Abby, who was sitting across from her, echo his heartfelt amen. Emma lifted her head, ready to count the minutes until the meeting ended.

Harold Davis stepped forward and briefly shared the vision of the ministry and then Pastor Wilde introduced each of the mentors. Emma recognized some of the men from church and a few others from town. Each one took a few minutes to explain why he was involved in the ministry and then went on to share some of his hobbies and interests. After that, the pastor encouraged the mothers to ask questions and express any concerns they had about the program.

Most of them were excited about their sons having a male role model, but Emma couldn't lay aside the doubts that swept through her mind. Jeremy wasn't rowdy or rebellious. Not a "handful"; the word she'd heard some of the mothers use to describe their sons. When he showed an interest in something, she encouraged him to check out a book or do an internet search on the topic.

Jeremy wasn't lacking anything. Was he? As his

mother, it was her job to protect him. He had already experienced the loss of his father. Was it wrong of her to want to shield him from situations—or people—that could hurt him?

A sudden commotion interrupted the meeting as the boys spilled out of the woods. Abby's fiancé, Quinn O'Halloran, had taken them on a nature walk to keep them occupied during the question-and-answer session.

"I think that's our signal to adjourn." Pastor Matt smiled. "But please, feel free to stay as long as you like. We've organized a fishing tournament for the boys and thanks to Abby, there is still plenty of food left."

"Oops, that's my cue." Abby leaned over and gave Emma a quick hug, surrounding her with the faint but distinctive scent of cinnamon. "I'll call you about that business card."

"I better help her get ready for the second wave." Kate stood up and pointed her plastic fork at Emma. "Stop by the café sometime." She lowered her voice. "People say that my pie is as good as Abby's."

"I heard that!" Abby called over her shoulder.

"You were supposed to." Kate rolled her eyes and aimed a smile at Emma, who couldn't muster one in return.

She'd been watching for Jeremy and her heart wrenched when she spotted him trailing behind the rest of the group, his hands clenched into fists at his sides.

This was what she'd been afraid would happen.

Chapter Six

Tamping down her concern, Emma waved to get Jeremy's attention. He saw her and ran over to the table.

"Is everything all right?"

"Look what I found!" Jeremy slid onto the bench next to her, his expression animated rather than upset. "Mr. O'Halloran said it's a real arrowhead. I found it when we were looking for deer antlers in the woods."

Emma looked down at the flat oval stone cradled in her son's grimy palm. The tiny notches on either side had definitely been put there by design, not accident.

"You don't stumble on one of these very often." An elderly man, whose dusky skin and coffee-brown eyes reflected his Native American ancestry, had walked over to examine the arrowhead. "Your son is quite the adventurer."

Jeremy's eyes glowed at the praise. "Just like we learned at camp. Right, Mr. Redstone?"

"I'm glad you remembered." The man winked at

him. "How are you doing with the rest of your explorations these days?"

"Good."

Daniel Redstone must have sensed Emma's confusion, because he turned back to Emma with a smile. "I volunteered with The Great Adventure Camp last month and Jeremy joined my group. All the boys committed to memorizing one Scripture verse a week."

Emma felt the same way she had after admitting to Abby that Jeremy didn't know how to swim. He had tried to tell her about the things he'd learned at the church-sponsored day camp but Emma knew she'd been less than receptive. As sensitive as Jeremy was, he must have picked up on her feelings. As the week progressed, he'd talked less and less about the things they'd done on that particular day. At the time, she'd been relieved. Now she was simply embarrassed.

"I don't understand some of them," Jeremy admitted. "The words are kind of hard to read in Mom's Bible."

Mom's Bible?

Emma swallowed hard. She didn't own a Bible... Yes, she did.

A palm-size edition, with print so small a person practically needed a magnifying glass to read it, bound in white leather. The clerk at the bridal store had given it to Emma when she'd purchased her gown. She vaguely remembered the woman smiling and telling her that it was the most important "accessory" a bride could have. After the wedding ceremony, Emma had carefully written Brian's name and her own in the front cover and recorded the date.

The beginning of their life together.

Emma hadn't seen the Bible for a long time. But somehow, Jeremy must have found it.

She pushed to her feet, overwhelmed by a sudden urge to escape. "We have to go."

"But, Mom!" Jeremy's voice rose in dismay. "There's going to be a fishing tournament. Can't we stay a little longer?"

"We agreed to attend the picnic," Emma said, careful not to look at Jeremy and see the disappointment in his eyes. "And the picnic is over."

She'd kept her part of the deal. Now Jeremy would have to accept her decision.

"Chief Sutton! Why do I get the impression that you aren't taking me seriously?"

Jake held the phone a few inches away from his ear but it didn't muffle Delia Peake's piercing soprano. Her voice sounded pleasant enough when it blended with the rest of the church choir but not when she was using it to drill a hole in his eardrum.

"I suppose I could take an impression of the foot—*paw*—print, Mrs. Peake, but it would be difficult to match it to a specific suspect…" Jake closed his eyes. "No, I must have missed that episode, but no matter what you saw on television, I don't think it's possible to trace the damage done to your garden to a *particular* raccoon."

A rap on the door brought Jake's head up. His prayer for deliverance had been answered.

Thank you, Lord.

"Mrs. Peake? I'm sorry, but my nine-o'clock appointment is here." Jake didn't know who that nine-o'clock appointment was, but it didn't matter. He was grateful for their arrival as he hung up the phone.

The door opened and Matt Wilde sauntered in.

Or not.

"To what do I owe this unexpected visit?" As relieved as Jake was at the interruption, an internal alarm went off at the sight of the serious expression on the pastor's face.

"I have a problem."

Jake's eyes narrowed as he leaned back in the chair. "Why do I get the feeling that your problem is about to become my problem?"

"I think you should rethink your decision to become a mentor."

"Matt—"

"Just hear me out. Please."

"Fine," Jake said irritably. "But only because you used the magic word."

Matt, like Andy, seemed to have a Teflon coating when it came to sarcasm. He dropped into the chair opposite Jake's desk instead of running for cover.

"We had a lot more boys show up yesterday than we anticipated, praise God."

Jake couldn't argue with that. It *was* a praise. New as he was to a life of faith, answered prayer still blew him away. But that didn't mean he trusted the look in Matt's eyes.

"I did volunteer for the prayer team, remember?"

"You can be on the prayer team."

"Good—"

"*And* serve as a mentor."

"What makes you so sure I can do this?" Jake's hands fisted on the desk.

"What makes you sure you can't?" Matt countered mildly.

Because I'm not sure I have anything valuable to offer, Jake wanted to say. How could he be a good influence on a person when he hadn't noticed his best friend drifting closer to the line between right and wrong? But he wasn't ready to share that story. Not even with Matt. The physical wounds he'd suffered had healed faster than the emotional ones.

"I have no idea how to relate to kids." Frustration leeched into his voice. "If God wants me to be involved in something, shouldn't it at least be something I'm *good* at?"

Something that didn't make him feel totally inadequate?

"You must be better than you think." Matt leaned back and crossed his hands behind his head. "One of the boys specifically requested you."

"Requested me?" Jake couldn't believe it. He hadn't mingled with the boys at the picnic the day before. He hadn't joined in the games with the pastor and Quinn O'Halloran. In fact, the only boy he'd had any interaction with at all had been...

Jake's head jerked up and he met Matt's amused gaze.

"That's right. Jeremy Barlow."

The name brought Jake to his feet. "Are you saying that Emma agreed to let Jeremy participate?"

"Not yet."

"You'll never be able to convince her."

"You're probably right." Matt's smiled turned smug. "That's why I'm hoping you can."

* * *

I'll trust that You know what You're doing, God.

Jake muttered the prayer five minutes later as he crossed Main Street. Veering toward the one-story brick building on the corner, he followed the cobble-stone walkway to the door and paused to read the bronze plaque before going inside.

The building had once housed the first one-room schoolhouse in the county. Vacant for years, it had been saved from being turned into a parking lot by a group of citizens who later formed the local histori-cal society.

The details were printed in letters so small that Jake had to squint to read them. But he did—because knowing local history was important.

Not because he was stalling.

And not because he was sure that he was the last person Emma expected—or wanted—to walk into the library.

Jake slipped inside the building, careful not to let the door slam shut behind him. It was the first time he'd been inside the library. Sunlight poured through the lace curtains, creating stencils on the gleaming hardwood floor. Bookshelves fanned out like the spokes of a wheel from the massive circular oak desk in the center of the room. The air smelled like lemon polish.

The order and tidiness reminded him of a certain librarian.

Jake looked around. There was no sign of Emma.

He was about to ring the bell when he heard a voice coming from the back of the room. Jake followed the sound through the maze of tables and suddenly felt as if he'd fallen through a rabbit hole. Everything around him suddenly shrank in size. The tables and chairs. The bookshelves.

Behind a portable room divider, painted in bright colors and cut out to resemble a storybook forest scene, he heard a soft giggle.

"'Watch what I do! I'll bake cookies and bread. Yummy pies, tarts and cakes,' Chef Charlotte said..."

The lilting voice sounded vaguely familiar.

Jake moved closer and peeked through a narrow gap in the divider.

A dozen children sat in a semicircle on a colorful rag rug. All eyes were riveted on the woman who sat cross-legged in front of them, holding a picture book on her lap. A snow-white apron shrouded her slim frame and a tall chef's hat was propped on the tawny head, but there was no mistaking the face that had been invading his thoughts. Even with the tip of her nose and porcelain cheeks dusted with something that looked like...flour.

The children, who had obviously heard the story before, all shouted together on cue. "What will you do with your cakes and bread?"

"'I'll give them away,' Chef Charlotte said." With a flourish, Emma waved a wooden spoon in the air as if it were a scepter.

Jake could feel his chin scraping against the floor.

What had happened to the Emma Barlow he knew? The buttoned-up woman who had worn a skirt and blouse to a Saturday picnic? The one who didn't seem to *like* people?

Or maybe, Jake had a sudden epiphany, it was just him that she didn't like.

"Who's that?"

Jake stepped back but not fast enough. The freckle-faced boy who'd spotted him pointed to the gap in the divider, giving away Jake's exact location.

"It's a stranger!" The little girl sitting closest to Emma let out a shriek with a decibel level high enough to break glass.

"Stranger, stranger!" The rest took up the chant.

Jake winced.

"No, it's not." One brave little soul had peered around the divider. "It's a p'liceman. He gotsa badge, see?"

Before Jake could blink, a pint-size posse surrounded him. He was, to use official police jargon, *busted.*

"Are you going to read us a story like Miss Emma?" A petite girl with melting dark eyes and a cloud of black curls tugged on his pant leg.

Jake shot Emma a panicked look.

"That's a good idea, Hannah." Emma's smile made Jake's blood run cold. "And I think I know the perfect one for Chief Sutton, don't you?"

"Sheriff Ben Rides Again!" The children hopped up and down, making Jake feel as if he were caught in a blender. They captured him before he could protest, towing him over to the rag rug Emma had occupied moments ago. Jake felt a little like Gulliver amid the Lilliputians.

Emma managed to work her way to the front of the jubilant crowd. Relieved, Jake smiled. But instead of rescuing him, she handed him an oversize picture book. And a stick horse with a tangled mane of red yarn and button eyes.

Jake couldn't believe she hadn't put a stop to this yet. She should be upset that he'd interrupted her story time…

Their eyes met over the children's heads and Jake suddenly understood.

This was a challenge.

And Jake never—*never*—walked away from a challenge. He unleashed a slow smile in Emma's direction.

"Don't *I* get a hat?"

Hat.

Emma suddenly remembered the chef's hat perched on her head. She swept it off and smoothed away some flyaway strands of hair from her face.

The bells over the door of the library usually alerted her if a patron entered the library, but the story she'd been reading was interactive and this particular group of five- and six-year-olds tended to be a bit exuberant.

As Jake would soon discover.

Emma almost felt sorry for him. Almost.

The man *should* be shaking in his boots for sneaking up on her like that.

How long had he been watching her? And why?

She had the uneasy feeling it wasn't because he needed a library card. And if he did, Emma doubted that he would stop in while on duty. Did his visit have something to do with the stolen property that Jeremy had found on Saturday?

The thought should have made her relax, but it

didn't. If she was uncomfortable, Emma deemed it only fair that Jake Sutton be uncomfortable, as well.

Except that Jake didn't appear uncomfortable at all.

Reggie, the boy who'd spotted Jake hiding behind the divider, retrieved a battered cowboy hat from the trunk of dress-up clothes and handed it to him. Jake tapped it against his thigh a few times, almost as if he were pretending to dislodge some invisible trail dust clinging to it.

"I can't see, Ms. Emma!" Hannah tugged on the hem of her apron.

Emma scooted to the side. She didn't even have to remind the children to take a seat. They dropped like stones onto the rug when Jake lightly cleared his throat. He opened the book and thumbed to the first page.

"'Sheriff Ben was getting old. Too old to keep the peace in a town like Cutter Bend,'" Jake read. "'His bones were tired and creaky and he got sore when he rode his mule into town'…" He paused and shot her a suspicious look. "Local law enforcement rides a *mule?*"

"Gracie!" one of the girls squealed.

"A mule," Jake muttered. "Named Gracie."

"Read it! Read it!" The words became a chant, coupled with a rhythmic pounding of little hands against the floor.

Emma nodded, pressing her lips together to seal in the smile she felt coming on. Any moment, Jake Sutton would find an excuse to flee like Snakebite Sam, Sheriff Ben's archenemy…

Instead, he flicked the brim of the cowboy hat and it settled on his dark head at a jaunty angle.

The crushed black felt had never looked so attractive.

Emma swallowed hard, her fist clenching the wooden spoon she still held in her hand. The fluttery feeling that started in her knees and worked its way to her heart whenever Jake Sutton came into view was unexpected. Unnerving. And totally unacceptable.

But acknowledging that didn't make it go away.

"'Sheriff Ben had achy bones and his eyesight wasn't as good as it used to be, but he wasn't afraid of anyone. Not even'—" Jake paused dramatically and all the children leaned forward in a hushed silence, eyes wide as they waited for him to continue even though they'd heard the story a dozen times "'—Snakebite Sam.'"

Chapter Seven

As the last of the children danced out the door, Emma took refuge behind the desk, putting something solid between her and Jake.

She thought he would leave when he realized how busy she was. But no. Jake had joined the story-time group for snack time. He'd lowered his lean frame onto one of the tiny wooden chairs and accepted a pink frosted cupcake in honor of Hannah Cohen's fifth birthday. He had sipped pretend tea from a pink teacup and politely declined the use of the lavender feather boa one of the girls offered to drape around his neck.

Emma would have thought the *sight* of a feather boa would have sent Jake running for the door.

But here he was. Prowling around her desk. Forcing Emma to turn a complete circle while she kept a wary eye on him.

"This is a nice library."

"Thank you."

"How long have you worked here?"

Emma moistened her lips. "Six years."

The answer hung in the air between them.

"I see," Jake said after a moment.

Did he, Emma wondered with a trace of bitterness. She glanced at the door, hoping someone—anyone— would come into the library and give her an excuse to escape. But now that the children had gone home, the noon hour tended to be slow. School would be starting in a few weeks and the last days of balmy temperatures would soon be a memory. People wanted to soak up the last bit of sunshine rather than check out a book to read.

Emma decided she had no option but to face his unexpected presence head-on.

"What can I do for you, Chief Sutton?"

"You can start by calling me Jake, remember?"

Emma wanted to say that wasn't a good idea, only she wasn't sure why. In a town the size of Mirror Lake, no one stood on ceremony. She'd even heard several people call Pastor Wilde by his first name at the picnic. But how could she explain to Jake that dropping his title felt as if she were removing a barrier?

A barrier Emma didn't *want* removed.

"Is this about the tools that Jeremy found? Does he have to make some kind of statement?" She hoped not. If Jeremy had to give a formal statement, it would mean a trip to the police department, and Emma had no desire to go there ever again. Just the thought tied her stomach into knots.

"No, this isn't about the tools—"

"Then if you'd like a library card, you can fill out this form." Emma gestured toward the applications stacked neatly in a plastic tray. "And I will need to see proof of residence."

"I stopped by to talk to you about the mentoring ministry that Church of the Pines started."

Emma's mouth turned as dry as the chalk she'd dusted on her cheeks before reading *Charlotte the Chef*. "I didn't realize you were involved."

"I'm on the prayer team." Jake's lips twisted in a wry smile. "But I also told the pastor I'd be willing to do whatever God wants me to."

Did he think that meant trying to change her mind?

"I planned to call Pastor Wilde today and let him know that Jeremy won't be able to participate." Although, knowing how disappointed he would be, Emma hadn't broken the news to her son.

"He wants to be involved, Emma."

Emma's heart gave a little kick when Jake said her name.

"He also wants to eat hot dogs for breakfast." She managed to lift her chin and meet that unsettling amber gaze straight on. "That doesn't mean it's good for him."

This was going to be more difficult than he thought.

Emma had scrambled for cover behind the desk the moment they were alone. Jake didn't know why she'd bothered. The rigid set of her shoulders and the wary look in her eyes proved effective enough barriers.

To anyone but him.

He might have been tempted to give up and walk out the door if the conversation he'd had with Matt wasn't still lodged in his head.

"Jeremy Barlow called the church an hour ago,"

Matt had told him. "That kid is something else. He said he's been praying about it and he is convinced that *you* are supposed to be his mentor."

"Did he say why?"

"No." Matt's smile had faded. "But it could have something to do with his dad being a police officer. It would make sense, wouldn't it? A boy that age might be curious about a man who pursued the same career as his father."

A career that had taken that father's life.

Jake had released a slow breath. There was a strong possibility that the reason Jeremy had chosen him as a mentor would be the same reason Emma would reject him.

She looked tempted to show him the door now. Fortunately, the library was open to the public so she had to endure his presence for the moment.

Okay, Lord, if this is Your idea, You are going to have to give me some wisdom here. I have no idea how to change Emma's mind.

Although it suddenly became clear to Jake that he wanted to.

What had started out as curiosity had undergone a subtle shift over the past hour. Maybe it had something to do with the fact that he'd seen Emma with her defenses down, waving a rolling pin as she recited a story for a mesmerized group of kindergartners.

To be honest, Jake had been a little mesmerized himself by the undercurrent of laughter he'd heard in her voice. The dusting of flour on the tip of Emma's nose that elevated her already pretty features to a winsome beauty.

She met his gaze, shields once again in place, but

this time Jake looked past the stubborn tilt of her chin and saw the vulnerable curve of her lips, and the fear crouched behind the defiant look in her eyes.

With a flash of insight that Jake assumed was an answer to his prayer, he heard himself ask, "How old was Jeremy when Brian died?"

The color drained from Emma's face and she flinched, leaving Jake to wonder how long it had been since she'd heard anyone say her husband's name.

Forget the barrier she'd put between them. In two strides, Jake was standing next to her. Not close enough to crowd, but close enough to catch her if she passed out on him.

Emma folded her arms across her chest. For a second, Jake didn't think she was going to answer. When she did, the word came out in a whisper.

"Four."

Jake had suspected Jeremy must have been close to that age when he'd lost his father, but hearing Emma confirm it twisted his gut.

What now, Lord?

In his former line of work, Jake had extracted information from people with the precision of a surgeon but now things had changed. *He* had changed. Jake knew he couldn't stir the well of Emma's grief and find the answers he was seeking without God's help.

"Does Jeremy ask a lot of questions about him?" he asked, feeling his way through unfamiliar territory.

"No." Emma hesitated. "He used to."

Jake read between the lines. Jeremy had asked questions until he was old enough to realize that it hurt his mother to talk about it.

"You're doing a great job with him, Emma," he

said. "Jeremy is bright. Curious. To tell you the truth, I'm a little intimidated by a kid who put down the word research under his list of hobbies and interests."

A ghost of a smile lifted the corners of her lips. "I've always encouraged him to study. To seek out the answers to his questions."

"That's what I mean." Jake was stunned by a sudden longing to see the rest of that smile. "I think Jeremy is at the age where he wants to test himself. Boys want to know what they're made of. Push the limits a little. And you want him to do that." He saw panic flare in Emma's eyes and added swiftly, "In healthy ways. Ways that will help him make a smooth transition from boy to man."

Emma remained silent.

"Emma?"

She looked at him and Jake could see the battle being played out in those expressive blue eyes.

"What are you afraid of?"

What was she afraid of?

There were so many things to choose from, Emma wasn't sure she could pick out only one.

She was afraid that letting Jeremy spend time with a mentor would prove that she wasn't doing her job.

She was afraid her son would need her less…or not at all.

She was afraid of letting Jeremy out of her sight because he was the only family she had left.

And she was afraid of the disturbing feelings that Jake Sutton stirred inside of her. Feelings Emma thought had been buried along with Brian.

He was close. Too close. Whenever Emma drew

in a breath, the clean scent of Jake's soap, mingled with a hint of lime, came with it, muddling her senses.

"I appreciate what Pastor Wilde is trying to do," Emma said stiffly. "I'm sure there are boys who would benefit from the mentoring program. But to be perfectly honest, I can't imagine allowing Jeremy to spend time with a stranger."

"What if the person wasn't a stranger? Would that make a difference?"

"I don't know." Emma tucked her lower lip between her teeth as she considered the question. "I suppose it might. But we haven't been going to church very long. Jeremy doesn't know many people."

And neither did she. Living in a small town, where it seemed as if everyone knew each other, had been intimidating to a young woman who had never settled in one place for very long. Emma had been more than content to remain in the background. After Brian's death, she had retreated even further in an attempt to avoid the awkward silences and the pity she saw on people's faces.

"He knows me," Jake said.

"You?" Emma almost choked on the word.

Jake didn't look offended by her strong reaction. "He called Pastor Matt this morning and requested that I be his mentor."

Requested. Jake Sutton.

Oh, Jeremy.

"But…" Emma pressed one hand against her forehead, trying to sort through this latest complication. "I don't understand."

But then again, maybe she did.

On her way to bed the night before, Emma had noticed a sliver of light under Jeremy's bedroom door. That hadn't surprised her. More often than not, she would find her son sound asleep with a book still propped up in his lap.

Only he hadn't been asleep. He'd been sitting up in bed, his gaze fixed on the arrowhead in his hand.

"And here I thought I'd find you reading up on Native American artifacts," Emma had gently teased.

"It's not the same." Jeremy had run his thumb over the jagged edges of the stone. The sparkle in his eyes had warned Emma that a change was coming. A change she didn't understand but knew she couldn't prevent.

He wanted to *find* arrowheads, not read about them.

That simple statement forced Emma to face her own limitations. Forced her to acknowledge that Jeremy needed something that she couldn't give him. She remembered the way Jake had boosted his confidence by letting him dig the hole for the apple tree.

How had Jake put it? That boys needed to test themselves?

The thought both terrified Emma and made her proud of her son at the same time.

But Jake Sutton?

A man who, like Brian, had chosen a dangerous career. A man whose scarred jaw and measured gaze were an unsettling contradiction to the one who'd clapped a battered cowboy hat on his head and completely charmed a rambunctious group of children.

If he saw Jeremy on a regular basis, did that mean she would have to see *him?*

Emma's knees turned to liquid at the thought.

"Would you consider letting Jeremy and me spend some time together for a trial period?" Jake asked. "After that, if you still believe it's a bad idea, you can withdraw him from the program. If you explained it to Jeremy, I think he would agree to that."

So did Emma. After all, as her son was quick to point out these days, it was *reasonable* for a person to check things out before they made a decision. If only she'd known her favorite saying would be used against her!

"A trial period," she repeated.

"How about a month?"

"I don't know." *I don't know you.* "What are your qualifications? Have you been involved in a mentoring program before?"

Jake looked up at the ceiling, providing Emma with a closer view of the pale grid of scars etching his jaw. "I don't have any experience with kids. This is all new to me, too."

It was the last thing Emma had expected him to admit.

"Then give me one good reason why I should trust you with my son."

"Because Jeremy wants you to."

Now who wasn't playing fair? Emma thought. Jake had to know that Jeremy was her reason for getting up in the morning. The last thing she wanted to do was deny her son something that put a sparkle in his eyes. Like the one she'd seen when he'd shown her the arrowhead…and talked about the crime that he and Jake had "solved together" on Saturday.

"Why do *you* want to do this?" Emma asked.

Jake's lips quirked. "Because Jeremy wants me to."

The same reason. Like it or not, concern for her son had become a connecting point between them.

"I'll agree to a month." Emma hoped she wasn't making a huge mistake.

"I'll tell Pastor Wilde." Jake started to walk away but paused when he reached the door. "And Emma?"

She forced herself to look at him.

"You *can* trust me."

As soon as the door closed, Emma sank against the desk.

Trust him?

At the moment, it was the feelings Jake stirred up inside of her that she didn't trust.

Chapter Eight

Jake's cell phone rang less than five minutes after he walked into the house.

He glanced at the tiny screen to read the name before answering it. It seemed that someone—and Jake had a hunch that someone's name was Delia Peake—had given his private number to everyone in Mirror Lake.

This time, however, it was safe to pick up.

"Whatsup, Bro?" Andy's cheerful greeting came over the line.

"Whatsup, *Bro?*" Jake echoed. "You've been spending too much time with the kids in your youth group."

But even as he gave Andy a hard time, Jake was glad the term "brother" came so easily. Jake had been twelve, Andy three years younger, when Jake's mom and Andy's dad had fallen in love. They had become linked together by their parents' marriage certificate, not blood. Jake and his best friend, Sean, had tormented the poor kid every chance they got, but Andy had never complained or tried to get back at him. Jake had thought of Sean as his brother, but when push came to shove, it had been Andy who hadn't given up on him. It was his prayers that had pulled Jake out of the darkness.

"There's no such thing as too much time with my kids," Andy said loyally. The thing was, Jake knew he meant it. "Are you on duty or off?"

"Am I ever off duty?"

"Should I get out my violin?" Andy paused. "Or my harp?"

"Did you call just to harass me?" Jake laughed, the sound of his brother's voice easing some of the tension that had settled in his shoulders after his visit to the library that morning.

"As entertaining as that can be, I called because God brought your name up while I was praying today."

"What time was that?" Jake asked suspiciously.

"This morning. About eleven o'clock."

Eleven o'clock. Roughly the same time he had gone to see Emma at the library.

Was he being tag-teamed?

"Really?"

"Yes, really. So, are you going to tell me why?"

Jake knew he could sum it up in two words. Emma Barlow. But he wasn't sure what would happen if he trusted that kind of intel to his kid brother.

That Emma had agreed—albeit reluctantly—to let him spend time with Jeremy on a trial basis had been nothing less than a miracle. Jake hadn't been quite sure how he'd come up with the idea…until now.

"Probably because I needed an extra dose of courage," Jake admitted.

"You?" Now it was Andy's turn to laugh. "The

undercover drug officer? The guy who walked into crack houses without a weapon? Made deals with the thugs whose pictures are on the bulletin board at the post office?"

Compared to Jake's newest assignment, his previous job *still* looked easier.

"The church I've been attending started a mentoring ministry. I got drafted."

And even more specifically, *requested.* In spite of his misgivings, that had been the reason Jake hadn't been able to say no.

That and two matching pairs of wide, gray-blue eyes.

"You? You're going to be a mentor to a…kid?"

"That's usually who needs a mentor. Are you laughing?" Jake demanded.

"No…" A series of muffled snorts followed the word.

"Uh-huh." Jake didn't have to be in the same room as his brother to know he was rolling on the floor. "I tried to tell the pastor it was a bad idea."

"What are you talking about?" Andy sobered immediately. "It's a great idea."

"You of all people should know that isn't true. Some people could question my judgment. My ability to be a good influence."

On the other side of the line, Andy expelled a slow breath. "You have to let it go, Jake," he said quietly. "No one saw the signs."

That wasn't much of a consolation. "I should have seen it. Sean was my best friend."

That was the thing about dwelling in the shadows

for so long. Eventually, they began to blur a person's perspective. Wrong started to look like…right.

"Sean made his choice. And if he'd had his way, we wouldn't be having this conversation."

A shared memory weighted the silence that fell between them. Andy's stricken face staring down at Jake when the paramedics wheeled him into the E.R. Both of them unsure if they'd ever see each other again.

As often as Jake had brushed aside Andy's faith or, even worse, poked fun at his brother for dropping out of medical school to attend the seminary instead, he hadn't felt as if he could appeal to God for help the night of the drug bust. The only thing Jake could do was look into the cold eye of the gun pointed at him and apologize to God for being stubborn. Tell Him that he wished he would have taken time to know Him when he'd had the chance—that he would do things differently if he could.

God hadn't only heard his prayer, He had intervened in a way that left Jake feeling a little like the apostle Paul on the road to Damascus.

Because the second bullet—the one aimed at his forehead—never left the gun. It jammed. And then the man holding it had crumpled to the floor, two feet away from Jake, before he could try again.

In his head, Jake knew what Andy said about Sean was right. It was taking his heart a little longer to catch up.

He rose to his feet and took a restless lap around the room. "For now, it looks like God wants me to spend some time with Jeremy, but I could definitely use some pointers."

"You're asking me for advice?" Andy's tone lightened, as if he sensed Jake's reluctance to talk about Sean.

"Don't let it go to your head. Kids are your thing, not mine."

"When do they match you up with someone?"

"They already did."

Andy's low whistle made Jake smile. "I told you that God wasn't going to waste any time. What's his name?"

"Jeremy Barlow."

"Troublemaker?"

"Not even close. Jeremy is on the shy side. Doesn't seem to have many friends. He's definitely a thinker."

"Rough home life?"

Rough home life.

Jake turned the words over. In his mind's eye, he could see an older house and the front porch that begged for a coat of paint. The twenty-year shingles on the roof that looked as if they'd been forced to last thirty. All home-maintenance projects that would have fallen on Brian Barlow's shoulders and yet they'd become another burden for Emma to bear.

He had no doubt the citizens of Mirror Lake would have chipped in to help if Emma had only let people know she had a need. He had a hunch that something beyond grief added to her resistance. No one could find fault, however, with her parenting.

"Emma is doing a good job but she can't do everything."

"Whoa, hold on a second," Andy said. "No need to get defensive. It was a question, not a judgment. And who is Emma?"

"Jeremy's mom. Her husband was a cop here in Mirror Lake. He died six years ago in a high-speed chase. Jeremy was only four years old at the time."

"That's rough. So how does she feel about you mentoring Jeremy?"

"She doesn't…approve of me."

"But you're one of the good guys," Andy protested.

"I'm not sure she thinks so," Jake said. "She's very protective. And she isn't sold on the idea of her son spending time with someone she doesn't know."

"I have the perfect solution for that."

"You do?"

"Let her get to know you."

"Jake wants to take me fishing, Mom!"

Emma's heart turned a somersault at the announcement. The fact that she knew this was coming, had even agreed to it, didn't seem to matter when faced with the reality of what she'd agreed to.

For Jeremy's sake, Emma tried not to let him see her reaction. "When?"

"Tomorrow night." Jeremy's thin frame practically vibrated with excitement. "But he said to make sure it was okay with you first."

How nice of Jake, Emma thought. She didn't want him to be thoughtful. Or considerate. It was easier to keep her distance when all she saw was a badge.

Jake had claimed he understood how difficult it was for her to let Jeremy spend time with him, and yet their very first outing was a fishing trip. Couldn't he have chosen something that didn't involve water? What was wrong with going out for ice cream? Playing catch at the ball field? Not that Jeremy *liked* base-ball, but still…

"You don't have a fishing pole." A weak excuse, but the only one she could come up with on such short notice.

"I saw one in the shed."

Emma turned toward the sink, blinking back the tears that blurred her vision. After Brian's death, other than a few special mementos she'd saved for Jeremy, Emma had given the rest of his things to a local charity. She didn't remember keeping his fishing pole.

"So, can I go?" Jeremy pleaded.

"I suppose."

He let out a whoop that rattled the light fixture on the ceiling. "Really? You won't be mad?"

The innocent question pierced Emma's conscience.

Had she really been that unreasonable lately?

Yes, she had.

Emma forced a smile. "I won't be mad."

Jeremy lifted the telephone that Emma hadn't seen clutched in his hand. "Mom says it's okay."

Jake was on the phone? Emma hadn't even heard it ring! She stifled a groan. Had he heard her pitiful attempt to discourage her son from going?

Probably.

"Okay." Jeremy's smile didn't dim. "Here she is." He handed her the phone. "Jake wants to talk to you."

"H-hello."

"Hi, Emma." Jake's husky voice raised goose bumps on her arms. "If I didn't have a city council meeting tomorrow after work, I would accept your dinner invitation."

Her *dinner* invitation?

"I...understand." Emma understood that she and her son were going to sit down and have a talk!

"I'll definitely take you up on it another time, though."

"Another time," she echoed faintly.

"I'll stop by around six o'clock to pick up Jeremy, if that works for you."

"He's looking forward to it."

"So am I."

Emma hung up the phone and turned on her son. "Jeremy Barlow—don't you ever invite someone to dinner without asking me first."

The guileless blue eyes widened. "But Mom, don't you like Jake?"

The unexpected question punched the air from Emma's lungs. "It doesn't matter if I like him."

"Yes, it does." Jeremy's worried expression heaped guilt on top of her anxiety.

"I like him." Emma pushed the words out. "He seems...nice." Inwardly she winced at the generic description. One that didn't begin to describe the man whose unexpected appearance at the library the day before had turned her world upside down.

The answer seemed to satisfy Jeremy, however, because his sunny smile returned. "I like him, too. A lot."

That was another thing Emma was afraid of.

Jake turned off the ignition and stared at Emma's house, wondering how he could convince her to let him tackle some of the minor repairs around the place. It had been difficult enough to get her to agree to let him spend time with Jeremy.

Window boxes filled with yellow flowers and rosebushes planted along the stone foundation added homey touches but couldn't hide the peeling paint or the porch that listed to one side.

As he got out of the car, the front door flew open.

"Hi, Jake!" Jeremy hurtled toward him.

"Ready to do some fishing?"

"Yup." Jeremy nodded vigorously. "I found a pole in the shed. It was my dad's."

The announcement stripped the air from Jake's lungs. He wanted to be there for Jeremy, but what if his efforts only succeeded in bringing back painful memories for Emma?

Then you'll be out of their lives in a month, he reminded himself.

For some reason, the thought settled like a weight on Jake's chest. What was the matter with him? He didn't form attachments easily and yet somehow, Emma and her son had already worked their way under his skin.

"The trunk is open. Go ahead and load up your stuff," Jake instructed. "I have to talk to your mom."

"Okay." Jeremy headed for the car. "She's inside."

Jake rapped on the door but didn't wait for an invitation before going inside. Emma might have had trouble keeping up with general maintenance on the outside of the house, but on the inside, pale yellow walls and white crown molding gave the interior a warm, welcoming look.

The foyer branched off in several directions so Jake picked the one that he guessed would lead him to the kitchen.

His heart tipped at the sight of Emma standing in

the middle of the room, hands propped on her slender hips as she stared down at an enormous wicker trunk. Tendrils of honey-streaked hair had escaped the wide gold clip at the nape of her neck and framed her delicate features.

Jake fought a sudden urge to smooth them back into place.

He'd deliberately scheduled some time with Jeremy right away—before Emma could change her mind—but the pensive expression on her face pinched his conscience. It was clear that even though Emma had approved the fishing trip, she was having second thoughts about letting her son go.

He braced a hand on each side of the doorway. "I did knock."

Emma visibly started at the sound of his voice. "Jake."

Finally. Jake had started to wonder if she would ever drop the title and call him by his first name. He nodded at the trunk. "Do you need some help with that?"

"Thank you." Emma's polite mask fell back into place. "It is a little heavy."

"Where does it go?"

"Wherever you have room."

Wherever *he* had room?

"You want me to take this along?" Jake had to be sure he understood.

Emma nodded. "I packed a few things in the picnic basket for you and Jeremy."

A picnic basket? It was closer to the size of a laundry hamper.

Jake clamped down on a smile. Even with his rusty

social skills, he knew it probably wouldn't be a good idea to point out they were only going to be gone a few hours. "What's in it?"

"Juice boxes. Oatmeal cookies."

"Healthy." Jake hoped that Jeremy would have room for an ice-cream sundae on the way home.

"Disposable washcloths."

"Always a good idea." When Jake saw Emma's frown, he decided it might be wiser to simply smile and nod.

"I don't have bug spray," Emma said. "Did you bring some?"

Jake had a hunch he was being tested. But fortunately, he knew the correct answer. Emma wasn't the only one who had come prepared.

"It's in the tackle box. Right next to the first-aid kit."

The flash of startled approval in Emma's eyes had Jake silently thanking the mother of twin boys who'd been standing behind him in line at the sporting-goods store. She'd overheard Jake talking to the cashier about his upcoming fishing trip and handed him the little white box.

"You'll need one of these," she'd whispered.

Jake had glanced at the red cross stamped on the cover—and then at the price tag. "Ten dollars for Band-Aids and antibiotic ointment?"

"Ten dollars for peace of mind," the woman had said with a wise smile.

Without another word, Jake had tossed it into the cart. Now he was glad he had.

Jeremy skidded into the kitchen. "I'm ready, Jake. Let's go!"

Chapter Nine

Emma laced her fingers together to stop them from shaking. She wished she could take back her decision. Wished that some things could stay the same.

But she forced a smile on the outside so her sensitive son wouldn't suspect that she was crumbling on the *inside*.

"Did you remember your jacket?"

"I have a sweatshirt. It's not cold out, Mom."

She caught her lip between her teeth. "I guess you're right."

"Why don't you get in the car, Jeremy?" Jake suggested softly. "I'll be right there."

"Okay." Jeremy ran over and locked his arms around her waist. "Bye, Mom!"

"Bye, sweetheart."

Jeremy squirmed in her arms and Emma forced herself to let go. Now if only she could hold herself together a few more seconds until Jake left.

Only he didn't leave.

"Are you all right?"

"I'll be fine." When they returned.

"I remember when I was a kid, my mom always wanted to know one thing if I made plans to do something. *Details*." Jake reached down and picked up the wicker basket. "Of course I didn't realize at the time that her 'one thing' really meant a lot of things. I thought I was getting off easy." He flashed the smile that never failed to set her pulse racing.

Emma wanted to return his smile. She stared at a point over his shoulder instead.

"Since Jeremy doesn't know what we're going to do this evening, I'll fill you in," Jake said, as if she'd asked. "We're not taking a boat out on the lake. Abby offered the use of her dock at the lodge. I'll make sure Jeremy wears a life jacket, since you mentioned that he doesn't know how to swim. I can though, by the way." He handed her a piece of paper. "Here's my cell phone number. Feel free to call. Just to say hello, if you want to."

Jake had read her mind.

Emma didn't know whether to be relieved or terrified. And she could see that he wasn't poking fun at her concerns, he was trying to ease them. Emma wasn't used to having someone who could read her thoughts so easily. Wasn't used to letting someone *close* enough to read her thoughts.

"Thank you." She focused on the number written on the piece of paper, silently willing him to go, but it was clear Jake wasn't finished with her yet.

"Now it's my turn to get some details from you. What time would you like me to bring Jeremy home?"

"How about eight o'clock?" Two hours should be more than enough time to catch a few fish, Emma reasoned.

"All right." Jake tilted his head. Studied her. And then, "Would you like to come with us?"

Emma didn't think she'd heard him right. "With you?"

"Sure. I don't mind and I'm sure Jeremy wouldn't, either."

Emma was tempted by the invitation. But the whole idea behind the mentoring program was to give Jeremy an opportunity to spend time with the mentor, not the mother.

"No, you two go ahead. Male bonding and all that." She ran damp palms down the front of her khaki skirt. "I have a project I'm working on for Abby."

"Are you sure?"

"I'm sure." She wasn't. Not at all. "I'll see you in a few hours."

"I'll take good care of him, Emma."

"I know you will."

Surprise flared in Jake's eyes but Emma couldn't blame him.

She'd surprised herself.

"When can we go fishing again, Jake?"

"I'm not sure." It was the second time Jeremy had asked the question since they'd left Mirror Lake Lodge, and now that his house was in sight, he was eager for an answer.

The porch light flickered a welcome as Jake parked the car in the driveway. Had Emma spent the entire evening staring out the window, counting the minutes until they returned?

Jake had made a point to get Jeremy home early. He knew what it had cost Emma to turn down his invitation to go fishing with them. She could have gone along and kept an eye on her son, and yet she hadn't wanted to get in the way of "male bonding." The last thing Jake wanted to do was damage the fragile trust she'd placed in him.

"I'll have to check with your mom first."

"You can talk to her now." Jeremy unbuckled his seat belt and bailed out of the car, leaving behind the faint but unmistakable scent of fish in the air.

He may have brought Jeremy home early but not exactly in the same condition the boy had been in when they left.

Not that he was, either.

A ribbon of light unfurled across the yard as Emma opened the door and stepped onto the porch.

"Hi, Mom! We're back!"

"I see that." Emma's smile bloomed in response to her son's enthusiasm. "How was the fishing?"

"Great." Jeremy swaggered toward her, the fishing pole balanced on his shoulder. "We caught a lot, didn't we, Jake?"

"We did." They'd lost a lot more, but that had been his fault!

"Jake's going to cook them up for us next time."

If, Jake thought, there *was* a next time. Maybe Emma had changed her mind and decided that two hours, not four weeks, was enough of a "trial period."

A breeze stirred the evening air and Emma's nose wrinkled. "I think someone is going to need a shower before bed."

"Okay." Jeremy grinned and turned to Jake. "I had a lot of fun. Thanks, Jake." He ran into the house, leaving them alone with the awkward silence that fell between them.

Emma backed against the door. Judging from the uncertain look in her eyes, Jake guessed she was torn over whether or not to invite him in. He made the decision for her.

"I'll get the rest of the things out of the trunk, but before I do, this is for you." Jake held out a plastic cup.

"What is it?" Emma cast a dubious look at the contents.

"It's an ice-cream sundae. At least it used to be," Jake amended. The maraschino cherry that adorned the top had sunk to the bottom and the ice cream had changed from a solid to a liquid during the short drive from the Grapevine Café to the house. "Jeremy mentioned that hot fudge is your favorite kind."

"It is." Emma finally reached out and took the cup but she continued to stare down at the sundae as if she'd never seen one before.

"If it makes you feel better, we ate the oatmeal cookies first."

Emma smiled and Jake felt the impact down to his toes. It wasn't the first time he'd seen it, but it was the first time she'd directed it at *him*. It also gave him the courage to discover the answer to the question that had been chewing at the edge of his thoughts all evening.

"How did you do tonight?"

"It was…hard."

She'd told him the truth, so Jake decided he couldn't do any less.

"What would you say if I told you that I was just as afraid to take him as you were to let him go?"

Emma lifted curious eyes to his face. "What do you mean?"

Jake wasn't sure if he could even put it into words. Sitting on the dock, listening to Jeremy's laughter stir the evening air. Watching his expression when he reeled the first fish in. Seeing those blue eyes light up whenever Jake praised his effort.

It had left him feeling…renewed.

Until now, Jake hadn't realized the toll his undercover work had taken on him. The subtle change that occurred when a man grew so accustomed to the darkness that he forgot what it was like to live in the light.

Let Emma get to know you, Andy had said. But there were some things he couldn't tell her.

But he *could* tell her this.

Unable to resist this time, Jake reached out and tucked a strand of hair behind her ear. He leaned closer.

"I've never been fishing before."

Chapter Ten

Jake left Emma standing on the porch, trying to make sense of his words. And his touch.

Dazed, she made her way upstairs just as Jeremy emerged from the bathroom, his hair damp from the shower. With the dirt removed and a damp towel draped over his shoulder instead of a fishing creel, he looked more like her little boy. To Emma's relief, he smelled better, too.

"Did Jake leave?"

Emma managed a nod.

"Did you like the sundae?" Jeremy spotted the plastic cup in her hand. "It was Jake's idea."

"That was very thoughtful of him." She was beginning to see that's the kind of man Jake was. The kind who talked about his faith with the easy confidence of one who believed it. The kind who took a boy fishing and invited his mother along in order to ease her fears.

If only the others could be put to rest as easily, Emma thought.

Jeremy darted into his bedroom and flipped on

the light on the nightstand. Emma followed, bending down to collect a trail of dirty clothes along the way.

"I'm glad you had a good time."

"You can come with us next time if you want to." Jeremy peeled back the comforter and dived beneath it.

"We'll see."

Emma decided to save that particular discussion for later. She reached for the light switch. "Do you want this off?"

"Not yet. I'm going to read awhile."

The librarian in Emma couldn't help but be pleased. "Let me guess—a book about fishing."

"Nope." Jeremy slid open the drawer in the nightstand and reached inside.

Emma sat down hard at the foot of the bed, her gaze riveted on the little white Bible Jeremy had tugged out of the drawer. "Where did you find that?"

"In a box of books downstairs." Jeremy looked surprised by the question. "Mr. Redstone told us that the Bible is one of the ways God talks to us, so I read it every night before I go to bed."

"I see." Emma moistened her lips, unsure of what to say. Or do.

A few days ago, she would have kissed Jeremy on the forehead and fled. Today, guilt weighed her down. She had always prided herself on having a close relationship with her son. Had always encouraged him to share his thoughts and ideas…until recently, since they'd started attending church.

Emma's conflicted emotions about faith clashed with the desire to understand her son's.

"What are you reading?"

Jeremy's shoulders relaxed and Emma knew she'd asked the right question. It hurt to realize that Jeremy hadn't thought he could share a part of his life that had become so important over the past few weeks.

"I'm reading the New Testament right now, but I told Jake that I'd look up his verse."

"*His* verse?" Emma said faintly.

Jeremy nodded. "He doesn't know many verses cause he's a new Christian, too, so he said he'd help me memorize mine if I helped him memorize his."

It didn't surprise Emma to discover that Jake was a Christian. He had volunteered with the mentoring ministry, after all. It was the "new" part that stirred her curiosity.

"Jake said his brother, Andy, told him to learn this one." Jeremy thumbed through the translucent pages with a speed that made Emma blink. "Andy is a pastor, like Pastor Matt, only he talks to kids. He's the one who told Jake about God."

Emma's head started to spin. Apparently Jake and Jeremy had done more than fish that evening. Judging from the amount of information her son was sharing, they must have spent as much time, if not more, in conversation!

"Here it is. It's in Ephesians chapter three." Jeremy squinted at the tiny words. "Do you want me to read it out loud?"

Emma nodded, not trusting her voice at the moment.

"'And I pray that you, being rooted and established in love, may have the power, together with all the saints, to grasp how wide and long and high and deep is the love of Christ.'" Jeremy read slowly, the tip of his finger tracing each word. "Wow, that's a long one," he said when he came to the end of the verse.

"Yes, it is." The room felt hot as the meaning of the words soaked in.

Why had Jake's brother chosen that particular passage of Scripture? Did it hold some sort of special significance?

Why do you care? an inner voice chided.

Emma brushed the question away, afraid of what the answer might be.

"It's time for you to get some sleep now," she murmured.

"Are you going to pray with me tonight, too, Mom?"

Emma saw the expectant look on Jeremy's face and couldn't turn him down, even though it had been years since she had talked to God. But she wasn't willing to let her own doubts and insecurities sever the closeness between them.

"All right."

"I'll go first." Jeremy bowed his head. "God, thank You that Mom let me go fishing with Jake. Thanks for all the fish we caught and that it didn't rain. Help Jake memorize the long verse, because he said it gets harder to remember things when you get older..."

Emma found herself smiling, until Jeremy's elbow nudged her side. "It's your turn, Mom," he whispered.

"Sorry." She'd missed her cue.

As she opened her mouth, a wave of panic crashed over her.

Don't be silly, she thought, *just say something. Thank God for the sunshine...*

"You can tell Him anything, Mom," Jeremy whispered. "Mr. Redstone told us in Sunday school that you can be honest with God because nothing you say is going to change how much He loves you."

What about the things you *didn't* say, Emma thought. What if you'd stopped talking to God because you couldn't find the words that described how you were feeling?

Or because you weren't sure He loved you at all?

She squeezed Jeremy's hand. At least there was one thing she could say with absolute certainty. "Thank you, God, for Jeremy. Amen."

"Amen." Jeremy burrowed deeper underneath the covers.

"Now good night." Emma planted a kiss on his forehead and stood up. "We have to be at the library by eight tomorrow."

"Okay." He stifled a yawn. "'Night, Mom."

As soon as Emma closed the door, she sank against the wall and let the tears spill over.

"Well? How did it go?"

Jake sighed into the phone and heard Andy chuckle. "That bad, huh?"

"Define 'bad.'"

"But Emma didn't change her mind, right? She let you take Jeremy fishing."

"This time." Right up until the moment Jake put the car into Drive, he hadn't been sure. He stepped out onto the deck and stared at the narrow strip of moonlight shimmering on the surface of the lake.

"Did the two of you get along?"

"Things were okay. Until I touched her—"

"Jake—"

"It wasn't inappropriate," Jake hastened to assure his younger brother. *The pastor.* "Her hair had come out of that little clip she wears and I just…"

Gave into the irresistible urge to see if it felt as soft and silky as it looked.

Jake gave himself another mental smack upside the head. If he wanted to earn Emma's trust, that hadn't exactly been the smartest way to go about it.

"Jake!"

"What?"

"I was asking if you and *Jeremy* got along," Andy said. "But if you want to talk about Emma, that's fine with me."

The undercurrent of laughter in his brother's voice warned Jake that he would never live this one down. "It's not what you think."

"What am I thinking?"

Jake's back teeth snapped together. "Can we *not* talk about Emma?"

"Sure," Andy said mildly. "But you're the one who brought her up. I was asking about Jeremy, remember?"

"Jeremy is a great kid." Jake grabbed at the opportunity to steer the conversation onto safer ground. "He didn't hold it against me that I promised to take him fishing and then, an hour later, I had to admit that I've never fished before in my life."

"That isn't entirely true, you know."

"I know you didn't believe this when I was *twelve,* and you probably aren't going to believe me now, but I wasn't trying to *catch* your goldfish," Jake grumbled.

"I found a string with a paper clip attached to it

next to the aquarium. It doesn't take a background in law enforcement to figure out what was going on."

"Circumstantial evidence," Jake muttered. "And you accused *me* of holding on to the past."

"You do," Andy said without malice. "But I have things that God is working on, too. Which means we're both under divine construction."

That might be true, Jake thought, but he had a long way to go to catch up to his brother. The foundation of Andy's faith had been built long ago, before their parents had even met. Not for Jake. God was starting from scratch with him. Most days Jake felt as if he were clinging to the cornerstone for strength, still surrounded by debris from the past.

"Jeremy would probably do better with someone who can answer his questions." And the boy had been full of them. In order to stop the flood, Jake had finally confessed that he was a new believer. But rather than being disappointed, Jeremy had seemed excited to discover they had something in common.

Go figure.

"If the Lord asks us to do something, He gives us the strength to accomplish it," Andy reminded him.

"See, that's what I'm talking about," Jake complained. "You always know what to say."

"Don't let the enemy convince you that you don't have anything to offer them," Andy had said right before he'd hung up.

At two-thirty in the morning, his brother's words cycled back through Jake's memory.

Offer *them?*

What had he meant by that?

He'd agreed to be a mentor because Jeremy needed someone willing to spend time with him.

But as Jake lay in bed, staring up at the ceiling, his thoughts drifted to Emma once again.

What did *she* need?

Emma didn't need this.

No matter how hard she tried to focus on her job, Jake kept invading her thoughts. And even when she wasn't thinking about *him,* the verse that Jeremy had read—*Jake's verse*—continued to play in her mind like the refrain of a familiar song.

Keeping her wayward thoughts in line proved difficult enough, but over the course of the day, Emma caught her gaze straying to the windows overlooking Main Street. In desperation, she began to contemplate rearranging the furniture in the library. Beginning with her desk.

By closing time, Emma couldn't wait to get home.

She locked the front door of the library and went to look for Jeremy. The last time she'd seen him, he had swiped a notebook and pen and disappeared into her office, a tiny cubbyhole located in the back of the building.

"Jeremy?"

"I'm over here, Mom," came the muffled reply.

She followed the sound of his voice to a corner at the far end of the library and found him sitting on the floor with his back against the oversize book section. "It's almost time to close up. Are you ready to go?"

"Almost."

Emma hid a smile as Jeremy gave her a distracted smile. The notebook lay open on his lap and he continued to furiously sketch something on the page. She tilted her head but it was difficult to interpret the drawing upside down.

"What are you working on?"

"The design for our raft," Jeremy replied without looking up. "Jake said he would get the supplies if I drew up the plans."

Raft. Jake. Supplies.

Emma's knees suddenly felt a little weak. She anchored an arm against the K–O shelf for support.

"The two of you are building a...raft?"

"For the contest during Reflection Days next weekend. We're going to win, too, because I have a really good idea." Jeremy nibbled thoughtfully on the end of the pen. "The raft that makes it all the way to the flag and doesn't sink gets a trophy."

Be. Calm.

"And Jake thinks this is a good idea?" Emma's voice thinned out.

"Uh-huh." Jeremy blinked up at her. "I just need five more minutes to think, Mom. Is that okay?"

"Sure, sweetheart," Emma said between gritted teeth.

Five minutes would give her plenty of time to make a phone call!

Chapter Eleven

"Go away."

Jake froze in the doorway of the café, pinned in place by Kate's scowl.

"All I want is a cup of coffee." He tried to bluff his way past her suspicions, but someone must have gotten to Kate first. The Grapevine definitely lived up to its name.

"Sure." Kate snorted. "You don't want coffee, you want to upset the delicate balance of my life."

"Phil said you love animals."

"I do love animals," came the prompt response. "I'm what is commonly referred to as a 'cat' person. In fact, I have two of them. And they rule over a very small house. Did you ask Abby?"

"I called her first," Jake admitted. "She said she'd love to take him, but when she and Quinn get married, they'll have Mulligan and Lady out at the lodge." Jake didn't add that he blamed Quinn O'Halloran for giving Abby time to come up with an excuse. Quinn had seen the dog turning somersaults in the backseat of the squad car after Jake had picked it up.

A thoughtful look entered Kate's eyes. "A dog like that needs a home in the country. And kids. Having a pet teaches responsibility. But not someone too young," she added quickly. "Ten or eleven is a good age. You know what they say about the bond between a boy and his dog."

Was it his imagination, or had she put delicate emphasis on the word "boy"?

Jake's eyes narrowed. She couldn't be thinking what he *thought* she was thinking.

"You don't mean Jeremy Barlow."

"Jeremy Barlow." Kate clapped her hands together. "Wow, that's a great idea, Jake."

"Oh, no." Jake was already shaking his head. "I can't show up at Emma's with a dog."

Especially *this* dog.

The campaign Delia Peake had single-handedly launched to capture the animal that had been terrorizing her neighborhood had come to a successful, if not surprising, conclusion. In the interest of maintaining public relations—and because he knew the woman wanted to gloat—Jake had responded to the call.

Upon his arrival, Delia had risen to her full height of four feet eleven inches, which brought her nose even with his badge.

"Chief Sutton." The tip of her pink walking stick had struck the ground with each syllable. "I don't care what you do with that garden-destroying, Dumpster-diving creature as long as you remove it from my yard. Immediately."

If Jake had known what he was getting into, he would have sent Phil Koenigs instead. Standing guard over the garden-destroying Dumpster diver had become his assignment for the rest of the day. Along with finding it a temporary foster home until more permanent arrangements could be made.

"Jeremy is an only child," Kate said, building her case with the finesse of a seasoned attorney. "He would probably love to have a dog."

Jake knew she might be right, but at the moment, Jeremy wasn't the one he was thinking about!

"Do you know Emma at all?"

"No, and I feel bad about that." Kate's expression clouded. "I went to school with Brian. His death hit everyone pretty hard—nothing like that had ever happened around here before. No one had gotten to know Emma and because she was such a private person, we didn't want to intrude on her grief. Maybe that wasn't the best thing. For the town, or for her and Jeremy."

She poured a cup of coffee—in a travel cup, Jake noticed—and handed it to him. "None of us has been able to get close to her. You're the first person to get your foot in the door, so to speak."

"If I show up with that dog, Emma is going to slam the door in my face," Jake muttered.

"Maybe. Maybe not."

Jake was spared further comment when his radio crackled. "Excuse me."

"No problem." Kate flashed an impish smile before flouncing back to the kitchen.

"Chief?" Steve Patterson's voice came over the radio. "Emma Barlow called the department about twenty minutes ago. I told her that you'd checked out for the day, but Mayor Dodd noticed your car parked in front of the café."

"Emma called?" Out of the corner of his eye, he saw Kate smile.

"She asked to talk to you, but she didn't say why she was calling."

Jake ignored the blatant curiosity he heard in the officer's voice. "I appreciate you letting me know."

The only problem was, Jake thought as he slid the radio back into the leather holster on his belt, everyone else at the department would know, too. If they didn't already.

Kate's head popped up in the pass-through window between the kitchen and the old-fashioned soda fountain. "The library closed ten minutes ago. You could probably catch Emma at home. The home that happens to be located on a dead-end road."

"I know where Emma lives," Jake said drily. "But thanks."

"Helping local law enforcement is my civic duty," Kate intoned.

Jake waited until he was outside before he rolled his eyes at the sky.

Tag-teaming again, Lord?

He slid into the driver's seat and turned on the radio to drown out the ruckus in the backseat.

"Take it easy, back there." Jake tried to sound soothing in order to stop the howling but the only thing he managed to do was turn up the volume.

Who was he kidding? Emma would never agree to take the dog in.

But she *had* called the department and asked to talk to him. Had Emma changed her mind because he'd crossed a line? Upset the delicate balance of her life, as Kate would say.

At least that evened things out between them.

Emma Barlow upset the delicate balance of *his* life, too.

Call him a glutton for punishment, but Jake turned off on Stony Ridge Road anyway.

He parked the car in front of the house but instead of going up to the door, he followed the soft strains of jazz music to the stone silo near the barn, thinking that Jeremy might be playing inside.

"Jeremy?"

No answer.

Jake ducked his head and slipped through the narrow doorway. He was about to call out the boy's name again when he heard the sound of glass breaking.

All his instincts kicked into gear as he lunged through another doorway into a small room attached to the silo. Jake stopped short as a glass missile hurtled toward the wall and broke into a rainbow of colorful fragments.

It wasn't Jeremy that he'd found. It was Emma. Streaks of gray cement covered her bare arms and the faded denim overalls she wore. It looked as if she'd been playing in the mud. Sunlight streamed through the windows, sparking off the gold threads in her hair.

"In another situation, this could qualify as disorderly conduct, you know."

Emma whirled around at the sound of his voice.

"What are you doing here?" she gasped.

Jake sauntered over to the radio and stabbed the tip of his finger against the power button. "One of the officers said you called."

"Yes, but I didn't dial 911," Emma said tartly.

Jake laughed, not put off by her response. She

looked too adorably rumpled to intimidate him. "I was on my way home and decided to swing by in person." He made a quick scan of the room as he spoke. An old wooden table, filled with baskets of broken glass and pottery, was centered along one wall. A pyramid of plastic buckets rose from a pallet in the corner. What the room lacked in space it made up for in natural light. A wall made up of tiny windows captured the sun like a prism.

"Is this your studio?"

"Nothing quite so lofty." Emma shook her head, the movement setting her ponytail into motion. "Like I keep telling Abby Porter, this is a hobby."

"Well, you're good at it." Jake studied the piece she had been working on. The top of a small, rather ordinary-looking table had been transformed with pieces of glass and colorful stone. At first glance, they seemed to be set into place with no particular thought or pattern. Jake looked more closely.

"It's the lake."

Emma stared at him in disbelief. "There's no blue in it."

"There doesn't have to be," Jake pointed out. "Water isn't always blue."

Without responding, Emma bent down and began to collect pieces of broken glass, the set of her shoulders an indication that Jake was once again guilty of trespassing. "You didn't have to drive over here," she finally said.

"I was on the way home. Your place isn't out of the way." Jake knelt down to help and the scent of strawberry shampoo teased his senses. "Did you need something?"

* * *

Yes, Emma thought. *I need you to leave me alone.*

Which didn't make sense, especially considering the fact that she was the one who'd contacted him. *By phone.* She hadn't expected Jake to stop by the house to talk to her in person. Or catch her in the middle of taking out her frustration on a box of innocent cups and saucers!

No one but Jeremy had ever seen her working on a mosaic. Not even Abby, who'd asked if some of her guests would be welcome to watch Emma work. Her response had been a polite but firm *no.*

Jake Sutton, as usual, hadn't waited for an invitation. He didn't hesitate to intrude upon the private areas of her life—and her heart.

Emma tried to resurrect some of the anger she'd felt after her conversation with Jeremy. "It's about this…raft contest," she sputtered, rattled by his closeness.

"Jeremy is pretty excited about it." Jake shifted his weight, bringing them close enough for Emma to see delicate flecks of gold leaf embedded in the amber depths of his eyes.

Concentrate, Emma!

"I'm sorry." He blew out a sigh. "I did warn you that this is all new to me. If you don't mind me asking, why don't you want Jeremy to compete in the race? I asked around today and a lot of boys his age sign up."

But not *my* boy, Emma wanted to protest.

"He's never even watched the events, let alone asked to participate in one of them," she said instead. "I don't understand this sudden interest in something he never seemed to care about before."

A heartbeat of silence stretched between them. "He's been interested, Emma, but he never pushed the issue because he thought *you* wouldn't want to."

"How can you say that?" Emma surged to her feet, her tone accusing.

Jake raked a hand through his hair. "*I* didn't say it. Jeremy did."

Emma didn't know if she believed him. But maybe it was because she didn't *want* to believe him. "But I've never told Jeremy that I didn't want to go to Reflection Days. Why would he say that?"

"Maybe because Jeremy is as protective of you as you are of him."

The quiet response splintered what remained of Emma's composure.

Jake must have misunderstood. If Jeremy had wanted to go to the Reflection Days celebration, he would have said something to her. Besides that, she had never come out and said they couldn't go. She just hadn't…encouraged it. And Jeremy hadn't seemed interested.

She *knew* her son. She was sensitive to his personality. His interests. Jeremy was an introvert, similar in temperament to her, so when it came to extracurricular activities or social situations, Emma hadn't forced him out of his comfort zone.

Because it would have forced you out of yours, too?

Emma closed her eyes, blindsided by the realization that Jake's interpretation of the situation could be right.

All this time, she'd thought that she was being sensitive to what Jeremy wanted, but Jake claimed that her son had been doing the same thing.

Taking care of her, protecting her, was a burden that Emma had never wanted to put on Jeremy's shoulders.

But apparently, Emma thought with a stab of pain, Jeremy had placed it on himself.

"Excuse me." She walked past Jake and stumbled out of the building into the sunshine.

That went well.

Jake took a moment to mentally beat himself up for the clumsy way he'd handled things.

If only he'd had a clue that Emma's concern about the raft race had prompted her phone call. Jeremy had been so pumped up about the upcoming Reflection Days celebration, Jake should have known he would mention it to his mother.

It might have helped if you would have mentioned it, too, Jake silently berated himself.

The night before, while he and Jeremy had been fishing off Abby's dock, a boat had skimmed past. Mayor Dodd and two other members of the city council had been on it. The mayor had waved a bright yellow flag and jovially explained it was time to put it in the water and mark the halfway point for the raft race.

Noticing the way Jeremy's attention continued to stray from the bobber floating in the lily pads to the yellow flag flapping on a buoy offshore, Jake had asked if he participated in any of the events held during Reflection Days.

Making conversation, that's all he'd been guilty of. He hadn't expected Jeremy to say he'd never even *attended* the celebration that had become an annual tradition in Mirror Lake.

It hadn't taken Jake long to discover that Jeremy was in a tough spot, torn between not wanting to upset his mother and yet wanting to compete in some of the events.

He hadn't expected Jeremy to put him in a tough spot, too.

The boy had asked if Jake had ever been afraid to do something. When Jake admitted that he had, Jeremy asked if being afraid should stop a person from doing something.

Naturally, Jake had said no. More times than he could count, he'd faced dangerous situations in his line of work.

Jeremy's thoughtful nod had made Jake feel as if he were getting the hang of this mentoring thing. Until Jeremy's next question had blindsided him.

"Then can we enter the raft race together?"

Saying yes had brought an immediate smile to Jeremy's face. Jake should have known that Emma would have a different reaction to the news.

Once again, he was going to have to convince her to trust him. If he could catch up to her. Emma was probably already in the house by now…

He strode outside and found her rooted in place, her gaze fixed on a point farther up the driveway.

She glanced at him, confusion replacing the pain he'd seen in her eyes a few moments ago.

"Is your car moving?"

Chapter Twelve

Jake had forgotten about the dog.

How could he have forgotten about the dog?

At the moment, however, he was thankful for any distraction that had erased the stricken look from Emma's eyes.

"Yes, it is, but I'd keep my distance if I were you."

Emma ignored the warning and quickened her pace, forcing Jake to increase his stride to keep up with her.

"What is it?"

"Mrs. Peake's tomato-eating raccoon."

Now she stopped. "You put a raccoon in the *backseat?*"

"I couldn't exactly put it in the trunk. As tempting as that was," Jake added darkly. "Don't get too close—"

Emma reached the car and bent down to peer inside the window. A furry body slammed against the glass.

She jumped backward, almost toppling Jake over.

A pink tongue swiped the window in the exact spot her face had been.

"I know you're from the city," Emma said cautiously. "But that isn't a raccoon, Jake. It's a *dog*."

"Tell that to Mrs. Peake." Jake shook his head. "She ordered a live trap for 'troublesome wild animals' and she's convinced that's exactly what she caught."

The dog, in a blatant attempt to cultivate sympathy, began to whine. A thin, pitiful sound that had Emma stepping up to the window again. "It looks like a Lab mix."

"And sounds like it swallowed a siren." Jake winced. "I've been listening to that all day. I tried to bribe him with food, biscuits, a rawhide chew and a rubber ball but no deal."

"Do you know who he belongs to?"

"No idea or he'd be back home, safe and sound, by now. No one has reported a missing dog and this guy has been on the loose for over a week. He's either lost or abandoned." Jake had a hunch it was the second. He tapped on the glass but the mournful wail continued.

Emma pushed her fingers through the opening Jake had left in the window and fondled a silky ear.

The whining stopped. Just like that.

"What did you do?" Jake demanded.

"I think he wants some attention, that's all." She reached in farther to scratch the dog's other ear. "You can let him out while we wait for Jeremy to come out. He probably doesn't like being cooped up."

Jake hesitated, remembering the condition of his office after he'd had the same thought. "It's probably safer to leave him in the car. He's pretty wound up. I shut him in the storage room this afternoon and he tried to dig his way out."

"What are you going to do with him?" Emma wanted to know. "The closest animal shelter is almost an hour away."

Jake didn't want to be reminded. In spite of Kate's brilliant plan to pawn the animal off on Emma, he doubted that she would be willing to take him in.

"I'm going to bring him home with me for the night. Tomorrow I'll call around and see if there's an opening at a shelter."

"He's not going to like being in a kennel there, either."

Emma opened the door before Jake could stop her. The dog shot out of the backseat as if someone had launched it from a cannon…and then dropped at her feet and rolled over.

Jake's mouth fell open.

"Definitely out of control." Emma's lips curved into a smile as she reached down to rub the dog's belly.

"He likes you."

"Don't be silly," Emma said briskly. "He likes attention."

"I gave him attention," Jake reminded her.

"You gave him toys."

Jake opened his mouth to argue…and then realized she was right.

"Hi, Jake!" The front door slammed and Jeremy bounded up, bypassing him and going straight for the animal lying prone at his mother's feet. "Cool! Is this your dog?"

"It's a stray I picked up today."

"A stray!" Excitement backlit the blue eyes. "Can't we keep him, Mom?"

Emma was already shaking her head. "He doesn't belong to us, sweetheart."

"But he doesn't belong to anyone else, either," Jeremy said reasonably. "So why can't we keep him?"

"I don't think that's a good idea."

"Why not?"

Why not?

Emma could come up with a dozen reasons. Well, at least two.

"You're starting school in a few weeks and I'm at work all day." Emma could tell she was weakening. Unfortunately, so could her son.

"How about a trial period?" Jeremy pushed. "To see if he likes us?"

Jake coughed but Emma knew he'd done it to hide a laugh. Emma's huff of exasperation covered one of her own. What was she getting into? She didn't even know if the dog was housebroken.

The dog licked her hand and whined, as if adding an appeal of its own.

"We're not really set up to take in a dog on such short notice." Emma scratched the furry muzzle and heard a contented sigh. "We don't have any dog food."

"I have a bag in the car." At her incredulous look, Jake lifted his hands. "Hey, it was either provide kibble or have holes eaten in the upholstery."

Emma raised an eyebrow. A comment like that was supposed to convince her to bring the dog into their home?

"It sure looks like he's settled down a lot, though," Jake said, immediately recognizing the error of his ways. "I don't think he's destructive. Like you said, he just needs some attention."

"I can give him lots of attention." Jeremy grinned up at her.

"We'll keep him for the weekend and see if we all get along. That's the only promise I'm willing to make." Emma only hoped she wouldn't regret the decision!

"I'll show him my room." Jeremy jumped to his feet. "Come on—" He looked at Jake. "What's his name?"

"You can do the honors." Jake lowered his voice. "I won't tell you what Mrs. Peake called him."

Emma hid a smile. Delia Peake served as the chairwoman of the library board. The woman had a backbone as strong as her pink walking stick.

"I'll think of one." Jeremy patted his leg. "Come on."

The dog looked at Emma, as if asking for permission. She wasn't fooled for a minute. This had to be some sort of conspiracy. She waved her hands. "Go on. You may as well let Jeremy take you on a tour of the place."

The dog rolled to its feet and grinned, the pink tongue unfurling like a ribbon.

"He knew what you said. He's smart, isn't he?" Jeremy said.

"He seems to be." Emma's eyes narrowed on Jake. The smug expression on the man's face had her wondering if this hadn't been his plan all along!

"You might want to give him a dish of water," Jake suggested.

"You aren't leaving, are you, Jake?" Jeremy's worried gaze shifted from Jake to his mother.

"I'll stick around for a few minutes."

"Mom, can Jake stay for supper?"

"Jeremy!" Emma choked on the word.

Her son looked at her, wide-eyed. "What? I asked you first this time."

Out of the corner of her eye, Emma saw Jake smile. He would realize that she'd been backed into a corner and offer her a way out.

"I'm sure Jake already has dinner plans." *Please have other dinner plans.*

The glint in Jake's eyes told her that he'd read her mind.

"I'd love to stay."

"What are you two doing out there?"

Jake winked at Jeremy as he handed him another nail. "Tell her it's guy stuff."

"It's guy stuff, Mom."

"Guy stuff, hmm? That explains why it's so noisy." Emma's sigh was audible through the window screen. "Supper will be on the table in five minutes."

Jake had waited until Emma disappeared inside the house before asking Jeremy if he would like to assist him in a small project. Just as Jake had suspected, Jeremy was more than willing to help. He had led Jake to the barn, where a rusty box held the tools they needed.

He wasn't sure how Emma would react to him fixing the loose boards on the porch. Especially considering he'd already turned her day upside down by signing Jeremy up for the raft race without her permission. And dumping a stray dog into her lap.

"How does this look?" Jeremy sat back on his heels.

Jake surveyed his work. "One or two more whacks with the hammer should do it."

Twin lines of concentration plowed rows between Jeremy's eyebrows as he followed Jake's instructions. "Is this better?"

"It looks great."

Emma poked her head around the door. "Come in and wash up now."

"We're fixing some loose boards on the porch, Mom."

"I see that."

Something in her tone told Jake that his list of misdemeanors was growing by the minute.

They trooped inside and washed up at the kitchen sink. The house boasted no formal dining area but Emma had tucked a small oak table in the corner. The table had already been set for three, the floral china arranged just so. Not a paper plate or plastic fork in sight.

Jake sniffed the air appreciatively. A pan of lasagna served as the centerpiece, the cheese still bubbling around the edges. A basket heaped with garlic bread and a salad completed the meal.

The comfortable setting was so far removed from what he was used to, he wasn't sure what to do next. As an undercover drug officer, the places he'd called "home" over the past few years hadn't been the kind that encouraged people to linger. The furniture, what there was of it, reeked of cigarette smoke. Dishes would pile up for days, waiting until someone came down from their high long enough to do a cursory cleaning.

"You can sit here, Jake." Jeremy pointed to the chair next to his.

"As long as I don't have to share my garlic bread."

Jake had meant it as a joke, but when he glanced at Emma, the color had drained from her face, making her eyes appear even more blue.

"Is something wrong?"

"No. Please, sit down." Emma glanced at the chair that Jeremy had offered him. The one at the head of the table.

Brian's chair.

Chapter Thirteen

He should have known better.

If Andy called tonight, asking for details, his brother would probably contact Matt and have him removed from the team of mentors.

"I'll sit here instead." Jake pulled one of the other ladder-back chairs away from the table and sat down. "That way, I can fight you for the garlic bread *and* the salad." He winked at Jeremy.

"Okay." Jeremy grinned but didn't reach for either one. "Should we pray, Mom?"

Emma's head jerked up and her gaze collided with Jake's across the table. "You go ahead, sweetheart."

Jeremy closed his eyes. "Lord, thank You for this food and thank You that Jake could stay for supper. Thanks for Shadow and I pray that he likes it here. Amen."

Emma might have offered up a thank-you for the food, but Jake wasn't sure she would have joined Jeremy in thanking God for the rest. Especially considering that he and the dog hadn't been on the guest list for the evening meal.

"You named him Shadow?" Emma looked up.

"He looks like one, don't you think?" Jeremy reached down and patted the dog on the head.

The dog's tail began to thump out a gentle beat against the floor, almost as if it approved of the name.

"He was as hard to catch as one," Jake said. "But he seems happy here."

If he didn't know better, Jake would have thought someone had switched dogs when his back was turned. The one who'd terrorized the police department all day now lay stretched out on the rug, the picture of contentment.

"I showed Mom the plans for our raft, Jake." Jeremy's smile glowed as bright as the candle burning in the center of the table. "We have to sign up for the race by Monday."

Emma's strong reaction to the raft race had left Jake hoping for another opportunity to discuss it with her. The last thing he wanted to do was undermine her authority as a parent.

"When we talked about the raft race last night, I assumed you had your mother's permission to enter," Jake said carefully.

Jeremy sank a little lower in the chair and peeked at his mother from beneath a thick fringe of sandy brown lashes. "Is it okay with you, Mom?"

Emma gave a short nod. "I suppose so. As long as Jake is willing to help you."

"He promised he would." Jeremy's expression shifted from relieved to anxious once again. "Didn't you, Jake?"

"Yes, I did." Jake was glad he could put the boy's

mind at ease now that Emma had given her permission.

Jeremy passed the bowl of salad to him. "The first thing we have to do is build a model of my design to make sure it floats."

"Can't you just build the raft ahead of time?" Emma asked.

"Uh-uh." Jeremy shook his head. "That's one of the rules. You have to bring the stuff to make it and build it right there. And you only get ten minutes to do it. You can't use parts of a real boat, either. Or sails. You have to paddle them. Some of the rafts tip over right away because of the uneven weight distribution, but I know a way around that."

Jeremy paused to take a breath and Emma squeezed in another question. "How do you know so much about the race?"

"I've been thinking about it for a few years now," Jeremy said matter-of-factly. "I just got tired of being afraid to *do* it. Jake said that being afraid shouldn't stop a person from doing the things they want to do."

Jake said.

The words hung in the air between them.

Great, Jake thought. Between the dog and the raft race, he'd probably worn out his welcome. The trouble was, he was in no hurry to leave.

He wanted to linger over the best meal he'd had in ages. And finish fixing the porch.

And spend more time with Jeremy and Emma.

While his head questioned whether he belonged there—with them—his heart seemed more than ready to make itself at home.

"You were afraid sometimes when you were undercover, weren't you, Jake?" Jeremy tucked into his lasagna, unaware of the growing tension at the table.

"That's right." Jake just hadn't expected it to come up again as dinner conversation!

Emma's eyes darkened in confusion. "But that was a long time ago, wasn't it? You must have had a desk job of some kind before you came to Mirror Lake. A patrol officer doesn't just skip to the rank of police chief."

She was right. But that "patrol officer" could skip a few rungs on the department ladder when God had a hand in things.

"Technically, I held the rank of sergeant when I left my last job."

"But why did you move to Mirror Lake? Do you have family in the area?"

"No." The innocent question pinched a nerve. Jake had limited contact with his family when he'd agreed to go undercover, telling himself it was best for everyone that way. Andy had tried to set him straight at the time, but he hadn't listened. Rebuilding a relationship had come more slowly with his mom and stepdad than with his stepbrother. "Mirror Lake is the place I'm supposed to be. I believe that God brought me here for a reason."

And now that he'd met Jeremy and Emma, that reason was becoming a little more clear. From what he could see, Emma's grief had formed a protective wall around both of them for so long, it almost seemed as if they'd become trapped inside of it.

Emma's smooth brow furrowed. "You think that God cares about things like that?" she asked hesitantly.

Jake met her doubtful gaze head-on. "I know He does."

"That's because God saved Jake when he got shot," Jeremy added helpfully.

Emma's fork clattered to the floor.

"You were...shot?"

Jake winced.

Yeah, come to think of it, he'd mentioned that to Jeremy, too.

Jake had been shot.

Shot.

Emma's gaze flickered to the crosshatch of scars on the underside of his jaw. Had a bullet grazed a path there?

The thought made her stomach pitch.

"No." Jake caught her staring. "I wish I could impress you with a heroic deed, but these particular scars were caused by stupidity." He scraped the back of his hand over the scars. "When I was eight years old, I decided to make a tree fort in the backyard."

"What happened?" Jeremy leaned forward, fascinated by the tale.

"It didn't work. I fell. But instead of landing in the sandbox, I bounced off the fence that separated our yard from the neighbor's. Mrs. Parker grew prize-winning roses." He winked at Jeremy. "But not that year. She also got the sympathy vote from my mother, which meant that I had to spend the entire summer weeding flower beds."

Jeremy laughed but Emma couldn't. She was still reeling from the knowledge that Jake had survived an injury much more serious than falling into a rosebush.

She excused herself from the table and went to get a clean fork. As it was, Jake saw too much—she certainly didn't want him to see the tears that had sprung to her eyes.

Tears that caused her doubts to surface once again. For the past six years, she had done her best to shelter Jeremy from the pain of losing his father at such a young age. Now, not only had she agreed to let Jake mentor her son, but she had just discovered that he was a living testimony of how dangerous his chosen profession could be.

Jeremy was already getting attached to Jake. Emma could see the hero worship in his eyes—hear it in his voice—whenever he talked about the man.

Jake had survived a gunshot wound once, but Emma knew from bitter experience that there were no guarantees he wouldn't be hurt again. Not even in a small town as idyllic as Mirror Lake.

How would Jeremy handle that?

How would you?

Emma pushed the unwelcome thought away.

This wasn't about her—this was about Jeremy and what was best for him. Wasn't it?

She walked back to the table, careful to avoid Jake's eyes.

"I think I'll take Shadow for a walk," Jeremy announced. "Who wants to come with us?"

"We should all go." Jake slanted a look at her. "After we help your mom clean up the kitchen."

Emma stiffened. She didn't *want* his help.

She didn't want to go for a walk, either. All she wanted was a few minutes alone to untangle the knot of emotions balled up inside of her.

"You two can go ahead without me. There isn't much to clean up." Emma sucked in a breath and held it, hoping Jake would take the hint.

"Jeremy, will you please take Shadow outside?" he asked. "I'll be there in a few minutes."

"Sure." Jeremy slapped his palm against his thigh. "Let's go, Shadow."

The dog launched to its feet and beat him to the door. Emma could hear Jeremy's laughter as it closed behind them. She should have gotten him a dog a long time ago, but she had always talked herself out of it.

"Supper was delicious, Emma."

"Thank you." She turned on the water and let the sink fill, acutely aware of Jake picking up the dishes and stacking them on the table behind her.

"No, thank you." His husky voice, and the fact they were alone, created a level of intimacy between them that should have made Emma uncomfortable. Especially after what she'd just learned.

It felt so strange to have him there, in her kitchen. Sitting at the table. Sharing a meal with them.

Emma had seen the understanding dawn in his eyes when Jeremy had offered him the chair at the head of the table. He must have assumed the look of shock on her face stemmed from the fact that she didn't want him to sit in Brian's chair. To take his place at the table.

But that hadn't been the reason. The truth was, Emma had suddenly realized that Jake's presence in her home, in spite of her misgivings, didn't feel wrong at all. In fact, somehow, it felt…right.

"No dishwasher?" Jake's voice rumbled close to her ear.

"No." A shiver danced its way down Emma's spine. "It isn't necessary for you to help me, you know."

Jake smiled. "I've already been in hot water a few times tonight… What's one more?"

In spite of the fact that she was struggling to find her next breath, Emma fought a sudden urge to smile. She covered it with a stern look as they switched places at the sink. "So you admit that it wasn't an accident, showing up with a stray dog?"

"I'll admit it was good timing." Jake rolled back the sleeves of his white dress shirt and began to wash the plates. "I had a dog and you had a ten-year-old boy who needed one."

Emma averted her gaze from the corded muscles of Jake's forearms. He'd locked his gun belt in the trunk of the car, but still wore his uniform shirt and badge. That—and the story about surviving a gunshot— provided vivid reminders of what he did for a living.

"You make it sound so simple."

Jake's shoulders lifted and fell. "Sometimes we complicate things."

And sometimes things got complicated without a person even trying, Emma thought. Like the feelings that Jake's presence in her home stirred up inside of her.

Feelings she didn't *want* to feel.

"Let me know the days you want to take Jeremy to work on the raft." She began to wipe down the countertop to put some distance between them. "Like you said, Reflection Days starts next Friday, so you don't have a lot of time."

"I know." She felt the force of Jake's smile. "That's why I thought we'd build it here."

Chapter Fourteen

"'Mornin, Jake. What got you out of bed so early on a Saturday morning?"

Jake, who'd been staring at a mind-boggling display of dog leashes and collars for the past ten minutes, turned at the sound of Phil Koenigs's voice.

A smile slid across the officer's weathered face when he noticed the yellow collar clutched in Jake's hand. "Don't tell me you ended up with that troublemaker? Aren't you supposed to delegate responsibility?"

Because it was Saturday, and they both happened to be off duty, Jake couldn't very well reprimand his second in command for insubordination. Although the grin on the officer's face definitely qualified.

"I did. And I found him a good home."

"No kidding." Phil glanced at the box of biscuits and the Frisbee tucked under Jake's arm. "Then what's all this for?"

"A guilt offering." Or a bribe. Jake didn't care what it was called as long as it changed Shadow's status in the Barlow home from temporary to permanent.

"So where did you drop him off? The county shelter?"

"No, I gave him to Jeremy Barlow." Jake hooked the yellow collar back over the metal arm on the display and picked out a red one instead. "How big do you think he's going to get? Medium, large or supersize?"

"Emma took him?"

The strangled question pulled Jake's attention away from the collars.

"That's right." He glanced up in time to see a strange expression shift the broad planes of the officer's face. "What's the matter?"

"I'm just surprised, that's all," Phil muttered.

From Jake's standpoint, there was more to it than surprise. Aisle three in the local lumber store seemed as good a place as any to find out what it was. This wasn't the first time Phil had displayed obvious discomfort when Emma's name came up.

"I've been spending some time with Jeremy through the mentoring program at Church of the Pines."

"Heard about that," Phil said shortly. "I just have a hard time believing that Emma agreed to it, is all."

He wasn't the only one, Jake thought. But that didn't explain why the senior officer couldn't seem to look him in the eye.

"Do you have a problem with Emma?"

Phil seemed troubled by the question. "Why do you ask?"

"Oh, I don't know," Jake drawled. "Maybe because you and the guys were drawing straws to decide who had to drop off a bouquet of flowers on the anniversary of her husband's death."

"It's more like Emma has a problem with us," Phil said. "I wish she would have moved away after…you know."

The admission stunned Jake. "Because it's difficult to see her still grieving?"

"Not only that." Phil shifted his weight as if adjusting the burden of guilt he bore. "We never did catch the person on the motorcycle that Brian was pursuing."

Jake let out a slow breath. "I'm sure Emma doesn't hold you or the other officers responsible for not making an arrest."

Phil didn't look convinced. "Brian and I worked together on third shift at the time. He came over the radio and said he'd just clocked a motorcycle going ninety miles an hour. I told him to let it go. Department policy states that for safety reasons, we aren't supposed to pursue anyone at those speeds." A shadow passed through his eyes. "Brian always was a bit of a cowboy but I never thought he'd take off after the cycle anyway. When dispatch tried to call him a few minutes later, he didn't respond. The accident reconstruction team figured Brian lost control on a curve and rolled the squad car. He died on the way to the hospital. Maybe it would have given Emma some closure if we'd made an arrest. Maybe she thinks we should have tried harder. Or gotten help for Brian sooner."

The undercurrent of anguish in Phil's voice made Jake wonder if the officer was imagining that Emma blamed him—because he blamed himself.

"You did the best you could. In a situation like that, you can second-guess yourself until you go crazy." Jake spoke from experience, even though he wasn't always successful when it came to taking his own advice. No matter how many times Andy reminded him that he couldn't take responsibility for Sean's decisions, there were times Jake questioned whether the outcome would have been different if *he* had done something different.

"It happened six years ago and there are still nights I lose sleep thinking about it." Phil grimaced. "Even if Emma doesn't hold us responsible, I think it's hard for her to see the badge and not be reminded of everything she lost. She's very protective when it comes to her son. I guess that's why I was surprised she agreed to let Jeremy spend time with you."

Now that Jake knew more of the details surroundings Brian's death, he couldn't believe she had, either.

"There you are! I should have known you'd found someone to talk shop with." Phil's wife, Maureen, rounded the aisle, the warm look in her eyes belying her scolding tone. "Good morning, Chief. You're up bright and early on a Saturday."

"Hi, Maureen."

Phil looked relieved by the interruption. After a few minutes of small talk, he put his hand under his wife's elbow and guided her away.

As Jake drove to Emma's house, the conversation with Phil kept cycling through his mind.

The truth was becoming more and more difficult to deny. He didn't want Emma to see a badge when she looked at him.

He wanted her to see *him*.

* * *

"We need your help, Mom."

Jeremy dashed into the outbuilding, where Emma was painting the legs on the mosaic table Abby had ordered.

When Jake had promised he would help with the raft, she hadn't expected him to show up at nine o'clock the next morning. At least he hadn't caught her sitting at the table in her pajamas, bleary-eyed while she waited for her first cup of coffee to take effect. She blamed the fact that she'd slept a little longer than usual on the amount of hours she had tossed and turned throughout the night.

No matter how hard she tried, she couldn't seem to dislodge Jake from her thoughts. And when he'd walked into the kitchen, looking way too attractive for her peace of mind in a pair of faded jeans and a butter-soft chambray shirt, Emma had bolted.

She'd been hiding ever since.

Fortunately, the table she was making for Abby provided a legitimate excuse to avoid the barn, the location Jeremy and Jake had claimed for their raft-building project. At least until now.

Emma rocked back on her heels. "What do you need me to do?"

"Time us," Jeremy said, holding up a stopwatch. "We're not sure how long it's going to take to put the frame together."

"I suppose I can do that," Emma murmured. "Let me wash up first and I'll meet you over there."

"Okay." Jeremy darted away, Shadow hot on his heels.

Apparently Jake had been right about that, too. A dog and a ten-year-old boy were made for each other.

Emma turned on the faucet and washed the paint off her hands. She was stalling, there was no point in denying it.

The fact that she wanted to see Jake made her *not* want to see him even more. And that kind of topsy-turvy thinking was proof of the effect the man had on her!

"Mom!" Jeremy's voice drifted through the open window. "Are you ready yet?"

"On my way." But only because she didn't have a choice in the matter.

Emma entered the barn and almost bumped into Jake, who was kneeling on the dirt floor. He rose to his feet and dusted his hands against his jeans.

"Sorry we had to interrupt you, but it's going to take both Jeremy and me to put this thing together and we needed a timekeeper. Shadow is very smart for a canine but I don't think he can help us out." Jake flashed that teasing smile, the one Emma had seen the day he'd slapped on the battered Stetson for story hour. The one that never failed to send her heart on a roller-coaster ride to her toes.

Emma's fist closed around the stopwatch as she resisted the urge to reach out and brush a swatch of tousled dark hair off Jake's forehead. In plainclothes, it was all too easy to forget what he did for a living.

Too easy to forget that, by his own admission, he'd been injured—no, not just injured, *shot*—while working undercover.

Jeremy hadn't seemed upset by the knowledge.

Emma, on the other hand, hadn't been able to put it out of her mind.

Jake had talked about how God had led him to Mirror Lake at the same time and she wondered how he reconciled what had to be a horrific experience with his strong faith in a loving God.

In order to hide her troubled thoughts, Emma pretended to study the eclectic array of parts scattered on the floor at their feet. "Tell me when you're ready and I'll start the clock."

"We have ten minutes to assemble the raft," Jeremy told her. "But the longer it takes, the less time we have to paddle out to the flag. We need to figure out how to reduce the time."

"Jeremy thinks we can do it in six," Jake added. "I think he's right."

The grin on her son's face reflected a confidence Emma had never seen before—at least not until Jake Sutton had entered their lives.

"Do you think Mom will be surprised when she sees what we did?"

"No doubt."

No doubt whatsoever, Jake thought as he surveyed their work with a critical eye.

Once she had finished timing them, Emma had promptly retreated to her workroom again.

That had been two hours ago, and Jake hadn't seen her since.

He and Jeremy had spent the next hour working out some snags in the raft's original design before taking a short break. Taking Shadow for a walk around the house had given Jake an opportunity to take a silent inventory of a few of the more pressing repairs that needed to be finished before winter set in. He might not have much experience when it came to home handyman stuff, but he was willing to try.

If he could convince Emma to *let* him.

At the lumberyard that morning, Jake had picked up a few extra boards along with the supplies needed for the raft. Jeremy, eager to test out the brand-new junior tool set Jake had given him, didn't mind putting aside that particular project for a while.

"I'm finished with this one." Jeremy rubbed his nose with the back of his hand. "Are you hungry?"

Jake could take a hint. "Are you ready for lunch?"

Jeremy leaped to his feet. "I'll get Mom."

"Your mom said something about finishing up a table for Miss Porter. How about we make lunch for her today?"

Jeremy considered the suggestion with the same thoughtful concentration he applied to other decisions. "I like hot dogs. Mom likes grilled cheese sandwiches and tomato soup."

"I think we can handle that."

"So do I." Jeremy grinned.

They straightened up the barn before walking back to the house. Shadow attached himself to Jeremy's side. Jake couldn't help but notice how quickly the pair had taken to each other.

The soft smile he had seen on Emma's face when she noticed the dog's brand-new collar had lingered at the edge of Jake's thoughts all morning.

Who was he kidding? Everything about Emma lingered in his thoughts, from the way her eyes darkened to an evening-sky blue when she was thinking hard about something to the gentle sway of her hips when she walked.

Grilled cheese sandwiches. Tomato soup.

Jake firmly rerouted his thoughts as they went inside.

"Mom usually does everything." Jeremy stood in the middle of the kitchen and looked at him for direction.

"Which is why we're going to give her a break today." Even as he spoke, Jake hoped Emma wouldn't show up until lunch was ready.

But she did.

She ventured into the kitchen less than ten minutes later. Jeremy was standing at the counter, buttering slices of bread, while Jake kept a watchful eye on the tomato soup.

Her cheeks flushed a delicate shade of pink. "Why didn't you come and get me?" she scolded them. "I would have made lunch."

"We wanted to surprise you." Jeremy inserted a piece of cheese between two slices of bread before carefully transferring it to the skillet.

"You did." Emma sidled into the kitchen. "I'll set the table."

"Already done," Jake said.

Emma glanced at the table and the uncertain expression tugged at his heart.

She took care of Jeremy, but when was the last time someone had taken care of her?

"There must be something I can do," she persisted.

"There is." Jake pointed to the table. "You can sit down. You've been working hard all morning."

Emma didn't listen. She wedged her way in between them and her gaze flickered to the wooden spoon in Jake's hand.

He lifted it above his head. "Don't even think about trying to disarm a police officer."

Jeremy giggled.

"I wasn't." Her blush deepened.

"Uh-huh." Jake let his skepticism show.

"I can't see the pan, Mom, 'cause you're in the way." Jeremy heaved a sigh.

"Sorry." Emma stepped back. "I guess I'll just…"

"Sit down." Jake and Jeremy said the words at the same time.

Emma laughed. "All right, all right. I'll sit down."

The unexpected sound rippled through the kitchen—and snatched the air from Jake's lungs.

Breathe.

"The sandwiches are smoking." Jeremy's announcement jump-started Jake's heart again. "Does that mean they're done, Jake?"

"Affirmative. And they look great." Jake ignored the crispy dark brown edges—*his fault*—as he flipped the sandwiches onto a plate. "I told you we could pull this off."

"Jake made tomato soup for you, Mom." Jeremy took the carton of milk out of the refrigerator and poured three glasses. "I told him you liked it."

"Hot fudge sundaes and tomato soup." Jake set a bowl down on the colorful woven place mat in front of Emma. "If you aren't careful, pretty soon I'll know all your secrets."

"That means I'll have to be careful then, won't I?"

Jake had been teasing. One look at Emma's guarded expression told him that she hadn't.

"I'll say the prayer today." Jeremy slid into his chair at the table and bowed his head.

Jake listened as the boy thanked God for the soup and grilled cheese sandwiches. And Shadow. And that they had put the raft together in a record-breaking seven minutes and thirty-four seconds.

After Jeremy's "amen," Jake tacked on a silent prayer of his own.

Thank You for showing me there is still laughter inside of Emma. Keep working in her heart. Show her that You haven't forgotten about her. That You love her.

Jake opened his eyes and found Emma staring at him. For a split second, all her defenses were down. He saw bewilderment and confusion—and a longing that both terrified him and gave him hope, all at the same time.

Or was what he was seeing in Emma's eyes simply a reflection of his own emotions?

Chapter Fifteen

Over the swish of the washing machine, Emma heard the muffled but steady tap of a hammer. Only this time, the noise wasn't coming from the barn. It wasn't coming from the porch, either, where Jake and Jeremy had fixed several loose boards the day before.

She would have thought Jake had projects of his own to attend to on a beautiful Saturday afternoon, but he seemed to be in no hurry to leave.

An image of him standing next to Jeremy in the kitchen, patiently supervising his efforts, surfaced in her memory again. Jake claimed to have no experience with children and yet he instinctively seemed to know exactly what would appeal to a boy like Jeremy, who wanted to learn new things.

Emma had shooed them out of the kitchen after lunch, assuming that Jake would take the hint. He and Jeremy had taken Shadow for a walk instead.

She stepped outside and followed the tapping to the back of the house.

Emma wasn't sure what she'd expected to find,

but the sight that greeted her momentarily stopped her in her tracks.

Jeremy sat cross-legged in the grass next to the back door, paintbrush in hand. The screen door had been removed. So had the screen, which someone had wadded up and stuffed into a garbage can.

Her gaze flew to Jake. He stood several feet away from Jeremy, hands propped on his lean hips as he stared up at the misshapen metal gutter that followed the roofline.

"I thought you two would be back in the barn, trying to shave a few more minutes off your time." Emma couldn't help the fact that her statement sounded like an accusation.

Both heads turned in her direction.

"We're taking a break," Jeremy explained.

"You're taking a break to *work*." Emma planted her hands on her hips. "I don't think I've ever heard of that."

He waved the brush at her, inadvertently spattering the grass with droplets of white paint. "Jake bought a new screen for the door."

"Did he?" Emma pinned a look on Jake that should have drawn another response other than the smile he flashed in return.

"I noticed the old one had a few holes in it," he said.

Fixing the back door had slowly been working its way up the project list, but Emma wasn't sure if she should be grateful or embarrassed that Jake had noticed its pitiful condition.

"He bought me my own set of tools, too." Jeremy

pointed to a toolbox gleaming in the afternoon sunlight, as shiny and red as a McIntosh apple.

"That was nice of him." Too nice. Except that
Emma didn't want Jake to feel obligated to buy Jeremy gifts. Or give up an entire Saturday to work on
projects that weren't his responsibility.

They weren't his responsibility.

"I made some lemonade." Emma manufactured
a smile for Jeremy's sake. "Jeremy, why don't you
bring the pitcher and some glasses out to the picnic
table and take a *real* break?"

"Okay." Jeremy jumped to his feet and transferred
the paintbrush into her hand before disappearing into
the house.

Emma quickly maneuvered the dripping brush
over the can.

"It's primer." Jake sauntered over, not looking the
least bit guilty at having been caught in the act of
another home-repair project. "I wasn't sure if you
wanted to repaint the frame the same color, so I didn't
pick up the paint for that yet."

Yet.

"You're Jeremy's mentor, not my carpenter."

Jake stuffed a rag in the back pocket of his jeans
and shrugged. "A boy should know his way around
a toolbox."

So that's what this was about. Another "teach-
able moment."

The things she had sheltered Jeremy from, like hot
skillets and hammers and raft-building contests, Jake
considered learning opportunities. Emma couldn't
deny that she had liked it better when Jeremy had

learned things from a book, but she couldn't deny that her son's confidence had been steadily growing.

"How much do I owe you for everything?"

"Nothing." Jake's jaw tightened.

"I can't let you pay for the supplies." Emma folded her arms across her chest and raised her chin. Jake would discover she could be just as stubborn as he was. It was bad enough he had taken it upon himself to make repairs, she couldn't let him absorb the cost.

"All right." He gave in. "If you insist."

"I do."

"The cost of the supplies is dinner."

"D-dinner?" Emma stammered.

"Jeremy mentioned that you make great homemade pizza. And since I don't specialize in homemade anything, that would be reimbursement enough."

"Pizza? That doesn't seem like a fair trade." And opening her purse would be easier on Emma's peace of mind than opening her home to Jake again.

"It's more than fair. Jeremy wants to help you. It gives him a sense of pride," Jake said.

Pride? What about her pride?

Emma was embarrassed by her inability to keep up with simple outside home repairs—and mortified that Jake had noticed.

Her gaze strayed from Jake to the siding that was practically begging for a fresh coat of paint.

"I've thought about selling the house." Emma couldn't believe she had said the words out loud.

Jake was silent for a moment, as if he'd been surprised by the admission, too. And then, "Did you and Brian live here while you were married?"

Emma nodded, surprised that the mention of Brian's name didn't flood her with painful memories. "It belonged to his grandparents. After Grandma Barlow died, Brian's grandfather closed up the house and moved to Arizona to live with Brian's parents. When Brian took the job with the Mirror Lake police department, his grandfather was thrilled. He called the house a wedding gift."

"A difficult one to return," Jake commented.

Emma couldn't argue with that.

"It was supposed to be temporary." Regret stirred the ashes of Emma's grief. "We planned to build a place on the lake eventually, but Jeremy was born premature and couldn't leave the hospital for two weeks. The bills piled up and it seemed wiser to stay put until we got back on our feet."

Their five-year plan.

She and Brian had had such a short amount of time together, Emma sometimes felt as if she had never really gotten to know her husband at all.

"Brian didn't have any other family close by?"

"An older sister, Melissa, but she had already graduated from college and moved to the east coast by the time we got married." Emma, who had always dreamed of having a sister, had been disappointed that Brian's only sibling had moved so far away. "She writes at Christmas and sends Jeremy a birthday card every year, though."

The shadow in Emma's eyes ignited a slow burn that worked its way through Jake as the truth became clear.

The very people who should have been there to lift her up had, in fact, let her down.

"Don't Brian's parents, or his sister, ever come back to visit?" he asked carefully.

Emma shook her head. "There isn't anything here for them anymore."

There's you, Jake wanted to say. *And Jeremy.*

From the way Emma described her situation, it sounded as if she and Jeremy had been...abandoned.

"I don't blame them," Emma said quickly, as if she'd read his mind. "The memories... It would be hard for them to come back here."

"You stayed."

"I didn't have much of a choice." Emma shrugged. "The house might have come with some flaws but at least it didn't have a mortgage. When Jeremy turned two, I started working a few hours a week at the library, just to supplement Brian's income a little, but after..." Some of the strength in Emma's voice ebbed away. "When Mrs. Morrison retired, she suggested that the library board offer me the full-time position because I had experience, even though I hadn't finished my degree."

"What about your family?" Jake felt compelled to ask.

The silence that fell between them lasted so long that Jake didn't think Emma was going to answer the question at all.

"My mom died in a car accident when I was six years old," she finally said. "Dad was in the military, so we never stayed in one place very long. After I graduated from high school, I decided to take some classes at a local technical college. The next time Dad moved, I was an adult, so he moved without me."

"Where is your father now?"

"He retired a few years ago but accepted a part-time job as a consultant with a civilian company overseas. He only makes one trip back to the States a year."

Which answered the next question that had begun to form in Jake's mind.

Something in his expression must have shown, because Emma stepped back. The guarded look returned.

"I'm sorry. I didn't mean to go on and on."

And she didn't want him to feel sorry for her, either. But Jake didn't. He felt sorry for all the people in Emma's life who had never taken the time to get to know her.

"Don't be sorry. It will help me get to know Jeremy better if I know some of his background." Jake spoke the truth but the brief glimpse into Emma's past had told him a lot about her, too.

But it was clear she was already regretting it.

"I read the guidelines for the mentor program that Pastor Wilde sent to me," Emma said slowly. "They state that mentors agree to spend four hours a week with the boy they've been assigned to. *Four hours.* You've put in your time and then some. I know you're busy. Please don't let Jeremy pressure you into spending more time with him than necessary."

"In the first place, I don't think of Jeremy as someone I've been *assigned* to," he said. "And I don't spend time with him because I feel pressured. I enjoy spending time with him."

And with you.

"It's nice of you to say that."

For some reason, the polite words rankled.

"Nice?" Jake repeated the word with a bite that caused her to flinch. "I'm not just saying it, Emma, I mean it."

He could tell by the expression on her face that she didn't believe him. "You said that you worked undercover," she said stiffly. "I realize that making grilled cheese sandwiches and fixing screen doors don't exactly provide the adrenaline rush that you must be used to."

"You're right about that," he agreed. "I slept on a lot of couches in houses that weren't exactly the picket-fence type. Saw things that I wish I could forget." *Had done things he wished he could forget.* "I volunteered to work undercover because I wanted to change things, but I got in so deep. I didn't realize that I was the one who was changing, until I...until God got hold of me.

"Fishing with Jeremy. Listening to him laugh. Making grilled cheese sandwiches. Fixing the loose boards on your porch. Those aren't ordinary things to me, Emma. They feel more like a a gift."

Chapter Sixteen

"Come on, Mom! It's almost time for church to start!"

"I'll be down in a minute." Emma felt a stab of guilt, knowing she wouldn't mind walking into the service a few minutes late. Then she and Jeremy could sit in the back row and avoid the fellowship time that took place in the foyer before the service began.

And Jake.

The conversation they'd had the day before came rushing back. Somehow, in the space of a few minutes, he had managed to coax her into revealing details about her life that she had never told anyone else.

Emma flushed at the memory. Jake Sutton hadn't charmed or forced his way through her defenses, either. Oh, no. One look into those mesmerizing amber eyes and she had practically invited him in!

Emma had reminded Jake about the mentoring guidelines in an effort to put some distance between them, but he had turned the tables on her.

"Those aren't ordinary things to me, Emma. They feel more like a gift."

She had been stunned by the sincerity in his voice. And the tiny current of awareness that had sparked the air between them. One that should have made Emma retreat rather than coax her to move closer.

Fortunately, the connection was broken when Jeremy, needing help carrying the pitcher of lemonade, called for help. Jake had opened the door for him—and provided Emma with an escape hatch.

He hadn't followed her that time. An hour later, from the safety of her workroom, she heard his car drive away. Emma had been able to breathe again.

At least for a little while.

The Sunday worship service would make another encounter with Jake inevitable, but a little distance, Emma reasoned, would give her a chance to put their relationship back into perspective.

Not *their* relationship.

Emma caught herself. She and Jake didn't have a relationship. They had an…an *agreement.* An agreement born from their commitment to Jeremy. He was the connecting point between them.

That's all it was.

"And it's enough."

If she said the words out loud, Emma thought, maybe she could convince her heart to believe them.

She drove into the church parking lot and Jeremy stuck his head out the window, his gaze scanning the rows of vehicles.

"I see Jake's car!" His entire body rose off the seat in his excitement. "Maybe he's waiting for us."

Emma hoped not. She could already feel a blush heating her cheeks at the *thought* of seeing him again.

As it turned out, they were a few minutes late.

The worship team had taken their place at the front of the sanctuary and the young woman at the keyboard had started to play the opening notes of a popular praise song.

Emma released the breath she'd been holding. They could find a seat in the back...

"I see a spot!"

Before she could blink, Jeremy was hiking down the center aisle, his destination the second pew from the front.

The pew where Jake was sitting.

The trouble was, unless Emma wanted to draw even more attention than they already were, she had no choice but to follow.

Jake had already risen to his feet by the time Jeremy reached his side. He must have heard Jeremy's voice—Emma had no doubt *everyone* in the sanctuary had heard Jeremy's voice—because everyone in the row was shifting to make room for them.

Emma kept her eyes focused straight ahead as she took her place next to her son. It was clear that she was going to have to have a talk with him—and apologize to Jake. He may have agreed to be her son's mentor, but it didn't mean he was obligated to give Jeremy all of his attention.

Pastor Wilde stepped behind the podium to open the service with a word of prayer, saving her from further embarrassment.

During previous services, Emma had been able to retreat into herself—planning the next week's menu or silently sifting through the books in the research section of the library. But she hadn't had Kate offering to share her hymnal. And the words of the songs about God's love hadn't touched a bittersweet chord inside of her before, filling the empty spaces that had been there as long as Emma could remember. Even before Brian's death.

By the time Pastor Wilde finished his sermon and the congregation rose to their feet for the closing song, it was all Emma could do not to bolt from the sanctuary.

She did manage to sidestep Kate in her haste to get to the door, but found her path blocked by Esther Redstone. The elderly woman belonged to a knitting group that held their monthly meetings in the conference room at the library. Whenever they burst through the door, toting bags of yarn and enough food to feed a small army, Emma thought they looked more like a troop of Girl Scouts on a camping trip rather than a knitting group.

"There you are, Emma!" The woman's friendly smile made her a tiny but formidable obstacle. "Do you have a minute to chat?"

Over the woman's chic little straw hat, Emma saw Jeremy trudging toward the car.

"Of course." Emma couldn't say no. Esther exuded a warmth and beauty that rivaled the blankets she and the Knit Our Hearts Together ministry created.

"Would you be interested in donating several of your mosaic garden stones for our booth at the craft show during Reflection Days next weekend? The proceeds go into a special Christmas fund for the missionaries the church supports."

Emma hesitated a moment before telling the truth. "I don't usually sell my work."

Esther wasn't deterred. "I know that, dear, but

when the committee met last night, Abby thought you might make an exception this time."

Abby. Emma should have known.

"When is the craft show?"

Esther's eyes began to sparkle like sapphires. "Reflection Days starts on Friday afternoon and the craft show is one of the highlights of the kickoff. We set up tents near the pavilion at the park."

"How many do you need?" Emma asked, even as she silently calculated how much free time she would have that week and how long it would take to design and create an order of stepping-stones.

"I don't know. One, two, three…" Esther peeked at her under the brim of her hat, sudden mischief dancing in her eyes. "A hundred."

In spite of her initial hesitation, Emma couldn't help but chuckle. "I don't think I could make a hundred in less than a week."

"Then we'll take as many as you are willing to donate," Esther said promptly. "I'm glad Abby thought of you. Thank you so much."

"You're welcome," Emma said automatically, even as she wondered at what point she had actually agreed to make the donation!

Esther patted her hand. "We could really use your help setting up that day, too. Kate mentioned that the library closes early on Friday afternoons."

So Kate was part of the conspiracy, too.

"Mrs. Redstone—" Emma gasped, the argument she was about to make cut off by the older woman's brief but exuberant hug.

"Wonderful! And please call me Esther, dear. No need to stand on ceremony when we'll be working together, is there? I'll see you at the pavilion at one o'clock on Friday afternoon." Esther released her and sailed down the hall.

Emma gave up. If necessary, she could let Kate or Abby know that she wouldn't be available to help. Since they'd been the ones who'd drafted her, they could find a replacement for her!

Making her way across the parking lot, Emma braced herself to face Jake again. They hadn't spoken after the service. Pastor Wilde had motioned to him after the closing prayer and Emma had immediately been caught up in the wave of people moving up the aisle.

But when she saw Jeremy, he was alone.

Emma resisted the urge to look around. "Are you ready to go home?"

"Uh-huh." Jeremy slid into the passenger seat.

On the drive back home, Emma could no longer resist asking, "Did you talk to Jake?"

"A little bit." Jeremy was staring out the window, so Emma couldn't tell if the conversation had been a disappointment.

"He has plans for this afternoon?"

"Uh-huh." Now Jeremy turned to look at her, eyes shining. "He's coming over for pizza."

Maybe, Jake thought, he shouldn't have accepted Jeremy's invitation to join him and Emma for lunch.

But then again, he *had* made a deal with Emma. Home-repair supplies for homemade pizza. And the truth was, even if Jeremy hadn't approached him after the service, asking when they were going to work on the raft again, Jake would have been hard-pressed to stay away and give Emma the space she wanted. Especially now that he was beginning to question whether "space" was what she *needed*.

The brief glimpse into Emma's past had left him shaken.

No wonder it was difficult for her to reach out to people and ask for help. Her family had never reached out to her. No wonder she was so protective of Jeremy. No one had protected her.

Her husband's family, locked in the grip of their own grief, hadn't been there for Emma after Brian's death. And from what Jake had learned about her father, his obvious indifference to her when she was a child had continued after she was an adult.

But it wasn't just the fact that no one had walked beside Emma through the pain of her loss, but the matter-of-fact tone in which she'd talked about it that stirred up Jake's anger. As if she hadn't expected it to be any other way…

"Jake?"

He felt a tug on his arm and found himself looking into a pair of wide, gray-blue eyes.

"Sorry, bud." Jake mentally shook himself. "What did you say?"

"I think I should ask Mom to time us again."

"You know what I think?" Jake looked down at the raft. "I think it's time we put this thing in the lake and take it for a test run."

Jeremy's eyes widened. "Really?"

"We have to make sure it floats, don't we?" Jake winked at the boy.

"Yes!" Jeremy pumped the air with his fist.

Jake smiled at his enthusiasm. "I'll check it out with

your Mom first, before we start loading up the car."
He had learned that particular lesson the hard way.

Jeremy had already dropped to his knees and
began to dismantle the raft again, not concerned that
they might not be granted permission to carry out
the mission.

Jake, however, had his doubts.

Emma hadn't said much when he had shown up for
lunch after church, but she had mentioned Esther's
request that she donate some of her garden stones to
the craft show.

He sensed a conspiracy. And if his suspicions were
on target, Jake could have hugged Esther. The women
were finding ways to gently coax Emma out of her
shell.

Jazz music drifted through the open window of
the outbuilding as Jake approached.

"Emma?" He called out a warning before entering
her work zone this time. He'd learned that lesson, too.

"Come in."

"Are you sure it's safe?" Jake paused in the doorway and looked around for flying dishes.

"I'll tell you when to duck. Maybe."

Jake felt the air empty from his lungs.

Emma was teasing him? Because Jake could have
sworn he saw a smile lift the corners of her lips before
she looked down at the mosaic she was working on.

His gaze skimmed over her slender frame. Jake
had thought Emma stunning in the dainty little sundress she'd worn to church that morning—he had
barely been able to take his eyes off her. But she
looked equally as fetching in tennis shoes, baggy
overalls and a faded gray T-shirt.

Focus, Sutton. You interrupted her for a reason, remember?

"Do you mind if I take Jeremy down to the boat landing for an hour or so? We're satisfied that we've got a good time making the raft, now we need to make sure it's going to hold us."

"All right."

"All right?" he blurted, a little shocked that she'd agreed so quickly. After all, he was asking her to trust him. Again.

"I realize you have to make sure it's…seaworthy." Emma pushed a piece of glass into the wet cement, adding to the row she had been working on.

But Jake didn't miss the little frown that settled between her brows.

It occurred to him that Emma was used to spending her free time with Jeremy. Jake didn't want to be the guy who took her son away from her.

"We could use a spotter," he said casually. "It's a beautiful afternoon. Hot and sunny. I've heard a nasty rumor there might not be many of those left."

The frown deepened. "I have to finish this before the cement dries."

"We can wait."

Emma looked out the window at the cloudless sky. "I'll meet you by the car in fifteen minutes."

"I knew it." Jake flashed an approving smile. "The woman is beautiful *and* sensible."

Emma stared at Jake's retreating back as he sauntered out the door. It closed quietly behind him and she sagged against the table.

Beautiful.

In stained bib overalls and battered tennis shoes? Her ponytail trailing between her shoulder blades like a damp rope?

And sensible.

Emma turned the words over in her mind.

She caught a glimpse of her reflection in the antique mirror over the sink. The woman looking back at her was smiling.

Oh. No.

That morning, she had been trying to come up with ways to avoid Jake. Now, when she would have had the perfect opportunity, she had agreed to accompany him to the lake.

What was wrong with her?

She had been afraid that Jeremy was getting too attached to Jake. Now she had to wonder if she was guilty of the same thing.

Chapter Seventeen

"Stopwatch?" Jeremy looked over at her and Emma held it up for his inspection.

"Check."

"Camera?"

"Check." She dug around in her beach bag and produced that, too.

"Oatmeal cookies?" Jake took up the questioning, his teasing smile playing havoc with her pulse.

Emma made a face at him, knowing that he was remembering the picnic basket she had sent along on their first fishing trip.

"Chocolate chip," she whispered. "And they're for later."

"I think we're ready, Mom. Count to three and then say go," Jeremy instructed.

Emma took a deep breath, heart still suffering the aftershock from Jake's smile. "One, two, three...go."

She watched in fascination as the two of them set to work with an efficiency that made every movement look as if it had been choreographed. In a little over six minutes they were transporting the raft down to the shoreline, ready to launch.

Emma followed, keeping an eye on the stopwatch. According to Jeremy, the winner of last year's competition had completed the entire race—from start to finish—in five minutes and eleven seconds.

Jeremy clambered aboard but when Jake jumped on, the raft tipped to the side, threatening to capsize them.

"What's the matter?" Emma stopped at the edge of the water where the waves licked at the tips of her bare toes.

"Too much weight," Jeremy called over his shoulder.

"Hey!" Jake pretended to look affronted at the suggestion. "Keep paddling. She'll stay afloat."

But "she" didn't.

One of the barrels came loose and started to drift away, upsetting the balance even more. By the time they admitted defeat, both were soaking wet. They slogged back to shore where Emma was waiting with dry towels.

And the camera.

When the flash went off, Jake and Jeremy swung accusing looks in her direction.

"That wasn't supposed to happen." Jake reached for the towel.

"Really? The raft wasn't supposed to sink?" Emma saw their disgruntled looks. And giggled.

"Mom, you aren't supposed to laugh at us," Jeremy grumbled.

"I'm not laughing." Emma clapped a hand over her mouth to muffle the sound.

Jake arched a brow at Jeremy. "Sounds like she's laughing to me."

"Me, too." Jeremy began to dry his hair but they heard a low but unmistakable chuckle from beneath the towel.

"Oh, well. Back to the drawing board." Jake peeled off his shirt and Emma's breath hitched in her throat as she stared at his bare chest. Not at the ridged torso, as smooth and golden-brown as teakwood, but at the crisscross of raised, angry-looking scars just below his rib cage.

Jake realized what he'd done when he heard Emma stifle a gasp.

Now that the pain of his injury had, for the most part, subsided, he no longer thought about the scarring.

Until now.

He grabbed the extra shirt he'd brought along and shrugged it on, fumbling with the buttons in his haste to cover up the wound again before Jeremy noticed it.

Unfortunately, it was too late for Emma.

She stepped between him and Jeremy, using her body to shield his injury from curious eyes, but not fast enough for Jake to miss the mixture of shock and disbelief in her own.

Emma knew he had been shot, but Jake supposed there was a difference between knowing it had happened and witnessing the results.

Would she let him explain?

Jake blew out a sigh as he acknowledged there was a bigger question.

Could he explain?

Other than Andy and Pastor Matt, not many people outside Jake's former precinct knew the details surrounding his injury. That was the way he preferred it.

In silence, they loaded the pieces of the raft into the trunk of the car.

"What's up?" Jake caught a glimpse of Jeremy's pensive face in the rearview mirror.

"I thought for sure it would float," he said. "My calculations should have been right."

"Well, I happen to know one thing you didn't calculate." Jake decided to take a page from Emma's book and try to help Jeremy see the humor in the situation.

"What?"

"You didn't add in the calories from the four slices of pizza I ate for lunch." Jake patted his flat stomach. "I'm sure that I weigh five pounds more than I did this morning."

That drew a smile.

"I ate that many, too," Jeremy confessed.

"So now we know. None of your mom's homemade pizza before the race."

Jeremy smiled, his earlier cheerfulness restored. Emma, on the other hand, didn't. Not only that, she had barely spoken a word since they'd left the park.

Jake had a hunch he knew the reason why.

By the time they arrived back at the house, the sun had started to set, outlining the trees in liquid gold. Shadow was waiting for them, wet nose pressed against the window and looking unhappy at having been left behind.

"Should I take Shadow for a walk?" Jeremy asked.

Emma shook her head. "It's getting dark. I can do

it. You should take off those wet clothes and jump into the shower."

Jeremy obeyed but paused halfway up the steps. "Are you coming over tomorrow after you get off work, Jake?"

Jake opened his mouth to answer but Emma beat him to it.

"Jeremy." Her voice was firm. "I'm sure Chief Sutton has other things that need his attention."

Jake winced inwardly. So they were back to his title again.

The boy's expression fell. "I guess so."

"Good night." Jake reached out and gave Jeremy's shoulder a comforting squeeze. "You do what your mom says and I'll put the raft back in the barn."

He was stunned when Jeremy's arms circled his waist and he hugged him before disappearing into the house. "G'night, Jake."

Emma appeared more troubled than surprised by the boy's unexpected display of affection.

"I'll unload the car," Jake said. "Shadow isn't going to let you forget that you promised him a walk."

She gave a brief nod and struck out across the yard, the dog streaking ahead of her.

Jake couldn't prevent a sigh from escaping. When it came to getting to know Emma, he felt as if he were on a treasure hunt.

The journey wouldn't always be easy, but he had no doubt it would be worth the effort if he didn't give up.

He wanted to hear her laughter. He wanted to see hope dispel the grief in her eyes. There were times he caught a glimpse of those things and knew God was at work in Emma's life.

If he—and his career—stopped getting in the way.

If only the scars on his chest could be explained away with a lighthearted story about a tumble into the neighbor's rosebush.

By the time Jake unloaded the last pieces of the raft from the trunk of the car, it was dark enough that he was forced to turn the lights on in the barn. He started to straighten things up and then chided himself for lingering, knowing that Emma wouldn't seek out his company.

He turned to leave and that's when he saw her. Perched on an old wooden chest just inside the door, knees drawn up against her chest. Jake hadn't even heard her come in.

He closed the distance between them and dropped down beside her on the bench. Emma continued to stare straight ahead, the flickering overhead light illuminating the delicate lines of her profile.

Silence stretched between them.

Jake didn't know what to say. Wasn't sure what Emma wanted to hear.

"Who did that to you?"

The soft question broadsided him. If Emma had asked *how* it happened, he would have given her an abbreviated version of the events that unfolded the night of the drug bust.

But she hadn't asked "how." She had asked "who." And that complicated the situation.

"I don't like to talk about it." An answer that wasn't an answer.

"Then tell me about your family."

"I don't—" Talk about them either, Jake started to say. Until he remembered that he had asked Emma the same question the day before.

Let her get to know you, Andy had said.

Jake decided to take his younger brother's advice, especially if it meant that he could avoid talking about his injury.

"I have a mother and a stepfather. A younger stepbrother."

"Andy," Emma murmured.

Jake couldn't hide his surprise that she knew his brother's name. "That's right. But up until six months ago, I could count on one hand the number of times I visited them over the past five years. And I lived in the same city." Jake paused, waiting for the stab of regret to subside. "I didn't see them on holidays. I didn't stop by for coffee on the weekends."

"I don't understand."

Neither had they, Jake thought.

"Usually when an officer is undercover, he does some surveillance, makes a few buys until an arrest is made. My assignment lasted almost five years. In order to prove that I was one of them, I had to fit in. Had to earn their trust. It wasn't easy but it was… necessary…to do my job."

"So you had to sever ties with your family?"

"I thought it was in their best interest," Jake explained. "We weren't just trying to shut down a few neighborhood drug dealers. This was bigger. It went all the way to the top of the food chain."

All the way to police department.

All the way to Sean.

* * *

Emma felt, rather than saw, a sudden memory that ripped through Jake. Made him shudder. Did he even realize that one of his hands had moved to his chest, covering the scars she had seen that afternoon?

"Is that how you got hurt?"

"Yes."

When it didn't appear that Jake was going to offer any more information, Emma was forced to ask another question.

"They figured out you were a police officer?"

"Only after someone told them that I was." Jake closed his eyes briefly. "The night of the bust, two people died. I was supposed to be one of them. I was viewed as a threat—the other guy, Manny, he was… dispensable. A nineteen-year-old addict who'd been on the streets since he was twelve. He liked to brag that he only looked out for himself. He refused a direct order to shoot me."

"What happened? After… Manny?" Emma had to know. Not for her sake, but for Jake. Something in his eyes told her that this wasn't a memory easily shared.

She understood. She had a few of her own.

"Something that I can't explain other than to say that God intervened."

"Intervened?"

"I got hit and went down. That was the first bullet. The second one jammed in the chamber." Jake stared ahead with unseeing eyes, as if caught up in the memory again. "When I was at the end of my strength, I called out to God. He reached out His hand and He hasn't let go of me since."

Bile rose in the back of Emma's throat. Not only because a young man had lost his life, but because Jake had come so close to dying.

"The person who shot you?" she whispered. "Did they arrest him?"

"The SWAT team heard the first shot and they took the second one."

"And the person who set you up? Did you find out who it was?"

"Sean O'Keefe." Jake's eyes darkened with fresh pain. Pain that Emma sensed didn't have anything to do with his injury.

"You knew him?"

A heartbeat of silence followed.

"He was my best friend."

His best friend.

Emma swallowed hard. Without thinking, she reached out and covered the hand that rested on his knee. Jake's fingers curled around hers.

"Sean used our friendship to keep tabs on me and he knew that I suspected some of the officers were taking bribes to look the other way. I never expected he was one of them, though." Jake drew in a ragged breath. "The dealer didn't think I'd live to see morning, so he decided to make me suffer a little before he killed me. He told me everything. How Sean betrayed me. And why."

Their eyes met and Jake must have seen the question in hers. "It wasn't just for the money. I think he got tired. Disillusioned. The things a cop sees can wear him down. Tempt him to give in rather than fight. I wonder sometimes…" His voice trailed off but Emma knew what he'd been about to say.

"You wouldn't have." She could say the words with absolute certainty.

Jake's hand tightened around hers. "There were days when things got…blurry. When I was under-cover, I walked a fine line between right and wrong in order to earn people's trust. There were times I stepped over it. It wasn't as hard to forgive Sean as it was to forgive myself for not realizing what was happening to him."

"But you did."

A smile lifted the corner of Jake's lips. "With God's help. I'd surrendered my life to Him, but when I was in the hospital Andy warned me that anger and bitterness could keep me stuck. Prevent me from moving forward. He was right. The weeks after Sean was arrested were a struggle, but I had made a prom-ise to God the night I was shot."

"A promise?"

"To do things His way. To follow where He leads."

"To Mirror Lake." Emma remembered what Jake had said the night that Jeremy had invited him over for dinner.

"Andy agreed that it would be a good place to heal."

"Have you?" she asked without thinking. "Started to…heal?"

Jake rose to his feet with an enigmatic smile. "A little more every day."

Chapter Eighteen

"The garden stones are beautiful, Emma!"

"What did I tell you, Esther?" Abby breezed into the booth with an armload of afghans. "She has a gift."

"Abby." Emma knelt down to adjust a canvas flap—and to hide her embarrassment.

"She's right." Esther smiled. "Some of the people who wandered through earlier this morning asked me if you took orders."

"Mmm." Abby tossed Emma a "so there" look over her shoulder. "I brought some flowerpots from the inn so we can display the stepping-stones as if they're in a garden. We can even have them leading up to the booth."

"That's a great idea." Esther nodded approvingly. "Emma? What do you think?"

Emma glanced at Abby and any reservations she may have had were overcome by the infectious sparkle in the other woman's eyes.

"It *is* a great idea," she agreed.

"I'll be right back. The flowers are in the back of my car."

Abby dashed off and a white paper stick topped with a gigantic puff of spun sugar was thrust under Emma's nose.

"Cotton candy?"

Kate had returned.

"I can't. Just looking at that makes my teeth hurt," Emma confessed.

"But it will make your taste buds sing." Kate grinned. "Where did Abby run off to so fast?"

"She went to get the flowers." Esther poked her head out from behind the curtain of the booth.

"What can I do?"

"Someone made a last-minute donation," Esther said. "The church van is filled with crocheted pot holders that we need to find a place for."

"I'm on it." Kate saluted her with the cotton candy before handing it to Emma.

"I wish I had half that girl's energy," Esther said as Kate bounded toward the parking lot.

Emma raised an eyebrow. "You do."

"There are days these old bones wouldn't agree with you." Esther began to drape the afghans over the rungs of the antique wooden ladder Abby had set up in a corner of the booth.

Emma opened one of the boxes on the grass and pulled a brightly colored knitted blanket out. "Who made this one? I love the pattern."

"I did," Esther said. "And between you and me, I had more trouble with it. I must have started over a dozen times. Almost gave up that many, too. The only reason I stuck it out was because my grandmother designed the pattern. She's the one who taught me how to knit."

"I would like to buy this one," Emma said impulsively. "If you don't mind selling it to me, of course."

"Sorry." Esther was already shaking her head. "I can't sell it to you."

"Oh—"

"But I will give it to you. As a gift."

"Esther, no. I would rather pay for it."

Esther considered her for a moment. "I suppose you would," she said at length. "But I don't sell my afghans to friends, I give them away. That's another thing my grandmother taught me."

Friends.

Emma offered a tentative smile as she hugged the blanket against her chest. "Thank you."

"You're welcome." Esther looked pleased as she finished arranging the display of afghans. She turned her attention to the garden stones Emma had brought over to the park after work. "You do beautiful work, too. Did your mother teach you how to do this? Or did you take a class?"

"I taught myself. It's just a hobby," Emma said. "Something to fill the hours after Jeremy goes to bed."

Esther acted as if she hadn't heard her. One gnarled finger traced the uneven fragments of glass in the design. "Broken pieces of pottery—something that most people wouldn't see any value in—is used to create something new and beautiful. I look at these and I'm reminded that God does the same thing in our lives when we trust Him."

The words, soft as they were, cut Emma to the

core. Maybe that was why she couldn't prevent the words that spilled out.

"I'm afraid to trust Him."

Emma couldn't believe she had said the words out loud. She glanced at Esther, knowing she would see disapproval. Or disgust. What kind of terrible person admitted that they were afraid to trust God? The creator of the entire universe?

But there was neither disapproval nor disgust on Esther's face. All Emma saw was understanding. And maybe a glimmer of humor. "Then I suggest you tell Him that."

Emma choked. "I can't!"

"You think it would surprise Him? When we tell God how we feel, we aren't telling Him anything that He doesn't already know." Esther smiled. "I love the story of the father who came to Jesus and asked Him to heal his son. The man tells Him that he believes—and in the very next breath, he asks Jesus to help him overcome his unbelief. He realized he didn't have a lot of faith but he knew who to turn to for help. That prayer was heartfelt. Honest.

"You want Jeremy to be honest with you, don't you? Not only do you want to laugh with him, you want him to come to you when he's hurting or upset. To share his heart with you. That's the kind of relationship God wants to have with *His* children."

Emma's throat swelled.

Her ten-year-old son had said the same thing the night they had prayed together. If only she could have that kind of faith. Simple. Uncomplicated.

Not at all like life.

She had always felt so…alone. Her father had

treated her as if she were excess baggage he was obligated to haul from place to place. Other than those
brief years with Brian, as long as she could remember, she had been alone.

"I just don't understand *why*," she whispered.

Esther's eyes filled with tears. "You can tell Him
that, too."

Jake spotted Emma talking with Esther Redstone
in one of the craft booths set up near the pavilion.

Caught up in the whirlwind of pre–Reflection
Days preparations, he hadn't seen much of Emma
over the course of the week. The few times he had
stopped by the house to spend time with Jeremy,
Emma had been in her workroom, making stepping-
stones for the craft show.

Or had she been avoiding him?

Jake hadn't meant to share so many details about
his past. If his goal was to get Emma to see beyond
his badge, he'd made a mess of it. All he had done was
give her more reasons to keep him at arm's length.

*Keep working in Emma's heart, Lord. I'll try to
stay out of the way.*

"Are you avoiding her?" Kate had managed to
sneak up on him.

Jake didn't bother to feign ignorance. Not with
Kate. "No."

"Is that the whole truth and nothing but the truth?"
Abby appeared beside her friend.

He'd been ambushed.

"I can arrest you both for disturbing the peace."
Jake scowled. "My peace."

Abby's smile remained serene. "You are welcome

to bring Emma and Jeremy over to the lodge tonight to watch the water parade. We've got the best view from the beach."

"Did I say I was going to the water parade?"

"Everyone goes to the water parade," Kate informed him.

"Everyone but Emma," Jake pointed out.

"Maybe no one's ever asked her."

Jake's eyes narrowed. "Emma doesn't like social events. I doubt I could convince her."

Especially now.

Kate grinned. "Mmm. If I remember correctly, that's what you said about the dog."

"Jake invited us to go to the water parade with him tonight. It's going to be awesome, Mom." Jeremy flopped down on the grass beside Emma. "Miss Porter is going to let us watch it from her dock and she's going to make s'mores and everything."

"Is she?" Emma shot "Miss Porter" a look.

"That's because Miss Porter's bed-and-breakfast happens to have the best view of the parade." Abby, busy arranging pots of autumn mums in front of the booth, didn't appear the least repentant.

"Can we go?"

"I don't know," Emma hedged. "I'll have to think about it. The parade doesn't start until ten. That's a late night."

"Think of it as a last hurrah before school starts," Kate interjected. "There's a bonfire at the park before the parade. A lot of people pack a picnic supper and make an entire evening of it."

"The water parade is beautiful." Esther joined the

chorus. "Some of the business owners get quite creative."

"Thank you." Kate dropped a curtsy and grinned. "The Grapevine did win first place in the most original category last year. The girls from my book club have been helping me decorate the float this year. And I need all my friends to cheer us on."

"See, Mom?" Jeremy's expression became earnest. "Kate needs us."

"That's right. Kate needs you." The café owner aimed a saucy wink at Emma.

"Jake's never seen the parade before, either," Jeremy added for good measure.

Everyone waited expectantly for her decision.

"It looks like I'm outnumbered." Emma sighed. "You can go."

Jeremy's smile dimmed. "But he wants both of us to watch the parade with him. He said so."

Emma wasn't so sure about that.

Several times during the week Jake had stopped over after work to help Jeremy with the raft, but he hadn't exchanged more than a few polite words with her.

Not for the first time, Emma wondered if Jake regretted telling her about his friend, Sean.

After he had left that night, Emma had stayed in the barn for another hour, thinking about what he had said. He had a reason to be angry. Bitter. Instead, he had turned to God. Gave Him credit for being able to release those feelings and move forward.

Emma moved over to one of the tables, her hands unsteady as she began to rearrange a display of stained-glass suncatchers.

If she were honest with herself, she knew that she had been holding on to those same kind of feelings. Six years had gone by since Brian's death but she was afraid to look ahead. Afraid that if she did, she would forget him. Afraid that if she let go of her grief, she wouldn't have anything else to hold on to.

He reached out His hand and He hasn't let go...

Jake's faith stirred up that familiar longing again. Was it that simple? Reaching out to God and trusting that He would be there?

"Mom?" Emma felt a tug on her arm and realized that Jeremy was still waiting for an answer. "I don't want to go to the parade without you."

"I'll go along. If you're sure that Jake invited both of us."

"He said he'd find the perfect spot for the three of us to watch the parade. And you're one of the three of us," Jeremy said.

"You can't argue that logic," Kate murmured.

Abby clapped her hands together. "And I can help you find that perfect spot to watch the parade!"

Chapter Nineteen

"Jake's here!"

After two weeks, Emma should have been getting used to hearing the familiar refrain but her heart reacted the same way every time.

"Don't forget your sweatshirt," she called as her son streaked past.

"I won't."

Emma forced herself to take a deep breath. It was silly to become rattled over the thought of spending the evening with Jake.

"Look what Jake got for us!" Jeremy had returned, only this time he was waving a T-shirt over his head. He thrust it into her hands. "Isn't it cool?"

Emma examined the garment. It boasted wide red, white and blue stripes. But mostly red. Emblazoned on the front in bold block letters were the words TEAM VICTORY. "Wow."

"I know. It's for the race tomorrow." Jeremy could barely contain his excitement.

"It looks a little big," Emma murmured.

"That one is yours." Jake sauntered into the kitchen.

"Mine?" The word came out in a squeak.

"I had one made for each of us."

"Wow." Emma said it again.

"I'll bet none of the other teams are going to have shirts like this," Jeremy said.

"Probably not," Emma agreed.

Jake winked at her. "You can thank me later."

"I…" Emma forgot what she'd been about to say, her thoughts dissolving in the warmth of his smile.

"What's the matter, Mom?"

"Nothing." Nothing that she could explain, anyway. Emma grabbed her purse. "We better get going."

Jake took one look at the line of cars lining the driveway at the lodge and figured Abby had invited the entire town, not just a few friends, to watch the parade from her property!

"Abby is amazing," Emma said, her gaze sweeping the landscaped grounds in disbelief. "She should have entered a float in the parade."

"She didn't have to," Jake said as he followed Emma across the yard. "Look at how many lights she used."

Luminaries hung from the branches of the trees around the lodge and white lights had been strung on the boathouse. The smell of a campfire permeated the air, dispersed by the warm breeze blowing across the lake.

As if on cue, their hostess breezed up to them.

"There's lemonade and cookies on the picnic tables," Abby said. "You can sit anywhere you want to but I promised that I would share an inside tip. The best view of the parade is from that little rise over by the cabins."

"Really?" Emma flicked a glance in that direction. "I don't see anyone else over there."

"That's strange," Abby said, the picture of innocence. "I guess you'll be the first ones."

Why did Jake have the feeling they would be the *only* ones?

"Thanks," he said drily.

She flashed a sunny smile. "Anytime, Jake. Now, I have to help Quinn make the s'mores. If you need anything, let me know."

Abby disappeared in the direction of the campfire, leaving the three of them alone again.

"There's Cody." Jeremy pointed to a shadowy figure waving to them from the end of the dock. "Can I go and talk to him for a few minutes?"

Emma didn't hesitate. "All right."

Jake wanted to hug her. He had noticed a tentative friendship spring up between Jeremy and Cody Lang and he wanted to encourage it. It looked as though Emma did, too, and was willing to put aside some of her reservations to let the boys get to know each other better.

"I'll be over there," she added, pointing to the spot Abby had suggested.

"Okay." Jeremy headed down to the lake and Jake fell in step with Emma as she moved toward the secluded spot under a circle of towering white pine.

He hadn't expected her to accept his invitation to the parade, but suspected Jeremy had had something to do with her decision.

Which was why Jake had asked him first.

There was a burst of applause as the first float in the parade chugged around the curve of the shoreline.

Strings of multicolored lights fastened to a frame transformed the ordinary fishing boat into a coffee cup,
complete with a curl of "smoke" fashioned from strips
of filmy white cloth that fluttered gently in the breeze.

"Look! That one must be Kate's."

Jake smiled at the note of excitement in Emma's
voice. He spread the blanket out under the tree. "Here
you go."

"Thank you." Emma sat down on the edge of the blanket, her gaze riveted on the line of boats as they came
into view. "I had no idea so much work went into this."

"Neither did I." Jake stretched out beside her.
"Mayor Dodd stopped by the department so many
times this week, checking on this and that, I considered deputizing him."

"He came into the library a few times, too. I think
he wanted to make sure I hadn't taken down any of
the posters."

Two more floats brought a loud chorus of oohs and
aahs from the spectators on the beach.

"Sounds like they're having fun," Jake commented.

"You don't have to keep me company, you know,"
Emma said quietly. "I'd understand if you'd rather
join the party."

"I am right where I want to be." It was the truth
but Jake wondered if he'd said too much.

There had been a few times when they were together that he imagined feeling a spark of attraction
between them, but Jake had convinced himself that's
all it was. His imagination.

He reached for the thermos of coffee and his arm
brushed against Emma's. She shivered.

"Are you cold?"

"N-no."

That didn't sound very convincing. Jake stripped off his denim jacket and draped it over her shoulders.

The coat almost swallowed her whole.

"Well, at the moment you look more like Sheriff Ben than Chef Charlotte." Laughing, Jake slid one hand underneath the frayed collar to free her hair. She had worn it loose today and it slid like satin between his fingers.

His laughter faded away. Without thinking, Jake cupped the back of her head in his hand and pulled her closer. Their lips met in a fleeting but gentle kiss that turned Jake's heart inside out.

A split second after he let her go, he saw the shocked look on Emma's face.

"I'm sorry." Jake released her. "I don't know why…" *Yes, you do.* "Excuse me a minute. I think I'll check on Jeremy."

He surged to his feet.

There'd been times he'd had to face a difficult situation and calmly stand his ground.

This wasn't one of them.

"What time is it?"

"Twelve-thirty." Jake padded to the sliding glass door and stared outside. "Were you sleeping?"

"Yes. Now my question is, why aren't you?" Andy yawned.

"I just got back from the water parade a little while ago."

"Ah." His brother sounded more awake now.

"What does that mean? *Ah?*"

"It means you were with Jeremy and Emma Barlow."

"They'd never seen it before." And he had sure made it a night to remember, Jake thought wryly.

"You're spending a lot of time with them."

"I'm Jeremy's mentor. That's kind of the point."

"So where does Emma fit?"

Jake had a mental image of wrapping Emma in his jacket. Pulling her into his arms. And the look of shock on her face…

He groaned.

"Uh-oh." Andy's voice was laced with amusement. "What did you do this time?"

"Nothing. I'd rather not talk about it."

"No talking about nothing. Got it." Another yawn. "You have feelings for Emma, don't you?"

"Andy." Jake gave a warning growl.

"Oh, that's the nothing you don't want to talk about. Sorry. I'm a little slow at…twelve fifty-three in the morning."

Jake rolled his eyes even as a smile worked at the corners of his lips. "Why did I call you?"

"Because you miss me," Andy said promptly.

Jake shook his head. "I'll let you go back to sleep."

"Jake?" Andy's voice became somber. "God is in control, and I don't say that because it's written in a pastor's handbook somewhere. He brought you to Mirror Lake for a reason and it wasn't an accident that you met Jeremy and Emma. Trust Him. And get some sleep. Isn't that big raft race you've been telling me about tomorrow morning?"

"Eleven o'clock."

"Let me know how it goes."

"Thanks, Andy."

"Anytime, Bro."

Jake hung up the phone and got ready for bed. He lay down, linking his hands behind his head as he stared up at the ceiling. As usual, his kid brother was right. He did need to trust that God was in control.

And he did have feelings for Emma.

Lord, I know You're at work in my life and in Emma's. I don't know what's going to happen, but I do trust You.

The next time Jake woke up, it was because his pager was going off.

Emma woke up and found two pairs of eyes staring at her.

One blue, one chocolate brown.

"Are you awake, Mom?" Jeremy whispered.

She smiled, reminded of the Christmas mornings when Jeremy would sneak into her bedroom before dawn and ask the same question. "I am now." Emma covered a yawn. "What time is it?"

"Six."

"Six?" She sat up and Shadow took that as an invitation to launch himself onto the bed. He turned a circle and flopped down, propping his chin on her feet.

"The pancake breakfast starts at seven, remember?" Jeremy plopped down next to the dog.

Emma groaned. She couldn't believe a town the size of Mirror Lake could pack so many activities into one three-day weekend. "I remember. But we don't have to be the first ones in line, do we?"

"How about the second?" Jeremy summoned the heart-melting smile that she had never been able to refuse. "Do you think Jake will be there?"

Emma's heart flipped over. "I'm not sure, but he'll

be at the park in time for the raft race. Why don't you take Shadow for a walk while I get dressed and have a cup of coffee?"

At the word walk, Shadow's ears lifted.

"Go on, now." Under the blankets, Emma nudged the dog with her toe. Shadow jumped down and followed Jeremy out of the room.

She collapsed back against the pillow and closed her eyes.

Jake had kissed her.

And she'd *wanted* him to.

That was what had taken her by surprise when Jake had drawn her into his arms.

There was no denying the truth any longer.

She had reluctantly let Jake into her life…and over the past few weeks he had somehow worked his way into her heart.

The day promised to be a warm one, so Emma dressed in denim capris and a lightweight floral shirt. There was no sign of Jeremy and Shadow when she came downstairs but a cup of coffee sat on the counter, cooling.

Ordinarily, the thought of attending any kind of social event, being surrounded by people, would have put Emma on edge. Filled her with dread. But this felt different. She was looking forward to seeing Esther Redstone. Listening in on Kate and Abby's lively banter. Watching Jeremy interact with some of the boys he'd met at church.

And seeing Jake again.

"Are you ready, Mom?" The screen door banged behind Jeremy and Shadow as they skidded into the kitchen.

"Ready to eat cold pancakes and sausage at a picnic table outside?" Emma grinned. "Can't wait."

Jeremy responded to her teasing with a grin of his own. "Don't forget the camera so you can take pictures of me and Jake at the race."

"I won't." Emma had already stashed it in her purse the night before. "If Shadow has food and water, I guess we're ready to go."

Shadow walked over to his dog bed in the corner and collapsed with a sigh, as if he knew he wasn't invited along on this particular trip into town.

"Do you have your T-shirt, Mom?"

Her T-shirt.

Emma gulped. "I'm not sure where I put it."

"I think it's in the laundry room on top of the dryer," Jeremy said helpfully.

So it was. Bravely, Emma pulled the shirt over her head and avoided the mirror in the front hall as she walked out the door.

The short drive to Mirror Lake seemed to take a lot longer than usual.

"I can't believe people get up this early on a Saturday morning," Emma muttered as she drove around the parking lot for the second time, trying to find an empty space.

"It's the pancakes, Mom. And people want to be here early and get a good spot to watch the race."

Emma finally found a narrow space between two pickup trucks and eased her car between the painted lines. Jeremy would have bailed out immediately, but she put her hand on his arm.

"Wait a second, Jeremy. I want to talk to you about something."

In spite of his eagerness to be the first one in the breakfast line, Jeremy settled back against the seat. "What is it, Mom?"

"The race." Emma wasn't quite sure how to proceed. "I don't want to discourage you, but you are competing against teams who do this every year. I just don't want you to be too disappointed if you don't win."

"I know. Jake told me the same thing."

Emma blinked. "He did?"

"Yup. Jake said it doesn't matter if we win or lose, that we had a lot of fun building the raft and that's the most important thing."

Jake said.

The very words that Emma had once thought of as a threat now made her smile. "I guess that's covered, then."

"*Now* can we eat pancakes?"

"Now we can eat pancakes."

They made their way over to the line of portable buffet tables, where Kate was doling out plates.

"You two are up bright and early this morning." She smiled as Jeremy almost danced through the line.

"*Jeremy* was up bright and early this morning," Emma corrected. "He's excited about the race but I'm surprised he didn't sleep longer, considering how late he was up last night."

"Last night," Kate mused. "The water parade was beautiful. Did you see it?"

"Of course I did. You were there…" Emma's voice trailed off when she caught Kate's not-so-subtle meaning.

"All I'm saying is that from my vantage point, it

looked to me like you were watching someone—I
mean *something*—else."

Emma almost smiled. "I'm leaving now."

"You can run, but you can't hide." Kate's lilting voice
followed Emma's retreat. "Nice shirt, by the way!"

As Emma searched for a place to sit, she spotted Esther Redstone and Abby sitting together under
the pavilion. Abby immediately waved and patted an
empty spot on the bench beside her.

"Over here, Emma! We saved a spot for you and
Jeremy."

The sweetness of the gesture stripped away any
apprehension that Emma had been feeling. They lingered over breakfast and cups of hot coffee. More
people began to arrive and Emma glanced at her
watch, surprised to see that over an hour had passed.

There was still no sign of Jake, but she wasn't worried. A few of the teams had begun to assemble down
by the lake, but he and Jeremy would have plenty of
time to set up before the start of the race.

After they finished eating, Abby left to track
down Quinn, who'd volunteered to help with security. Emma decided to check on Jeremy, who had gone
to the playground with Cody Lang.

Jeremy broke away from the group. "Is Jake here
yet?"

Emma scanned the people setting up lawn chairs along
the beach. A flutter of uneasiness skated down her spine.

"Not yet."

Chapter Twenty

"He'll be here." Jeremy didn't look the least bit concerned that the start of the race was drawing closer.

"Let me check my cell phone. Maybe he tried to call." Emma opened up her purse and fished around inside but all that turned up was her checkbook, sunglasses and a tube of lip gloss.

In her haste to leave, Emma realized she must have left her phone on the nightstand.

"Is there anything I can help you with?"

"We can unload the trunk now, I guess." Jeremy looked around. "The other teams are starting to get ready."

Daniel joined up with them on the second trip to the car and helped them carry the rest of the supplies down to the beach.

"Well, folks, the annual raft race will be starting shortly." Mayor Dodd, armed with a microphone on the makeshift stage, boomed out the announcement. "You may want to grab a lawn chair and make your way down to the lake. This event is a Reflection Days tradition and we've got two more teams signed up this year…"

Abby drew Emma to the side. "What's the matter?" she whispered.

For Jeremy's sake, Emma had tried to hide her concern over Jake's continuing absence. But the race would be starting in less than half an hour and it was getting more difficult not to panic. If Jake didn't show up, Jeremy would have to forfeit.

"Jake should be here by now." Emma kept her voice low so Jeremy wouldn't overhear. "I left my phone at home, so I don't know if he tried to call."

"Here. You can borrow mine." Abby retrieved her cell phone from the tapestry bag looped over her shoulder.

"Thank you." Emma took a few steps away and dialed the number. Out of the corner of her eye, she saw Abby whispering something to Quinn. Her fiancé glanced at Emma and nodded before he strode away.

Emma closed the phone and handed it back to her. The question in Abby's eyes had Emma shaking her head. "There's no answer."

By quarter to eleven, the mayor bellowed a first call to the teams signed up for the race.

Jeremy wilted against her side, eyes bright with unshed tears even as he struggled to keep a brave face. "I don't think Jake is coming, Mom."

Emma tamped down her rising panic. "Don't worry, sweetheart. We have a few minutes yet. He'll show up."

He *had* to show up.

Five minutes later, however, she was beginning to doubt her own words.

"All teams should begin to line up behind the yellow tape." The announcer's cheerful voice came over the loudspeaker.

"I'm sorry, Emma." Abby's soft voice barely cut through her panic.

Anger rose up inside of Emma, weaving through the anxiety that had already tied her stomach into knots. Jeremy had been counting on Jake. So had she. What was she supposed to tell her son? That all the time and effort he had put into planning for the race had been for nothing?

Abby squeezed her arm. "What should we do?" Her expression mirrored the helplessness that Emma was feeling.

"I think we can make room on our raft." Quinn stepped forward. "Jeremy can race with me and Cody."

Emma felt a tug on her arm and looked down at her son's face. The tears were still there…but so was a look of determination.

"Did you hear Mr. O'Halloran?" Emma tried to keep her tone upbeat. She couldn't let Jeremy see how upset she was by Jake's absence. "He offered to let you race with them."

"Thanks, but that's okay." Jeremy flashed a shy smile at Quinn even as he turned down the invitation.

"Two minutes!" the mayor bellowed.

The onlookers moved closer together on the beach, the noise subsiding into a hushed anticipation.

"Jeremy, you're under thirteen. The rules state you have to have an adult with you," Emma reminded him.

"I know. You can go with me."

Emma's knees buckled. "Me?"

"We can do it, Mom." Jeremy sounded so confident that Emma almost believed him. "You watched me and Jake put the raft together a million times."

Not even close, Emma thought wildly. It had been three or four at the most, every time they'd asked her to time them.

She balked, her gaze locking on the yellow flag flapping offshore. For some reason, it looked a lot farther away than it had the day Jake and Jeremy had tested it out. "Jeremy…maybe you should just withdraw from the race."

Even as she spoke, Abby was adjusting the straps on a bright orange life jacket. Emma gasped when she felt Abby put it over her head and fasten the buckles around her waist.

"You know I don't like the water," she told her son in a terse whisper.

"You aren't going to be in the water," Jeremy said. "You're going to be on the raft."

"But what if we lose because of me?" A very real possibility, to Emma's way of thinking.

"That's okay." Jeremy tugged her toward the Team Victory flag stuck in the sand. The one that matched their T-shirts. "You and Jake said that doesn't matter. The important thing is to have fun, remember?"

Of course she remembered. But this wasn't exactly her idea of fun!

Emma looked over her shoulder, desperate to spot a familiar figure striding toward them. Tried to convince herself that Jake had somehow lost track of the time…

"Come on, Mom. It's going to start."

"Number four, Team Victory," the announcer called.

Heads swiveled in their direction.

"Team Victory," he repeated.

"Okay." She drew in a ragged breath. "Let's do it."

Jeremy raised his hand for a high five and Emma smacked her palm weakly against his.

The announcer read through the rules one more time. Emma's gaze traveled over the pieces of the raft and she tried to remember the order in which Jeremy and Jake had constructed it.

Where is he, God?

"Three…two…one." A whistle blew and Jeremy gave her a hammer.

Emma worked quickly, guided by memory and the occasional instruction from Jeremy. A few minutes later, she heard a splash as one of the rafts launched. Jeremy didn't spare a moment to glance up to see who was ahead of them.

"Ready." They pulled the raft across the narrow strip of sand. "You're going to have to paddle, Mom."

Emma summoned a smile. "It'll be fun."

Jeremy flashed a grin.

Even as Emma positioned herself on the raft, she looked around to see if Jake had arrived. Kate, Esther and Daniel stood next to Team Victory's flag, waving their arms and shouting out encouragements.

The raft dipped to accommodate their combined weight and water flowed over the side. Emma gasped as it soaked through her clothing.

A collective groan rose from the group of onlookers as another raft capsized. A small rowboat immediately went to the contestants' aid.

They were in first place.

As they drew closer to the flag, Emma put her paddle across her lap. Her fingers trembled as she fumbled to untie one of the bright red bandanas from the buoy.

"I've got it. Let's go!" Emma shouted as soon as it was free.

As they turned the raft around, another one bumped up against them. The jolt pitched Jeremy to the side and Emma's heart followed suit.

She made a grab for his arm but he righted himself. "I'm okay," he gasped.

Paddling furiously, they passed several more rafts bobbing toward the flag. Some of the contestants lay on their stomachs, using their hands and feet to paddle.

As the cheering grew louder, it occurred to Emma that they were going to win.

"We have to tie the bandana to our flag," Jeremy said as the underside of the raft scraped against the sand. "Otherwise we're disqualified."

"I'll let you do the honors," Emma said. "You're faster than I am." And once the adrenaline wore off, she wasn't sure her legs would hold her upright!

They bailed off the side of the raft into the shallow water and dragged it onto shore. Jeremy sprinted ahead of her with the bandana.

Jeremy was knotting the bandana on their flagpole as she reached his side. But the small group of people clustered around him weren't jumping up and cheering.

Emma's heart dropped like a stone when she saw Quinn standing next to Officer Koenigs. The man's ordinarily placid expression now reflected a grim resignation.

A sudden flashback weakened her knees.

She had seen that look before.

"First place goes to Team Victory," the announcer said. "Jeremy and Emma Barlow. Come over here and get your trophy."

"Jeremy—go get the trophy for us," Emma said hoarsely.

Fortunately, her son hadn't sensed anything amiss. With a grin, he loped over to the judge's stand.

Abby came alongside Emma and gave her arm a bracing squeeze.

Emma moistened her lips. Her gaze cut from Quinn back to Phil Koenigs. "What happened? Is it… Jake?"

The officer nodded reluctantly. "About six o'clock, the sheriff's department received a call that a vehicle in front of them was driving erratically. The caller followed the car until it turned off on a dead-end road about ten miles out of town." Phil paused and cleared his throat. "By the time the officer arrived on the scene, the occupants of the vehicle had gone into a cabin. He saw stolen property in the backseat of the car and called for backup."

"Why would Jake respond?" Emma stared at the older officer in confusion. Jake wasn't a county deputy, nor would a police chief be expected to respond to a routine call.

Unless it wasn't a routine call.

"Whoever was in the cabin shot at the officer," Phil explained. "For the last few hours, the officers have been in a standoff with the two men inside. Several departments in the area responded. From what we know, they're either drunk or strung out on drugs. I've been out of town the last few days visiting my daughter, but when I heard the call come over the radio, I drove back. I'd just stopped home to change into my uniform when Quinn tracked me down. He thought I should be the one to tell you what was going on so you'd hear the truth. Rumors are already starting to go around."

Most of the words filtered through Emma's mind. The ones that stayed turned her heart cold. *Shot at the officer. Strung out on drugs.*

"Thank you." Emma could feel a strange numbness seeping into every pore. The rushing sound in her ears made it difficult to concentrate on what the officer was saying.

"I have to get back there now," Phil told them. "Hopefully we'll get this thing wrapped up soon."

"We'll be praying for you and the other officers," Abby promised softly.

"I appreciate that, Miss Porter." Phil looked at Emma, his eyes dark with regret. "I'm sorry, Emma. I wish I didn't have to be the bearer of bad news."

Again.

The word hung in the air between them.

How could she have forgotten that this was what it had felt like? The uncertainty. The waiting. Living with the knowledge that at any moment, a situation could change. Your life could change.

"I appreciate you taking the time to come down and tell me." Emma reached out and shook his hand.

Phil nodded curtly. "I'm sure Jake will get word to you as soon as he can."

"Look at the trophy we won!" Jeremy skidded up, holding a small gold trophy. His bright gaze searched the faces around him. "Is Jake here yet?"

Spots danced in front of Emma's eyes.

What was she going to tell her son?

"Not yet." Daniel answered the question. "Something came up this morning and he had to go to work."

"Work?" Jeremy's brow furrowed. "He's okay, though, isn't he?"

Emma swallowed hard. "I haven't heard from him yet." At least, Emma thought, she was telling the truth.

At the moment, she didn't dare consider the alternative.

"What a way to spend a day." Phil Koenigs leaned against the wall in the department break room, weariness etched in every line on his face. "Maureen will be glad when I call her and tell her to fire up the grill."

Steve Patterson shed his uniform shirt and draped it over a chair before casting a guilty look at Jake. "Sorry, Chief. No disrespect, but I'm beginning to offend myself."

"You were beginning to offend the rest of us, too," Trip muttered.

Jake listened to the officers, knowing the banter was their way of releasing stress. The men had been strategically placed around the perimeter of the cabin, forced to remain nearly motionless in the hot sun for hours.

The call came in shortly after Jake's alarm had gone off that morning. Shots fired at a cabin north of Mirror Lake. With several county deputies on vacation, local departments had responded to the scene to help out. He got the directions from dispatch and called Emma on the way to the scene, sick at the thought of having to explain that he might not be there for the raft race.

The call had gone right to her voice mail and Jake hadn't had another opportunity to get in touch with her after that.

The standoff had lasted all day, until one of the young men had finally staggered out of the cabin shortly before dusk. He was worried about his friend, who'd been passed out for several hours.

He was taken into custody while the other man was transported to the hospital. Jake had remained at the scene until an inventory of the stolen property was completed and the car impounded.

The sheriff had contacted Jake after the young man gave a statement, letting him know that both men had been involved in the rash of cabin burglaries.

Jake was relieved it had turned out the way it did. Bad guys in custody—no one injured.

But would Emma see it that way?

Chapter Twenty-One

"I'm going to take Shadow for a walk, okay, Mom?" Jeremy appeared in the kitchen doorway.

"All right. I'm sure he'd like that." Emma forced a smile. She didn't blame her son for needing some time alone to think.

Once they had heard the news about Jake, neither one of them had felt like staying at the park for the rest of the celebration. Emma had done her best to hide her feelings from Jeremy, but he had been quiet on the drive back home, resistant to her attempts to draw him out.

She heard the front door close and laid her head on the table.

I don't understand, God.

The silent cry burst out of a place deep within her.

They'd gone through this before. By letting Jake into their lives, she had put Jeremy in a situation where he could be hurt again. For six years, Emma had done everything within her power to protect her son…

She closed her eyes and drew in a ragged breath.

Maybe that was the trouble. She had done everything in *her* power.

When I came to the end of my strength, I called out to God. He reached out His hand and He hasn't let go.

Jake's words. Said with absolute certainty.

Emma had always believed in God, but after Brian died, she had pulled away from Him, too.

She felt like that father in the story that Esther had told her. And she'd said that nothing in the heart was hidden from God, so Emma didn't bother to hold anything back this time. Even as she stumbled through the prayer, peace settled over her, a kind of peace she had never experienced before.

I'm here, God. And I'm reaching out to You. I'm tired of doing all of this alone. I need You. I want to trust You. Esther said that we can be honest with You, so here it is. I'm scared to death but I'm going to trust You. I'm going to trust that You're not going to let go of me, either.

"Mom?" Jeremy's soft voice intruded on her prayer. "You're crying."

"I'm praying." She sniffled.

"For Jake?"

"And for me."

The look of hope on her son's face was humbling. She drew him close.

"Do you mind if we pray together?" he asked.

"I think that's a great idea," Emma whispered.

They went into the living room and sat together on the couch, heads bowed, Shadow sprawled at their feet.

Jeremy's simple but heartfelt prayer struck a chord in Emma's heart.

"I know that Jake has to help people sometimes, God. That's his job. But me and mom are worried about him, so please keep him safe. Amen."

"Amen," Emma echoed.

The sound of a car coming up the driveway pushed them both to their feet. Jeremy raced to the window and brushed the curtain aside.

He twisted around to look at her. "I think it's Mr. Redstone."

Daniel?

Emma peered out the window and saw not one car, but three, lined up in the driveway. Behind the Redstones' pickup truck she recognized Abby's red convertible. Kate sat in the driver's seat of the vintage Thunderbird parked behind it.

By the time Emma reached the door, people were already filing in.

"We had all this leftover food," Abby informed her cheerfully. "So we thought we'd drop some off."

Daniel ruffled Jeremy's hair. "And I had to see the dog that Mrs. Peake has been talking about. He's a local celebrity."

"Shadow," Jeremy said.

Emma's throat swelled. No matter what they claimed their reasons were, she knew why they'd come.

When Brian died, people had reached out to her and she'd backed away.

This time, she opened the door wide and let them in.

Jake pulled into the driveway, surprised to see a line of cars parked in front of Emma's house.

After going home to shower and change his clothes, Jake had been tempted to crawl into bed, close his eyes and slip into oblivion for the next ten hours. But he couldn't. Not until he apologized to Jeremy. And to Emma.

The front door opened as Jake got out of the car and Jeremy hurtled toward him.

Jake didn't think twice. He caught the boy up in his arms and gave him a hard hug.

"You're okay," Jeremy gasped.

"I'm okay." Jake's heart wrenched. Until this moment, he wasn't sure if Jeremy would look at him with resentment for not being there when he needed him. "I'm sorry that I didn't make the race this morning, bud."

More sorry than he could say.

"I know you had to work. Officer Koenigs told us," Jeremy said, inadvertently twisting the knife in Jake's heart again.

He had talked with Phil several times over the course of the day, but the officer hadn't mentioned he was the one who had told Emma about the standoff.

Jake glanced toward the house. For all the cars, there were no signs of life. No sign of Emma, either.

Would she even want to see him?

"We won the race."

"What?" Jake dragged his gaze back to Jeremy's face.

"We won." Jeremy repeated the words with a proud grin.

Relief swept through Jake. Someone had come through for Jeremy when he hadn't been able to. He sent up a silent thank-you to the Lord looking out for him. "Who signed on as first mate? Was it Daniel? Quinn?"

"Nope. Mom did."

Jake couldn't have heard him right. "Your mom?"

"She was the only one who knew how to put the raft together," Jeremy reminded him. "She did good, even when I almost fell into the water when I was untying the bandana from the buoy."

If Jake had wondered if Emma would forgive him, Jeremy's matter-of-fact comment provided him with the answer.

Now he regretted giving in to the urge to kiss her even more. It only created another bond that had to be severed. Because if Emma ever did fall in love again, it wouldn't be with someone who brought pain and uncertainty back into her life.

"Do you want to see the trophy?" Jeremy was already tugging him toward the house.

"I don't want to intrude if you and your mom invited company over."

"We didn't invite them," Jeremy said blithely. "And it's just Mr. and Mrs. Redstone and Miss Porter and Kate."

Another twist of the knife.

If they had shown up without being invited, that meant they'd been worried about Emma, too.

"Quinn must be here." Abby rose to her feet when they heard a car door slam. "He said he was going to stop by after the park closed."

Emma hoped Abby's fiancé would have some word about Jake. As the day had stretched on, she had battled fear. Doubt. Familiar adversaries, only the difference was, she didn't feel as if she were facing them alone anymore.

At Daniel's suggestion, they had all prayed for Jake's safety and the safety of the other officers. After that, the man had proved to be a welcome distraction for Jeremy, taking him and Shadow on a long walk around the property.

Abby had taken over the kitchen, putting on a pot of coffee while Kate and Esther dished up plates of food. Their concern had wrapped around Emma like a warm blanket.

"I'll pour a cup of coffee for Quinn." Kate was on her way to the kitchen before Emma could stand up.

It was a good thing she wasn't standing.

Because the man Jeremy led into the living room wasn't Quinn O'Halloran. It was Jake.

Jake's heart stalled when he saw Emma.

Her face was pale. Her eyes red-rimmed and puffy.

He had done this to her.

"Praise God." Daniel clapped him on the back and everyone surrounded him. Everyone but Emma.

Jake hadn't expected to have an audience when he apologized to Emma, but maybe it was a blessing they weren't alone.

Kate herded him over to the sofa. "Tell us everything."

Not a chance, Jake thought. Instead, he briefly summarized the past fourteen hours, careful to gloss over certain details. Like the young man staggering out of the cabin with a loaded shotgun.

There was no point in putting that image in anyone's mind.

Fortunately, no one asked him to elaborate when he finished the story but Jake had no doubt that Emma, of all people, could fill in the details he had left out.

"I have to get something." Jeremy dashed out of the room and returned a few minutes later with a gold trophy.

"This is great." Jake summoned a smile as he took the trophy and turned it over in his hands. "I knew you could do it."

He tried to give it back but Jeremy shook his head.

"I want you to keep it."

"I can't do that. It belongs to you—and your mother." Jake couldn't look at Emma again. Not yet.

"But you helped me build the raft. You're part of Team Victory."

"But I wasn't there." Jake felt at a loss, knowing he didn't deserve something that meant so much to Jeremy.

"That's why I want you to have it. Mom said it's okay."

Jake felt as small as the gold letters stamped on the bottom of the trophy. "How about we make it a traveling trophy? I'll keep it for a month and then I'll give it back to you."

"And Mom can take it for a month, too."

"Right." Jake cleared his throat.

"Would you like a cup of coffee, Jake?" Kate waded bravely into the awkward silence that fell.

"Or something to eat?" Abby chimed in.

"No, thank you. I just stopped over to apologize to Jeremy and Emma for missing the race this morning." Jake backed toward the door. "I'm pretty exhausted."

Jeremy followed him to the door. "Are you coming over after church tomorrow?"

"I don't think I'll be able to." Jake pushed out a smile. "But I'll call you and we'll set something up, how's that?"

"Okay." Jeremy grinned. "Take good care of the trophy."

"I will."

At least that was one promise he could keep.

Emma looked out the window and saw Jake's car pull away.

For the past two weeks, he had followed the mentoring guidelines to the letter.

Once a week for four hours.

No more, no less.

School had started, so Jake had started to pick up Jeremy in the evening and take him into town or back to his cabin. If he did talk to her, he maintained a polite but careful distance.

It was driving Emma crazy.

Something had changed between them. The night of the parade, he had drawn her into his arms and kissed her. Now he treated her as if they were barely acquaintances.

More than anything, she wanted to tell him that she had surrendered her heart to the Lord. That she understood the freedom that came from trusting Him. In some ways, Emma felt as if she had come back to life again.

Did Jake realize that trusting her with his story had, in turn, helped her put her trust in God?

"Hi, Mom." Jeremy wandered in, lacking the

bounce Emma had gotten used to seeing after he spent time with Jake.

"Did you have fun?"

"Yeah."

"You don't sound too sure." Emma gave him a playful nudge. "What did you and Jake do tonight?"

"He helped me with my leaf collection for science class." Jeremy scuffed the toe of his tennis shoe against the concrete floor.

"You must have enjoyed that."

Jeremy shrugged. "I guess."

Emma put an empty mold into the sink and propped a hip against the table. "Want to tell me what's bothering you, sweetheart?"

"It's different now."

"What's different?"

"I like hanging out with Jake, but I liked it when he came over here, too."

So did Emma.

"Maybe you should tell him how you feel," she suggested cautiously.

"I did. He said that 'it's for the best.'" Jeremy knelt down and wrapped his arms around Shadow's neck. "But it doesn't feel like it's for the best."

Emma frowned. What had Jake meant by that? The best for whom?

"I'm going inside to work on the rest of my homework." Jeremy rose to his feet. "Come on, Shadow."

Tears pricked Emma's eyes. Not just for Jeremy, but for both of them.

Whatever his reason, Jake had walked away. Emma decided it was time to find out why.

Chapter Twenty-Two

Jake glanced at his watch. If Matt didn't show up at the pavilion in five minutes, he was going back to the police department.

Maybe he would cut it down to three minutes.

The pastor had called earlier that morning and said he wanted to talk to him, but for some odd reason, had suggested they meet at the park instead of the church office.

Because Jake had a pretty good idea what the topic would be, he was reluctant to meet with Matt at all.

The night before, when he had dropped Jeremy off and saw the lights on in Emma's workroom, it had taken all his self-control to drive away. And it hadn't helped that Jeremy had asked him why they no longer spent any time at his house—and why they were only getting together once a week.

Jake had given him a vague answer about school starting and it being for the best, but the truth was, it was killing him to stay away from Emma and cut down on the amount of time he spent with Jeremy.

He sat down on one of the benches overlooking the

water and tried to pray. Lately, Jake's conversations with God had been a struggle, too.

"I'm surprised you're still here." Matt jogged up to him.

"You had another two minutes and twelve seconds."

The pastor smiled, but it didn't quite reach his eyes. "I believe you."

"So what's on your mind?"

"Skipping the small talk, huh?" Matt shook his head. "I'm all for that—what's going on with you and the Barlows?"

Maybe he would rather discuss the weather, Jake thought. But it was too late now.

"Did Jeremy talk to you?"

"Actually, I got a call from your brother."

"You talked to Andy?" Jake lifted a skeptical brow.

"That's right. He's concerned about you. And so am I," Matt added.

Unbelievable, Jake thought. Or maybe not, considering what his brother and his friend did for a living. "I'm a big boy. I don't need you guys hovering around me like I'm a five-year-old learning to ride a bicycle."

"Hovering?" Matt snorted. "We were arguing on the phone about which one of us gets to do the honor of smacking you upside the head."

"I didn't make this decision lightly," Jake growled. If anything, it was killing him. Over the past week, he'd been careful to stick to the four-hour time block he'd agreed to upon joining the mentoring program.

"Why *did* you make it?"

Jake couldn't believe he had to ask. He plowed

his fingers through his hair and speared Matt with a look. "You know why."

"Humor me."

"I saw Emma's face that day. It was like sending her back in time to the day Brian died, right down to Phil Koenigs giving her the news." Even now, Jake's composure staggered under the weight of it. "For a while, I thought there could be something between us—something good—but I can't promise her that I'll always be safe. That I'll always come home on time or…that I'll come home at all. I'm not going to put her and Jeremy through that again."

"Are you sure that Emma is the one you're protecting?" Matt asked quietly. "Or are you protecting yourself?"

"Maybe I'm protecting all of us." Jake stared at the water with unseeing eyes. Even if Emma shared his feelings, he couldn't stand it if, down the road, those feelings changed. Better to make a clean break now. "This is for the best."

"If you're making a decision about us, don't I have a say in what's best?"

Jake froze at the sound of Emma's voice.

He shot an accusing look at Matt, who shrugged. Not at all repentant—or surprised—that Emma was there. That she might have overheard some of their conversation.

"What happened to confidential meetings with the pastor?" he muttered.

"Oh, those take place in my office," Matt said with cheerful disregard for the dark look Jake tossed his way. "The park is open to the public. I have no control over who comes and goes. And if you'll excuse me, I'm going."

Jake's mouth dropped open, but he couldn't get a word out. Not that it would have mattered. Matt was already halfway to the car.

"Jake?"

He couldn't look at her. It *hurt* to look at her.

"I should be used to being set up by my friends." Self-preservation sharpened his tone.

Emma flinched and guilt arrowed through him. This wasn't her fault, Jake reminded himself.

"Don't be upset with Pastor Wilde. I called the church this morning and asked if I could set up an appointment to talk to him. He said he wouldn't be able to see me until this afternoon, because the two of you were meeting."

"At the park."

"He might have mentioned that, too." Emma took a step closer.

Jake couldn't help it. He braced himself to absorb the pain and looked at her now. The luminous smile on her face stole his breath.

"How much did you hear?"

"Enough to know that you're wrong."

"Am I?" Jake's lips twisted. "So you weren't upset with me for standing Jeremy up on the day of the race? Resentful that I had to put my job ahead of him? Worried about me when you found out that I was in a standoff with a drunk kid holding a shotgun?"

"You're right." Emma's voice trembled. "I was all those things. At first. But the thing you are wrong about was that you put me in a situation I'd been in before. I wasn't. And that *was* your fault. Because of you, I didn't go back to that place because I'm not the same person I was six years ago. I'm not the same person I was a month ago. I wasn't, what your verse says, *rooted in love*. I didn't trust God—now I do. I know He'll never leave me.

"You told me that spending time with Jeremy was a gift that you didn't deserve, but you didn't see that you are as much of a gift to us. To *me*. You questioned whether you had anything to give but you gave me something that I'd lost. Hope."

Emma searched Jake's eyes, looking for a sign that something she'd said had made a difference. Made him change his mind.

She hadn't meant to eavesdrop on his conversation with Pastor Wilde, but when she'd heard the anguish and regret in Jake's voice, she hadn't been able to take another step forward.

Was it possible he didn't realize what he had brought to their lives?

He had pulled away from her and Jeremy, not because his feelings had changed, but in order to protect them from pain.

"I'm afraid," Jake said flatly. "Afraid that I'll let you down. Afraid that I don't know enough about raising kids or about making you happy. About not being what you and Jeremy need. I told you I was new at all this."

He started to move away, but she caught his hand.

"It feels new to me, too," she admitted. "I told you the truth when I said I'm not the same person. We're going to make mistakes, but I think… I think if we both stay close to God, nothing will come between us."

Jake pulled her against him and buried his face in her hair. "I love you, Emma."

She clung to him, absorbing the words like summer rain. "I love you, too."

"I'll admit I've been afraid of something else."

"What?"

The flecks of gold in his eyes sent a shiver of heat rippling through her. "I've been afraid to kiss you again."

"I've heard you aren't supposed to let fear stop you from doing the things you want to do," Emma said a little breathlessly.

Jake smiled that heart-stopping smile as he drew her closer. His lips took hers in a searching kiss and Emma melted against him, this time telling him without words how she felt about him.

When they broke apart a few minutes later, Jake stared down at her, a dazed expression on his face. "Thank you for helping me overcome my fear."

"I'm just returning the favor, Chief Sutton." Emma leaned against his broad chest, pressing her face against his heart.

His arms tightened around her. "You're the brave one. I was ready to walk away."

"You wouldn't have gotten very far." Emma chuckled. "If I had to, I was going to remind you that you had a week left on our trial period."

"Are you saying that you want to extend it?"

The teasing look on his face made Emma respond in kind. She pretended to consider the question. "I think we should. How long do you think it should be this time?"

Jake drew her back into his arms. "I was thinking maybe...forever?"

"What a coincidence." Emma smiled up into his eyes. "That's exactly what I was thinking."

Epilogue

"You look kind of nervous, Jake." Jeremy tipped his head as Jake paced the floor in front of him.

"I need to talk to you about something."

"Okay." Jeremy leaned back against the sofa cushions. "Go for it."

Go for it.

Those three little words were the reason he was so nervous in the first place.

"All right." Jake took a deep breath. "I want to marry your mom," he said. "But before I ask her, I have to know how you feel about it."

Jeremy folded his arms across his chest.

Okay, so Jake had been half hoping he would leap off the sofa and give him a high five. Shake his hand. *Something.* But one of the things he loved about the kid was the way he approached everything—from breakfast cereal to a proposal of marriage—with thoughtful concentration.

"You better sit down, Jake."

Jake sat.

"If you and Mom got married, where would we live?"

"Well, your mother will have something to say about that, of course, but I thought we might want to stay here. You have your room fixed up the way you want it here and Shadow has space to run. We could fix up the barn and turn it into a studio for your mom, especially now that Abby talked her into teaching classes for the people who stay at the inn."

"And the apple tree is here," Jeremy added.

The apple tree.

Jake thought back to the first time he had met Emma. When she had opened the door, he had had no idea his life was about to change. No idea that he had been coming *home*.

God, You are so amazing.

"That's another thing." Jake felt his throat tighten. "Your dad loved you and your mom very much and I'm not trying to take his place. I don't want you to forget him…but I hope we can add new memories to the ones you have."

"Are you going to have more kids?"

"I don't know." Jake slumped back against the cushion, trying to hide the fact that the innocent question had turned his bones to liquid. "Your mom and I haven't talked about…adding on to the family. But how would you feel about it? A brother or sister?"

Or, Jake warmed to the idea, maybe one—or two—of each.

"I think it would be cool—as long as I don't have to share my room if it's a sister."

"Sisters in the spare bedroom. Promise."

Jeremy was silent for a few minutes and Jake could almost see the wheels turning in his head.

"Do you have a ring?"

Jake hid a smile.

"As a matter of fact, I do." In his pocket, waiting for the right moment to slip it on Emma's finger.

Jeremy held out his hand.

"Oh. You want to take a look at it." Jake fumbled in his pocket and retrieved the tiny velvet box. He presented it to Jeremy.

"It's a good one." Jeremy pronounced after inspecting it carefully. "Mom will like it."

Jake hoped so. He had purchased the ring a week ago, hoping that Emma would understand the significance of the slender gold band set with three diamonds—one for each of them.

"So, what do you think?"

When Jeremy didn't respond right away, Jake felt a pang of concern.

"Jeremy, I can't promise that I won't make mistakes," he said quietly. "But I love your mom…and I love you, too. I believe that God wants us to be family."

"I know." Jeremy looked down at his hands.

"You have another question, I can tell. You never have to be afraid to tell me what's on your mind. Go ahead and ask me."

"After you and mom get married, do you mind if I call you Dad instead of Jake?"

Jake's vision blurred. "I would love that."

Jeremy grinned.

"So…" Jake's self-control finally buckled under the pressure. "Does that mean I have your blessing?"

"Yup—"

The front door opened and they heard Emma call out a cheerful hello. A second later she appeared in the doorway.

"What's going on in here?"

Jake couldn't answer. As usual, seeing Emma took his breath away. In the past few weeks he had seen a transformation in her that he could only attribute to the Lord. The grief had thawed, leaving behind a radiant warmth in her eyes.

"We're having a talk," Jeremy said smugly.

"A talk? That sounds serious." Emma breezed into the room, depositing purse and keys on the table near the door. She leaned over and squeezed Jake's hand. "What about?"

"I'm going to bed now." Jeremy launched himself off the sofa. "Jake will tell you. Maybe you guys should take Shadow for a walk. There's a full moon tonight."

"Thanks, Jeremy. I'll take it from here," Jake whispered.

A full moon? And take what from here?

Emma looked at Jake, puzzled, but he merely shrugged.

They were both acting strange.

"I'll be up to pray with you in a few minutes." Emma dropped a kiss on her son's head.

Jake held out her jacket and she slipped it on, resisting the urge to turn into his arms and not let go.

"Come on. We don't want to miss that full moon," he said.

Shadow disappeared ahead of them into the shadows.

"How did everything go tonight?" Jake took her hand and the warmth of his skin chased away the chill in the October air.

"Esther is convinced she can teach me to knit but I think I'll stick to mosaics." Emma chuckled as she remembered her first attempt that evening when she joined the Knit Our Hearts Together group. "Kate almost gave up, too. She said something about using her knitting needles as plant stakes."

When Jake didn't smile, Emma stopped and planted her hands on her hips. "All right, what's going on? Is it something with Jeremy? You two looked pretty serious when I walked in. What were you talking about?"

Jake's silence—and the fact that he withdrew his hand from hers—added to Emma's concern.

"We were talking about this," he finally said.

Emma glanced down and saw the velvet box cradled in Jake's palm. The light from the porch illuminated the diamond ring in the center of it.

"I love you, Emma. Will you marry me?"

Emma stared down at the ring, overwhelmed by love for the man standing in front of her. She'd sensed that Jake was taking things slowly out of respect for her but Emma was ready to start their life together. She'd even confided to Kate and Abby that if he didn't propose soon, she was going to have to propose to *him*.

"Jake—"

Emma paused as the front door opened and light spilled across the yard.

"Well?" Jeremy peered at them from the doorway.
"What did she say?"

Emma started to laugh and Jake smiled.

"Well? What did she say?" he whispered.

Emma smiled up at him.

"She said *yes*."

* * * * *

Dear Reader,

I hope you enjoyed getting to know Emma and Jake (and, of course, Jeremy and Shadow!) during your visit to Mirror Lake.

As a police officer's wife, I know it isn't always easy to send my husband off to work every day, not knowing what situations he will have to face. Like Emma, I've learned that staying close to God and trusting Him brings peace. I hope you have found the same, no matter what your circumstances.

Be sure to plan another visit to Mirror Lake. Matthew Wilde's life is turned upside down when a "black sheep" wanders into the fold. Everyone is talking about Zoey Decker...but will the pastor listen to gossip—or his heart—when it comes to Mirror Lake's prodigal daughter?

I love to hear from you! Please visit my website at kathrynspringer.com and sign up for my quarterly newsletter.

Blessings,

Kathryn Springer

THE WORLD IS BETTER WITH

Romance

Harlequin has everything from contemporary, passionate and heartwarming to suspenseful and inspirational stories.

Whatever your mood,
we have a romance just for you!

Connect with us to find your next great read, special offers and more.

f /HarlequinBooks

🐦 @HarlequinBooks

www.HarlequinBlog.com

www.Harlequin.com/Newsletters

HARLEQUIN®

A *Romance* FOR EVERY MOOD™

www.Harlequin.com

JUST CAN'T GET ENOUGH?

Join our social communities
and talk to us online.

You will have access to the latest
news on upcoming titles and special
promotions, but most importantly,
you can talk to other fans about your
favorite Harlequin reads.

Harlequin.com/Community

Facebook.com/HarlequinBooks

Twitter.com/HarlequinBooks

Pinterest.com/HarlequinBooks

HARLEQUIN®

A *Romance* FOR EVERY MOOD™

Stay up-to-date on all your romance-reading news with the *Harlequin Shopping Guide,* featuring bestselling authors, exciting new miniseries, books to watch and more!

The newest issue will be delivered right to you with our compliments! There are 4 each year.

Signing up is easy.

EMAIL

ShoppingGuide@Harlequin.ca

WRITE TO US

HARLEQUIN BOOKS
Attention: Customer Service Department
P.O. Box 9057, Buffalo, NY 14269-9057

OR PHONE

1-800-873-8635 in the United States
1-888-343-9777 in Canada

Please allow 4-6 weeks for delivery of the first issue by mail.